EIGHT

Unfrozen Four Series
Book Two

WEEKS

Eight Weeks
Copyright © 2022 Joelina Falk

You can find me here:

http://www.joelinafalk.com/
https://www.instagram.com/authorjoelinafalk/
https://twitter.com/joelinafalk

To those who believe in soul mates...
This one's for you.

PLAYLIST

When You're Ready — Shawn Mendes ♡

see you later (ten years) — Jenna Raine ♡

Wildest Dreams (Taylor's Version) — Taylor Swift ♡

WYD Now? — Sadie Jean [feat. Zai1k & Zakhar] ♡

Favorite T-Shirt – Acoustic — Jake Scott ♡

Let's Fall in Love for the Night — FINNEAS ♡

Chills — Why Don't We ♡

Full Time Job — We Three ♡

Make You Mine — PUBLIC ♡

It'll Be Okay — Shawn Mendes ♡

Heart To Heart — James Blunt ♡

Last First Kiss — One Direction ♡

Chapter 1

"and I thought I'd be happy, but I'm barely breathing"—
Falling Up by Dean Lewis

Sofia

"THIS IS THE FINAL BOARDING CALL for flight 375A to New York City. Please proceed to gate six immediately. The final checks are being completed and the captain will order for the doors of the aircraft to close in approximately five to ten minutes. I repeat. This is the final boarding call for flight 375A to New York City."

I'm starting to regret my decision to leave for a couple of months. Sure, I've always dreamed of studying abroad, but never have I imagined that being my final year of university.

I'm also not quite sure how good of a decision it was to choose St. Trewery University. I had so many options, and yet I chose to go to the one university in the city I ran away from.

I hadn't really had a choice anyway. My father got a better job offer in Germany when I was seven, of course, he took it. My mother figured we shouldn't have to live four years without seeing our father, so we tagged right along.

And I guess I'm returning for a little under half a year.

But… all my friends are here. So is my family. Well, part of my family. I'm only really close to two of them, though.

Still, it's good to finally get far away from my ex-boyfriend for a while.

Exactly, Sofia. Stay positive.

We don't allow negative thoughts. Especially not when you're trapped in an airplane for the next twelve hours of your life. That is if the plane doesn't crash and you'll die.

Aaaand there the negativity is again.

Breathe in. Breathe out. Everything will be alright.

Just ten minutes ago I had to say goodbye to everyone I love. And I doubt I'll get to see them again before Christmas. Maybe not even then.

Flights are expensive. Especially ones that get you across the ocean.

I can literally feel the elderly lady next to me judge me. She probably wonders why Satan decided to punish her by seating her next to a twenty-year-old.

Correction, a *bawling-her-eyes-out* twenty-year-old.

She might as well have been seated next to a toddler at this point.

It's not that I'm necessarily afraid of flying. Maybe I am. But the fact that I miss everyone already plays a huge role for my tears as well.

Alright, and perhaps the fact that my anxiety goes crazy when I'm in the air. Something about flying just doesn't seem right to me.

I'm not only a whole day late, but I'm also homeless now.

Things couldn't get any worse.

Well, at least my classes don't start before Monday. And as it's only Saturday, I have about one and a half days left to find a place to stay.

I was supposed to get a room assigned at St. Trewery's dorms, but as it seems, they're full. Why would they promise me a room when, clearly, they have no space for me?

Literally. It took them a whole six months and me already being stuck here to find out I cannot stay at the dorms.

And to make matters worse, I started my goddamn period on this damn flight here.

But, hey, I did say I lived here once. I'm just praying my aunt is still around. I haven't talked to her in what must be decades. Maybe not decade*s*, but at least ten years.

I take out my phone, seeing it only has about five percent battery left, but it'll have to do. I certainly won't get to charge it any time soon.

I look up her contact in my phone, praying to every single God out there that she's still got the same number.

Dialing her number, my blood starts rushing through me at lightning speed, my hands shaking. Why am I so anxious about talking to my aunt? Perhaps because if she says no or doesn't live here anymore, I seriously don't know where else to go.

Luck seems to be on my side for once, seeing as someone actually does pick up the phone.

"Sofia?" the voice of my aunt comes through the phone. She sounds as surprised to hear from me as I was hearing I will be homeless.

"Hey, yeah, it's me." *Awkward.*

My aunt keeps quiet. As I said, we haven't talked in at least one decade. I must have been ten by the time living on the other side of the globe just got too much to stay in touch with everyone else. So, I'm not surprised she has no idea what to say.

"Look, I have a problem…" I walk up and down the little pathway in front of a grocery store, not knowing how to ask someone I haven't talked to in ages for such a huge favor.

"Spit it out, dear."

"I'm in New City," I say. "I was supposed to stay at the dorms of St. Trewery, but as it seems, they no longer have a room available for me. So up until I—"

"Oh, dear, I don't live in New City anymore." *There goes my only hope.* "I do live in Wesley Hills, though. You remember your childhood friend... What's her name again? Liliana?"

"Lily?" Her name sends an instant chill through my body. I haven't heard her name in so long, it's strange realizing certain people in my life actually remember her, talking to me about her.

"Yes, yes. Her mother lives right next to me."

I'm not sure why she's telling me this. "That's cool. So uh, listen, Nicole. I know this is a lot to ask... but could I stay with you for a short while? Only until I found an apartment close to St. Trewery?"

"Sure. I'll text you my address. Just go and knock at Victoria's door and ask for the key to let yourself in. She has a spare one. I'm at work, otherwise, I'd come pick you up."

Oh, thank fuck. I already pictured myself spending the night sleeping on a park bench. Though, I might want to take care of my whole getting-my-period problem before I seat myself in an Uber.

Chapter 2

"look death in the eyes like everyday"—CHXSE Up by
Chase Atlantic

"MISS, YOUR CARD WAS DECLINED."

I just wanted *one* quiet birthday morning. And yet I find myself in a drug store, buying a last-minute present for my sister.

After Colin's text last night, saying Lily would be staying with us for a couple of days, I need to get this present before they get home. I wanted to buy one shortly before leaving for Brites, but Lily would have found out I kind of forgot to get her one. So, it had to be now.

Funny how we share the same birthday and yet I somehow forgot to get my twin sister a birthday present.

Anyway, being here wouldn't be such a bad thing, if that woman at the register next to mine wasn't about to explode.

Looking at what she's buying, that poor cashier has it coming. Feminine hygiene products, chocolate, and a declined card… that *screams* outraged woman.

"You cannot be fucking serious," she speaks in a much calmer voice than I anticipated. "They said it would work here!" *There it is.*

"I'm sorry, miss, but like I told you before, we don't take bank cards from other countries. And what the hell is an 'EC-Card?'"

"I don't have cash on me. I just landed good two hours ago." Whatever she says next stays a mystery as she switches languages. It does sound awfully a lot like an insult though, so that's interesting.

I pay for Lily's present, and since I feel charitable today, I walk right over to the other register.

The guy looks up, furrowing his eyebrows as I slap my credit card in front of him.

"I'll pay for it."

"You really don't have to," the woman says. Only now do I allow myself to look at her.

She's got brown hair and dark eyes. She looks tired, *really* tired. And a lot like she's just gotten off an hours-long ride from somewhere. The three suitcases next to her only confirm it.

Her skin is tan enough to not look pale with that hair of hers, but not tan enough to look sun-kissed either. So, she's not from the west coast or Florida, I'd say.

I might be hallucinating, but this woman standing in front of me reminds me a lot of someone I used to know. Someone I promised the world to, and too many other unrealistic things. Someone that always meant and will always mean more to me than anyone ever could.

"That's like five dollars. Don't worry about it." And besides, I have two sisters. I know how cranky they can get when they're on their period.

Doing a little favor and buying tampons and chocolate for someone that needs it really isn't a big deal.

"Thank you," she says, giving me a quick smile.

As soon as I get my card back, I walk off, ready to get the hell home and wait for Colin, my best friend and apparently boyfriend of my twin sister, and Lily to come home. I'm not sure where they're at, but I'm assuming at his parents' house.

Just as I reach my car, I notice the brunette woman sitting on one of her suitcases in front of the store.

My mind tells me to keep on going about my day, but something else within me tells me she's in deep shit and could use a helping hand.

I mentally beat up myself when I walk up to her again. If I end up getting murdered, at least I'll be joining my sister.

I come to a stop in front of her, noticing she's crying. *Oh, boy. This is going to be a mistake.*

"Hey, do you need anything else?" I find myself asking when instead I should be running to my car and get back home.

She doesn't look up, but she shakes her head anyway. I suppose she's done with her life for the day.

What I should do right now is leave, but for some reason, my legs stay put. And my mouth seems to make itself useful. Or… unuseful. "Do you need a ride home?"

That gets her attention way too quickly. But instead of saying yes or no, she chuckles ironically. "If I had one."

"What do you mean?" Please don't tell me she's homeless. That's something I for real cannot deal with today. I mean, I could offer her some money, maybe a hotel room. It won't hurt me. But I don't usually walk around shoving money down poor people's throats.

A long and deep rush of air leaves her. "Not that you really care, but I just got off a twelve-hour flight, took on another hour-long car ride here, only for my university to tell me they've given my room to someone else because I'm a day late. So now I somehow have to get to my aunt's house without money. Plus, and this is going to be a little TMI, I've gotten my period in the car and I have absolutely no opportunity to fucking change."

"Where does your aunt live?" That's the only thing I dare ask. I don't need to hear about her period. As normal as it is. But seriously, I do *not* need to know about some stranger's cycle.

"Roven Rd, Wesley Hills."

I exhale heavily, knowing I will regret the words that are about to leave my mouth. "That's sixteen minutes from here. I can drive you." *But you shouldn't, Aaron.*

"No, that's fine," she says. "I cannot afford to get blood all over your car seats."

"Seeing as you cannot even afford tampons and chocolate, I'm not surprised to hear that."

She snorts a laugh, nodding her head. "What's your name anyway?" She looks me up and down, kind of like she's checking me out.

I'm not going to lie, if she didn't provide me with far too many, far too intimate information about her period, I totally would have tapped her.

"Aaron. What's yours?"

"Sofia." Aw, well. Now I certainly can't tap her anyway. If Lily ever finds out I've had sex with someone named Sofia, she will rip my organs out.

The name Sofia is… a no-go. Too many fun memories are connected to someone with the same name.

If I ruined said memories by choosing to add another one...nope.

Who am I kidding? This isn't about Lily and her memories. It's about *my* memories. Ones I would rather not have but can't quite find the courage to paint over by using another girl named Sofia.

"Well, Sofia. I happen to live about two minutes from here. You can come with me, get all… cleaned up, change, and *then* I can get you to your aunt's house. If you'd like."

Sofia is shaking her head almost instantly. "Hell no. I've watched far too many documentaries. Pretty boys like you *always* have some shit up their sleeves. A knife, most likely."

I swing my arms around like a fool. And—surprise—nothing comes falling out of my sleeves. "I only kill women on the second date."

"It'd be way less obvious to do on the first date with *another* guy she's dating. They'd question him first."

I'm not even sure why I'm taking in her words as deeply as I do, genuinely thinking about it. I am *not* a murderer. And I never planned on becoming one. But I suppose she does have a point. A great one even.

"Well, do I have to be scared for my life if I take you home with me?" I ask, pushing my hands into my jeans pockets.

"Always."

CHAPTER 3

"but just for this moment / let me live in my head"—Made Up Story by Andi

Sofia

I HAVE TO SAY, Aaron is ridiculously handsome.

He fits right into the beauty standard. Athletic, blond with eyes that could blind people with their brightness. Though, they're not blue but green. He hasn't really smiled at me yet, but even so, I can tell he has a pretty one.

Personally, I never really understood why that's the standard in the beauty industry. But I'll admit, he sure is good-looking. Could make it as a model if he tried to.

"If you want, you can take a shower, too," Aaron tells me right after he knocks on his bathroom door.

It's kind of crazy how my first day here sort of started with me meeting a guy with the same name as the one I'd said goodbye to last before leaving.

I shouldn't take the offer, but I feel more than disgusting. "Thank you!"

"My best friend could come home any minute, so maybe try not to take more than ten minutes." I suppose that's his way of telling me he wants me to get lost. I can't even blame him for it.

I don't try to react to him, as rude as that might come across. I wouldn't even know what to say, to be honest.

All I want to do is freshen up and—Wow.

My eyes move over to the variety of shower products, only to land on women's shampoo. He even has women's body wash here. If it weren't for the typical 3 in 1 man's one, I wouldn't assume he's taken and rather believe he prefers the smell of fruits than *men*.

But:

Dude has got a girlfriend and casually invites some stranger into his house. I wonder what she would say if she knew I was here.

Men don't usually have a whole shower full of shampoo, conditioner and God knows how many hair products. At least I've never come across one. There's still a chance he's one of the few that do, but again, judging by the 3 in 1 men shower gel, I doubt it.

As I get out of the bathroom, freshly showered and no longer feeling as though blood is running down my legs, I find Aaron's bedroom empty.

I'm not sure how rude I am allowed to be by walking out of the room to look for him, but I also don't want to wait here for him to come back.

So, I do what my subconscious tells me not to do and walk right out of his bedroom. The room door on the opposite side of Aaron's is open, and because I seem to be nosy lately, I peek inside.

Aaron is putting something into the drawer beside the bed, but that's not what I'm really paying attention to. It's the picture frame I find on the other nightstand.

"Who's that?" I ask before the thought of asking even entered my brain.

Just like that, Aaron flinches slightly but turns around to find my eyes. Then he looks over to the other side of the bed, smiling. "That's my sister."

His sister looks so much like… Lily. Like *my* Lily. Just older and far less smiley.

She's no longer *my* Lily. Lily and I haven't been in touch for thirteen years. I doubt you can call that a best friend anymore.

"She's my best friend's girlfriend, apparently. Though he did ask me to put that picture away before they get here. As it seems, he doesn't want her to know how crazy he is about her."

My eyes follow him over to the other side of the bed, as he snatches the picture and shoves it inside yet another drawer.

As he turns around, my eyes involuntarily zoom in on his muscles as his shirt rides up when he stretches. Muscles I'd love to lick.

Woah. Hold on there.

I shake my head, needing to get rid of this intrusive thought. I don't even know where it came from, but I sure as hell do not want it.

You swore off guys after Leon, remember? And he has a girlfriend.

Or does he?

"Do you have a girlfriend?"

Aaron comes walking out of his best friend's room, closing the door behind him. "Nah. The things in my shower are from my ex, Winter." Aaron gestures for me to walk downstairs, which I do gladly. Me being at a stranger's house is bad enough. No need for me to keep on finding things out I shouldn't *want* to find out.

"Are you hungry?" Aaron suddenly asks, just as we both reach the last step. I shake my head at him. I'm starving, but he's been far too hospitable already. I mean, he let a goddamn *stranger* use his shower. Who does that? "Are you sure? I could swear I heard your stomach yell at me while you were in the shower."

I turn around to face him, cheeks burning up so quickly, even if I tried to stop the pink color from spreading on them, I wouldn't stand a chance. "You did?"

Aaron starts to laugh, holding a hand to his stomach as he does. "No, Sofia. I didn't hear it. But I assumed you'd be hungry after God knows how long you've been on the road."

13

"I can eat at my aunt's house. It's not a big deal." And it isn't. I bet she's got edible food at home. Everyone does, right? Perhaps not the best bread in the world, but I won't get to eat that until I'm back in Germany anyway.

"Good, because I can't cook to save my life. But I would have called my best friend over to do so," he says, offering me nothing but a quick shrug. "You good to go then?"

I nod, though I do wonder why he wants to get rid of me so quickly. I suppose it makes sense, given how we've met and all, so I shouldn't get offended by it.

Like he could read my mind, Aaron says, "It's my birthday. I still need to figure things out for tonight. You should come. My sister and I are celebrating at *Brites*. It's a sports bar just down the road. Have to warn you though, the team is a bit crazy."

"The team?"

"I play hockey for St. Trewery University. *That* team. They're loud and all, but we're like one big family." Hockey? Seriously? This city is just throwing hints at me now, isn't it?

I mean, c'mon. How obvious can it possibly get? Aaron. He's a hockey player, too. This city just wants me to find them, doesn't it?

CHAPTER 4

"it was only perfect in the past / 'cause a first love never lasts"—First Love Never Lasts Up by Kira Kosarin

Aaron

"JUST STOP RIGHT THERE," Sofia says, pointing toward a red-painted house.

"You know, it doesn't make a difference if I stop in front of your aunt's house, or her neighbor's."

Sofia glares at me like I just said her dog died. She unbuckles her seatbelt and gets out of the car the second the car stands still. "I have to get the keys from Mrs. Reyes's house. My aunt and she are great friends and she's got a spare one."

Mrs. Reyes?

As Sofia starts to walk around the car to get to the trunk, I jump out as well, feeling as though I need to give her at least one helping hand. I mean, this woman has three suitcases with her. Surely, she could use some help.

"So, do *you* know Mrs. Reyes?" I ask carefully. Sofia nods instantly, then shakes her head a second later. "Which one is it, Sofia? Yes or no?"

"Yes *and* no. I used to be really close to her daughter before my fami—" Sofia doesn't get to finish her sentence because someone comes walking out of "Mrs. Reyes'" house. Or rather *two* some-one's. My twin sister and my very best friend.

"You shouldn't have been born, Lily!" my, who would have guessed it, mother yells right before the door slams shut.

Lily and I may be twins, have the very same parents… but we grew up in two entirely different households. Whereas I was lucky enough to stay with my father after our parents split, Lily desperately wanted to have both of our parents in her life. She ended up staying with our mother and only being allowed to see me and Dad every Sunday.

Now to the more heartbreaking part… our mother hates Lily. Loathes her to death.

I haven't talked to my mother since I was five years old, and even I know they're not on good terms.

But what's even worse, my sister is suicidal, and this woman has the audacity to tell her own daughter to die. *Disgusting*.

As I watch Colin wrap his arms around Lily while she sobs, my brain suddenly starts to do its job, working.

Sofia. She knows "Mrs. Reyes". She was friends with her daughter "before…"

"Sofia."

Remember when I said there are memories connected to some-one named Sofia? Yeah, let me introduce you to Sofia Michelle Carlsen. The very one that's standing right in front of me, with her hands held on her waist, her long brunette hair with the top part of it stuck back to get the strands out of her face. And, not to forget, the Sofia trademark; The ribbon that's tied into a cute bow just where her hair is supposed to hold in place.

I can't believe I didn't connect the dots earlier. Who even walks around with a bow at the back of their head? Also, why the hell did she stick to it?

Sofia had always worn bows in her hair, ever since I can re-member. I didn't think she'd still wear them. But then again, I didn't exactly follow up with her on social media, for my own sanity.

Sofia moved away when we were eight years old. Her father had to move for his job, got stationed in Germany.

I've always liked Sofia, sometimes maybe a little too much. But to be fair, we were children, so that doesn't count. Little boys are stupid. Older ones too, but on a different level.

She turns to look at me, evidently having been able to connect the dots as well. "Is that..."

As she attempts to make a step toward the house, probably to get to her long-lost best friend, I reach for her wrist, holding it in my hand, and pull her out of sight from my best friend and sister.

"Oh my god, Aaron. Let me go say hello to Lily!" she whisper-yells. "I haven't talked to her since—"

"Shut up, would you." If there is one thing Lily doesn't need at the moment, it's finding out her childhood best friend is back in town. Not while my best friend is trying to save her life.

"What do you mean shu—" I press my hand to her mouth to keep her from speaking.

"Just shut up for a minute, would you, *Icicle*?" As I hold her close, I can't stop my eyes from traveling down her neck, trying to find that one piece of jewelry I gave her just before she left for Germany.

It's silly, I know. I haven't been wearing the other half of said jewelry for years. There is no way she's wearing it still.

And she doesn't. At least I don't see a silver chain around her neck at all.

Only half-heartedly, I manage to not look around the corner to see what's happening between my best friend and sister. No matter what they are, fake-dating or not, it's none of my business. Well, it will be when that douchebag of best friend of mine breaks her heart. But as of now, he didn't.

Once I hear a car door close, followed by another, I remove my hand from Sofia's mouth. An engine starts and soon after a car drives away. That's when I finally get up from the floor, ignoring Sofia. Or I try to.

"Aaron, what was that all about? Why can't I say hello to *my* best friend?" she demands. Sofia pouts at me, her eyebrows dipping, finding together in the same frown she used to have when we were young.

How did I not recognize her?

Sliding a hand down my face, I let out a long breath. "She's not your best friend anymore, Icicle."

"Oh, wow. I see," she says, chuckling disbelievingly. "You still haven't found your humanity." She goes to unload her suitcases from my trunk, scowling like whatever I've said was the ultimate insult to her ever.

"Need I remind you of what I've done for you today?"

She shakes her head then tilts her face up to the sky as she inhales a deep breath before her eyes meet mine again. "Thank you, Aaron. I mean it." I know she does. Sofia Carlsen is incapable of being mean. She's always been like that. Though, she might have changed. It's been thirteen years since I've talked to her after all.

"You're very welcome. I'm always there to help out an old friend of mine."

CHAPTER 5

"a clock ticks till it breaks your glass and I drown in you again"—Clarity — Acoustic by Foxes

"CAN YOU BELIEVE IT?" Miles, best friend number two out of three, asks as I scoot next to him in our booth. "Carter actually seeming to *like* a girl?"

No, I cannot believe it, but I sure hope he's being sincere. I cannot deal with having to cut off my best friend because he broke my sister's heart which then ends up in her death. If it doesn't end with her death either way.

Just a week ago I had to find out that my sister wants to die. And I mean, she doesn't just say she wants to die, she is *planning* her death. She is full-on writing her goodbyes. As it seems, Colin found out as well.

Lily and Colin have been spending an awful amount of time together this past week, and they didn't even know each other a week ago. So I assume Colin is trying to save her life. At least I hope he fucking is, otherwise I will end him.

The worst part is, I cannot even talk to my own sister about it. She will most likely talk her way out of my confrontation.

That doesn't matter today. My sister is safe with Colin, I know that. So there is no need to worry right now. Tonight, I will have fun. I will get drunk and forget the little sex scene I had to witness this afternoon when I came back home from Wesley Hills.

I didn't think I'd ever have to drink myself into oblivion to forget having seen someone have sex, but here we are. Even if it's just about some finger fucking but seeing your best friend having his hand shoved in your twin sister's pants... no thank you, I definitely need a couple of drinks after that.

"Let's do another round of shots!" I cheer loud enough for the entire rest of my team to holler. They know tonight's on me. Or more like Colin Carter. That guy promised to give me his credit card if he didn't have to get me a present.

He didn't have to get me one either way, but I mean, he sure can afford a couple of drinks.

Don't get me wrong, I have had the privilege to grow up rich. But Colin Carter tops pretty much everyone at St. Trewery. His father is a hockey coach. Though, not just *any* coach... he's coaching the New York Rangers. Well, not right now. Currently, he's a pain in our asses.

Colin said Mr. Carter wants to stay close to his family for a while which is why he took a break from the NYR. Not that I really care. Coach is coach. They're all pains in our asses. Though, *this* one, he's extra assy.

Grey, best friend number three, also known as the mother in our friend group, has his tongue stuck in his boyfriend's mouth, which is why Izan and Grey are the very last to even acknowledge the next round of Tequila shots that are being handed out to everyone.

On the count of three, we all lick the salt off the back of our hands, down the Tequila shot, and shove a slice of lime into our mouths.

The second my shot glass hits the top of the table my eyes shoot toward the entrance doors. I normally don't care who enters this bar, don't bother to check even if it's some college chick marching in here, but I do *now*. I do care because the woman walking inside is Sofia, wearing anything but what I was expecting her to wear.

It's October, and this woman decided to wear a black dress that doesn't go past her mid-thighs. The dress is skin-tight with triangles cut out right around her waist up to her ribs. And the cleavage… whom the hell let her go out dressed like this. Without a bodyguard, I mean.

She looks flaming hot, no doubt, has my dick hard in mere seconds. And by the looks of the other single men in this sports bar, I believe they agree with me.

"Is she new in the city?" Miles asks, looking Sofia up and down, but for once he seems far too uninterested. Usually, Miles is the first to tap a woman the second he gets a chance to. Call it dealing with emptiness.

Miles King needs something, or rather someone, to fill up the void in him ever since Millie died, leaving him with a daughter to care for at the age of eighteen. Now, at the age of twenty-two, Miles is the biggest manwhore I know—without taking or offering money for it, that is. And for what? So he can shut off his brain for a hot minute and forget that Millie is no longer in his life.

"Yes and no," I answer quickly. Quickly, because Sofia has spotted me and is making her way over to us.

She's wearing a big white smile on her face, at least until some guy whistles after her. At this very point, Sofia turns around, looking for the guy that is staring at her boobs rather than her eyes.

The second she's turned around, my eyes land on the wisteria-colored bow on the back of her head.

Always got to have that damn ribbon in her hair.

"Have you never seen a woman?" I hear Sofia ask, even over the voices of other people around and the music playing in the background.

Archer Kingston keeps awfully quiet now. God, I've had him on my blacklist ever since he laid a hand on my sister just an hour ago, and now he's crossing another line. "Dressing like that is calling for it."

"No, it is not," Sofia says as a matter of fact. "I'm not asking to be cat-called just because I show a little bit of skin. The question you should be asking yourself is if *I* want *you* to make some disgusting comments about how hot I look in my dress and how desperate you are to get it off of me, or if you're just thinking like a rapist."

Her chest is visibly rising and falling as she breathes a little too heavily from what I'd assume must be rage. "But let me guess, you play football for the sake of getting girls? How's that working out for you?"

Not good at all. Everyone knows that.

Archer might have a pretty face. And yes, he does get some attention for his face and body but the second he opens his mouth… it's over.

He's unapproachable, hard to crack. At least that is what he told his football friends who spread said rumor. But he isn't. Not in the slightest.

"Working out just fine."

Sofia laughs right into his face, brushing her hair back behind her shoulders. "So that's why you're sitting all alone at this table, huh?"

I stand corrected, Sofia *has* changed. A whole lot. But I'm not sure I like that very much. She's no longer the innocent girl that backs away from loud noises. She's no longer the Sofia I knew. But I bet she thinks the very same about me.

I've changed too. That's what happens when you grow up.

On second thought, maybe the mouthy Sofia could be an adventure.

"Where do you know her from anyway?" Miles's voice makes it through to me. I turn my head only to find him taking a sip from his beer.

"Why would you think I know her?"

"Alright, I think you've had enough alcohol, Marsh," he says, pushing my glass filled with some kind of mix over to Grey. Honestly, I barely even remember what I ordered. "I asked if she was new in the city, you gave me an answer. Oh, and she's on her way over here."

Just as the words leave my best friend's mouth, Sofia approaches us. "Aaron?"

Looking away from Miles, I turn to look at Sofia, meeting her eyes dark eyes. "Be my guest, Sofia. Take a seat." I gesture toward the only other free seat at our booth.

Thanks to Lily and Colin leaving early, we have some extra space here. Naturally, a booth doesn't sit up to twenty-five people, so the team kind of spread all around the bar, but it doesn't matter. I'm with my closest friends and their companies.

Sofia looks at Grey, smiles widely then takes a seat next to him, right across from me. "I know it's after midnight already, but… happy birthday, Aaron."

"Thanks, Icicle."

"Stop calling me that."

Sofia lays her hands down on the table, interlocking them. I reach over, placing my hand right over hers. The cold instantly travels over my skin. "You're still as cold as one." Withdrawing my hand from hers again, I now lean back in my seat, holding my hands by my nape.

She glares at me. Clearly, she doesn't like hearing her nickname again, but that's just why I call her that, why I've always called her that. Sofia has hated the nickname from the second I came up with it, and the scowl on her face has always been a great reason for me to keep on calling her "Icicle".

"Whatever, *Nix*." Sofia grabs the glass Miles pushed away from me two minutes ago and takes a sip. "What kind of girly drink is this?"

If I had to guess, about everyone at this table is currently looking at Sofia with more than three question marks above their heads. I know for sure I didn't order some "girly drink", whatever that may be. "It's Vodka Cran."

Sofia shakes her head. "It's Cranberry, that's what it is. Maybe one percent vodka, or half a percent."

"Yeah? How are you the alcohol expert here?" Grey asks, offering Sofia a smug smile. That's so not like Grey. Grey is quiet and sweet. He's not challenging or smug. Guess alcohol doesn't do him any good.

"I haven't introduced myself properly yet," Sofia says then turns to look at Grey. She holds out her hand, waiting for him to take it. "I'm Sofia. I spent my entire teenage years in Germany. Our legal drinking age is eighteen. Beer and wine, however, that's legal at the age of sixteen. But if you live in a small town or even better, a village, chances are, you start drinking at the age of twelve."

Grey shakes her hand, bobbing his head with a downward smile like he's impressed.

"Germany?" Miles blurts out like he wasn't expecting that at all. "You don't even have an accent."

"That's because I was born here. My parents are both from New York City, though I lived right here until I was seven years old. That's where I know this dwarf here from." She points her finger at me, then instantly gets up. "Let me show you what *real* drinks are."

"If you down this, I'll pay for all of your drinks," I say, pushing the *Prairie Fire* toward Sofia.

My head is spinning from all the shit I've downed thanks to Sofia. There is no way in hell that I would *ever* drink a shot made of vodka, whiskey, and Tabasco, and let's not forget the pepper taste. Nope. Not going to happen.

What started as a bet who dares to drink the weirdest shot mixtures is now a wish to die. Clearly. And I do not have one of those. However, I will if I have to drink *that* thing.

And besides, Sofia doesn't know I am paying for all the drinks tonight. For hers especially since she's not twenty-one yet. Without me, she wouldn't even get a single drink here, apart from non-alcoholic ones.

"Seriously? Aaron, that's like a hundred dollars."

I shrug. "For someone that can't afford—"

Her hand collides with my arm as she slaps me. "Remind me of it *again* and I will do worse to you than just slap you."

Smirking, I ask, "For instance?"

"I'll inject e-liquid into your bloodstream, and you best hope you'll make it out alive."

"I have to say, Icicle, if that's your way of trying to flirt with me, it's not going to work. Threatening to poison me, that's not really a great move. What happened to asking for a kiss first?"

I lay my hand on her thigh, feeling her tense at my touch. Her breath comes out a little more ragged, uncontrolled.

So I do have some kind of effect on her after all.

"Let me put arsenic trioxide on my lips first, maybe then you'll get one." *That sounds like a challenge to me.*

"Is that the sugar look-alike?" She nods. "Too obvious, Icicle. Try something without color. And perhaps anything that wouldn't kill you in the process. Unless of course, you plan on dying with me, in that case, you're good to use arsenic trioxide."

Sofia swats my hand away from her thigh, grabs the shot glass, and downs the contents in the blink of an eye. Her face doesn't even *twitch* at the explosion that must be happening inside of her.

CHAPTER 6

"met a lot of people but nobody feels like you"—*It's You by Ali Gatie*

Sofia

"TELL ME ONE MORE THING ABOUT HIM!" Miles begs as his friend Kya pulls up in front of my aunt's house.

I shrug. "Wouldn't know what to tell you."

I never thought that on my first day back in New City, I would walk right into my childhood crush, then find out he's somewhat popular and far more good-looking than I had remembered. I also didn't think I would end up in a bar that night or get a ride home from a friend of said childhood crush's friend.

"Tell me embarrassing stories about Aaron. I *have* to have something against him."

I truly wish I could tell Miles more, but I don't know that much about Aaron. He's all grown up now. He's still into hockey, that much I figured. But aside from that… nothing. I doubt he still plays with *Hot Wheels* or his sister's Barbies because he's being forced to occupy her. I don't think Aaron still goes out every Monday to pick a flower off the ground and give it to his mother. I also don't think he still sings along to *"Too Little, Too Late"* by *JoJo* while brushing his teeth.

There is nothing I can tell Miles. And the little things I know from when we were younger, I will gatekeep them forever.

"I haven't spoken to him in thirteen years. Even if I wanted to tell you more, there is nothing to say." Except for the fact that we both have one half of a necklace. But he isn't wearing it anymore.

It doesn't surprise me. He's probably had ten girlfriends by now. Plus, a promise made at the age of eight cannot last. Especially not when you're worlds apart from the other.

"You done? I promised Eira I would be there at six. We still got an hour and a half to drive, Miles," Kya says. Kya seems to be all okay. I haven't been talking to her, but she was kind enough to give me a ride home, even though Wesley Hills is in the other direction from New York City.

"Who's Eira?" I ask, my mouth being faster than my brain. I shouldn't ask because this is none of my business.

"Colin Carter's sister. I tutor her because she can't attend school anymore. Not a clue why it has to be at six in the morning on a Sunday, but I suppose it's better than never seeing her again." Giving me a quick smile, she turns to look at Miles again. I get the feeling she's kind, but not to everyone. Like, for some unknown reason, she just hates me even though she doesn't know me at all. "What are you doing in New York this early anyway?"

I hop out of the car before I could hear his answer. I'm not here to make friends. It's only eight more months until graduation. I am here to study, get my degree, and be done with school shit for the rest of my life. Plus, I swore to stay away from the hockey crowd shortly after I left for Germany oh so many years ago.

I've gotten my heart broken by one hockey player, and I wasn't going to risk that happening ever again. Not by friends of said heartbreaker anyway.

You guys were eight. Just get over it already.

I unlock the front door of my aunt's house. She said I could keep the spare key as long as I'm staying here, so at least I don't have to ring the doorbell all the time.

As I enter, I am greeted by a cloud of smoke. The living room lights are turned on, yet all I really see is—*surprise*—smoke. Not a fire kind of smoke. Cigarette smoke.

"Nicole?" I call out, but as she doesn't respond, I know this can only be Hugo, my uncle. Well, technically he's not my uncle as my aunt isn't married to him. I have absolutely no idea how Nicole can keep him around.

I haven't even been here for a day, and I want to wrap my hands around his throat and squeeze tightly.

"Germany, is that you?" Hugo asks from the living room at the same time as another wave of smoke rushes through the air. "Come here, pretty face. Say hello to your uncle."

I don't bother going anywhere near that smoked-up living room. "Sorry, I'm really tired!" As fast as I can, I rush up the stairs, into my provisional bedroom, locking the door right behind me.

It's one thing to live with people that are strangers to you by now, and another when one of these strangers is a pedophilic asshole.

I believe my mother has tried getting rid of Hugo more often than Nicole has.

When we used to live here and Nicole stopped by for a visit, accompanied by her "picture perfect" boyfriend Hugo, my mother would tell my sister and me to change into clothes that don't show too much skin.

Imagine having to worry about your sister's man looking at *children* in a way he definitely shouldn't. *Nuh-uh.*

If my mother knew he is still around, she would book the next flight to New City and drag my ass out of this house faster than I could blink.

As I open my suitcase to find some more comfortable clothes to wear, I notice a carton box right under the bed with the inscription: *"Sofia"*

It's my handwriting, well, the one I had when I was seven. I must have written it shortly before we moved. One of the few boxes my parents decided not to take with us as they were "unnecessary".

In a matter of seconds, I'm changed into a big shirt and shorts.

My hair is just thrown up into a bun that definitely won't survive the next thirty minutes, but who even cares.

Reaching underneath the bed, I pull out the box, almost choking on the wave of dust that comes my way when I blow it off as much as possible.

You know the feeling, when you investigate and find out some information you could have lived without?

Opening this box is one of those moments for me.

This box contains all of my old pictures with Lily, Aaron, and me. Even a picture of the three of us when Aaron had just bought us matching frog stuffed animals. He got them for us as a friendship present. Well, his father bought them, but Aaron made him do it, okay?

I remember looking for that thing the entire day before I moved away, and as I couldn't find it, Aaron gave me his.

He said, *"Keep it so you will never forget me, Icicle."*

Oh, how could I ever forget him? Even without having the frog sitting on my bed daily, I would have never been able to forget him.

I pick up one of the pictures, the one that was taken just before I left the Marsh's house for the last time.

Chapter 7

"if this is what it's like falling in love / then I don't ever wanna grow up"—Kid In Love by Shawn Mendes

October 2008—Age Seven

"SOFIA, SWEETIE, WE HAVE TO GO," my mom says as she comes walking into my now empty bedroom.

My sister Julia is happy that we're leaving. She said she didn't like our home anyway, but I like it here. I don't want to leave for Germany.

I heard it's cold there and all the people are mean. My older brother Lukas told me that. And I believe every word Lukas says because he is smart. He is already going to middle school. But Julia is a lot smarter because she started high school this year. But Lukas is my favorite sibling, so I trust him more.

But the good thing is, I already know a little German. My mom is from Germany, so she taught me before.

"I don't want to go," I tell her through tears. This is so unfair. All of my friends are here. I even go to school here. I don't want to take the plane to school every day. I would much rather walk with my two best friends in the whole wide world.

Tears stream down my face when I look up at my mother. "I don't know where Phoenix is."

Phoenix is my favorite stuffed animal. He's a frog and I don't like frogs, but Lily does. Aaron, Lily's brother, gave him to me as a goodbye because he knows I will leave very soon.

Want me to let you in on a little secret?

I named him Phoenix because that's Aaron's middle name, but Lily can't know I named him that. She doesn't want me to like Aaron, so I don't. But I still named him Phoenix.

"Did you forget him at Aaron's house yesterday?" Mom asks even though she knows I wouldn't remember it even if I did forget him there. I shake my head, convinced that I had Phoenix still when I got back home. "We'll stop by at his house on our way to the airport, okay, sweetie?"

Seeing Aaron one last time before we leave? That I can do. I *have* to do.

I will miss Aaron a lot. He annoys me sometimes, or rather every time when I see him, but he's my best friend's brother and I like him. We always skate together, but not as often anymore because Lily can't see him. We still meet up though.

I don't know why that is.

Now we only ever skate together every Monday and Friday for a little while because he has hockey training. I'm already at the ice rink because, before his hockey training, I always meet with my Coach and Lily for practice.

I love skating, especially with my best friend.

But you know what I don't like? Aaron always calls me "Icicle". It's so annoying. My name is Sofia, not Icicle. Don't tell Aaron, but I kind of like that he has a nickname for me.

We're at Aaron's house now, but Emerson said he isn't inside yet. He went outside to have an eye on Ana because her mom had to use the restroom. Lily said we don't like Ana.

Ana is still a baby, of course, we don't like her. Babies are loud and cry a lot. I know because my brother told me I always cried when I was born.

"Icicle!" Aaron yells all excitedly when he comes running into the house. "I thought you already left for Germany."

I shake my head quickly. Aaron makes me nervous. I never know how to act around him. I really like Aaron a lot, but I can't tell Lily.

"We're on our way now, Phoenix," I say. I always call him by his middle name because it makes him look at me madly. He doesn't like being called Phoenix.

"Don't call me that!" His eyebrows dip into a mad frown just at the same time as he crosses his arms over his chest.

I giggle because that is what he makes me do a lot. But then I start to cry because I remember why I'm here. Almost instantly Aaron wraps his arms around me.

"Don't cry, my Sofia. We'll see each other again, I promise." I smile but he can't see that. Aaron doesn't know whether we'll see each other again or not, but I love that he promised we will. "When I'm old enough, I will come looking for you, my Sofia."

I hope he will. Even though I'm only gone for a few years.

"I lost my frog," I tell him. I didn't tell Aaron I named the frog Phoenix. I'm scared he would make fun of me for it.

Aaron looks at me, then smiles widely. "That's not a problem, Icicle. You can have mine."

He takes my hand in his and pulls me upstairs into his room. Aaron has a huge bedroom, but I don't like it very much. His walls are covered in posters of hockey players, and he has clutter all over his floor. Mostly pucks he stole from the arena or hockey games his father took him to. He even has sticks all around his bedroom, but very few toys. But I know he has a lot of toy cars around here somewhere.

"I will give it back, okay?"

"No, keep it so you will never forget me, Icicle," he says as he hands me his frog. It's not the same I have. Well, it is, just in different clothes.

Mine wears a hockey uniform, which is another reason why I

named him after Aaron. Aaron's frog wears a light purple dress. He insists the color is called *wisteria*, but we all know it's light purple.

It doesn't matter because this color is now my very favorite one.

"What's her name?" I ask, taking the frog from him.

"Uh"—Aaron kicks a sock on his floor into the next best corner—"Violet."

"Are you lying?" He is lying. Aaron would *never* call the frog Violet when he insists the dress is wisteria.

"Yes."

"Sofia!" Aaron's dad yells from downstairs. "Your mother is waiting."

Why can't I just stay with the Marshs? Or with Lily. I don't want to go so far away from home.

Aaron and I both walk downstairs, holding each other's hand. I'm still crying, more than I was before. And it only gets worse when we reach the last step where Aaron hugs me one more time.

Right before my mom and I leave, Aaron kisses my cheek after he whispers, "Remember, we'll get married one day."

I hear a *click*, but I ignore it because Aaron is giving me one more thing.

"I forgot to give it to you yesterday," he says as he lays a necklace into my hand. "It's one half of a heart, I have the other one. Promise you won't ever take it off."

Looking at the *Lego* piece attached to a thin silver chain, I feel a teardrop drip from my nose. "I promise."

Chapter 8

"and when you're in the trenches and you're under fire / I will cover you"—Brother by Kodaline

"YOU'RE SUPPOSED TO HIT THE NET, MARSH!" Coach Carter yells, angrily throwing his clipboard right onto the ice.

He's in a cranky mood lately, but it's sort of given when his daughter died last Wednesday, and his son, the one that tries his best to go pro after graduation, would rather spend his time at a mental hospital to visit my sister than show up for practice.

To be fair, Colin probably had other reasons not to show up today. For instance, because his sister died, he might need longer to deal with it and such. But I do, however, feel better knowing he still cares about *my* sister. Even after he got her far enough to be wanting help.

Doesn't mean Coach should let his anger out on me though.

Now, I know Tobias Carter sees a hell lot of potential in me, which is quite the ego boost coming from a Coach that's usually coaching the pros. And I like that he tells me when I could do better, but fucking hell. I missed the net *once* and he goes on yelling at me for it.

For the next thirty minutes, half the team spends it skating up and down the ice while the other half comes crashing into them. Coach said it's a great way to practice taking control over sudden anger outbreaks and aggressive attacks from opponents on the ice. I think it's complete bullshit.

"What's up with him lately?" Miles holds his hand out for me to help me back up. That asshole just ran right into me… and we're on the same side of the team-split here.

I take his hand and make myself a lot heavier than I am just for Miles to struggle a little bit. But of course, he doesn't.

"Not a clue." Well, I do know, but I promised Colin I wouldn't say a word to *anyone* yet.

"He's acting like me when I don't fuck at least once a day." He's not wrong, that I have to admit. "Anyway, you think he'd let me go early when I ask nicely?"

I shake my head. "No way."

"That's what I thought." Sighing heavily, Miles looks at the digital clock on the other end of the arena. He seems a bit nervous, but I'm not sure why.

"What's up? I can vouch for you if needed."

Another headshake, but this time it looks sadder than I've ever witnessed Miles act before. "Maeve is giving me a hard time with Brooke."

Miles usually doesn't talk about his daughter with the rest of the team around, or anyone really, which tells me exactly how bad the situation is right now.

The team knows of Brooklyn, but Miles still prefers to keep her away from everyone. Only on rare occasions does he bring up his daughter with everyone around or involves her in plans when the rest of the team is there as well.

"She gave me a fucking ultimatum."

Before I get the chance to speak, Coach Carter blows his whistle, then shouts, "King, Marsh, I didn't say you could go on a coffee break! Get back to skating!"

But I don't. As any good number one alternative captain would, I sit back down on the ice to protest. I don't care if this is going to get me benched for the next game, but today's practice is just bull-shit.

Miles looks at me as though he's trying to tell me I'm crazy. Perhaps I am, but I'm doing this for him. If his sister gives Miles an ultimatum, it doesn't matter what it's about, the situation is serious. Miles needs to leave, so I'll help him to get out early. Not giving a shit anymore, Miles sits down right beside me, deciding to protest with me together.

"What the hell is that about?" Coach asks, making his way over to us. As he stands in front of me, he asks again.

"I demand we leave early today. Clearly, you have other worries than getting us ready for our next game, Coach. Today's training *sucks*. It's complete bullshit." *Way to go, Aaron*. I should be a little less cranky with this man, but hell does it feel good to say it out loud.

"Yeah, Coach. What's up with practice today? It doesn't make sense."

I can watch as the Coach balls his hands into fists and then loosens them up again before calling out for the rest of the team to gather around.

Moments later, we're all standing on the ice like little kids waiting to get handed some ice cream. Just that we're not getting handed some ice cream but devastating news.

"You all remember Eira, right?"

The team nods because we do. Maybe not the new ones, but last year, for Eira's fifteenth birthday, the team planned everything. And I mean *everything*. From the location to entertainment, meals, snacks, etcetera. A handful even went to go dress shopping with her. Eira has always been a good vibe when she watched us, cheered for us. Everyone loves her.

"My daughter had cancer, as most of you knew. But unfortunately, there was nothing more to do for her." A few gasps sound through the silent arena, aware of where this is going. "Eira died last Wednesday, which is why practice was called off all week. Her funeral is this Friday and it's a little stressful to make every wish she had for it reality." In translation, the Coach lets his stress out on us through stupid practice because he knows it'll torture us.

"Colin wanted to be the one to tell you, but due to the situation with his girlfriend, he found it far more important to be there for her than attend today."

"You've got a visitor," Grey says, slapping me on the back before pointing across the parking lot of the arena.

After protesting and arguing with the Coach for good fifteen minutes, he finally let us go. Mind you, a whole hour earlier than practice would be off.

Sofia standing on the other side of the parking lot most likely has nothing to do with me.

"Did you know about Eira?" Miles suddenly asks. He's not the type to be sentimental, at least not that I know of. The concern in his voice is pretty unexpected if you asked me.

"I did."

"That she was dying, too?"

I nod. "I suspected it. Colin never said anything, but she didn't exactly look healthy the past couple of weeks. I already had my guesses when Colin said their parents pulled her out of school due to medical reasons though."

"She got sick pretty young, didn't she?" Miles rakes a hand through his hair. "Like fourteen?"

Not sure where he's going with this, but I do have an idea. "They noticed something being off when she was thirteen, but she's been diagnosed at fourteen." The only reason I know so much about Eira's cancer history is because whenever I was over at Colin's childhood home, Eira wouldn't stop talking about *every-thing*. Including her cancer.

"How did they notice something was off?"

I finally find the strength to look away from Sofia. My eyes first meet with Grey's, looking as confused and suspicious as mine probably do. Then we both look at Miles at the same time. We even ask, "You don't think Brooke has leukemia, do you?" at the very same time. Two different phrasings, but it still gets the same question across.

"No, but what if she does and I simply don't think about it being possible?"

Grey lays a hand on Miles's shoulder. "Do you have any *reasons* to suspect she might have leukemia, Miles?"

Miles shakes his head. "But Maeve said she has been pretty tired and moody lately."

Hence whatever ultimatum she gave Miles. Maeve might be Miles's stepsister, and she might have taken in his daughter while Miles is still going to college, but we all know Maeve would much rather never talk to her brother ever again. And when *his* child starts being difficult… of course she would find something to make Miles feel miserable about it.

For just a second, my eyes wander over to Sofia. She's still standing on the opposite side of the parking lot, waiting. She keeps on looking at me too, so at least I'm not the only one that can't stop checking.

"Brooklyn knows you're her father and Maeve is only her aunt, right?" I hear Grey ask, followed by a quick confirmation from Miles. "Did you ever consider that maybe Brooke would much rather live with her father than her aunt?"

"Sure, but I can't really change it. I'm not graduating before May."

"She can stay with us, Miles. I told you a million times. I don't mind her being around." Grey and Miles have rented a house together, just like Colin and I have. The best part about it, we're even neighbors. Our houses are connected by a garden that we have to share. But since Miles and Grey are over at Colin and my house daily anyway, it's only convenient for them. Makes it easier to get to the other side of the street.

"But I can't take her to class with me. And she hates daycare. I've tried."

An idea pops up in my head. Not sure if it's a good or bad one, but it most definitely is *an* idea. "We don't always have classes at the same time. I can take care of her while I'm off. Bet Grey would gladly be a helping hand as well." Because Grey is the best. "Colin has different hours too. He can do something good for once as well."

"What about hockey? We're all there at the same time."

I smirk while looking at Sofia. Miles follows my eyes, but he instantly shakes his head. "I am *not* letting my four-year-old with a complete stranger."

"No, but I have a sister. Brooklyn met Lily before. Briefly, but they met. Plus, you know Lily. *I* know Lily very well. Colin is in love with Lily. And Grey never said anything bad about her, so that's also a good sign. And there is a high chance Lily *and* Sofia would gladly spend their time watching your daughter while we're at practice."

CHAPTER 9

"I haven't been by your side / in a minute but I, think about it sometimes"—What A Time by Julia Michaels, Niall Horan

WHY CAN'T HE TAKE A GODDAMN HINT?

I've been standing here for good fifteen minutes, looking at Aaron while he's talking to his friends. I mean, I guess I can't take it badly. If I wanted to talk to him, I might as well walk up to them and ask for his time. But I am not doing that. I keep standing here like a coward, waiting for Aaron to walk over here.

I'm not even sure why the thought of talking to Aaron gets me this nervous? He's just… Aaron. Phoenix.

He's the guy that owned my heart a long time ago. Emphasis lies on a *long time ago*.

Thankfully I don't have to wait much longer for him to get the hint. On second thought, I want to run away because the smirk on his face, as he approaches me, screams danger.

"Hey there, Icicle," he says, clapping his hands together. "Whatcha doing here?"

You got this, Sofia. He's *just* Aaron. "Do you know where Lily's at? I've tried finding her all week but she's unfindable."

His arms cross over his chest, his tongue pressing into his lower cheek as he continues to smirk. "Why?"

What does he mean by "why?" Lily is my best friend. I've never called her anything but that even when we haven't been speaking for ages. "Because I need to see her. I need to talk to her."

"Not sure where she is, but you can come home with me and ask her boyfriend. He definitely knows where she's at."

I should say no and continue to look for her all around campus daily. Something about Aaron's tone tells me he is lying. It's the same one he always used when we were younger, and he was being dishonest. Though, these days it's a bit deeper as his voice deepened over the years.

But what comes out of my mouth is, "Doesn't he play hockey, too?"

Aaron nods. "He skipped practice." As far as I heard, Colin Carter is the captain of the hockey team. A pretty unreliable one if he skips practice just like that. "I actually have a really important favor to ask you, Sofia."

My alarm bells start ringing. The last time Aaron and I spoke was the day I got here, and before that when we were eight. Whatever favor he wants to ask for, it's nothing he should be asking me so early on. I mean, you don't just go around asking for favors from people.

"What favor?"

"I'll tell you when we get home. I have to ask Colin the same one, no need to say it twice."

"I'm not sure if he's home yet," Aaron tells me as he unlocks the front door to his house.

It's weird being back here. Granted, I've only been here once, but that doesn't make it any less weird. At least this time I'm not here to use his shower and change my clothes.

"How am I supposed to ask your best friend a question when he isn't even here?"

Aaron holds the door open for me and I follow him inside.

"You're not just here for him, Icicle. We have some catching up to do, don't you think?"

Considering that I didn't even think he'd ever want to talk to me again, I didn't believe so, no. Now that he indirectly says he *wants* to talk to me, I certainly do.

Just as I open my mouth, the same handsome-looking guy I've seen exit Mrs. Reyes's house comes sprinting down the stairs. "You're hom—Who the hell is this?" He points at me but doesn't bother to look at me.

Aaron takes out a bottle of water from the refrigerator and takes a long sip before he even cares to answer. "She's someone that can so easily steal your girlfriend from you, Carter."

Right, because Lily and I are oh-so-close these days.

Don't get me wrong, I really wish we were. Losing my friendship with Lily has been the hardest fucking thing to go through in my entire life. I hated every day I lived in Germany for the simple fact that Lily wasn't there with me.

Sure, I got used to not having her around. I found other friends, too. It's not that I've been lonely without her.

It's just… Sometimes, losing your best friend hurts more than anything you've ever felt before. Especially when you don't have an actual cut in the friendship. When your friendship just drifts further and further apart and there is nothing you can do about it. It feels like stabbing a knife into your heart so you could die… only that you keep missing the heart and stab over and over again.

Not being able to find peace in a situation sucks.

"Steal my Lilybug from me?" He laughs, once. "Impossible." All of Colin's humor is gone just after the last word leaves his mouth. Eventually, he looks at me, or rather his eyes follow up my body. "Don't tell me you're his new on-again off-again fuck-buddy."

"Winter and my fucking was never on-again and off-again. Our relationship status was." Details that I do not need to know. "But, my friend, to answer your first question, this is Sofia."

I can see as Colin's body freezes from shock. It's like my name alone is poison in his mind. "Sofia?" he asks to make sure. "*The* Sofia?" He's now watching me more deeply, analyzing every inch of my facial features.

Whatever he might see on my face, I don't think he likes it.

A second after Colin finishes staring at my face, his eyebrows drip and he looks as though he's in pain. "Like, the one that moved to Germany—Sofia?"

I don't know who talked about me, but one definitely did. There is no way this guy would know this otherwise. Not sure if I want to entertain the idea that both of my long-lost friends talked about me to someone that has no idea who I am.

"That would be me."

Colin's body sags as he exhales so deeply, he might as well be blowing out more air than what was inside of him. "Are you planning on stealing my girlfriend from me? Because I'm not sure I won't use some of my contacts to stop that from happening."

I shake my head instantly. Unsure if I should be terrified or find that adorable. "Aaron just took me here so I could ask you a question."

"Right. Icicle, Lily isn't attending classes these days. She's at— she's somewhere outside of New City at the moment. Won't come back before Friday of next week," Aaron says way before I even get to voice my question for Colin.

What the hell though? Why didn't he just tell me that before he took me here? Because, clearly, he knew.

"You could've just told me that right away, *Phoenix*."

"Phoenix? Now that's getting interesting." Amusement dances on Colin's words. He leans back against the wall, just watching Aaron and me.

Aaron holds up his middle finger, flipping both, Colin, and me, off like we're eight years old again. "I could have, but where's the fun in that?"

"I have things to do."

"Like what? Look for your best friend all around campus when she's not there?"

I've listened to enough true crime podcasts to know how to murder him without getting caught. Never thought this would come in handy, apparently, it will very soon. "You're such an asshole, you know that?"

"That's not how you should talk to an old crush."

Alright, let's start a list of things I need in order to make his death look like an accident.

"I never had a crush on you." That's not entirely true, but you know, at the age of six to eight, every guy you meet is either disgusting or you pin after them for no reason. I can easily play this off.

Aaron chuckles, winking at me before he says, "Anyway, now that you're both here… Colin, Miles needs our help and you do not have any other choice but to be okay with it. It's about Brooke. And Sofia, the favor I needed to ask you… I kind of need you to watch a little four-year-old for an hour or two, daily. Together with Lily, of course. It's just for the time while we're at hockey practice."

That's a lot to ask, don't you think?

"Obviously I'll owe you for that. But here's the thing…"

To sum up his explanation, his friend needs help to keep his daughter around without making her attend his classes. And Aaron doesn't want Lily to take care of a toddler all by herself for whatever reasons. Which is where I'll come into the picture. Being a helping hand.

There are about two handful of reasons why I should say no.

But there are also a few reasons why I cannot say no.

Reason number one: A father needs help with his child. And as it sounds, he is depending on his friends for it.

Reason number two: I get to spend time reconnecting with Lily.

Reason number three: As much as I want to murder Aaron for being an asshole, he's been a great friend once. Annoying, but a great one nonetheless. I may not be helping him out, but someone important to him.

Chapter 10

"I don't want to say goodbye 'cause this one means forever"—In The Stars by Benson Boone

THEY WANTED A SMALL THING. Only family and Eira's closest friends. But Eira didn't want that. Of course, she didn't want a small thing.

I just bet Eira Carter began planning her own funeral the day she's been diagnosed with leukemia. Not that anyone can blame her, really. She knew there was no chance of surviving it, it's what the doctors have been telling her from day one.

Doesn't make it any less sad.

The entire St. Trewery hockey team had to get their asses over to New York to make it to Eira's funeral. Excuses to miss today weren't accepted. *Everyone* had to come. Okay, except for the freshmen. They didn't even know Eira. But everyone else… yup, they are here.

As Colin's best friend, I had met Eira a hell of a lot more times than the rest of the team did, which got me a spot right in the front row.

I hate funerals. Haven't been to a lot yet, but the ones I did attend, I can't say I was thrilled to be there.

I'm not saying some people's deaths are worse than others, but I am kind of saying it anyway. I mean, did anyone grieve over the death of a serial killer? I don't think so.

That's a bad comparison to what I was about to say.

What I meant to say is, I attended my grandpa's funeral a couple of years ago. He was old, fragile, and sick, it was bound to happen. But Eira was young. She was sick too, but barely above the age of sixteen. I'm convinced her young age has my heart torn into pieces worse than it was when my grandpa died.

My sister is standing right next to me, holding onto my hand tightly while I assume Colin does the same with hers.

It's a miracle she was even allowed to be here.

Lily is supposed to be at a mental hospital, getting help for her suicidal thoughts and depression. *Professional* help, not just Colin taking her out on dates. It took about three parents, a whole hockey team and the letter from a sixteen-year-old, *dead* girl to convince the staff from said hospital to let my sister out for the day. Of course, she's being accompanied by two social workers, watching from afar, but it's still better than my sister not being able to attend a funeral she is needed at.

Not that she is needed for the funeral, but she is needed to console her grieving boyfriend, the one that is trying his hardest not to let tears slip past his eyes as the clergy says a few words. And well, the letter did say Eira wanted Lily here, so there's that too.

Soon after the clergy is done with his eulogy, family members follow, but I barely pay attention to what is said. At least until Colin stands in front of everyone, his hand still holding onto my sister's for dear life as he tries to gather himself before speaking.

I can't believe I didn't even notice when Lily let go of my hand. But I guess when I was busy trying to sound out the voices of people talking and refusing to let myself get consumed by the ache in my heart, it makes sense.

"Eira was a lot of things," Colin starts, looking over the crowd of people. "Wow, okay, I didn't think I'd find seeing people at a funeral dressed in bright colors astonishing, yet here we are." None of us is dressed in black as Eira wanted colors. He smiles at the lack of the color black, then proceeds.

"As I was saying, Eira was a lot of things. Mainly loud. She was so loud, I just bet people in L.A. could hear her laughter. I don't think I've ever witnessed Eira complain about her illness. Sure, she had her days when she was sick of it, but other than that… my sister was living her best life even through everything that was happening. She kept smiles on her face, talked about how excited she was to start a new adventure. Because as we all know, when you die, you start another one."

It's not a proven theory, but it's what Eira believed.

"My sister was so sure she was put on this earth for one reason, and she fulfilled her goal which is why she was supposed to die early. I have no idea what that reason was, besides clearly breaking my family's heart, and then telling us to haunt us when we shed tears. God forbid her family actually loves her. But you know Eira, tears weren't her thing. Neither was sadness. But she did love a good amount of drama."

People chuckle through tears as Colin glares toward his sister's casket. He lets go of Lily's hand then walks right up to Eira's dead body. He looks inside, then shakes his head letting out an extra-heavy sigh.

"You really had to come into our lives like a bomb and then dip out when it got interesting, didn't you, *enana*?" He turns back to everyone, then rolls his eyes. "The audacity of this girl, I swear. She had us fooled. She was all about the drama, wanting to be the center of attention, she even made like a hundred people show up to a not-so-happy get-together about *her*. And guess who doesn't bother being here? Exactly, my sister."

"For so many reasons, I hope she's going on a great new adventure. I am praying for her that her new life is going to be so much longer, that her new family gets to spend more time with her and appreciates it as much as we all did. Maybe she'll be re-born with a great singing voice, God knows she loved singing. Wherever she may end up, or already ended up, I hope she is okay." Colin lets out a deep sigh. "But I'm telling you, if she's still in ghost mode right now, she might as well be laughing at every single tear she has seen today. Or roll her eyes, cuss you out for wasting tears."

Only Colin could make people laugh at a funeral. Though I know, despite the slim smile on his face, whatever is going on inside of his head and heart, it's far away from happiness and laughter.

I know I'm far from it. *My* chest is hurting, my head is spinning in hopes for Eira that everything she expected death to be like... it's just like it.

A couple more people go up on that tiny stage to say a few words, and with every other person, the heaviness around us seems to lighten as people no longer talk about how sad it is that Eira is gone, but about how much she loved laughing, how she would fall onto any soft surface all dramatically when she was about to ask a question, she knew wasn't going to draw a good reaction out of the other person. They talked about her happy memories. The little moments in life people tend to overlook.

An hour later—I believe—the whole ceremony is over. The team is awfully quiet for once, yet they still somehow crack jokes despite looking like they've been run over by ten trucks and had bees sting their eyes.

We're all invited to the Carter's house for a little party in Eira's honor. Yes, a *party*. Just like she wished.

Tears aren't allowed, so she said herself. Repetitively. She wanted everything glamorous, big, and happy. Eira didn't want to go with people crying over her death, she wanted them to celebrate her life.

As we all make our way out of this cemetery, a wisteria-colored bow on dark chocolate-colored hair catches my attention.

She's kneeling by a grave, currently exchanging old roses with her favorite flowers.

I don't have to see the woman's face to know it's Sofia.

I have absolutely no idea why she's here, whose grave she is visiting, but I do know I won't stop thinking about it until I get an answer.

But that answer will have to wait.

Today is about Eira, not my weird connection to my old child-hood crush.

CHAPTER 11

"shooting for the stars when I couldn't make a killing"—
High Hopes by Panic! At The Disco

Sofia

"HOW'S IT GOING?" my brother asks after I finally pick up the phone at five in the goddamn morning. "Did you hear the news already?"

"What news?" Clearly, I didn't.

"The ones about Leon and Julia."

"No, but I'm sure you'll enlighten me very soon, Lukas." Lukas is five years older than me… and yet *he* is the one that loves gossip. With his twenty-six years on this earth, you'd think he finds gossiping childish. Well, he doesn't. Especially not when it's about our sister and that fucker that used to be my boyfriend.

If I'm being honest, I've always preferred Lukas over Julia. I never thought he preferred me over her though, given that they're closer in age than we are. But the second I told him Julia fucked *my* boyfriend while I was still with him, he turned against her instantly.

Now, I know siblings should always stick together and have each other's backs and such. But I refuse to call Julia my sister at this point.

She's twenty-seven years old. Leon is my age. She knew very well that we were dating, and she still went and seduced him.

I'm not upset we're no longer together. In fact, I knew Leon and I wouldn't work out the second we started dating. Doesn't mean she can go and fuck him while he's in a relationship with me though.

And to make matters worse, they're now a couple.

"Leon is going to propose to her on Christmas morning," Lukas tells me. "As far as I know, Julia knows of it. They're planning the proposal to make *you* feel bad when you come back for the holidays."

Only Julia would be this cruel.

She's always been heartless. Even more so when we moved to Germany. In a country where people tend to take words too seriously sometimes, she definitely fits right in. That is unless you move to a small town in the countryside and the townies are all chirpy and not saying hello while passing someone on the streets is counted as being rude.

Such a nightmare for my dear sister. A definite laugh for me.

"I'm not even sure I can come," I say. The thought of having to watch my sister get proposed to by a guy I've dated before just gives me one more reason not to have time to be home for Christmas. "I'll probably have tons of homework etcetera."

"No, Sofia. You *will* be there. I need you here. You think I can get through that act all by myself? If I'm the only one wasted, Dad will make me clean our barn for a whole month. You know I can't keep my mouth shut when I'm drunk, so I would tell Julia how much of a bitch she is only to get punished by our parents at the age of twenty-six." He sure would. Our father is a little stricter than our mother, and yes, somehow, he still thinks punishing his *adult* children is acceptable.

Still. "I don't know, Lukas. Everyone is going to look at me with pity in their eyes. They know what happened. It's a small village we live in, word gets around. And then Leon *proposes* to my sister? They'll assume I'd be devastated."

"So get a boyfriend and make him top Leon's proposal."

I chortle. "Doing what?"

"Propose to you a second later with a far bigger ring," he says. "Or no, I've got something better. Just ask a man that looks better than Leon to be your date. You were always far too pretty for him anyway. Julia will be jealous, try to snatch that guy away from you but he will humiliate her by calling her out."

That sounds awful. Hilarious, but awful.

"Where the hell am I supposed to find a hot guy that will pretend to be my boyfriend, fly to Germany with me for the *holidays* and act as though he's head over heels in love with me?" *Impossible*.

Lukas is quiet for a whole minute, just thinking.

While he thinks of an answer that won't come because it is simply impossible to make *that* happen, I decide to go through the box containing the pictures one more time.

I didn't get all too far last time as memories flooded my brain.

The first picture that catches my eye is from December 2007. More specifically, my seventh birthday.

Lily, Aaron, and I are sitting at a table, my face covered in cake because a certain someone figured it was funny to push my head into the purple-frosted birthday cake. Luckily for me, the candles were already blown out. Unfortunately, the purple frosting left an ugly stain that took a whole day to wash off. Imagine what the food coloring would have done to someone's teeth.

Back then, I thought this was the worst thing to ever happen to me. But thinking back now, that birthday was probably the best I've ever had.

"I got it!" he screams into the phone. "A male escort. But instead of using him to fuck, you'll get him to be your date. Easy. I'll pay."

What? I burst out into horrific laughter, a holding-my-hand-to-my-stomach kind of laughter.

"You're right, bad idea. Julia would definitely snatch that guy away. But I have another option for you. What's that guy's name again? Adam? Alan? You know, the hockey guy you liked so much. Didn't he live in New City? You think he still lives there?"

"No."

I can *feel* him smirk. "No what? No, he didn't live there; no, he doesn't live there anymore; or no, this won't happen?"

"Just no."

Chapter 12

"I'll promise you to give my all"—I Still Love You by The-Overtunes

Aaron

"ARE YOU FUCKING KIDDING ME!" my sister yells the second I walk into our house. As far as I know, she'll be living with Colin and me now.

Admittedly, I like it better that way. Won't admit it to her, but it's the truth. At least when she's here on a daily, I can keep an eye on her without excessively having to hunt her down on campus, call or text her five times a day to make sure she's still breathing.

She might have gotten the help she needed, but depression and suicidal thoughts just don't leave in two weeks. Or so I believe. So having her around is easing my nerves at least a little bit.

"Not sure I know what you're talking about, Lily." She's just gotten released from the psych ward a couple of hours ago, came to watch our game, and then went straight home with Colin. Now they're sitting on the couch in the living room watching a movie. "But it's great to have you around again."

"You *knew* Sofia was back!" She jumps off the couch, but Colin wraps his arms around her hips and pulls her back down. "She's been back for weeks and I'm only finding out *now*."

"You had other things to worry about." And that's the truth. Between Colin trying to get her to stay alive and her release from the psych ward, she didn't have time for a best friend reunion. Plus, there was no need in upsetting Lily by rubbing a person that she knows loves her, right in her face when she wanted to die. "Besides, you will meet her tomorrow. You guys are kind of babysitters now."

"Babysitters?!" she blurts out at the same time as Colin starts to laugh.

He shouldn't have.

Lily turns around to look at him, her eyebrows fallen into a mad frown. If looks could kill, I just bet Colin would have been dead about five times by now.

"Miles needs a helping hand with Brooklyn. Sofia agreed on watching her with you whenever we've got practice." To be fair, Sofia wasn't needed for this at all. But for some selfish reasons, I figured if Sofia was around during practice, I could at least catch a glimpse of her every now and then.

Despite what I've been telling myself all these years, my heart has always been stuck with her. It's why Winter and I could have never happened even if I wanted us to work out. I made a promise to Sofia so many years ago, and for some reason, I'm still holding on to it.

It won't happen, I just know it won't, but I also hate breaking promises. Sure, it was a promise made when I was eight, but a promise is a promise either way.

Sofia and I are two different people now than we were back at the age of eight. She's lived her whole life without me, I've lived mine without her. I know absolutely nothing about her anymore, same way that she has no clue who I am.

As much as I'd love to continue where we left our friendship off, it's impossible.

"It's one half of a heart, I have the other one. Promise you won't ever take it off." Not even I held on to that promise. But at least I still own that wisteria Lego necklace, so that's one good

thing, isn't it? Or pathetic.

Let's be honest here, if I just randomly started telling Sofia how much I've missed her and how glad I am that she's back, it would scare her off more than it would do us any good. Plus, it's just embarrassing for me.

But maybe… If we slowly start to get in touch again through my sister and her having to be around me, perhaps there is a chance that we can get to know each other all over again. And who knows? Maybe we can light an old flame.

"You're not still having a crush on her, do you?" my sister asks, causing me to swallow the wrong way and end up coughing like a maniac.

"Aaron having a crush?" I hear Colin laugh, seeing as he leans his chin on Lily's shoulder. "I'd like to see that."

"It was *so* obvious they liked each other."

"We were *eight*," I veto. "I found her annoying and nothing but that."

Lily never liked the thought of Sofia and I even *standing* each other, which is why I made sure to be mean to my sister's best friend. Unfortunately, Sofia took my rudeness as something completely different. And as it seemed, I liked her more than I wanted to admit.

Up until I found out she had to move away. That's when I ignored my sister's wishes and made promises I knew I couldn't keep.

And yet here I am, still holding on to them.

"Sure. And you also *need* her to watch Brooklyn with me because *I* want Sofia around, not you."

Chapter 13

*"don't want to say it but I really think that I miss him"—
chaotic by Tate McRae*

Sofia

"PLEASE CAN WE CUT THE 'let's get to know each other'-bullshit? I've had enough of that the past weeks," Lily says the second she steps out of her boyfriend's car and walks up to me.

"Gladly." Approximately half a heartbeat later, Lily wraps her arms around me so tightly, I think my lungs stopped working for a whole minute.

I've been waiting in front of the hockey arena for half an hour, worrying about what to say and how not to make this awkward only for Lily to shriek in excitement and hug the devil out of me.

Lily is nothing like I imagined. She's always been the loud one, laughing and full of joy. We've just met two minutes ago, and something tells me the fire that was always burning within her is no longer alive.

She seems awfully quiet, though still excited. If we'd been in touch for far longer than the two minutes, I'd ask her what the dark cloud above her head is about, but I don't feel comfortable enough to ask yet.

Aaron gets out of his car just when Lily and I pull away from our hug.

"You are so pretty," she says, taking my hands in hers like she can't believe I'm actually standing in front of her. Truthfully, I can't believe she is standing in front of me either.

I've been imagining what it would be like to reconnect with my childhood best friend, what it would be like when we meet again. None of the scenarios that went through my mind came close to this.

Even though we haven't had the chance to really reconnect yet, it still feels like we've never spent time apart.

"Oh my god, Sofia"—Lily looks at Colin then back at me—"This is Colin, my boyfriend."

He nods his head at me once, giving me a small smile before he wraps his arms around Lily from behind.

"I know, I've met him before."

"I just wanted to say it. I never had the chance to do that before." Lily giggles at something Colin whispers into her ear, then quickly shakes her head.

The things love can do to a person… It all seems so perfect, like love is the easiest thing in the world when in reality the honeymoon phase will be over sooner than later and what comes next is fights over fights. Giggling at something whispered in one's ear will appear as often as one can see a cockroach in the sky.

I once read that as soon as the honeymoon phase is over, you start seeing the flaws in your partner. And apparently, looking past them and still finding the person you love is pretty damn difficult. Hence couple parting ways rather early on in their relationship.

Still, seeing Lily this in love makes me happy. She definitely deserves it.

Suddenly I feel the bow on the back of my head loosen up. When I reach my hands back to tighten it, my fingers collide with someone else's.

Turning around, my eyes land on Aaron's. He's grinning down at me, licking his lips before opening his mouth. "Can't believe you still wear these things." Only when he twists the satin ribbon in his hands do I notice that he pulled the whole thing out of my hair.

I snatch it away from him, narrowing my eyes when I say, "Go fuck yourself, Phoenix."

"No need to get all feisty with me, Icicle. I always liked the bow in your hair. It's like your trademark."

"You *always* made fun of me for wearing it." He also kept pulling the ribbon out of my hair. Every. Single. Time.

"I wasn't making fun of it. I merely thought it'd look better in my hair than yours." He winks, then gives me a lopsided smile.

"Stop bothering Sofia, Aaron. Don't you have hockey practice to get ready for?" Lily asks, coming up beside me.

"Coach isn't there yet, so I've got some more time to annoy her."

"I'll take care of him." Colin bats his lashes at Lily, then looks at me for just a second and back at his girlfriend, like he couldn't keep his eyes off of her even if it would save his life. "Miles and Grey should be here any minute. Think you can wait for them without me, *mi sol*?"

Lily rolls her eyes and then nods. "I'm not four, dumbass."

"Just asking." He then leans in to kiss his girlfriend before swinging an arm around Aaron's shoulders and forcing him to walk inside the arena. Aaron tries to look back, but Colin turns Aaron's head to face forward.

As soon as the entrance doors close, Lily turns to me.

She lays her hands on either side of her jaw, looking at me through her lashes while refraining to smile. "I'm sorry, I just can't believe you're actually here."

"I almost wouldn't."

"Aaron said they just gave your room away." I nod. "So now you live with *Hugo*?"

For a second there I'm wondering how she knows that my aunt still lives with him, but then I remember that her mother and Nicole are neighbors. "Unfortunately."

"You could have my room. Colin and Aaron insist on me

staying at their house, so I no longer need my room at the dorms." It certainly would make my life a whole lot easier. Living with my uncle… it's like living in a bar filled with pedophiles. "You'd have a roommate. She's a bit much sometimes, but I think you could handle her pretty well. Just think about it."

I want to tell her that no matter how difficult her roommate is, she'll be a lot better than Hugo. But before I get the chance to open my mouth and speak, a car stops right next to us.

"These are Miles and Grey—"

"I know. I've met them before."

Lily groans. "I hate that everyone got to see you before me. That's simply not fair." We both laugh because it's true. I should have met Lily before everyone else. She should have been the one to introduce me to everyone and help me get comfortable at St. Trewery.

We watch as Miles helps a little blonde girl out of the car, closes the door, and holds her hand while they walk up to us. She giggles at something her father says, then scrunches up her nose as she looks up at him with admiration in her eyes.

As soon as they come to a stop in front of Lily and me, little Brooklyn hides right behind Miles's leg. Miles doesn't exchange many words with us either. All he voices is a quick, "Thank you for doing this for me." Then he gives us a short but information-filled rundown on things Brooklyn hates—*movies that don't include princesses*—and stuff she loves—*anything with princesses*—before he moves on to allergies. She doesn't have many, but she does have one. She's severely allergic to strawberries, but she keeps insisting on not being allergic so she could have anything strawberry flavored.

He also asks us not to wear anything strawberry scented because she's reacting to artificial scents too. Fortunately, neither Lily nor I wear anything strawberry-scented today. He probably should have given us a heads-up about *that* though.

As quiet as Brooklyn has been when I first met her, I'm quick to find out that she's quite the talker.

Lily and I keep trying to keep her occupied with drawing something, but she insists on *standing* on top of the seats to watch her father's hockey practice. And whenever he passes us, I almost get a heart attack because I think she might fall off the goddamn seat from excitement.

She jumps up and down, twirling around like the little princess she is.

"Remind me to never have children, please," Lily laughs, sighing in exhaustion. We've been watching Brooklyn for *one* hour, and yes, I, too, am exhausted. Then suddenly, Lily no longer watches the ice, her head snaps toward me like her life was depending on it. "Do you still skate?"

"Sometimes, yes. Not while I'm here though."

My Coach was ready to tie me to the rink when I told her I'd be gone for five months. She tried telling me figure skating was more important than my education, and that I'd need the training if I wanted to continue winning medals and such. But I never even wanted to become a professional figure skater.

Sure, skating is fun. I loved skating while Lily and I were partners. I loved it when I started from scratch in Germany, too. Everything was new and exciting. I love it with all of my heart, but it's not what I want to do. Skating is a hobby, not something I can see myself doing until my limbs give up.

"I'm sorry," Lily whispers like it's her fault. "I've been wondering if you quit because I tried googling you so many times, but I never found anything."

A chuckle leaves me faster than my mind could comprehend her words. *She tried googling me.* "Did you check the *German* websites?" I know for a fact there are articles about me on the internet.

Don't get me wrong, I'm not some much talked about figure skater, but I've won my fair share of medals and prices over the last couple of years.

Lily slaps a hand to her face. "No," she laughs. "I wouldn't have understood it, so I skipped them."

"So, you followed up on me?" I raise my brows at her.

"Obviously. But I couldn't find anything. I even made Aaron try and find you, but he said you were unfindable."

"Where the hell did he look for me? ICQ?" *But he looked for you. It's more than you could say about him.*

I *did* look for Aaron. In some ways. I tried finding him on Facebook *once* at the age of fourteen. I couldn't find him. So the most unrealistic fairytale built itself up in my mind. That being Aaron coming to find me in Germany, apologizing for taking so long but he was searching through the entire country to find me. And now he had finally found me.

But like I said, it was just unrealistic. Even I knew it.

"I'm not sure, he never said anything. But I was convinced if one of us would find you, it'd be Aaron."

I'm so close to asking why that is when Brooklyn decides to cut in. "My uncle Aaron?"

Uncle Aaron. I figured the four of them were close, but I honestly didn't think close enough for Miles to give either of the guys the title of his daughter's uncle.

"Yes, Dimples, your uncle Aaron," Lily says while she boops Brooklyn's nose.

She giggles in response. "DADDY!" Just like that, Brooklyn stands on the seat again, waving at Miles as he skates past us. He waves back, but I doubt he heard her yell for him.

I use the moment of distraction wisely. "Why would he be the one to find me?"

Lily's eyes snap back to mine, softening when she notices my confusion. "Please." She reaches toward my neck, pulling out the necklace from underneath my shirt. She holds the Lego pendant in the palm of her hand, smiling. "He never took it off. Not until he was eighteen and Winter threw a whole tantrum about it. If she didn't, I bet he'd still wear it today. Daily."

I took mine off earlier than he did then. I'm only wearing it now because I wanted to see if Aaron would notice. He didn't. If he did, he didn't say anything.

"Lily…"

"Look, it's been *ages*. I don't think you two could still have feelings for each other, if you do, then you're certainly destined for one another. I hated it once; you know how weird the whole thing was for me with my parents. Sure, we were young, and you probably didn't understand the situation. I also hated that you saw him more often than I did, which is why I didn't like the two of you together. Then again, we were *children*. I didn't even know what that thing was between the two of you. It doesn't matter anymore. Aaron can date whomever he wants, so can you. If by some miracle, you two find together, I'll cheer you on."

Where the hell does she get all this from?

"Did your relationship mess up your brain?" I ask, trying not to laugh. "I don't have feelings for your brother. That is even more unrealistic than my dreams."

Lily shakes her head holding her hands up like I was holding her at gunpoint. "I'm just saying. He was in a perfectly good relationship with the most annoying person ever. He broke up with her because she demanded he take off the necklace."

Like he could sense us talking about him, Aaron suddenly slaps his hand against the tempered glass to get our attention. When Lily and I both look up, he points toward the exit doors.

His eyes stay on me the whole time. Even when Lily gets up and walks up to him, slapping her hand against the glass right where his forehead leans on. And even when he feels the vibration, his eyes still stand connected with mine.

Something passes between us. Something oddly familiar but also completely new.

It's a strange feeling, one I've never felt before. A shiver that doesn't just touch the surface of my skin but also digs deeper.

It's like my whole blood has been exchanged with lava, but not hot enough to kill me either.

The way his eyes linger on mine, then slowly wander down my

neck leaves my skin burning. At least until I realize why he keeps looking at me with such intensity.

The. Goddamn. Necklace.

CHAPTER 14

"you're fucking with my head so shamelessly"—Hoping
by Alycia Marie

Aaron

SHE'S WEARING IT.

Sofia is wearing the necklace. *My* necklace. The very one I gave her and said to never take off.

Guilt tugs on my heart when I realize how happy this makes me, knowing I haven't worn mine in years. And she's wearing hers still. Even after all these years.

I shower and get dressed in record time. For once, I don't even wait until everyone else has showered, one thing I usually do because I cannot shower with people around.

As soon as I wear the most necessary clothes—shirt, pants, and shoes—I'm out the door. So is Miles, but he has a whole other reason to leave as quickly as possible.

And yet our destination is the same.

"Will you be there tonight?" I ask Miles as we race down the hall toward the exit of the arena. Even though it's Monday, the guys are meeting up for drinks tonight at Brites. Call it the celebration-of-a-new-week drinking.

Miles shakes his head. "No. I promised Brooke a movie night."

And you know how much I hate leaving her in the hands of a stranger."

True. And he certainly can't bring her to the bar. Guess we'll see a lot less of Miles from now on. Or not. He's our best friend after all. That means parties will from now on be held at our houses. At least team-celebratory parties. Nothing too wild. One has to keep a certain four-year-old in mind.

Lily and Sofia are standing right outside of the arena. My sister has little Brooke in her arms, trying to soothe her as she's crying. And just like that, Miles is out the door even faster than I could blink.

As soon as I make my way out as well, I hear Miles say, "What happened?" when he takes his daughter from my sister.

I don't wait to hear an answer even though I'm interested to find out why she's upset. I don't have the time to find out because the person I'm desperate to talk to is making her way across the parking lot to get away as fast as possible.

"Sofia!" I yell after her, but she ignores me. Not sure why the hell she would ignore me now. I haven't done anything to her, and I truly just want to *talk*.

Catching up with her isn't going to be difficult, though I do have to say, she seems to be quite the fast walker. I actually have to jog after her instead of taking bigger steps only.

"Sofia," I repeat the second I reach her, laying my hand on her shoulder to stop her from walking. She tenses at my touch and doesn't turn around. It's as though she is praying that if she doesn't react, I'll just go away.

Tough luck, that's not how I handle things.

"Let me drive you home," I offer, walking around her so we would be standing face to face.

"My uncle offered to pick me up." Her lips twitch at her obvious lie.

Why does she have to be so stubborn? I just want to talk to her about the necklace.

If she is still wearing it, do you think she is still hoping that one day we'd end up together like I promised we would?

I'll admit, she was the first girl I had ever been interested in, even after she moved away. I had to force myself not to follow up on her on social media for my very own sanity.

Truth be told, around the age of fourteen, my father was seconds away from sending me to a doctor to figure out what was wrong with me. I refused to let go of Sofia, even years later. I still held on to the thought of us together, still dreamed of seeing her again.

Eventually, I had to give her up though. Not voluntarily, but I had to. It was better for me.

Whatever Sofia had planted inside of my brain when we were kids, it made sure to fuck with me. I barely even wanted to spend time with people outside of school or hockey practice. Especially girls.

I wasn't interested in girls because there was only one that I was interested in. The same one that was living across the ocean and hadn't talked to me in years.

And now that I finally let go of the thought of us, she's here. She is here to fuck with my brain all over again.

But I won't let this happen. She's just here for a couple of months and then she'll be back in Germany. She'll go back to her friends, her family. We will be apart once again.

Digging up feelings that I know will be there if I look hard enough won't do me any good. Hell, I don't even have to search for said feelings, they'll be there on a fucking shrine I built.

Talk about obsessions; she's mine. Has always been and I doubt I'll ever stop obsessing over her.

That might not be very healthy but it's not like I would ever try to force Sofia into my life or keep mine on hold. Well, I no longer keep mine on hold for her.

"Please, let me drive you home, Sofia." I know she doesn't have a car here. I mean, she barely found a place to stay, and I doubt her aunt lets her borrow the only car she has to get to school or any-where, really. Which means Sofia is most likely using public transport.

Using public transport isn't a bad thing. Not at all. But she's here because I asked her to be, so driving her home is the least I could do.

"I wanted to visit my mother. Since you live next to her, it's more than convenient." Like I ever planned on visiting that godawful thing of a human being. Guess I am now.

Sofia looks away from me, her head tilting up to the sky as she lets out a sigh. "Alright, but only because you're heading there anyway." *I wasn't.*

I gesture toward my car, refraining from commenting anything, just in case that would make her run away.

Only when we're in my car, doors locked with no way for Sofia to escape can I talk to her about the necklace.

So when we're both seated and, on the road, I carefully ease into *the* conversation. "You're still wearing the necklace." *Or not so careful after all.*

"I always wear a necklace," she says. "I was studying, forgot the time, and had to rush out the door. It was the only one I could find."

"Ah, yeah. I, too, would rather wear a necklace with a Lego pendant than not wear one for a couple of hours." She might be able to fool other people with that excuse, but not me.

One wouldn't just choose to wear a necklace that used to have a great meaning to two people, right? Plus, we have to take into consideration that Sofia's belongings are in Germany. She chose to take the necklace with her to the U.S.

I mean, I keep mine around as well. I have it at home in my nightstand, waiting to be worn again. But I couldn't bring myself to do it. The meaning behind the necklace, the value it has... it's nothing I would wear again just for the sake of wearing a necklace.

"What does it even matter, Aaron?" she asks, not bothering to even look at me. I couldn't look back at her as I have to keep my eyes on the road, but she could at least *try* to show some interest in me. "It's a necklace."

"A necklace I gave you."

"I've received multiple necklaces as presents over the years, it's not that big of a deal."

But it is. "Yeah? And did everyone else promise you to come after you once they're old enough? Did everyone else promise they'd you'd be the only one for them when they gave you their present?"

"You were eight. You barely knew what the words you said meant."

Perhaps she's right. Still, they meant something to me.

Chapter 15

"but I got you this rose / and I need to know / will you let it die or let it grow?"—**Roses by Shawn Mendes**

Sofia

AARON AND I DON'T SPEAK FOR the rest drive over to Wesley Hills after my comment.

I don't expect him to say something. It was a mean thing to say, though, was I that far off?

It's embarrassing enough that he caught me wearing the necklace, even if I was hoping he'd see it. I didn't expect him to want to talk to me about it. I suppose it does make sense.

Aaron is right, it's a necklace one wouldn't just wear for nothing. And I didn't wear it for nothing. I wanted to see if he would react to it. He did, and I all but almost insulted him for it.

I panicked, okay?

If he finds out I was still holding on to his promise for far too many years, this is going to get really embarrassing for me.

As soon as we reach my aunt's house, I'm ready to sprint out of the car. Unfortunately for me, Aaron is keeping the doors locked.

I decide to look at him, see what is keeping him from unlocking the doors only to find him staring at his mother's house. It seems as though he's stuck in his head, and from the way his hands clench into fists, I doubt he's thinking about anything good.

I'm about to reach my hand over to his when my phone chimes.

Aaron's eyes snap over to the phone in my hands, yet all I can focus on are his green ones. The same I used to think about when I felt lonely and needed to escape my reality.

I always wondered what he would look like when he was older. I expected a chiseled jaw, though the same noodle arms he had back when we were eight. I guess I didn't think he could ever manage to get some muscles, but boy was I wrong.

Sometimes, I even wondered if he would dye his hair, go dark and try a new look. I can't be sure he has tried, but he doesn't have dark hair now, so if he did, it is grown out by now.

I was wondering if he'd grow a beard to look like his father or if he would shave it all to have smooth skin. I would wonder if he had a lot of admirers if he admired others as much as I did him.

Did he ever pursue his dreams or is at least trying to get there?

I would wonder if Aaron ever thought about me. Was he missing me as much as I missed him? Maybe he was even imagining us in a field of flowers together, holding hands, talking for hours on end while I could smell his sweet scent and he could smell whatever I would smell like, just like I did.

On rare occasions, I even allowed myself to imagine his voice; would he sound like his father, have a very deep voice with a slightly smoky rasp in it, or would it stay pure, only a slight octave deeper?

Aaron is nothing like I imagined he would be, and yet he is everything I could ever picture.

He is tall, muscular. His voice isn't too deep, but it also didn't stay that high. He doesn't smell sweet, but he smells like soap, musk, and a slight hint of cinnamon. Aaron doesn't grow out his beard, he shaves. He *is* trying to achieve his dreams, become a pro athlete. I've never been prouder of anyone ever before.

Stop thinking about Aaron, Sofia!

Almost impossible when he sits right next to me. And when I sit in *his* car. The very car that smells more like him than I remember.

In hopes to distract myself, I take a glance at my phone, praying someone is coming to my rescue.

Lukas: I have an update for you. Leon is proposing on your birthday!

Lukas: During dinner, I believe. Perfect to let everyone forget you exist.

Just fucking great.

"Who is Leon?" Aaron asks, not even seeming to be ashamed to have read my text.

"A prick that loves to ruin my life." My eyes slowly wander up Aaron's body before they meet his. "He's my ex-boyfriend. Cheated on me with my own sister. He's planning on proposing to her on Christmas Eve. Most definitely just to ruin my life even more."

"How so?"

I let a chuckle slip out of my throat. "I live in a small village. Word gets around easily. The people there know I've been cheated on, but according to them, it was meant to be because Leon and Julia were destined for one another. I wasn't sad about Leon and my breakup, and he is pissed because of it. Ever since then, every single one of my birthdays, he makes sure to do *anything* to ruin my night."

And it's not a lie. Last year, Leon gifted my sister a trip throughout Europe for two whole months. And guess why? Right, because my birthday then no longer mattered since my sister received such a great gift. It was all my family talked about; my birthday long forgotten.

"He's not a prick, Icicle. He's far worse. Who even *does* that?" Aaron speaks through gritted teeth, his jaw clenching like the thought of Leon doing me wrong irks him. Perhaps it does, but I won't get my hopes up too much.

What hopes, Sofia? I am not allowed to have hopes. Not with Aaron. It's just going to rip open wounds I barely even closed.

I shrug. "It's not that big of a deal. I didn't plan on going home for the holidays anyway. Now I have an actual *reason* not to go."

Aaron shakes his head. "Take me with you. I need to talk to this *Leon*. I need to feed him my fists or something. How fucking *stupid* can someone be?" Aaron reaches for his steering wheel, clenching his hands around it like he might beat whoever comes across him next if he didn't. "Swear to God, Sofia, if I was him, I would have worshipped the ground you were walking on. Hell, I would have even gone to a flower shop to get you these awful wisteria-colored flowers you love so much, *daily.*"

I'm praying he said all this just to get a reaction, not because he truly feels that way. My heart wouldn't be able to take it if he meant it.

I can't let emotions show, not the ones he might want to see. What I can do, however, is react to the flower comment. I know exactly which ones he is talking about. "Lilacs?"

"Is that what they're called?"

I nod, keeping a slight smile on my face.

Aaron always made fun of me for liking them, or even liking the color. Even though I'm still convinced it's just a light purple, lilac if you will, whereas he *insists* the color is called "wisteria". I can't believe he still insists on it.

"Yeah, Nix. That's what the flower is called." I chuckle softly, then feel the sudden need to address his offer. "You don't have to come to Germany with me. I'll be fine. I'll stay here and study."

"No. We're going to Germany together. It's about time I reconnect with my in-laws."

Chapter 16

"you're losing control a bit, and it's really distasteful"—
Fuck You by Lily Allen

Aaron

I SHOULD HAVE LEFT. Telling Sofia I was going to meet my mother was a lie. She wouldn't have found out if I actually went to see her or not, and yet here I am.

My mother is blowing her cigarette smoke right into my face as she just stares at me, not saying a single word. I am seconds away from puking at her rudeness.

First of all, who blows their goddamn cigarette smoke out in someone's face?

Second of all, what kind of mother just stares at the child they gave birth to for a whole five minutes without saying a single word? Especially after they've seen said child for the first time in sixteen years.

"Your sister alright?" she finally asks once her precious cigarette is finished.

"Not that you care," I answer. Perhaps I should be a little nicer, given that she's my mother and all. But then again, is she really?

Liz raised me. Well, my father did but Liz has been there all these years as well. She may only be my stepmother, and yet she's been more of a mother to me than the woman giving birth to me has ever been.

"I do care, Aaron." She puts off her cigarette in the ashtray, giving me a quick smile as her eyes land back on mine. "She is my daughter."

"Question is: are you her mother?"

"Of course I am. I gave birth to the both of you. I am hers as much as I am yours."

I shake my head, pressing my lips together as I refrain from saying things I would regret eventually.

I am here for closure, or so I keep telling myself. I haven't spoken to this woman in sixteen years, and it never seemed as though she cared much about not knowing how her son was doing.

As much as I removed her from my life, a part of me still stayed with her. There's always been this part of me that had hopes. Hopes that she might come back into my life, apologize for the things she's done, apologize for her stubbornness, her pride. But the apology never came, never will come.

"Lily is dating your friend, isn't she? I thought he was the gay one at first, but then it was only the brown-haired one," Victoria says, almost making me choke on my own saliva.

Alright. So, she has been stalking me and my friend group, wow. That is… insane. Disgusting.

Besides. "None of my friends are gay." At least not that I know of it. Grey isn't labeled, he just dates whomever he feels like. And I believe it's disrespectful to put a label on him when he doesn't do it.

"Sure one is. I saw him with a guy. It was very strange seeing that."

"Strange?" I think my eyes just popped out of my head.

She nods. "It's unnatural."

"Oh, for God's sake. Fuck you."

She gasps. "Don't talk to your mother like that."

"Don't be homophobic then."

"I am your mother, Aaron, whether you like it or not. So treat me with some respect." She waves me off, obviously being done with the topic and me calling her a homophobe. If I didn't have a reason to despise her already, I sure as hell would have one now.

I would leave, but I have questions. A lot of them.

My father answered as many as he could but getting answers about my mother from the woman herself might give me the peace I need.

"There is a difference between giving birth and being a mother." I didn't come here to criticize her parenting. She's a shitshow of a mother, we all know that. "Why did you never try to get in touch with me?"

She shrugs. "Your father wouldn't let me."

"Bullshit." My father tried *everything* to stay in touch with Lily. He tried everything to let me stay in touch with my own sister. He had custody over both of us. Full custody over me and shared one over my sister. He was legally meant to have my sister every other week, and yet he had to settle for seeing her every Sunday for a couple of hours only. All because my so-called mother was being difficult. "I want the truth."

"Aaron, it *is* the truth. Your father wanted me to stay away from you, so I did."

"You're a shitty liar." And that she is. The lies might roll easily off her tongue, but the twitch on her face says anything but. "Why didn't you want me in your life?"

She looks away from me, and quite frankly, I'm not mad about it. I don't need the eyes of my birthmother on me now when she didn't try to look at me growing up either.

Suddenly, I can hear the faint escape of breath from her lungs as she collects her thoughts. "I'm sure you're aware of the fact that your father and I split everything in half after our fallout."

Their *divorce.* It wasn't just a "fall-out".

"I'm aware." And yet, separating children, treating them like objects isn't exactly what I'd call great parenting… from either of my parents. They should have known better. Though, I do know my father tried his very best to keep both children in his life, unlike a certain mother.

"I couldn't have given you the life you wanted, Aaron. All the hockey practice and extra ice time were far too expensive. Your father, however, he could give you all that." She sighs deeply, wiping away a tear that never even threatened to slip out of her eyes. "You were always a good child, but I could do far more with your sister. I knew how to handle girls. I knew how to take care of her. With you... you had a greater interest in your father anyway. I wouldn't have wanted to force you away from him."

Am I the only one noticing that she doesn't make any fucking sense? How could Lily live with her? All her life, too. I'm here for an hour and almost lose my mind. Lily has lived with her for good eighteen years. Until she moved into the dorms to get out.

I finally understand why she desperately wanted to get out.

For years I've been making fun of my sister for living at the dorms when our mother lived close by, and she could've easily taken the bus to school or driven herself when she got a car. I also could have picked her up and drove her. Then again, our father lives close as well, I, too, could have stayed home. The difference is, however, I moved in with my best friend, off-campus.

"Long story short, you just weren't interested in me, Victoria," I say what she wouldn't. She doesn't deny nor confirm, but staying silent is enough of an answer, don't you think?

"I always knew what you were up to." Her voice is surprisingly low, filled with regret and guilt.

Something strange tugs on my heart. It's not sympathy for her or anything that shows I have any kind of love for this woman inside of me. It's *hatred*. There's nothing I feel but hate for her.

The woman that was supposed to raise me, love me, care for me... the same one that threw me away like I was never her child had the guts to follow up on me, yet she could never reach out to me.

Knowing that doesn't make me feel sad, it makes me angry.

"Good for you, Victoria." I stand, being done with this conversation. I may not have gotten the questions answered I came here with, nor did I get to voice them… but I got *one* answer, the one I needed the most.

My mother never cared about me, will never care, and even though she might pretend to feel guilty, she doesn't *want* to change anything.

That's enough for me to be done with her.

I never truly had the desire to have her in my life. Sure, when I was younger, I was sad she was gone, but it wasn't like I was *missing* her as much as I should have. And now that I am an adult, being able to understand what went down between my parents, understanding that my own mother never had the desire to be close to me, closes the chapter for good.

CHAPTER 17

"I don't want somebody having what we had"—What We Had by Sody

Aaron

COLIN LOOKS AT ME WITH AS MUCH confusion on his face as I feel inside of me.

One second the girls at our table talk about getting their nails done, going to some kind of spa somewhere in New York, and now they're talking about Sofia moving into Lily's dorm room as she no longer needs it. Which, frankly, seems like a bad idea judging by the look on Winter's face.

Even though Lily no longer considers Winter her best friend and is trying her very best to stay away from toxic people, she even cut off her entire friend group because they were too emotionally draining for her, Winter is still sticking around. But of course, she would.

Winter isn't easy to get rid of and trust me, I say this with years of experience.

I've tried getting rid of Winter a long time ago, but as it seems she's quite good in bed and pretty persuasive. So for all of my college years, I've had this on-again, off-again relationship with her.

Alright, fuck buddy relationship.

To avoid any misunderstandings, the sex was great, and as bad as it sounds, the only reason I stayed in our strange fuck-buddies arrangement.

She was simply draining me with the amount of self-love this woman has. And I mean, loving oneself is never a bad thing, until it gets to the point where all they want to talk about is themselves and how great of a person they are.

I had occasional fucks every now and then, but whenever I wasn't up for the chase, I knew Winter was only one call away. And she was always down for a good fuck with me. Especially since she never really got over her crush on me. Or love for me? I mean, we did date for a couple of months before it turned ugly. Not one of my proudest times in life, but it is what it is. At least she *knew* we were fuck buddies and nothing more.

Didn't stop her from seeking a relationship with me though.

I know I should have called it off, not led her on. She was a great distraction, and if I looked beyond all her self-love, I knew she is a good person. Somewhere deep within her is a woman that I might've liked if it weren't for her self-centeredness.

"What are they even saying?" Miles asks, not bothering to look up from his phone. I'm not even sure if he is talking to me and Colin, or to Grey who happens to be on the phone as well.

As nobody answers, he looks up and repeats his question. "I only heard moving in or something like that."

Colin sighs. "My girlfriend is giving her dorm room to Sofia."

Miles laughs, loudly. Eventually, he stops, his eyes moving from Sofia to Winter and back to me.

We're all seated at the same table, Miles, Grey, and me on one side, the other four on the other. For a second there I'm wondering why nobody is back home with Brooke when we're all off right now. But then I remember that she's probably with Emory.

I suppose it would have been fair if the guys sat on one side and the girls on the other as we're seven people in total. And with four huge jocks and three tiny women… they deserve to have their space and not be forced to be squeezed.

But Colin *had* to have his girlfriend sitting on his lap. I doubt Lily is allowed to sit anywhere else but on top of him.

It was obvious that Sofia would sit with Lily, and apparently Winter as well. Of course, only to appear less in love with me. The glances she sends my way give her feelings toward me away pretty easily.

"You do know she has a name, right?" I point out.

Colin flips me off with a grin. "Jealous your sister likes me more than you?"

"The hell I am." Seriously, she can't like my best friend more than me, can she? "I'm her favorite."

That seems to be getting the girls' attention because oh-so suddenly, all three of them are looking at me. But the only eyes I truly care about are Sofia's.

Her honey brown eyes always seem to be getting my attention even if that's the last thing I want to give her.

Seriously, after I offered to go to Germany with her out of total stupidity, one would think our friendship shifted into something less tense. It hadn't. I think I made it even worse.

We haven't exchanged a single word ever since then, and we're getting dangerously close to Thanksgiving. We're only a week away, two weeks away from December. If I'm supposed to accompany her, I should probably book a flight very soon before there are no more available seats. But I refuse to buy a flight ticket to God knows where in Germany she lives, spend hundreds, if not good over a thousand dollars to be her fake date only for Sofia to not even want me there.

I may have a hell ton of money shoved up my ass thanks to my father and Liz, but I am not wasting it on a flight ticket I might not even use.

"There's a high chance I'm her favorite," Miles jokes only to be a part of it. He knows he's not.

"Sofia is my favorite," Lily says, patting Colin's chest with her hand as his jaw drops. "She's my best friend after all."

My eyes instantly travel over to Winter, just in time to catch her jaw twitching in anger.

I'm not going to lie, it was cruel of Lily to say this in front of her, but it's not like Winter hadn't called literally *anyone* her best friend right in Lily's face before either.

Miles gestures between Sofia and Winter then says, "That's going to be interesting. You guys have to keep me posted." The smuggest smile I've ever seen is currently plastered right on his face as he looks at me.

"What's going to be interesting about this? We're just roommates." Winter keeps a false smile on her lips, one that doesn't quite reach her eyes. If I had to put a label on the spark in her eyes, I'd say it's anger with a hint of *I'm-going-to-murder-Aaron-Marsh* in it.

Well, at least Winter doesn't kno—Never mind. I've told her about Sofia… and Sofia knows I've dated someone named Winter.

Yup, this is going to get really interesting. For everyone else. For me, it's going to be a pain in my ass, I can sense it.

Sitting here sure does make my head spin for other reasons as well, though.

Seeing as Winter keeps catching a glimpse of me with either jealousy or a murderous hint in her eyes, I do wonder if Leon is just like her. I doubt it, given that he's a cheating asshole, so I've figured, but there is a chance that he once did love Sofia.

And if he did, I am not sure I won't make him acquainted with my fists and feet. Nobody was supposed to love Sofia like I once did. Granted, eight-year-old love isn't the same as the one would have been when they were dating at a later age, but I still never wanted *that* to happen.

It was always supposed to be Sofia and *me*. Not Sofia and God knows who.

She wasn't supposed to be happy with anyone else.

The pinch of jealousy in my heart when I think about Sofia being as happy with any other man as I always wished we could have been, is almost unbearable.

Mostly pathetic.

Did she tell him the same jokes she told me? Did they skate together and do races? And if so, did he let her win every single time like I did her because I knew she would end up smiling at me. The one cheek-y-smile I loved so much.

It's always been my favorite. Whenever Sofia would smile a little too widely, her cheeks would get all chubby. I loved that smile especially because I knew it was genuine. I knew that when I saw those chubby cheeks, she was happy. And nothing made me happier than seeing her happy.

"Turn that frown back around, Aaron." Miles nudges his elbow right into my side. "Are you okay?"

I nod, though in my mind I am shaking my head.

How am I ever going to be okay again after Sofia leaves?

CHAPTER 18

"and once we start there ain't no stopping"—*Can I Kiss You? by Dahl*

Sofia

AS FATE WOULD HAVE IT, my aunt was busy at work and couldn't help me take all of my belongings over to the St. Trewery dorms, which means I needed someone else to drive me. I couldn't possibly take a couple of suitcases on the bus, and I barely even had enough money to pay for said bus. Which meant calling an Uber is not an option at all.

My mother is going to send me some more money within the next couple of days. We both forgot how expensive everything is over here, though, Germany isn't *that* much less expensive. But to be fair, I didn't think I would have to pay for housing at my aunt's, she's my aunt after all. I just bet Hugo had his say in that decision.

Anyway, since my aunt can't drive me, I asked Lily if she knew someone that would willingly help me. I'm not going to lie, when she said she knew just the right person she could persuade into helping me, I was thinking she meant her boyfriend. From what I have witnessed the past couple of weeks, I have the feeling that he can't say no to her.

Imagine my surprise when instead of Colin a certain blond guy with the most magical green eyes stands in front of me as I open the door to my aunt's house.

"Glad to see you too, Icicle," he says, clearly taking my stunned expression as a triumph of some sort. "Didn't I *just* help you move in here? Leaving me already?"

"Shut up, Nix." I open the door wider for him, granting him access to the house even when all I want to do is slam the door right into his handsome face. "You know very well why I have to leave this house."

"Germany, did your friend get here now?" As if on cue, my reason to leave makes himself noticeable. "Is it a *she*?"

I freeze. Every single inch of my body becomes stiffer than it has ever been. This man is the definition of the word "disgusting". If I knew I would get away with murdering him, he would have been dead a long time ago. Unfortunately, in this case, murder is considered a crime and I would not get away with it. Even if it was for the greater good.

"Don't be disrespectful, Germany. Answer me!" From the *thud* that's coming from the living room, I'd say he just threw his precious remote control across the room, like he does so very often when things don't go his way.

Seconds later, I can hear footsteps coming from behind me. I turn around just in time to see that slobby grey-haired man approaching Aaron and me.

He looks even more disgusting when he isn't sitting in his armchair. The stains of old food on his shirt, not bothering to wear any pants because the only times he gets up from his armchair is when he uses the bathroom, gets a new beer, or goes upstairs to sleep. The beard that probably hasn't been cared for in years, and the sickening dirty fingernails… it all comes into view when he actually stands in front of me.

"Not a cute girl friend after all," he says, his voice filled with disgust as he takes in Aaron's figure. "Pretty faces don't get far in life. I had one and look at me now." His arms open as he turns around once, showing himself off.

My stomach turns, not only from having to look at this man but from the *smell* of him.

Hugo smells like he hasn't showered in weeks, and from the looks of it, he probably hasn't. The smell of sweat with a mixture of beer, rotten food, and whatever the hell one would define his breath as causes instant nausea.

My stomach is *hurting* from the smell of him, my eyes stinging.

It pains me so much, I willingly move to Aaron's side and lean my head against his body so I could smell him instead. And boy does he smell nice, even when a mere 6.5 feet away that smelly something stands, staring at my breasts.

Aaron must have noticed where Hugo's eyes linger because when Hugo's hand reaches out—even though he couldn't reach me from that far away—Aaron instantly tugs me further into his side, turns me so most of my front would be covered by his body while his arm around me does the rest to cover up my breasts. Well, his hand does most of the covering.

I'm not even wearing anything tight to show off my body and my breast isn't big at all, I'm not sure what he is seeing. I wouldn't *dare* showing any skin here with Hugo around. God knows what would happen if he saw just that tiny bit too much of it.

"Hey, hey, now. No need to be so uptight," Hugo says, dropping his hand.

My mind is trying to find words to say, trying to come up with anything that would shut him up, but for once I've got nothing.

Back in Germany, having good comebacks and a big mouth was what got you through school if you didn't want to be at the receiving end of arrogant wannabe Ariana Grandes. I know how to make myself heard, how not to let words too close to my heart, and yet with every word Hugo utters, all I manage to come up with is a repetitive mantra of "Do not puke."

"Where's your room, love?" Aaron's hand grazes the side of my breast, but he quickly moves it a tad further away from my body.

The short touch sends an awful lot of strange tingles through my entire body, waking up every single muscle. I'm well aware that he didn't mean to touch me, I even appreciate the fact that he respects me enough not to do so even though everything would be so much better than having Hugo continue to stare at me like he is seconds away from jumping me. But I do have to admit, I wouldn't mind Aaron touching me a little longer.

I point toward the stairs, telling Aaron to make his way up there. Thankfully he does without me having to say a word. Only when we made it inside of my room does Aaron let go of me and takes a step back. I almost laugh at the sudden loss of his warmth, but I'm not crazy enough to actually let it slip out to get questions thrown at my head.

"Thank you," I say, not only talking about him helping me take my suitcases over to the dorms but also for what he did with Hugo. Not that he did much or said anything specific to scare my not-really-uncle off, but he helped nonetheless.

Aaron leans back against the closed door, crossing his arms over his chest, smirking at me while his eyes flicker back and forth from my chest to my eyes. "You know, if you don't want your pe-dophilic uncle to stare at your boobs, maybe you should wear a shirt that isn't see-through."

"See-through?!" I run over to the wall-length mirror in this room, looking at myself only to find out that my shirt is, in fact, see-through. Not entirely but enough since the white fabric is still damp from my earlier escapade. That's what I get for wearing a white shirt when I have to wash off a stain from my aunt's bed-sheets.

I barely had the time to change before Aaron rang the doorbell and I forgot about white fabric actually turning see-through when it gets wet.

"Turn around!" I whisper-yell, looking at Aaron through the mirror. The smirk on his face doesn't fade, especially not when his eyes fall back down to my chest. "Nix!"

He doesn't turn around. Instead, Aaron finds it to be a great idea to walk up to me, coming to a stop when his front is so close to my back, I can almost feel the heat from his body on mine.

I'm pretty sure my heart just sank to the floor, trying its best to hide from the only guy I know has enough power over me to break it into a million pieces with just a couple of words.

He frightens me. Having him this close to me, feeling his breath on my skin, his heat warming me, and his eyes on mine has my blood run cold, freezing every inch of my body to the point where I can no longer move. And yet all I want to do is run away from him.

It doesn't even make sense. Aaron this close to me makes as much sense as a butterfly in a beehive. It's not supposed to be that way.

He grabs my shirt in his hand, pulling on it only to make it cling to my front even more than it already does. The wet shirt pressed against my body lets my skin show even more than before, granting him a much better view on my breasts than just outlines and shadows.

My nipples peak at the cold of the shirt, and even if I didn't feel it, I can see it in the mirror. And if I can see it, so can Aaron, but he doesn't comment on it.

"You're wearing it again," he says in such a low tone, I have to double-check if it's really Aaron here in the room with me. *It is*.

His free hand finds my neck, his finger hooking into the silver chain as he pulls it from underneath the shirt.

"Aaron…"

He lets go of the necklace, letting the Lego piece dangle between my boobs, his eyes following.

From what it looks like, Aaron is the calmest I've ever seen him. Yet the heat in his eyes says anything but.

"Did you ever think we had a chance?" he asks, meeting my eyes.

I shake my head. "We were kids." Our gazes stay locked, though I wish they wouldn't. "Whatever we had at that age, it was ephemeral, Aaron."

His lips flatten, eyes closing like he doesn't want to hear me say this. I'm not even sure *I* want to hear myself say this.

"You weren't supposed to be gone for so long, Sofia."

He's right. I've been told it'd only be four years. Four years and I'd be back in New City, back with my friends and family. But our plans changed after the incident.

Aaron lets go of my shirt but is quick to tilt my head into my neck while he looks down at me. "Why did you stay away?"

My eyebrows dip into a sad frown. Hearing the pain, the betrayal in his voice tugs on my heart with all the guilt in the world. It's like stepping on a bug and then wondering if the family of said bug will miss it, but ten times as bad.

He turns me around in just a second, pressing my back into the mirror while his arms hold me hostage. I'm pretty sure I could get out of his cage if I wanted to, but I don't.

"Why didn't you reach out, Sofia? Why didn't you tell me it'd take longer for you to come back?"

"I didn't think you cared."

Aaron takes a deep breath, his eyes shut as his head turns to the side for a moment. "I did care. More than you could ever imagine."

I want to reach my hands up, cup his face, and apologize for my decisions, but I don't regret staying in Germany. The only thing I truly regret is never having *tried* to find my favorite twins. I knew where they lived. I had their addresses. Even if I couldn't find them online, I could've sent letters and explained everything. I know they would have understood.

But I didn't.

His eyes are back on mine when he asks, "Can I kiss you?"

My breath gets stuck in my lungs, my brain officially playing tricks on me. Aaron Phoenix Marsh did not just ask me if he could kiss me. This is all just a bad dream, isn't it?

It can't be real. That would be one of the cruelest fucking things life is throwing my way.

Aaron and I can't ever be together. We live in two whole different countries, different continents, an ocean apart. I will go back to Germany in a few months whereas he will start his career as a pro hockey player here.

I'm sure he has a spot on a team already or has at least gotten an offer. If his best friend's father is coaching an NHL team, I'd assume it's safe to say he has a good chance of going pro after graduation.

Life is all about having the right connections, is it not?

With him on the road for games and me stuck in Germany, there is no space for a relationship of any kind.

"Why?"

Aaron brings a hand to my face, stroking his thumb over my cheek. "Because I need to know."

"Need to know what?"

"If it's there." Both of his hands now hold my face in them, his eyes burning holes into mine. "I need to know if it's *still* there. The chance of an 'us.'"

"Aaron…"

"Please."

Whatever theory he wants to test with a kiss, he won't get very far. I can give him answers to all of them, probably.

If he wants to know whether or not my insides would explode when his lips lay on mine, the answer is yes. I'll even add that, no matter how shitty the kiss would be, it would be the best kiss of my life simply because this is Aaron kissing me. I didn't hold on to the thought of him and me for nothing, and I wouldn't let it go any time soon. I know I have to, but as of now, I am not strong enough to do so.

If he wants to know whether or not I could picture a life with him, the answer would be yes, because I can. I always have.

There are differences though. Dreams and reality don't always align. Ours don't.

If he wants to know whether or not we end up together, the answer is no. We won't because our lives are too different.

We both want different things in life. Whereas he wants to become successful and chase his dream to become a pro hockey player, I want to stay as far away from here as possible. I want to write books and create new worlds to escape my reality because reality sucks. And it sucks that I can't write my *own* life in the way I want it to play out. If I could, I would've written myself to be with Aaron a long time ago.

He dreams big, has huge goals, and does everything to get there, and I write it. I write about people just like him. Single-minded people that chase the high and end up reaching their goals after struggling for a little while. When in reality, I am a coward hiding behind my stories.

"Please, let me kiss you. Just once. Just one taste, Sofia. I need to know."

Instead of answering Aaron, I move my face closer to his until he gets the hint and gently connects his lips with mine.

My heart begins to beat so rapidly, it might as well be jumping right out of my chest. I try to play it cool, act like the soft lips pressed to mine don't affect me whatsoever, but the flush creeping up on my cheeks is betraying me more than someone getting the last piece of pizza when I've been the one it was promised to.

My chest presses flush to his torso, his hands sliding down my body to hold me by my waist, pulling me further into him. Bolts of electricity shoot right through my body, making the hairs on my arms stand from the intensity of butterflies running wild in my stomach.

My arms loop around his neck, needing him to be even closer although that seems to be almost impossible at this point. We're already standing as close as it gets.

I knew I shouldn't be kissing him. I knew it would be wrong, but c'mon, you can't blame me for doing so anyway. Being kissed by Aaron has been on top of my list for years, and I know this is going to be the first and only time this will ever happen. Of course, I would jump at the opportunity, no matter how wrong I know this is.

Our tongues mingle, and I can't help but crave more of him. His kiss is perfection, the best I've had in my entire life. I'm not even *just* trying to convince myself of it. It's the truth, and I hate it more than anything.

His forehead leans against mine as soon as our lips part, my eyes still closed to stay in my little bubble, far away from reality, even when he lets out a soft sigh.

Aaron brings one hand to my chest, pressing his palm flat over my heart. "Did you feel that, Sofia?" he asks in a soft tone, seemingly still in the same bubble as me, afraid to step out of it.

I did feel it. All of it.

I felt the sparks, the butterflies, the warmth when he forced himself into my heart all over again. Yet despite feeling all of this, I shake my head for his own good. "I didn't feel anything. It was a kiss like any other." Just that it wasn't.

As the words settle into his head, Aaron's forehead leaves mine, his hands on my body following suit. The loss is felt instantly. His heat no longer warming me but instead, everything is so cold. The air around us is less dense than ever before, freezing.

"You're breaking my heart, Icicle."

I'm breaking my own heart.

CHAPTER 19

"if you're gonna let me down, let me down gently"—Water Under the Bridge by Adele

Sofia

AARON HAS BEEN AWFULLY QUIET since the kiss, not that I can blame him for it. Lucky for me, he still helps me with my new room. There's not much to do, but when I told him I'd have to somehow manage to build up a shelf all by myself, he offered to do it for me.

Since my handiness skill is at about minus ten, I let him.

So while Aaron is in my room, I try to make an effort in getting to know my roommate, if she'd let me. Lily has told me Winter is a bit challenging but she's nice. I'm just praying she isn't anything like the arrogant wannabe Ariana Grandes back in the small village I live in.

Though if she is, I at least know how to handle her.

"Are you sure you don't mind me staying here?" I ask. There is no need for me to introduce myself as Winter knows me already thanks to Lily.

"It's not like I have a choice anyway. I'd get a new roommate either way," she says, setting down the glass she's holding. "So, how do you know Aaron?"

Winter's awfully blue eyes don't meet mine, her gaze lingers on my body, searching for flaws, I'd assume. At least that's what the scowl on her face tells me.

"We used to be friends when we were younger." Thanks to my best friend I know Winter has no idea that Aaron and Lily are twins, so I won't let it slip out either. Not sure how anyone *can't* know they're related because if one took a look at them, you'd know.

"Used to be," she repeats to herself. "I do have to warn you, Sofia. Aaron is over quite a lot because we're dating and well, you know." She shrugs, grinning widely. "I hope you don't mind when certain activities get a bit louder."

Hearing Aaron having sex? Yeah, I think I will pass. It's not like it is going to happen, right? Aaron said he was single, Winter is his ex-girlfriend, and it doesn't seem like he's still interested in her, otherwise, he wouldn't have kissed me, right?

"Just tell me when to leave and I will."

"Will do." She turns to look at the TV, seemingly done with our conversation. I'm about to leave and check on Aaron, or my shelf when she speaks up again. "And Sofia, I suggest you keep your hands to yourself. Aaron is my boyfriend. I know he's hot and all, and I'm sure you'd love to spend a night with him. But he's taken, and too busy to build up shelves for some random girl he used to know."

What the fuck? This woman is *crazy.* No wonder she and Aaron didn't work out.

"Clearly, he's not too busy to do that, otherwise he wouldn't be here right now, would he?" Is it wrong to start a fight with your new roommate? I don't think so. Not in this case, anyway. And besides, *I* didn't start the fight, she did.

"I think I know my boyfriend better than you do, *Sophie.*"

"Could've fooled me with your ability to remember names," I mutter. "My name is *Sofia.* You better remember that because you will see a whole lot of me. Of me and Aaron *together.* And, FYI, he isn't your boyfriend, everyone knows that."

"He isn't yours either."

I lift my shoulders, forming my mouth into a line. "Never said that, now, have I?"

"Said what?" a deep voice asks from right behind me. As I turn around, I am greeted with two green eyes staring at me. Aaron doesn't even bother to acknowledge Winter, despite the little shriek that left her mouth right after he showed up.

"I think we need to talk, Aaron, baby."

He shakes his head, still not bothering to look at Winter as his eyes remain on me. "Swear, if Winter annoys you, give me a call and I'll take care of it."

"With sex?" Winter blurts out, but Aaron and I ignore her, *again*. Perhaps she should be taking offense that he just called her annoying, but all she cares about is getting laid by him. I'm pretty sure that's an obsession that should be checked out professionally.

"So, about the holidays…" His eyes flicker over my shoulder, taking a look at Winter for the first time today.

Aaron takes a step closer to me, his hand reaching behind my head where he pulls on one end of the ribbon in my hair to loosen up the bow. I want to complain about it when I'm getting distracted by Aaron wrapping my favorite ribbon around his wrist, stealing from me.

"Can I come with you?"

I nod, barely even realizing what he's asked as I'm too perplexed still.

Aaron Marsh has just taken my favorite ribbon from me. The one string of fabric I use daily to tie into a cute bow at the back of my head to keep my hair out of my face. He *knows* it's my favorite one, the color gives it away.

But what shocks me even more, I didn't stop him, nor am I asking for it back.

"I'm keeping that, Icicle. And you better never take off that necklace ever again." He pulls on the necklace around my neck, letting it dangle down *over* my shirt.

"Aaron…" I know he's just trying to get me attached to that

thing again, get me attached to *him* again. But it won't work. It won't because I've always been attached to this necklace. The greater challenge will be not getting attached to him.

"I saw the frog on your bed, Sofia. You cannot fucking tell me you kept that thing all those years for nothing. I don't believe that bullshit. So cut it out."

"I kept it for the memories. It means things to me. But that doesn't mean I still feel the same way about you the way I used to years ago."

He winks at me, not even *trying* to look hurt by my words. His goddamn ego must be bigger than I thought, probably the size of the sun.

"Winter, can I talk to you for a second?" he then says, the smile on his face disappearing with every word that leaves his mouth.

"Sure. I was just about to ask you the same thing."

And just like that, they're gone into her bedroom, away from my ears to hear them talk.

To my horror, I catch myself wondering what they're talking about. Is he *officially* going to end things with her? Is he going to get back together with her? Is he telling her to behave and not try to murder me in my sleep?

I even consider eavesdropping, but I won't sink that low. If they wanted me to hear what they're talking about, they would've stayed in this room and not walk off to her bedroom.

Only when thirty minutes pass and I no longer even hear voices, that's when I start to get nervous. Occasionally, I can hear sounds, but they're more like thuds and definitely nothing that comes remotely close to *talking*.

The picture my brain is painting at those sounds has my blood boil in seconds. Jealousy streams through my veins at a speed I never thought possible. But I have to remind myself that I am not *allowed* to get jealous.

Aaron has never been my boyfriend, he isn't now, and he won't ever be. I never had any claims on him. I shouldn't care whether he's fucking his ex or not.

But I do anyway. I do because I care.

It was always supposed to be Aaron and me. Us.

It was supposed to be us against the world. *Us* in a relationship with each other. We were supposed to be a couple, get married, have kids. It was never him and someone else. It was never me and someone else. It was *us*.

Well, that dream also kind of crashed like a flight going wrong when I came back to New City years ago and asked my parents to return to Germany and never come here ever again.

Chapter 20

"I'll move mountains if I can / just to make you understand"—For Your Love by Gunnar Gehl

Aaron

WINTER HAS RUINED MY GOOD MOOD.

My mood was already going downhill after my childhood crush broke my heart into a million pieces using a ruler rather than a knife. Fuck, even cutting my heart up with a butterknife would have been less painful.

I know Sofia was lying, the kiss we shared couldn't have meant nothing to her. Besides, I know when she's lying.

Her words still sting though.

Luckily, today is Saturday, meaning there is most definitely a party *somewhere*. And if not, I'll go to Brites and get the fuck wasted. I'm in need of it tonight. And tomorrow. And all the other days Sofia will be here.

I'm not saying I'm in love with her, because I'm not. One can't just be in love with someone they haven't seen in over a decade and had a crush on years ago. However, I am saying that I want to get to know her again. I want her in my life, steal my breath again. Dammit, I want her to steal my *heart* and make it hers. I want us to be *us* again. Just Nix and Icicle.

Guess she doesn't feel the same way.

As soon as I get back home, I'm pleased to find my best friends—and my sister—already in the living room, having cracked open a beer or two.

It's only six p.m., but that's late enough to pull out some liquor and get wasted.

If it weren't for that one little blonde girl curled up right next to Miles.

Brooklyn smiles at me as she spots me, her grin so wide, she might reach Jupiter with it. "Uncle Ron!" She jumps off the couch, running toward me. I kneel instantly, holding my arms open for her. As soon as her tiny arms are on my torso, I close her in for a tight hug.

There's nothing better than to get greeted by your best friend's daughter after a day like I had. Truthfully, I'd steal her from Miles and keep her as my own child if I could. But I guess I will settle for being "Uncle Ron".

"What are you doing here, little princess?" I ask, knowing very well what she's doing here. Miles is here, which means so, is she. It doesn't bother me when she's around. I love this little blonde girl more than I ever thought was possible.

I swear, sometimes I even think I'm going to be stricter as her uncle than Miles is going to be as her father. Like, imagining her being with someone once she's old enough—nope. Not happening.

Brooke giggles, pressing her face right into my chest. "To play games with you."

"Games?" I gasp in shock, exaggerating just a little bit for her sake. "But I'm a sore loser, princess. And you always win."

She pulls away from the hug, tugging on my hand now. "That's okay, Uncle Ron, I let you win this time."

"Sofia's not coming?" Grey asks, his eyebrows pull together in what must be confusion.

I shake my head. "I'm not sure I even asked if she wanted to. She has plenty to do with Winter and moving into the dorms."

"I'll text her," Lily says, instantly taking out her phone.

"Actually, can you send me her number?"

Lily's eyes snap toward me, as so do Colin's. The only difference is that my sister looks at me with sympathy, my best friend wears a smug smile on his lips.

"Let me ask you something a *very* good friend of mine voiced that one time I asked the same question," Colin begins, his smirk giving me an unusually intense desire to let my fist get acquainted with his face.

"You're taking her out on a date, and she didn't even give you her number?" The question that left my mouth when Colin asked for my sister's number. The same that'll haunt me now for the rest of my life. I never even asked for Sofia's number, nor am I going on a date with her. Yet it feels like I should've gotten her number the moment we met at the beginning of October.

Phone numbers end up in my possession almost magically. I enter a bar and won't get to leave said bar without a least three snippets of papers in my jeans pocket. So I'm sorry if not having Sofia's number yet somewhat throws me off.

Colin waits a second before he continues, only so he can take in my expression a little longer. "Or maybe not, you look like you're about to cry."

"Are you okay?" Lily asks, tapping her hand on the couch to tell me to sit down.

I do. I take a seat next to her, leaning my head on her shoulder even though Colin is almost growling in my ear for stealing his girlfriend for a moment. Like I care, she is my *sister*, for fuck's sake.

"I'm great."

"You don't look great," Grey remarks, instantly handing me something to drink. "Can't offer you anything stronger before a certain kid is asleep."

A sacrifice we are all willing to make for Miles, so I won't complain even though I could use something stronger right now.

"Is this about Sofia?" Lily digs deeper, leaning her head right against mine like she always used to do when we were a little younger and I came to talk to her about my problems. Mostly hockey related.

"Nah. Winter. She's out of her goddamn mind." After everything she said in her bedroom, it's safe to say she's also a big reason for my current mood.

Good two hours pass before Lily jumps up from her seat to run to the door and opens it, only to return to the living room with Sofia right by her side.

Our eyes meet only briefly, awkwardness taking the upper hand. I don't want things between us to be awkward, but I can't really help it either.

"You're just in time. We're playing truth or dare," Colin lets Sofia know while pulling his precious girlfriend back in his lap, hugging Lily like she was gone for years.

"Truth or dare?" Sofia repeats, taking a seat across from me. There's plenty of space to sit beside me, but of course, she'd go as far away from me as humanly possible.

Talk about a setback.

At least we're going to Germany together in a few weeks, right? That gives me a couple of days to... to what? Talk to her? Have her to myself with no way to escape me?

"Yes, getting Grey's mind off of his breakup."

Wait, *that's* why we're playing this game? I thought Brooke wanted to play it. Miles put her to sleep in my bedroom half an hour ago, and I thought we're only proceeding to play because we don't know what else to do.

I swear, I'm the worst best friend ever. I didn't even know Grey and Izan broke up.

"When the hell did that happen?" I query, hearing of it for the first time in my life.

Grey shrugs. "Yesterday. We wanted to go out for dinner, and we encountered a little bit of an... Asian stereotypical racism confrontation. I don't think he even thought about what he said, and I personally didn't feel all too attacked, but after what happened with Lexi, I refuse to stay in a relationship that has minor hits towards racism, you know? God, it was about fucking *rice* and me not being in the mood for it that night, but it doesn't change the fact that I hated the way he phrased it and—"

I lay my hand on his knee. "Breathe." He does. Inhales deeply, exhales twice as long. "It's okay, you know. No need to justify your breakup. If you couldn't stay with him for whatever he said, then don't force it."

He nods slowly. "So yeah. I'm officially swearing off *any* human. I'm staying single for the rest of my life. Who knows, maybe I'll adopt a few dogs and cats."

Grey and swearing off dating? I doubt it. He's a sucker for romance.

"Anyway," Miles laughs. "Now that everyone is here, we can proceed. I think it's only fair that it's Sofia's turn now. To be asked, I mean, not to ask."

The first couple of rounds go all smoothly. We're all having a clear head—mostly, anyway—and the questions stay as PG13 as possible, as so do the dares.

It isn't until Colin takes out his phone, downloads a Truth or Dare app, and sets it on 18+ that it takes a turn.

Miles seems surprisingly uncomfortable with that decision. He's usually the one to live after "go big or go home". But I suppose when half of us are drunk, two are tipsy and he's the only sober one, I, too, wouldn't like the idea very much.

Colin types all our names into the app, letting technology randomly decide whose turn it is. A second later, he looks up and smirks at me. "You're the first victim," he says. "Truth or dare, Aaron?"

"Truth." I am not fucking with technology. Not when it comes to truth or dare. God knows what the dares will be. Could be anything from drinking a beer all at once to stripping in front of everyone and remaining naked for the rest of the game. Even illegal shit isn't off the charts.

He rolls his eyes as he reads the question on his screen. "That's a boring one. Are your first and last crush similar appearance-wise?"

My eyes connect with Sofia's. The mix of curiosity and anticipation doing wonders for my dick. Never in my life has the way someone looked at me gotten me hard in seconds. Let alone an *innocent* look.

I grab my glass filled with overpriced whiskey and take a sip. If I'm going to answer this question honestly, I'll need the liquid courage. "Same person, but older now."

I'm not sure if Sofia's reddened cheeks are from alcohol or if she's blushing because she knows very well I am talking about her. Either way, she looks amazing. But as it seems, she always does.

"What a surprise," Lily chirps then sighs deeply.

It's the kind of sigh *I* can feel in *my* bones. It's like she feels all the frustration I do, only that I might feel it a million times more intense.

Everyone's looking at Colin as he lets the app choose the next victim. It so happens to be Sofia. She chooses truth, just like I did.

"In your opinion, who's the hottest person in this room and would you make out with them or not?"

I had my eyes on her when I answered my question, now Sofia has her eyes on me when she answers hers. Torturing me when she takes a little too long to answer. "I'll have to go with the second hottest because the first one is in a happy relationship."

Colin smacks his hand against my back, laughing loudly. "How badly did that bruise your ego?"

Too fucking much. "Not at all." My jaw tightens as Sofia smirks at me, then has the audacity to keep her eyes locked with mine while taking a sip from her cup. It's like she can see right through me, knowing her words affected me more than I am admitting.

"Please," Lily says. "You almost cried when Winter told you she'd choose Colin over you if he was interested."

I did not. I was pissed because my girlfriend—mind you, at that time we were an actual couple—straight up told me she would rather be with my best friend if he would have wanted to.

"Answer the actual question, Icicle."

Mischief gleams in her eyes when she says, "Grey. He's the second hottest, and yes, I'd fuck him if I had the chance to."

Grey leans back in his seat, one arm resting on the back of the sofa behind me. "By all means, Sofia. I'm down if you are."

What the hell is happening?

Drunk Grey really is a whole other version of him. One that's thinking with his dick rather than his brain.

Colin proceeds with the game, most definitely sensing that I'm about to explode from all this.

I have never felt jealousy, *ever*. And if that thing will always feel like I want to rip my best friend's head off only because Sofia chose him over me, then I wish to never experience it ever again.

Miles is the next victim. Dared to kiss one person in the room he feels would be an awesome kisser. It's one of the less bad dares. Not ideal, but it could've been something worse.

However, Miles is not stupid. He looks at each of us for a second, going at this logically. Something the rest of us lack right now thanks to the alcohol.

If I would have gotten this dare, you best believe my lips would be attached to Sofia's right now. And for the rest of our li—*Fuck no. Don't go there.*

Sofia is the only option for him though, so I'm not sure why he takes so long to decide. If he chooses Lily, Colin will throw his fists. Or the couch. Since Sofia is single, there won't be anything thrown his way when he kisses her.

Except for my whole body, maybe. If I can't restrain myself.

Expecting Miles to turn toward Sofia, I already dig my fingers into my thighs, waiting for me to go off like a bomb. But then Miles shrugs, turns toward Grey instead, cups Grey's face with his hands, and pulls him in for a kiss.

My mouth falls open, so does Colin's. I was expecting *everything*. I was counting on Miles backing out of this, him kissing the only woman I have ever had genuine feelings for, or fuck, Miles, trying to kiss himself using a mirror. But I was not expecting him to kiss Grey.

And I definitely wasn't expecting their kiss to last as long as it does.

We play a couple more rounds after that but then Miles decides it's time for him to leave and get Brooke to sleep in her own bed rather than mine. Before he goes to get upstairs Miles mumbles something about him not wanting to ruin *my* night.

Not quite sure what he means by that, but I sure hope to find out.

Once Miles and Brooke left, that stupid app decides to come up with worse dares. Dares like "Striptease for Grey".

Guess whose dare it is. Right, Sofia's.

Now guess who does *not* like the dare at all. Right, me.

Colin turns on some music at the same time as Sofia gets up and makes her way around the coffee table to Grey. As soon as she stands in front of him, every single brain cell of mine screams at me to do something.

So I get up, throw Sofia over my shoulder, and carry her upstairs into my bedroom, despite her efforts to get me to let her down.

CHAPTER 21

"every time we talk, it just hurts so bad / 'cause I don't even know what we are"—That Way by Tate McRae

I CLOSE THE DOOR BEHIND US when we enter my bedroom.

Sofia is still trying to fight me, but I couldn't give more fucks right now. If she wants to strip in front of a friend of mine, she shall do so without me being around. As we established, if I am around, I'll do everything in my power to stop this from happening.

I throw Sofia on my bed, her back hitting the mattress. Before she gets the chance to get up and run, I'm quick to hover over her, pinching her arms over her head with one hand while holding myself up with the other.

"Aaron, let me go."

"No," I bite out, my head dipping down until my lips are a breath away from hers. "What the fuck is wrong with you, Sofia?"

"With me!" She moves her legs around, desperately trying to get out from underneath me. "You're the one holding—"

I cover her lips with mine to shut her up. Not the best thing to do, but the only thing I could think of with an alcohol-induced brain.

Her lips are the softest I've ever felt against mine. Earlier she tasted like cherries, now she tastes like liquor, but not bad at all. I could kiss her forever and never get bored.

I'm not sure what kind of spell she has cast over me, but I am certain I've been bewitched. No normal person would be this crazy about someone they've once known, once liked.

It's not healthy, I'm sure of that, but I can't help but want to have her around me. I can't help but want to taste her on my tongue, want to feel her skin on mine, want her in my life, give her my heart, and never let her leave me ever again.

I want to know everything about her. Does she have allergies? What's her favorite color? Does she prefer eggs or pancakes in the morning? Would she rather go out in daytime or at night? Does she sleep with her hair up or down? I even want to know whether she still does a happy dance when she eats her favorite food or not.

Like I said, I want to know everything about her.

But that's impossible if she won't let me get to know her.

Sofia is as much interested in me as I am in her. I know she is. If she weren't, Sofia wouldn't still be kissing me. She wouldn't push her tongue into my mouth, or groan at the loss when I pull my lips away from hers.

But alright, she wants to pretend she doesn't feel the same way I feel about her, nothing I can do about that. I can, however, pretend to be just as uninterested in her.

But not now. Right now, I need to find out if she's as affected by me as I am by her.

Slowly, I move the hand that was holding hers, down her body, aiming to get under her skirt. If she wanted me to stop, she'd have enough time to tell me. But Sofia doesn't speak, she only gasps when my fingers graze the curve of her breast. Her breath comes out more ragged the farther my hands slide down.

My dick is pressing against my zipper, threatening to poke right through my pants. I can tell the moment she feels my erection press against her thigh because she lets out a soft breath that could be considered a moan.

Eventually, my hand reaches the hem of her skirt, my fingers following the fabric over her thigh until my hand dips underneath.

She holds her breath, eyes locked with mine the closer my fingers get to her pussy.

My fingers skim over her inner thighs, her skin so hot, I'd think I'm in Hell if I wasn't looking into Sofia's face. A face that wasn't made in Hell but in Heaven.

I give her one last chance to tell me to stop, but when nothing comes, I push her panties aside and slide a finger through her lips, finding her wet and ready for me.

I don't usually come fast, nor in my pants, but right this second, I could swear I'm about to come like a fucking teenager.

Sofia lets out a soft whimper when I circle a finger over her clit, her arms wrap around my neck for some stability. For something to hold on to when I give her a much-anticipated orgasm.

I want to give that to her. So badly, I could come from just the feeling of her pussy pulsating around my fingers when I push two of them knuckles deep inside of her, hearing the sweet sound of Sofia's moan leave her mouth.

My lips are dying to reconnect with hers and it takes all my willpower not to give in to the temptation. Having my fingers inside of her pussy is ruining me plenty as it is, no need to kiss her through all of this as well.

I pull my fingers out of her only to push them back inside, her nails digging into my shoulders.

My thumb finds her clit, slowly drawing circles as I stimulate her. I shouldn't have. Finding out what she feels like, what sounds she makes when my fingers are inside of her was just as bad of an idea as kissing her because now I want more. *Need* more.

Sofia's eyes are half-closed, but she tries to keep them locked with mine, even when I push my fingers into her faster, my thumb picking up its pace too. Not all too much, but enough to have her moan out louder, gasping for air when I can feel her walls clench around my fingers.

Her head moves up, her lips desperate to find mine… but that's when I draw the line.

117

"On second thought"—I pull my fingers out of her and move off her—"maybe Grey could use the distraction." She wouldn't go after Grey, I'm sure of it.

"What? Why? Aaron."

I insert my fingers into my mouth, sucking off her wetness while making sure I keep looking at her.

Sofia's mouth opens for a second as if she's about to speak but closes again. Her eyes follow my body when I walk across my bedroom, to find something for her to wear to bed. I don't care if she goes to sleep in one bed with Lily and Colin, but she won't be going home tonight. Not with the number of drinks she had.

She sits up, her arms folding over her chest. "Why did you stop? I thought that's what you wanted."

I shake my head, take one of my shirts out of my closet then throw it over to her. "You were right. Kissing you doesn't feel right. It's just like any other kiss. We'd cross a line I'm not willing to cross with you when we have sex."

Faintly, I can hear her sharp intake of breath, wincing at my words. If they hurt her, she doesn't say. "I should go home."

I throw a pair of shorts over to her, ones that'll probably be far too big for her, but unless she wants to sleep without pants, they're all I have. "You're staying. I won't let you Uber home when you've had a couple of drinks too many. I can't drive you because, again, I, too, had a few too many drinks. So had Colin, Lily, and Grey. And well, Miles can't leave because of Brooke. You're stuck here for the night." I don't think she even cares that much about staying far away from her new roommate. Winter isn't much of a great one.

"I can ask Lily if she has some better-fitting shorts for you," I offer, suddenly remembering that my sister lives in this house, too.

She glares at me, then chooses to ignore my offer. "You know, what you just did might be considered as rude."

"Offering my sister's clothes to you?"

"Starting to fuck me and not go through with it."

"My apologies, Miss Carlsen." I walk over to her, grasp her chin with one hand, and force her to look up at me. "I think I'm allowed to be rude when you're the one playing games."

"I'm not playing games."

"No? Well then, admit you do like me. Admit the kiss we shared earlier meant something to you. Tell me it wasn't *just* a kiss."

She stays quiet, her eyes trying to look anywhere but at me. So I squeeze her cheeks a little harder.

"You can't, can you? Because some fucked up part in your head tells you it could never be real, *we* could never be real." I let out a humorless chuckle. "Perhaps that part in your brain is right. We could never work."

I let go of her face, rushing toward my bedroom door to escape the room, fuck, escape the whole house. Tonight, I'll be cozying it up with Grey. I'm sure he won't mind me sleeping in his bed, he never has before.

Chapter 22

"No one can lift me, catch me the way that you do"—Still Falling For You by Ellie Goulding

Sofia

I HAVEN'T SEEN AARON ALL WEEK.

That's not true. I saw him at hockey practice because Lily and I are still babysitting Brooklyn while the guys have to be there. He knew I was there... and Aaron tried his very best to ignore my existence. He didn't even so much to look my way. Only if it was necessary, which was never.

Winter has been awfully weird to me as well. She tries to be out of the dorm before I wake up and only comes back after midnight in hopes I'm asleep by that time. It's almost ideal because I don't want her around me either. Having her avoid me doesn't bother me nearly as much as Aaron avoiding me does.

He wouldn't ignore you if you told him the truth, Sofia. The whole truth.

That doesn't matter right now. I could tell Aaron the truth knowing it wouldn't change anything at all, or I keep him at a safe distance and avoid a second heartbreak.

As I stare at my ceiling, trying my best to fall asleep early and ignore all my problems, my phone starts to ring. For a second, I debate to ignore the call, pretend to be asleep, and stay away from unwanted conversations. Just for tonight.

But when I see it's my mother who's calling, I don't have much of a choice. She'll get worried if I don't pick up. So I do.

"I hope I didn't wake you up," she says, sounding far too cheery for it being six in the morning in Germany. Though she's a morning person, so it shouldn't surprise me as much.

"You didn't. What's up?"

"Listen, your dad wants to book your flight back home. When's your last day exactly?"

"December seventeenth." As much as I want to leave New City and go back home, I cannot spend a whole two weeks with my family *and* Aaron. If he still wants to come with me, he'd be on the same flight as me. If he doesn't decide to leave early, my dad will book my flight to New City to be *after* New Year's, adding my time with Aaron up to over two weeks.

Two very dangerous weeks.

"Perfect. He'll try to get you on a flight on the eighteenth then." *Perfect…* right.

"Mom, I might be bringing a friend, is that okay?" I mean, I do have to ask eventually. I wouldn't let Aaron stay at a hotel for two weeks when he's supposed to be my fake boyfriend. And let's be honest, the second my mother finds out I'm bringing *Aaron*, she would smack me back to New City if I let him stay anywhere but our house.

"A friend? Why?"

Because that shit-face of an ex-boyfriend of mine is going to propose to your other daughter right on my birthday, that's why. "We're dating." Can't have her believe anything else. If my fake relationship is supposed to fool my sister and Leon, then not even my mother can know it's only a game of play pretend.

"DATING!" I'm sure she just woke up the entire house with her scream. "Tell me more. Now. Name? What's he like? God, Sofia, send your mother a picture next time!"

"His name is Aaron." No need to tell her it's *the* Aaron yet. I'm kind of curious to know if she'd recognize him. I didn't.

"Sofia…" She sighs heavily. "Another Aaron? You barely got over your crush on—"

"We don't talk about that, Mom. I'm going to sleep now. Have a wonderful day!" Without waiting for a goodnight on her part, I hang up the phone.

I'm not tired but listening to my mother talk about how much I used to like Aaron Marsh is not going to happen again. If I weren't still traumatized from all the late-night-talks we've had about him and how much it upsets her to see me cry over a guy I don't even know anymore… maybe it would only be half as bad.

But now that I got a date for my departure, I might as well send Aaron a text and let him know.

Sofia: Are you still interested in being my fake boyfriend for the holidays?

I don't expect Aaron to answer me right away, but surprisingly, he does.

You'd think after he ignored my existence for a whole week, he'd at least have the decency to apologize or sound less uninterested… he doesn't.

Aaron: Yeah, sure.

Sure? Unbelievable.

Sofia: Your enthusiasm is blowing me away, Nix. Careful, otherwise I might think you're excited to spend Christmas with me.

Aaron: I'm not coming for you. In any way possible. When do we get back?

Sofia: I'm not sure. I'll be back sometime after New Year's, but you might be dead when that time comes around. That attitude of yours is screaming for a knife in your heart. You can try to leave early if you want.

Aaron: And miss out on the family drama? Fuck no. I'm already spending the holidays with you, might as well see how it all plays out the week after.

Aaron: By the way, Icicle, stabbing someone isn't the smartest move to kill if you want to get away with it.

Aaron: Hey, do you mind if I call you? I'm cleaning my bathroom right now and texting isn't exactly helping get the task done.

What the hell?

First, he ignores me, then acts like a total dick when I ask if he still wants to accompany me, and now he wants to call me. I didn't even plan on continuing to text him.

Before I have my response typed out, my phone starts to ring. I would decline, but I'm curious to hear what else he has to say, so I pick up.

"How are you?" he asks right away. No hello, yet again no apology, no questions asked about our stay in Germany.

"I'm good, why are you asking?"

I hear the faint sound of a spray bottle in the background when Aaron replies, "Around this time two months ago, you were too broke to afford tampons, so I was going to ask if you need me to buy you some again. Glad to hear you're good."

My spit goes down the wrong pipe, making me cough as I choke on my very own saliva. How the fuck does he remember that?

I didn't think it was that memorable. He's done a good deed, saved me from having to rob the store for two items. There is no need to remember my embarrassment.

"I wasn't 'too broke', I didn't have any money on me yet. And the store did not accept my EC card."

Aaron chuckles. "Anyway, if you need anything, just let me

know. My card does work here and I'm happy to help a friend in need."

Would it be wrong to go over to his house and wrap my hands around his throat, squeezing just that tiny bit too hard? I don't think so.

"So uh, Sofia… I have questions about *my* stay in Germany." Didn't expect anything less. "Do I need to book a hotel? It wouldn't be a problem, but I need to know."

"My mother would decapitate me if I let you stay in a hotel." Besides, I don't think *Baierbrunn* even has a hotel, nor do the villages around.

"Huh. Yeah, makes sense. I, too, would like to decapitate you."

Of course, he would. I have the very same desire with his head. "Look, I don't have much information about the flights yet, but I'll let you know. I can ask my mom to ask my dad to pay for your flight since you're kind of coming for me."

The sound of a flushing toilet overtones his response, but he seems to notice when I don't react to whatever he said. "Sorry," he says, chuckling. "Uh, it's alright, Sofia. I can afford the flight."

"You sure? Flights from here to Germany and back are expensive."

"Hope your dad books first-class for you, because I won't sit in economy, and it would be a shame if I couldn't annoy you on our flight," he says like he means it.

I roll over on my bed, lying on my side. I turn my phone on speaker and lay it down beside me. Guess I'll be stuck with him on the phone for a while, so might as well get comfortable.

"I mean it, Nix. If you want me to pay, I'd totally get it." It certainly would make more sense. He's doing me a favor by being my fake boyfriend. Paying for his flight is the least I could do.

"And I'm telling you I'll be in first class. I haven't been in economy for years, Sofia. Trust me, I can afford a flight. Tell your dad he doesn't need to book yours; I'll do it. Call it a treat from your *boyfriend*. It's going to be your birthday the week after anyway."

He is out of his goddamn mind.

We keep arguing about the flights for another *hour*. I end up giving in, letting Aaron pay for my flight to Munich. I'm tired, so sue me for not wanting to keep on arguing. But there is one more thing we need to discuss.

"We need rules," I say.

"I got one. Pretty simple too." He sounds a bit far away, kind of like he laid his phone down somewhere to do something else. But then he's back in full volume when he continues. "Do whatever the hell we want because we're supposed to be in a relationship. Relationships don't have rules."

"That doesn't sound efficient."

"Alright. You want to talk about a stupid no kissing and no touching rule because that's what the people do in all these romance novels you like to read? Well, then you know as good as I do that these rules are made to be broken."

He's not wrong… much to my dismay. Wait, how the fuck does he know I like reading romance novels?

"You want to kiss me, fucking do it, Sofia. Want to get touchy, I have a body you can touch. Feel like sucking someone off, be my guest, I have a dick that would love your attention. Want to get fucked? You just have to ask, and I'll gladly be the one to do the job."

I'm quiet for a whole ass minute, needing a moment to process whatever words just left Aaron's mouth. Only my silence seems to give him another kick to speak.

"If you want to fall in love with me, Sofia. Do so, *please*," he adds. "We don't need rules to follow only to break them. Whatever you want to happen, I'm happy to make it reality."

"Okay," I say a little breathless.

I guess that settles that, but instead of hanging up the phone, Aaron and I keep talking about everything and nothing at all. He tells me about how he's gotten an unofficial offer from the NYR but isn't allowed to talk about it yet, then adds that the offer is definitely going to be made official after graduation because, well, his best friend's father is the Coach of the team and has quite the connections to the owner of the team. It's good to know Aaron has faith in Coach Carter's power.

It's also great to know that Aaron will be living the life he's always dreamed of. That makes one of us, but one is better than neither of us.

I tell him all about Leon and what went down between us, not because I want to tell him, but because he asked. He said he should know so he can come up with better comebacks if needed. I have total faith in Aaron crumbling Leon's ego if he has to.

He doesn't comment much about the whole relationship we had, only snorts disbelievingly every now and then.

"You know, you could have just hit me up instead of giving yourself to a fucker that was out for pussy and nothing else," Aaron mutters a little sleepily as I finish telling him about my first time and how I got persuaded into it rather than me actually being into it.

"Ah, yeah? And say what exactly?"

He hums, thinking. "I don't know. Something like 'Aaron? Mind getting your ass over here because I kind of want to lose my virginity and my only other option would be some wannabe hockey guy that had his dick in tons of other girls before'?"

I lick my lips, smiling to myself. "Because you didn't?"

"I didn't say that. But I sure wouldn't have told you the shit about *needing* to lose your v-card to be cool. Plus, we both know I was on your mind the entire time anyway."

That cocky fucker.

Aaron truly believes he's been in my head this entire time, huh?

He's right, of course, but still. It's the principle here, people.

"Uh-huh." I roll over, needing to reposition. "He was jealous of you, though. So, I give you that."

"How? I wasn't even in the picture."

That he wasn't, not literally, at least. "I had pictures in my room, and well, the necklace was a huge giveaway that he would never mean too much to me."

I can *see* the proud, self-confident smile forming on his lips, even without having to actually see his face. And the second I realize my mistake, it's already too late.

"My, my, Sofia. That sounds a little *insane* if I do say so. You had a boyfriend and still figured keeping your head with me was the way to go? I'm a little turned on by that, to be honest."

If I could, I would slap him for this very comment. Yet at the same time, he is right. It was insane. "Wow, if me saying the necklace you gave me got another guy jealous makes you hard, I'm really sorry for all those women you slept with. Must have lasted a second, tops."

His chuckle sounds through the phone, a little heavier than I remember, but it still somehow brings a shiver to run through my body.

"Not even a second," he says eventually. "It was all head in and done."

"I'm not surprised."

More time passes, some minutes pass by without either of us saying a single thing, others filled with conversations like we've been in touch all these years.

When I check my phone to see what time it is, I notice we've been on the phone for a whole three and a half hours.

"I should hang up and go to sleep," I say, yawning right afterward.

He groans like he's in pain or more like he simply doesn't want me to hang up yet. "Stay on the phone, please."

"Why?"

"Because… you know. So I can wake up with you still there."

CHAPTER 23

***"I've got myself a missing puzzle piece"—Like All My
Friends by Francis Karel***

Sofia

"I GET THE WHOLE THING WITH your ex and that you want to get
back at your sister," Lily says, her eyes focused on her boyfriend
as he skates past us. "But isn't it kind of cruel to your parents?"

The scoreboard reads 3-1 for the opponents, whoever they are.
I don't care much about hockey, but Lily asked me to come, and I
couldn't say no. As far as I know, Brooklyn is with her aunt today,
which means we don't have to take care of her during this game,
so truly, if it weren't for my best friend, I'd be in my dorm room
studying.

"Why would it be cruel to them?"

Lily sighs, turning her head to look at me just when Aaron
goals. She doesn't even acknowledge the crowd going wild. "They
loved Aaron. I'm sure your mother will be sad when she finds out
you two 'broke up'. Especially after seeing you act all in love for
two whole weeks."

I really don't care. "She wasn't sad when I told her Leon
cheated on me."

"Leon isn't Aaron."

That he is not.

I didn't spend years crying about Leon, but I spend an unhealthy number of years crying to my mother about how much I miss Aaron and Lily. Almost every single night for at least five years, I used to tell her how Aaron is going to come find me eventually, how everything is going to turn out just the way I always dreamed of. I grew older, so after the age of thirteen, I kept these thoughts to myself.

"I'm sure my mother will get over my fake breakup." She would, but I sure will hear a hell lot of questions over said breakup.

Lily hums like she's not sure whether she should believe me or not. "Are *you* going to be okay after the breakup?"

Our eyes meet. Hers calling me out on whatever bullshit I'm about to tell her, mine probably telling her a million different stories at once. "Sure. It's not like we're dating. No commitment. No feelings. We're just putting on a show for my family and that's it."

"You know, Colin and I were fake dating."

"You were?" My eyebrows quip up in surprise.

"Ah, well… sort of. He tried keeping me from committing suicide and was a little scared Aaron would murder him if he was just 'playing' me. And I kind of found out Aaron didn't want Colin to fuck me unless we were together, so there's that too."

Committing suicide? What the fuck. Like, I guessed something bad happened to Lily. The Lily I knew was never this quiet, but I didn't think she was trying to fucking kill herself. And how could she say it so… casually?

"Lily… I had no idea."

She shrugs. "It's fine, honestly. I am happy now. I have a great boyfriend, and his friends are actually really awesome, too. I have you back as well. And, yeah, maybe sometimes it's still a little difficult, but then I just rant to Colin, and he'll make me feel better." Lily nudges me with her elbow. "But back to you. You're so totally going to fall for him."

Lily's lips press together into a thin line as she keeps herself from either smiling or calling me out. It wouldn't matter if she were to call me out because I have to believe what my mouth says.

I cannot get Aaron and my relationship confused.

"I gave you enough time to regret your decision from last Saturday, so tell me… do you really think Grey is hotter than Aaron? I mean, I do think that but I'm Aaron's sister so it would be weird if I thought he was—" Lily shakes out her body at the thought of saying her brother was hot. Maybe if I didn't have a brother myself, I'd find it questionable, but as someone with a brother, I can totally relate to the shudder of disgust.

"He's an Asian *God*. Of course, he's hot."

Lily starts to laugh but stops as the guys sitting behind us shush her madly. "What about Miles?"

"Miles isn't ugly either," I say. It's the truth. Miles is good-looking. He has blond hair, just like Aaron, maybe a bit darker. His eyes are blue instead of green. He doesn't have freckles, but I don't think they'd suit him anyway.

Miles has a sharp jawline, cheekbones that could cut you. His face is a bit too symmetrical for my liking, but he's still handsome.

But Aaron has all that too… not the *too* symmetrical face, but he's near perfection.

Yes, Sofia, keep comparing guys to Aaron. You always looked for reasons to dislike someone.

Lily looks toward the ice again, mumbling something unintelligible as she scans the players to find Colin. "Before Colin and I were dating, he hated Miles being around me. Not when Colin was there, too, but you know, when Miles was alone with me."

Can't blame him. The first week of me staying at the dorms, I had tons of other girls warn me off of Miles, said he'd only use one for sex, and then disappear. I'm not sure if the rumors are true, but as far as I can tell, he's busy taking care of his daughter all day. There's no time for fucking everyone on campus.

"But you only said Grey to annoy Aaron, didn't you?"

Sighing, I nod. It's useless to lie to Lily. Sometimes I think she has developed the ability to read minds because as it seems, she always knows exactly what I want to say or how I feel.

We spend the rest of the game not talking about Aaron and me anymore, not that there is an Aaron and me. Lily made up her own mind about us, and no matter what I will tell her, she won't stop holding on to what she believes. She's always been stubborn like that, doubt it has changed.

When someone starts knocking on the tempered glass, I first think it's Aaron, to tell us practice is over, but I'm surprised to find it's Colin.

He nods at Lily, and when I look at her, I find her smiling brighter than the sun.

Colin yells something, but it's almost incoherent with all the sounds in the arena, the glass between him and us, and his helmet that also has yet another layer of resistance plastic.

Immediately, Lily shoots up from her seat and jogs over to the extra door that leads to the ice. It opens, only for Colin to pop his head out.

He takes off his helmet, then quickly presses his lips to Lily's before he gets yelled at for doing anything but participating on the ice, by his own father.

The sight of them being so disgustingly in love makes me nauseous. I'm happy for them, truly, but being this crazy in love sure has everyone around them roll their eyes.

And yet I can't help but wonder when it's finally going to be my turn. When will *I* find this kind of love? The gut-wrenching, feel-good kind of love I read and write about.

CHAPTER 24

"if we walk down this road / we'll be lovers for sure"—
The Other Side by Jason Derulo

Sofia

"AARON, WE'RE GOING TO MISS our goddamn flight!" I yell at him as I speed through the airport, only ever looking back to see whether he's following or not.

He is… in slow-fucking-motion.

If there's one thing I would not like to deal with, it's my outraged father when I tell him that I missed yet another flight. He was close to chopping off my head when I missed my flight to get to New York, imagine what he will do if I have to tell him I missed the one back home as well.

This time it wouldn't be my fault though. It would be Aaron's and Aaron's alone. *I* wanted to get here hours earlier, *he* said ten minutes before boarding will do.

Clearly, it will not fucking do.

They called out for the end of boarding ten minutes ago, which leaves us with approximately five more minutes to get to our gate and on the plane. If it's not too late already.

"Chill, Icicle, it's just a flight. We'll take the next one then," Aaron says as he—finally—catches up with me. "Besides, we're not boarding like normal passengers."

What the hell is that even supposed to mean? Just because he got us first-class tickets doesn't mean the airline gave us some VIP passes that allow us to catch up with the plane mid-air.

"What are you talking about?"

Aaron shrugs.

A minute later we finally reach the check-in and I'm quick to realize that it's too late. *Far* too late. Even if they're still boarding passengers, check-in will take some time.

I sink down to the floor as I watch a couple check in for their flight, fighting the urge inside of me to cry.

Letting out a heavy sigh, I take out my phone, muttering something along the lines like, "I'm texting my father." Someone will have to let him know that Aaron and I won't be there tonight but—if we're lucky—tomorrow morning, or evening. Fuck, maybe the day after tomorrow or even later.

Everyone's traveling for the holidays, so catching flights is an extreme sport at this point. Christmas might still be a week away, but that doesn't stop some people from getting to their loved ones early. Like it wouldn't have stopped me if it weren't for Aaron.

"You done crying?" Aaron asks, scrolling through his phone like missing a flight isn't a big deal.

I guess it isn't. We still have a week to get to Germany and it's not like we're missing an important event or something. But think about the money Aaron spent on these two tickets only for them to have been a waste since we're not even on the plane.

I inhale deeply, slide my hands down my face before I finally choose to get up from the floor. "We have to ask for the next available flight."

Aaron shakes his head. "Why?"

"WHY?" My hands ball into fists by my sides, ready to beat the living hell out of this guy for being stupid. "I want to see my parents, Aaron. If you don't want to come with me, that's fine. You're not obligated to. But *I* need to get to Germany as soon as possible."

He chuckles like all of this is nothing but a game to him. Then he takes my suitcase, continuing to walk through the airport as if he's about to sneak us onto another plane or something like that.

Maybe I would complain, but I don't quite remember what I was mad about when Aaron's jacket slides up and I catch a glimpse of the light-purple-colored ribbon around his wrist. The same ribbon he has stolen from me mere weeks ago.

"I used my best friend privileges," he tells me as he leads me somewhere across the airport. "We're flying private."

Sofia, focus.

I stop in my tracks, jaw dropping down to the floor. Did he just say what I think he did or are my ears lying to me?

"What kind of best friend privileges are those?"

Aaron turns to look at me, smirking. "Colin's dad is still an NHL Coach, and his mother works as a surgeon, I think. Truthfully, I didn't think they own a jet but apparently, they do, not that it should surprise me. Have you *seen* their house?" I shake my head because, obviously I haven't. "If I had to guess, eighty percent of their flooring is marble. Their kitchen is made of marble, countertops, the island, everything. The stairs to go upstairs have built-in LEDs. It's amazing, totally something I aim to build for myself one day."

"You don't want to go pro anymore?"

He laughs. "Sure, I do. But I don't study architecture for nothing. The least I can do is come up with a house for myself. Otherwise, my degree would have been for nothing, right?" There is a certain spark of determination in his eyes, one I would think is about hockey but could also be about building his very own house.

I'm not even going to question his dreams at this point. What I've learned very early on about Aaron, when he's passionate about something, he'll make sure to live his dream out.

"Guess that makes sense."

"Anyway, Colin offered the jet to me when I told him we'd be going to Germany together. Guess it was just his attempt in offering us more privacy because… well, doesn't matter. I'd be stupid to say no to a private jet all at no cost to me."

That he would be. Still, it doesn't keep me from feeling bad. After all, Colin or his parents still pay for the flight, or the fuel, pilot, and flight attendants. Just because it's free to us doesn't make the whole experience free.

"What would we need more privacy for?" I ask carefully.

"Conversations, obviously." He offers me a smug smile, followed by a wink.

"Are we really taking a jet and have it all to ourselves?" Aaron nods, though I still don't want to believe it.

Only as we reach the private check-in facility, actually checked in, are told where to go next, and meet up with the captain of our aircraft do I start to believe it.

Chapter 25

"girl you're driving me wild, but baby don't stop"—Freak Like Me by Hollywood Ending

Aaron

SOFIA GAVE ME A PRETTY DIFFICULT TASK. *Don't freak out when you see my family.*

Apparently, she wants to know if her parents will recognize me. As much as I'd like to know if they would, I hardly have it in me to keep myself from smiling like an idiot when I spot Karin and Peter standing by the entrance doors to the airport.

All this time I thought I missed Sofia like crazy, but fuck, I suppose I missed her parents too.

I always liked them, they were nice to me, took me to their picnic dates every Saturday morning so Sofia wouldn't be all that alone. But there was always another aspect I liked about them; their admiration for Lily.

I hated it when someone couldn't stand my sister, but Sofia's parents invited Lily *and* me over to sleepovers after our parents split up, even though they knew Sofia and I would spend half the time arguing and Lily would babble for hours on end.

But I can suck it up. I'm a grown man now, I can approach old acquaintances without smiling and going nuts.

It seems Sofia spotted her parents as well because her hand interlocks with mine without any hesitation. My heart skips a couple of beats at the contact, so many, I have to tell myself—yet again—to keep it down. I'm here to help Sofia, not to fall in love with my once childhood crush.

Not that I was planning on falling in love just right now.

"Sofia!" Karin waves at us, her smile wider than anyone's I've ever seen. Before we even get to approach Sofia's parents, about a million different emotions run over Karin's face. She goes from happy to confused, to surprised and God knows how many more.

Peter, however, just looks me up and down and nods like he couldn't care any more if he had to. He then whispers something to Karin only to have his eyes back on me a second later.

"Why didn't you tell me you were talking about Aaron *Marsh* on the phone!" Karin says the second we're standing right across from Sofia's parents.

Does this mean I can get visibly excited now? I think it does.

The corners of my mouth tip up into a subtle smile. *Still got to keep it casual, don't want to come off as strange.*

"Look at you all grown up." Peter slaps me on the back as he chuckles. "Cleaned up nicely."

"Peter!" Karin glares at him with a warning.

Sofia sighs, banging her forehead against my shoulder as if she's regretting all her life decisions. Too fucking bad, she's stuck with me now. At least for the next two and a half weeks.

"It's nice seeing you again, Mr. and Mrs. Carlsen."

Just like that, I earn myself another slap on my back but this time a less greeting one. "Don't tell me you forgot our names, son."

I have not. How could I? Ever.

Honestly, I couldn't tell you what I thought was going to happen if I ever met Sofia or her parents ever again, but it wasn't anything like this.

I gave up on expecting Sofia and I ever meet again, but we did. We don't get along the way I thought we would, and we certainly don't have the relationship I dreamed of having with her years ago.

But at least she's back in my life.

And her family? Well, I didn't think they'd welcome me with open arms.

After giving me a tour of their house, we stand in a pretty blank guest room. All white walls, a well-made bed, sort of empty room. I suppose guest rooms don't have to have character or signs of someone living there, but that doesn't keep me from wondering why they didn't add *some* color.

The rest of the house isn't all too colorful either, but it's lived in. There are pictures of all three kids everywhere, wedding photos from Karin and Peter, anything you could think of. So why is there *one* room with nothing but white walls, a dresser, and a double bed?

"You can stay here," Sofia says. "I know it's not much but—"

"Here?" Peter's eyebrows fall into a confused frown. "I thought Aaron is finally your boyfriend?"

Finally. So she did think about me a lot when we were apart? Or maybe not. There's a chance Peter just always saw her with me, which, I know my father did.

Sofia doesn't answer her father. She rolls her eyes and shrugs him off.

I look at Sofia, holding a hand to my heart when I say, "Yes, Icicle, I thought I am your *boyfriend*. We slept in one bed many times before, why can't we now?"

Sofia narrows her eyes at me until my blood stops rushing through my veins. I'm sure if she had a knife, said knife would have been stabbed me a million times by now.

I just bet she expects me to say I'm okay with staying in the guest room, which I would be… if Sofia and I weren't supposed to act like we're in love.

So instead of feeling intimidated by her murderous glance, I smile at her and reach a hand of mine up to the necklace I am wearing for her.

Sofia has mumbled something about making this relationship seem more realistic when we wear the matching Lego necklace that turns into a heart when connected, but let's be honest, I would have worn it even without that pity argument of hers.

It's the first time I'm wearing it again ever since I took it off, but I can't see myself not wearing it ever again.

"If you think me staying in a different room will keep my hands away from you, you're wrong. I'm addicted."

Peter chuckles. Karin shakes her head at my words but at least she keeps a smile on her face. One of the kinds of smiles that are unreadable because they could mean a million different things at once. So either she's glad to see Sofia and I reunited again, or she regrets having been okay with Sofia bringing someone for the holidays.

As we arrived at around eight p.m. at the airport and still had to take on another fifty-minute car drive to their house, plus the tour they gave me… it's around ten thirty p.m. when Karin kindly lets us know that dinner's ready.

I've been dying to get some food inside of my stomach. Forgive me, but I usually work out half the day when I'm not busy with assignments or hockey, hence I eat a lot in between. Not having eaten yet, when it would be almost four in New City right now, is killing me.

But thankfully dinner's ready now and I no longer have to die on the inside.

"Leon is going to be there," Sofia tells me at the same time as I get up from her bed, ready to sprint downstairs. "He's always around, making sure to rub his 'perfect' relationship right into my face."

Right. *Leon.* A fucking asshole I'll be making sure has a deformed nose before Sofia and I go back to America.

I mean, who goes about and fucks their girlfriend's *sister* while still in said relationship? Who even fucks anyone when they're in a relationship? Unfortunately, too many people, that much I know.

No matter how strong my urge is to give the guy a new nose—maybe even a whole new face—I can make sure of one thing without any consequences: making Sofia shine. Making sure her sister and that fucker named Leon are envious of her and her relationship because that's what Sofia wants, or maybe needs. To show two disgusting people that getting rid of the weight of some guy only ever brought good things to her life. *Me.*

I'm the best anyway, so that won't be all that difficult.

I hold my hand out to Sofia with a soft smile on my lips. Whenever I look at her, my heart tightens, laughing at me because I know she will never be mine. But that's not what's important right now. "Once a cheater, always a cheater, Icicle. His relationship isn't perfect at all."

Sofia takes my hand, the contact of her skin on mine sending sparks through my body as I've never experienced before. It's like that static shock when touching someone, just that Sofia's touch doesn't shock me for just a nanosecond, it burns my entire body.

"We got this, Sofia, I promise. By the time we leave for New City again, your sister will wish she never even started dating your ex because she'll envy what you have now. I'll be the best fake boyfriend you'll ever have."

I do plan on putting my whole body, heart, and soul into the next two and a half weeks, even if that means putting myself and my feelings last. And fuck knowing that I'll spend a whole two weeks and two days pretending to be in love with Sofia when all I want to do *is* fall in love with her for real.

Chapter 26

"and I'm ready if you're ready to go / just say the word, just say the word"—Vibes by Chase Atlantic

My parents didn't tell me Lukas was coming for dinner, but fuck am I glad he's here.

I probably missed my older brother the most, and with two siblings and two parents, there are a lot of people to miss when you're an ocean apart from them.

Unlike my parents, Lukas doesn't immediately recognize Aaron, but why would he? Not even *I* did, and I have my bets on my parents only being able to because they were already grown-ups with better memories and abilities to recognize faces when we moved. Well, or they secretly followed up on him, which I doubt.

The first thing Lukas does when he enters the house is stand himself in front of Aaron, eyes narrowed with his chest puffed out as if he's about to show who's the boss. *He definitely isn't.*

"So, you're the *boyfriend*?" Lukas asks, fully aware that it's bullshit. After all, he was the one suggesting I bring a fake date. "I'm Lukas, Sofia's *older* brother."

One corner of Aaron's mouth tips up, but he is quick to press his lips together to keep himself from smiling too widely, "I know,

Lukas. We've met before. Quite often, actually."

My brother is a bit startled for a second, keeping his eyes narrowed at Aaron like he's trying to match any other face to the one in front of him. And then, his head snaps toward me, eyes widen with shock. "You found him!" He claps his hands once, letting out one loud "*HA!*"

"He found me… sort of?" It's true. Given the way we met at the grocery store, him paying for my tampons and chocolate, smiling at me like he's some knight in shining armor… yes, he found *me*.

Lukas turns back toward Aaron, tapping his hand on my fake boyfriend's shoulder. "Well, then I don't need to pretend that I hate you. I know Sofia is in good hands with you. You wouldn't do stupid things to her like a certain other guy"—his eyes wander over to Leon, glaring at him—"did."

Aaron brings his hand up to his chest—the one that still has my ribbon wrapped around his wrist as his bracelet—drawing a cross with his finger right over his heart. "Cross my heart, I'd never hurt my Icicle."

With a sneaky look toward Leon, I notice his jaw clenching like he's about to jump over the table and slap the living hell out of my brother *and* Aaron for… for what? Getting along?

Lukas never liked Leon. Not even when he *didn't* go and cheat on me yet. And any other guy I got close to; Lukas immediately disliked. Leon *knows* that.

"You still call her that? Damn, you must have some nerves."

After another short chatter, we *finally* sit down at the table, ready to eat.

If there's one thing I missed more than Lukas, it's definitely the food. Well, the bread. *Real* bread. Not the white bread from America, the same that Germans would laugh at when they hear it being referred to as "*bread*". When we first moved here, I was confused as to why people laughed at me for calling it bread, but the longer I lived here, the more I understood.

Conversations over dinner are surprisingly less awkward than I thought they would be. My parents mainly focus on Aaron, asking

God knows how many questions about him and how he's been, if he's still aiming to go pro like he always wanted to, and more. The good thing is, the more questions they ask, the less I have to find out myself in some strange ways.

Plus, Julia seems to hate the attention he is getting. Usually, she's the one being the center of attention. Well, tough luck.

Leon tries to calm her down whenever she speaks, and my parents brush her off because they're too invested in conversation with my boyfr—*fake* boyfriend.

"How's Lily?" my mother eventually asks, earning a bit of a wince from Aaron in response. Ever since Lily kind of, somehow really casually, let it slip out, I do finally understand his reaction whenever someone asks about her.

Aaron inhales deeply before plastering on a charming smile. "She's adapting. Starting new and, you know, figuring life out. But it's not my story to tell."

His response is monotonous like he spent hours in front of a mirror practicing how to say these three sentences with sounding as convincing as possible.

My mother shrugs it off, probably noticing that Lily is a topic Aaron does not like to discuss for whatever reasons he may have.

I know they're close, so it's not that he had a big fallout with his sister, and I'm sure my parents don't think it's that. But it's none of their business asking about a topic he doesn't feel comfortable talking about.

"Are you seriously going to eat that too?" Julia scrunches her face up in disgust, motioning a hand toward my extra slice of bread.

Leon chuckles, leaning back in his chair to comfortably watch the anticipated fight to start. Yes, *anticipated* because it happens every single time we sit at this table for *any* meal.

My sister always has to comment on how much I eat because God forbid, I have a stomach to fill. I do sports like five times a week. Not recently as I'm studying abroad and don't really have the chance to skate daily and practice jumps etcetera.

Julia, however, does *nothing* all day. Her best workout consists of walking down the street to go buy some new clothes at the only local clothing store. And I guess going to work.

That wouldn't even be a problem. So then I eat more than she does, big deal. You don't see me commenting on her habits, on the little she eats, or how badly she pisses me off. Not out loud, at least. It is a problem though, because my sister thinks she's the best person in the universe and everyone has to live life how she wants it.

Breaking News, Julia, the world doesn't revolve around you.

I don't bother responding, instead, I shove a fork full of potatoes right into my mouth.

"How can you even still move on your skates? No wonder you're the slowest of all of them."

Leon licks his lips, marinating the fucking stupid words that are about to leave his mouth. He leans over to my sister, whispering, "You see why sex with her was the worst? There was never any spice in it. Always the same boring positions because she's just too…" loud enough for everyone at the table to hear.

Always the same lame words, especially when I'm far from what he makes me out to be. Sure, I have some curves, like any fucking body does. It's like he has nothing else to call me.

Worst is, Leon *wanted* Aaron to hear it. If he didn't, he would have said it in German since I'm sure he's aware that Aaron doesn't understand a single word.

Aaron snorts a laugh, his hand finding my thigh to hold on to. "Or maybe you're just not good enough in bed."

My parents quickly flee the room like they would every single time Leon and Julia start this discussion. Instead of, I don't know, tell them to stop. They tried before but it only ended with me getting insulted even more, so I can't blame them for letting us handle this on our own.

"How does it feel knowing you weren't her first?" Leon puts on a smug smile.

With a quick glance toward Lukas, I find him suppressing horrific laughter from slipping out. He knows very well that although Leon might have been my first, my mind wasn't with him at all.

Aaron shrugs. "Don't think you were either. Not mentally, at least. You sure Sofia's head was with you and not me?"

What the fuck. I said this to him in confidence.

Leon's eyes zoom in on the necklace around my neck then move over to Aaron's. He's known of the necklace, asked me to get rid of it because he felt uncomfortable knowing I still held on to someone else while dating him. Seeing now both halves of the necklace must help him connect the dots. "*Du verdammte Schlampe.*"

Maybe I would be a little more furious if Aaron wasn't stroking his thumb over my thigh, having my body react in ways I'm not sure it ever has.

It's calming, even when my ex has just called me a bitch.

"I have no idea what you said, but I'm certain it's an insult. A lame one if you have to go about insulting my girlfriend in a language I don't understand. That's pretty low, don't you think? Only cowards would even go as far as using insults to feel better about themselves." He gets up from his seat, holding his hand out for me to take. And I do. I take it not only to appear like we're an actual couple but because as it seems, I enjoy holding his hand.

The slip-up at the airport earlier was me panicking, desperate to make us seem like a couple. But fuck, the tingles rushing through my blood at the contact had me wondering if it's always going to be like this when Aaron's skin is on mine.

It's a good kind of rush that speeds up my heart rate, makes my breath hitch, and long for him… maybe not so good after all.

Chapter 27

"but if it ain't you, it's a lie"—Always Been You by Jessie Murph

Aaron

FOR SOMEONE WHO CLAIMS TO BE SMART, I sure as hell am stupid as fuck.

Who in their right mind says sharing a room with the woman you're attracted to is alright? Mind you, a woman that you're fake-dating and wants absolutely nothing to do with you otherwise. Except for being friends, maybe? Even *that* is cutting it.

Sofia wanted to go to sleep the second we went back to her room after dinner, which, frankly, I understand given how it went down. She was pretty quick to fall asleep, too. Or maybe she pretended to be asleep so I wouldn't speak to her. Either way, she is asleep *now*.

I've been lying in bed for hours, trying to fall asleep as well. It appears to be impossible. Not sure if it's jetlag or the mere fact that Sofia is lying too close to me. I'm not kidding, she is far too close. So close, my blood is starting to rush to a certain area that is not supposed to get up while her ass is a couple of inches away from my crotch.

I don't have it in me to turn over, facing the other side. It has many reasons, one being I don't want to move too much because I don't want to risk waking her up. And two, I simply don't want to face the other way. When I do, I can no longer look at Sofia, even if it's just the back of her head. But sometimes she turns over and I get to see her face. She looks so peaceful when she's asleep and far too beautiful. Who the fuck looks good *sleeping*?

Anyway, I grab my phone to check the time, praying it has only been a couple of minutes that felt like hours, but to my horror, it's five in the morning. I haven't closed my eyes even once, not sure if it's a smart idea to try now. I'd sleep in and never get used to the time difference.

Might as well get up then. I hear someone talk in the hallway, so if I'm lucky, maybe Sofia's parents are up, and I have *someone* to talk to.

Though, just as I am about to sneak out of bed, Sofia turns over in her sleep. My breath gets lost in my lungs when she swings one arm over my body, followed by a leg.

I freeze, being so still, I can hear my own heartbeat.

Sofia's head presses against my chest, and for a short moment there I pray to everything holy that she will never leave again.

The heat of her body rolls over my skin, tickling on the surface and bringing a surprising calmness to me. I can feel her deep in my bones, every inch of my body begging me to never let her go ever again. Screaming for me to keep her safe, protect her from her stupid sister and that godawful ex-boyfriend of hers 'til the end of time.

When she sniffles and mumbles something in her sleep, my muscles relax, and I give in to her touch. Allowing her to use me as her pillow. When I think about Sofia ever using her actual pillow ever again, I would love to rip that pillow into a million different pieces until her only available option is me.

But that might be a step too far.

I'm not a jealous man. I don't care who someone talks to or hangs up with. What they wear and how many other guys stare at them. But apparently, when it comes to Sofia, I gladly become a pillow serial killer.

"All my fault," she mutters, her body twitching. I can assure that flinch was *not* her being cold but caused by whatever the hell is going on in her dream.

Even when we were younger, Sofia used to stammer one word or two when she was asleep. Lily used to tell me all about it, and I had experienced it sometimes when Sofia spent the night at my house or I at hers. But never had she been twitching or clutching her hands together.

Her grip on my shirt tightens, soft whimpers leave her. They almost sound like the tiniest of sobs.

My arms find their way around her body, holding Sofia tightly against me, as I hope it will somehow make her nightmare go away.

I wish I could climb into her dream and fight whoever or whatever makes her cry in her sleep.

Never have I thought I'd be the possessive kind of guy but holding Sofia in my arms right this moment proves me differently. Knowing she's comfortable enough with me to fall asleep in one room with me, then subconsciously rolling over in her sleep to find shelter in my embrace sure as fuck makes me want to rip off everyone's head that dares disturb what's mine. She might not be mine yet, but she will be. Eventually. Hopefully.

After a little while of me gently stroking a hand up and down Sofia's back, she eventually calms. Her tense body relaxes, bringing instant relief to me as well. I don't want her to be afraid of anything, not even in her dreams.

Another couple of minutes pass, me just holding Sofia close to me while she sleeps in peace… at least until she detangles herself from my body and rolls over again. The loss of her body pressed to mine almost makes me pull her back into my embrace.

But I'm not that crazily obsessed. If we're somehow finding a way together, it won't be because either of us forced it.

Finally, I sneak myself out of bed, stretching when I stand. For a moment there I want to rush out already, escape a sleeping Sofia and force my eyes to look elsewhere because I cannot fucking take it anymore. But then I remember that I promised myself something.

I promised I would help Sofia. I promised I would do anything imaginable to make *her* look good. Make her seem more loved than her sister could ever imagine possible for anyone. Make Sofia's birthday next week as special as it gets with no way of a proposal being able to top it.

And if making all this possible means allowing myself to fall, then so be it. Even if this will end in heartbreak.

So, I take a deep breath and grab some fresh clothes from my suitcase—the one I don't plan on unpacking. With trying to make as less noise as possible, I quickly change, grab my wallet, and rush out of the room to find the bathroom, brush my teeth, and go downstairs.

I'm happy to find Peter and Karin awake, sitting in the living room just casually talking because I need to ask them for directions. As soon as they notice me, Karin's face lights up with a smile before she motions for me to sit. Having a talk with my fake girlfriend's parents wasn't planned, but I suppose it is on the agenda now.

However, I don't walk over to them. I decide to keep some distance between Sofia's parents and me. They wouldn't hurt me, I know that much, but still. I am not taking risks here.

"You're up early," Karin says. "I'm just going to assume it's jetlag."

I nod, though I'm only half convinced it's that. "I'm not used to being six hours ahead of my usual time."

Karin chuckles, appearing to be the nice mother I remembered, all the while Peter looks at me with narrowed eyes. It's like he's waiting for an explanation from me. I wouldn't know what he wants me to explain, so as long as he doesn't ask questions, I'll keep my mouth shut.

"Where are you headed?" Peter then asks, nodding toward the wallet in my hands.

I look down, fidgeting with said wallet before my eyes meet his again. "I was going to ask you for a flower shop nearby…"

His eyes narrow even more. I swear, he barely even sees me anymore, that's how narrow they are. "A flower shop?"

I nod, slowly. "Yes, uh…, I just want to get Sofia some flowers. She seemed a bit too upset for my liking after dinner, so I figured why not put a smile on her face right after she wakes up."

"You and your gifts," he chuckles, shaking his head. "You know she still has that frog you gave her."

"I have mine too." Well, I have *hers*, technically. I snatched it from her before they left for Germany. I know I had one that I put into some clothes Sofia would always wear, at least color-wise, but I needed something of *hers* with me while she was gone.

"You do?" Karin smiles widely. I only manage to nod before she speaks again. "There's a rise lantern festival tonight. A few villagers are getting together for it. It's nothing big, but I'm not sure if it might be a bit much for you, but we would love to see you there."

Please. "I still play hockey, some of my games are televised. I think I can handle a festival."

"Not sure, son," Peter says. "Not everyone here speaks English. Well, mostly the older people don't. And Sofia's friends can be a bit… much. People will stare at you and Sofia and talk. They're nice and all, but it's not the kind of festival you're used to. Besides, televised hockey games aren't the same as people being all up in your business at a festival."

I shrug. If Sofia is going, so will I. Then there will be some people talking about me, staring, and do God knows what… big deal. I'll get through it. Hopefully.

Eventually, Karin tells me the name of the nearest flower shop, offers to type it into google maps for me so there's no way I'll get lost. I happily hand my phone over for that. I'd rather run around with freezing hands as it's felt like twenty-three degrees outside than get lost in the cold… in the dark.

I'm not afraid of the dark, but I like to be cautious walking around a town I've never been to at five in the morning with snow covering ninety-eight percent of the paths.

"Get a hot drink from the bakery next door. They sell amazing hot cocoa, though you might want to try using a translator app to order it. I doubt Martina speaks English," Karin tells me, handing me back my phone. "You can try, but she might throw you out instantly." *Just great.*

Chapter 28

"you say we're just friends, but I swear / when nobody's around"—Better by Khalid

Sofia

I WOKE UP HALF AN HOUR AGO to an empty room. Don't get me wrong, I don't expect Aaron to stay around when he wakes up, but I did expect him to come back eventually.

Who is keeping him away for that long? If it's Leon... fuck, he'll need someone there.

Even though I'd love to spend some more time in bed, regretting my life choices, I do end up getting up to put on some more presentable clothes. I refuse to go downstairs in shorts and a tank top. Not with Leon around.

I only get to pull my shirt over my head halfway before I freeze to the sound of my bedroom door opening. To make matters worse, I don't even see *who* just entered my room thanks to my shirt being around the same height as my head, but I do know they have a splendid view of my boobs right now. A second later, the door closes, but I just know someone is still in the room with me. Someone; most definitely Aaron.

He just tends to have great timing when it comes to seeing my goddamn boobs. Start to think they're some fucking magnet field for his eyes.

"My, my, Icicle. If you wanted me to fuck you, you just had to say the word," Aaron jests. I'm about to drop the shirt back down my body when two hands touch my arms, stopping me. "Sofia…" His voice is low, breathy. His hands move to my shirt, pulling it right over my head and arms before he tosses it over into my hamper.

Aaron's eyes meet mine, pupils dilated and filled with lust that he tries to blink away. As soon as my arms sink to my sides, I contemplate covering myself up but then conclude that it's useless as he has seen my boobs already anyway, so why hide them?

After a little while his eyes follow down my neck, settling on my boobs. His gaze burns my skin. If I didn't know it's physically impossible to burn skin using one's eyes, I'd be convinced Aaron is leaving some third-degree burn scars on my body.

"Do you have a breast fetish?" I ask at the same time as his hands grasp my waist and he pulls me closer into his body. "I mean, you do so happen to like looking at them."

"Generally, no. For yours, definitely."

Oh, okay.

His hands on my waist slide up until his thumbs brush the underside of my boobs. While Aaron is too busy ogling my breasts, I use the opportunity to ogle him, take mental images of his face to savor them until I die.

Why does he have to be so goddamn handsome?

His hair seems to be fluffy, a dream come true for my hands. Long and voluminous. His skin is a tad too light but suits his freckles and light leaf green eyes. His lips are far too kissable for my liking, but enough to make me crave them on mine. Aaron's jaw is chiseled, defined like I've had yet to see one. And the dimple on his right side whenever he smiles… I could die looking at him.

A shiver runs down my spine when one of his thumbs brushes over my skin ever so softly, it might as well be a brush of air.

His eyebrows dip into a frown—nothing mad but confused, maybe? A frown of interest? "What does it mean?"

What does *what* mean? His touch? The fuck if I know. I'd say it means he's interested in my body. What does it mean that I let him touch me? I'm sure it means I'm just as interested in his… and I don't seem to have enough strength in me to fight it right now.

"The tattoo, Sofia," he chuckles, clearly having noticed my inner conflict. "What does it mean?"

Oh. The tattoo. I totally forgot I had it.

Suddenly, I really miss my shirt or any shirt. Even a blanket around my torso would do.

Finally, I manage to step back from Aaron, walking over to my closet to find a shirt to wear. Without looking at Aaron again, I speak. "It just says *'breathe'*. It doesn't have a meaning." Only that I have crippling anxiety and need to be reminded that it's okay to take a break every now and then.

"I think it does. But alright, if you don't want to tell me yet, I won't make you."

Oh lord, why does he have to respect me this much? Or anyone for that matter? Couldn't he be a total asshole? Being an asshole would certainly make hating him less difficult.

Imagine he wouldn't give a shit about what I wanted, how I felt. How differently I would think if he wasn't still the sweet guy he was at the age of eight; loving to tease but respectful. Only now he also knows how to tease me in ways that have not only my head smoking in anger but also make my body act like a complete fucking traitor.

Once I'm wearing a hoodie and exchanged my shorts for some black leggings, I allow myself to turn around again, finding Aaron standing by my dresser. He must be looking at the pictures, wondering why I have them here and why I would frame them and put them up.

My words are my worst enemy. I keep saying the kiss Aaron and I shared meant nothing, that he and I could never work… and yet I have pictures of us when we were younger standing on my dresser like some fucking shrine. It's kind of like my own personal temple, or so people could think if they looked at it.

Suddenly I'm glad I threw in pictures of my closest friends here in Germany as well. Only like two, but that's better than none, considering that there must be three *framed* ones of Aaron and me alone, then approximately six other ones of Lily, him and I hanging on the wall somewhere between all the other ones. The other ones being six in total, at most.

"See anything interesting?" I ask, figuring that I have to say something.

"I talked to your mom." Aaron turns around, now holding a bouquet of fucking flowers in his hands. Or so I assume. They're covered with an extra sheet of white wrapping paper. *Where the hell did he get those from anyway*? "She said *you* wanted to stay here."

The ultimate betrayal.

"I like it here." I do. I hated living in the center of Munich. Big crowds and everything being so busy weren't my thing. But then we moved here, into this small village. Everyone knows the other, the people are kind and always there for one if needed. They're like one big family and I loved the closeness. I never felt uncomfortable here, never had to worry about random men groping me when I walk alone at night, because word would get around quicker than anything.

If one of the villagers hates you, you're doomed. Your entire family is doomed, actually.

Aaron hums as he takes a step closer to me. "I don't blame you. It's beautiful here, though I bet it looks better in the summer."

It does. Everything is far greener, more fun. You can do other things than try not to slip while walking up the hill and end up sliding down instead.

"Did you mean to walk away from New City?"

I nod. There's no use in denying it. "I had nothing there anymore. I basically grew up around here. And after what happened when we came back to America… I just—"

Aaron's eyebrows draw together. "What happened?" he interrupts.

My heart begins to beat faster, hands shaking as I realize my mistake. I swore to never speak about it ever again. I swore to never *feel* the way I felt when it happened ever again. "Get me drunk and you might be able to get an answer."

Without trying to argue, Aaron takes yet another step toward me, holding the bouquet out for me. He doesn't press for an explanation, which I love about him.

Not love. Like. It's what I *like* about him. Cherish, appreciate, value, if you will. Any other adjective in the book. But definitely not *love*.

"I figured you could use something beautiful in your life, apart from me, obviously."

This guy... I'm at a loss of words for his cockiness.

I take the bouquet, immediately lifting the top paper to look at the flowers only to have my breath get sucked right out of my lungs. Beautiful fucking soft purple lilacs staring back at me like they're the sun shining down on me.

There's one thing I should do, like thank him, cry while being overrun with joy, but what comes out of me are six whole other words. "Are you out of your mind?!"

"I thought you'd be happy to get flowers, your favorite ones, mind you. I suppose I was wrong."

My head shakes all by itself, mouth slightly opened in either shock or disbelief, perhaps a healthy mixture of both. "One stem alone costs good four dollars, give or take. These must be what? One hundred stems?"

"Is this a bad time to tell you I've got more?"

"LILACS?"

He snorts a laugh. "No, presents."

I let out a deep breath, taking steps back until my legs hit my bed. Sitting down, I stare at the flowers in my hands, blinking away tears. I refuse to let some of those salty traitors run down my cheeks, telling Aaron just how much I love these. *Appreciate*. How much I appreciate these.

No one has ever gotten me flowers, especially not lilacs. Given the price of one single stem, I understand why no one has ever bought me lilacs. But fuck, I never even received a daisy, and everyone knows you can literally pick them off the grass outside.

Looking up to meet his eyes, I smile at him softly. "Thank you for these," I say, using every ounce of strength in me not to cry *or* smile like a child seeing candy. "This means the world to me."

"You'll get more." He offers me a nonchalant shrug, grinning widely at the same time as he goes to grab a gift bag from beside my dresser. Once he's back in front of me, Aaron sits down on the floor, crossing his legs while handing me the bag. "Now, I know you love romance novels, but I didn't know which one would be a surprise to get you, so I had to ask the owner if she knew you and all. She recommended something. So, in case you don't like it and it doesn't surprise you at all, it's not my fault."

I chuckle, even though I'm unsure of what he's talking about. At least until I open the gift bag and peek inside, finding a hardcover book staring back at me. Gasping, my eyes snap to Aaron's. "You did not."

"Did what?"

"Get lilacs *and* a hardcover! Do you know how expensive both things are?" I mean, hardcovers are definitely less expensive than lilacs, for sure.

Aaron runs his fingers through his hair. "Can't say I checked the bill."

Of course, he didn't. Honestly, I don't think I'd check it either, too afraid of my heart stopping to beat when I see the number on the receipt.

I pull out the book from the bag, experiencing yet another minor heart attack when I see it's a fucking first edition of *Pride and Prejudice*. I was well aware our local bookstore sold it, but none of the villagers could ever pay for that thing.

I mean, spending hundreds on a book or food... yeah, I think everyone chooses food over books.

"Does your money have any boundaries?" I regret asking instantly. It's rude to ask about money, but honestly, can you blame me for blurting out the question?

"For you? No." Aaron takes the gift bag from me, setting it down on the floor. He then lays the book on the bed beside me before taking my hands in his. "I got access to my trust fund when I turned twenty-one. My dad wants me to use the money to buy a house or do anything smart with it, invest or, you know… things like that. But I figured spending it on stuff that'll bring a smile to your face will do."

Aaron Marsh has officially lost his mind.

"No, Aaron. I'm thankful you got those for me, truly. However, if you could get a refund for these"—I nod towards the lilacs—"I would make you get it… but as that's impossible, I have to ask you not to spend so much money on me anymore. The money is for something important. It's for your future. Think of the dreamhouse you want. You could use the money to buy a piece of land and build the house you've dreamed of."

He shakes his head. "*You* are important, Sofia. More important than any dream I have ever had or will ever have."

Please, I need him to just stop this. Stop breaking my heart with every word he says that isn't proving his hatred for me. He has not once shown me he hated me, but fuck, I need him to. It'll make leaving him behind when college is over so much easier.

He leans a little into me, not all too much but enough for my pulse to go nuts.

"I was going to get you one of those porn books you seem to like," he says, his voice a little hoarse when he speaks. "But I couldn't think of any book you don't already have that intrigued me to buy."

A pink flush appears on my skin, I'm sure of it. "How would you know about my 'porn books'?"

His hands lay on my knees, a shiver rushes through my body. And then he winks. He. Fucking. *Winks*. And to make matters worse, he adds a smirk.

Hi, God, it's me again.

CHAPTER 29

"you know you could tear me apart"—Shivers by Ed
Sheeran

Aaron

"PIA, EMMA, JANE," SOFIA SAYS, smiling at her friends, "*das ist Aaron, mein Freund.*" Her hand squeezes mine, I'm not sure why, but I'm not here to complain about it.

I mean, the girl I've been crushing on for felt like forever is holding *my* hand, squeezing it. It doesn't matter if it's for comfort, a sign of her lies, or any other reason.

Also, I'm not quite sure what Sofia just said, but it sounded awfully a lot like an introduction. I could make out some names, so it's the only logical option, right?

Sofia's friends look me up and down, smirking. I swear, one even has some horny eyes going. The brunette, to be precise. Not sure what her name is, but I'm guessing one of the ones Sofia just said.

As I don't want to acknowledge the heated looks from the other women, I look around the barn. Yes, a fucking *barn*. Who the hell hosts a party inside of a barn? I'm glad we're somewhat inside as there must be at least a foot of snow on the ground, but a *barn*?

To my surprise, the barn is heated with what I assume must be a portable heating or a few of them.

The barn is big enough to allow the entire village inside and still has enough space for everyone to breathe and walk around properly. The entire interior is held cozy; hung-up fairy lights, blankets in case someone gets cold, tables with rows of food and drinks, hay bales all over the place, and a surprisingly great number of tables and chairs.

It is different from what I know, but nothing I wouldn't be able to get used to.

"He doesn't speak German," I hear Sofia say at the same time as she tugs on my arm and looks up at me. "Jane asked what you like most about Germany so far."

"Sofia." Most obvious answer. No matter where I am at, my answer will always be Sofia. That is if she's there with me. "Nothing more beautiful than her."

The black-haired girl—probably Jane—gapes at me. "Fuck, where'd you find that guy? Can one buy those somewhere?"

I do have to say, she's beautiful. Jane's got a beautiful face, not too symmetrical, deep brown eyes that seem almost black without the light hitting them. Her nose isn't crooked, but rather pointy, her legs long and slim.

And yet when I thought someone like her is just my type, my attention remains on a certain brunette with some curves in the right places, honey-brown eyes, a cute little nose, and red, kissable lips.

Sofia giggles then leans her head against my arm, her free hand now holding onto me as well. "Doubt it. And don't go on boosting his ego. He's a hockey player, Aaron's ego is the size of Alaska already."

"A hockey player?" The redhead's interest is piqued, eyebrows rising until they disappear underneath her bangs. "I thought Leon was a lesson to you."

Why the hell is everyone so obsessed with that cheating bastard?

"Aren't they all the same? I doubt one sports guy could stay faithful to their partner, especially when they're on the road for half the year," the very last of Sofia's friends adds, eying me curiously.

I shake my head at her, truly not understanding how either of them can make such bold assumptions. I'm sure there are some athletes out there not wanting to commit to someone else, but I'm not one of those.

Well, I have been, that much I have to say. I barely committed to Winter, but I suppose we can all agree on the same reason why that is.

Anyway, being in a fake relationship with Sofia or not, I wouldn't think of being with anyone else. She's it for me, has always been. So then I might have to find a more complicated way to get us to our happily ever after, but I will.

No matter how long it'll take, I promised, not only her but me too, that Sofia will end up with me. I'd be pretty stupid to jeopardize her trust in me with cheating. If she were to be in love with me, which she is not *yet*, I'd also be out of my mind insane to put that on the line for a silly fling.

I know what I want from Sofia, but I'm yet to make her understand, make her trust me enough to want the same.

"Fortunately, I'm not yet playing for the pros, so I'm not really on the road that much. Though, even if I were, Sofia is the only one that had ever held the key to my heart. She literally had me in a chokehold since we were seven. So much to thinking of another woman has me want to beat myself up." I wink at the blonde for the mere purpose to provoke. "Perhaps you simply haven't found the right man yet if you guys think every single athlete, or guy for that matter, would rather cheat than be loyal."

The girls' eyes snap over to Sofia's, one of them saying something in German. I'm not even sure I want to know what she said when I see Sofia rolling her eyes shortly before dragging me away from the three menaces.

Sofia leads me past the buffet table, to the fridge filled with drinks where she grabs a bottle of wine before leading me to one of the back corners of the barn. She then releases my arm, looking up a wooden ladder, one that looks like it's going to break when one steps foot on it.

"Are you planning on dragging me up there?" I ask at the same time as she clamps the bottle of wine between one arm and her side while using the other to hold on to one step of the ladder to climb up. In what must be seconds, I take the bottle from her, shaking my head as if to tell her she's insane.

I mean, come on. Climbing up a ladder—that seems to be older than her—with one hand, and not to forget that there are more missing steps to the ladder than present… no. I will not let her risk falling, breaking bones, or simply hurting herself in the slightest. In any way.

"It's safe. I've been using this ladder to get up there since I was ten. Nothing ever happened to me."

"Just because it never has doesn't mean nothing ever will happen. Did you *look* at that thing?! That is a safety violation."

Sofia bites her bottom lip, trying to keep the smile from showing but it doesn't work. Slowly, she's making her way up that ladder. Halfway up, she looks down at me, grinning. "If you're too scared to come up here, that's your problem. I'm not a coward."

She is going to be the death of me, won't she? In every single sense imaginable.

As she reaches the top, Sofia lies down on the wood, reaching a hand down to take the bottle from me. I hand it to her.

I'm well aware that I don't have to prove to Sofia that I'm far from scared, far from being a coward, and yet despite the uneasy feeling in my stomach, I follow her up the ladder.

Every other step creaks, screaming at me to get down. This is far from safe; nobody can convince me otherwise. Not even Sofia.

As soon as my feet are on solid—*creaking*—ground, I'm a little more relieved. I'm sure the thin layer of this wood could give in at any second and have Sofia and me fall at least eight feet, but I'm not here to back out of spending some alone time with Sofia… that is *if* I could find her.

Where the fuck did she go? I swear, I was right behind her and now she's—Oh. Found her. "What the hell are you doing sitting on a hay bale in the darkest possible corner?"

She shrugs at me, taking a sip from the wine, right from the bottle before holding it out to me. "Want a sip?"

Making my way over to Sofia, I shake my head. I don't like wine. Never did, never will.

Before I sit down beside her, I grab my phone from my pocket and send a quick text to a group chat consisting of my three best friends and me. You know, just to let them know that I might die very soon.

Aaron: Not to be dramatic, but I might die.

"Are you okay?" Sofia presses her lips together to stop herself from laughing. "You're a bit pale."

"That's the light." It's not, I'm sure of it.

I might be majoring in architecture, but that's all it is. Designing houses. I don't like heights.

In an attempt to calm my nerves, I finally take a seat, taking deep breaths. *Everything will be fine. This barn isn't that unsafe. The wood might be old and falling apart, but that's fine… it won't just break. Hopefully.*

"Nix?" Sofia's hand lies down on my thigh. "You're shaking. And I can assure you, it's not cold here. What is wrong?"

"Just not a fan of heights," I admit. Fuck, I never admitted that to anyone. I know it's common and nothing to be embarrassed about, but I'm not the guy to get scared. I don't admit to having weaknesses.

My phone chimes, my eyes instantly snapping to it to keep my head occupied.

Grey: Why, did Sofia beat you at hockey?

Miles: Stuck it in the wrong hole and now she's beating you to death?

Colin: Nah, he's too much of a pussy for that, Miles. Bet he wouldn't touch Sofia if she begged him to do it. He probably just poked his thumb with a needle. We all know he can't see blood.

Miles: Right. Hockey's just *the* sport for him.

Grey: Damn, I think he might actually be dead. He's surprisingly quiet.

Colin: Your friends will miss you, Ron! Lots of love. x

Grey: Hey, just because you fucked once doesn't mean we will *all* miss him.

Miles: Seriously. Ron wouldn't miss us either. *You*, he will miss you though, for sure.

Colin: You're just jealous.

Grey: Not going to lie, I am.

"You had sex with Colin?" Sofia's voice pulls my eyes away from my phone. My blood rushes through me a little quicker, my brain forgetting every single word known to the English language. "Aaron?"

I shake my head, not in an attempt to deny her question, but to clear up the fog that built up. "For the experience. You know, trying things out and all."

She bobs her head lightly, comprehending my words before she starts to laugh, leaning her forehead against my arm. I'm not quite sure if I am supposed to run for my life, be offended, or laugh along with her. Either way, hearing Sofia's giggles eases my nerves a tiny bit.

Though I know Sofia isn't the type to judge, it's still a little nerve-wracking to try and find out what the fuck her laughter means in this situation.

"This might be a little too personal, and I'd understand if you don't want to answer, but please tell me he bottomed. Or don't, whatever you feel comfortable with. But you don't seem like you're one to take something up your ass," she says, fidgeting with her fingers. She avoids looking at me the moment the words leave her mouth, and I just bet she's mentally beating herself up for having asked.

Oh, okay. She was laughing because she was picturing it, I guess?

"We didn't go there," I tell her, laying my hand on her thigh to hopefully ease her nerves a little. "Just sucked each other off and called it quits. I wasn't going to let Colin in through my back door, and he sure wasn't letting me do that either. Can't say I even wanted to, to be honest." I'm sure even if either of us volunteered to sacrifice their ass, we wouldn't have gone that far.

With a hint of an awkward smile, Sofia nods slowly. "Does Lily know?"

"I doubt it. Though she did ask me if I was attracted to Colin, so who even knows." What I do know, however, is that I am not in any way attracted to the male species. Dicks aren't my thing.

I think experimenting and finding out what is, and what isn't on your likes list is important. Colin thought the same, clearly. We weren't drunk or anything, not even tipsy. Hell, we had absolutely no alcohol intake that day whatsoever. It just so happened. One little talk between two guys and a silly idea and shit just went down. Nothing dramatic.

Sofia then moves away from my arm, the loss of her making itself noticeable instantly. The cold, that's not even cold but chillier now without her warmth on my body, digging through my sweater, sending a strange chill down my spine. It's like my body refuses to feel warm without any goddamn part of Sofia pressed to mine.

She takes yet another sip from the wine, once again holding the bottle out for me. I still don't take it despite the eye-roll I earn for it.

I won't drink tonight. One of us has got to be the sober one, and since it won't be Sofia, it's now my very responsibility to make sure she gets home safe, that she will be okay, that she won't do anything stupid. I will be her protector. If she wants me to or not. But then again, I will always protect her—drunk or not.

"You know, if I were you and had the chance to fuck Colin, I probably would have done the same thing. He's hot," Sofia admits, sighing deeply.

"He's dating your best friend. You shouldn't say things like that." I wouldn't care, truthfully. Sofia and I might not know one another that well anymore, but I would bet all my father's money on her, having every ounce of faith that she wouldn't try shit with Colin.

He wouldn't let it happen anyway. Colin is head over heels in love with my sister, which is a little disgusting, but I'm glad it's him and not some junkie Lily picked up on the streets,

Anyway, I happen to think *Rihanna* is pretty good-looking, and yet I'd never try to hop into bed with her.

Oh, and I also feel this cruelty in my guts. The cruelty I know is called jealousy but won't admit it to myself yet. I am *not* jealous just because the girl I have had a major crush on since I was a stupid five-year-old thinks my best friend is hot.

Nope. Not jealous.

I also don't feel the urge to punch my best friend in the face in hopes that it would fuck up his pretty face. Totally not.

Sofia smirks at me, then starts chugging down another few sips from the wine, drawing my eyes to her kissable lips. Lips that are red tonight. A bright, rich red that had my cock standing strong when I looked at her for the first time after she applied her lipstick.

Red is definitely her color, and yet I prefer her in that stupid wisteria color she loves so much.

"You're hot, too, you know?"

She can't say things like that. As much as I've been longing to hear her say it, praying she finds me attractive since the day she arrived here, my brain can't take it. Fuck, my *heart* can't take it.

"Of course, I know. I'm the most handsome guy you'll ever come across."

Her eyes narrow at me, one hand coming up to my face where she'd grip my chin between her fingers, taking a closer look at me while moving my head from side to side.

"Meh. You're missing some color. Maybe red would look good on you."

If you think red will look good on me, Sofia, I will wear red every single day for the rest of my life.

"Shit, really?" She nods. "Kiss me then."

Chapter 30

"I swear my whole world is turned around"—Upside
Down by Austin Moon

Sofia

"Kiss you?"

"Yes. You want to see red on me, kiss me." His eyes drop to my lips then meet mine again. "Or are you scared you might fall for me if you kiss me?"

Asshole.

I'm a competitive person. I have to be if I want to make it through skating competitions without losing my head. The losers always end up on the receiving end. Being competitive and working your way up to be better than everyone else sure helps never being at the bottom of the rank.

So, tell me I can't do something and I'm likely to do it just to prove the other person wrong.

Setting the bottle down on the floor for a hot second, I place both of my hands on either side of Aaron's face. He smirks at me, either anticipating the kiss or thinking I won't go through with this.

I inhale deeply. *Here goes nothing.*

Moving in closer, I barely get the chance to catch another breath before Aaron's mouth crashes down to mine, lips locking soft and gentle, yet it feels like they're on fire.

My heart skips a beat or two when his hands grip my waist, pulling me from beside him right over in his lap. My legs are on either side of his body, seeking stability from the hay bale we're sitting on. I try to hold myself up, not sitting down on his legs for my very own sanity. I'm not sure if it's unfortunate, or fortunate when Aaron pushes my hips down, seating me right on top of him.

My brain sinks into my pants when I feel his dick press against my thigh. Can't believe I'm saying this, but I sure would love to know what he would feel like inside of me.

As soon as his tongue slips into my mouth, my brain shuts down. Thinking about whether or not this is wrong, that we shouldn't kiss or be anything but friends isn't important anymore. What's important is that we both want this. So why the hell not give in to the temptation?

People's ways part all the time for various reasons, but if we never try to explore the unknown, we'll never find out, right? Who even knows, maybe Aaron and I could be as good together as I prayed we would be. Maybe not.

I know we won't last forever because I could never move back to New City. Getting a part of him for a little while will have to do. It's all I can ever get, all he can ever get from me, and it sure is better than not having had the other at all, right?

Though there is one thing I refuse to do, lie to Aaron. He needs to know that this won't be going anywhere. No future. No strings attached.

He is attracted to me, that much is obvious. The question is whether he is interested in a friends-with-benefits kind of relationship or not. I would be. Maybe it's not the very best for my heart, but again, it's all I can offer.

I can feel my nipples harden as I rub against him. Aaron groans into our kiss, pushing his tongue into my mouth to claim me. Like I'm not already his.

"Aaron." I gasp for air, but before I know, his lips are back on mine. His hands slide from my hips to my ass, giving it a firm squeeze.

"There you are."

Aaron and I break apart, my head instantly snapping toward the direction my mother's voice came from. She just stands there, a smile on her lips, her arms crossed over her chest. My sister is standing right next to our mother, her hands balled into fists on either side of her body.

"I told your father he'd find you here, and I was right."

Given that I've been hiding up here since we moved to *Baierbrunn*, one would think my father knows this. I always come here to write. This barn has been my escape ever since. It's cozy, warm. It's quiet with nobody around. It's just what one needs when they need to get away from everyone and everything. And well, nobody ever came up here, so I did instead.

"People are asking for you, Sofia," Julia says, her voice scornful. "But I suppose they're used to one of us being the disappointment of our family."

"Julia," my mother warns, drawing in a deep breath. Her patience level must be through the roof with Julia and me recently.

Well, *recently* is an understatement. I've never been too fond of Julia, thanks to our age gap. She has always been more interested in other things, things that didn't include me. She never made an effort in getting to know me. And as her younger sister, I didn't think *I* would have to be the one getting to know *her*. Anyway, our mother had to be patient with us since I was born, and it only got worse when I found out she slept with my boyfriend and didn't even regret it.

"Yeah? How does that feel?" I ask Julia. "I mean, you already took the spot for the bitch that sleeps with taken guys. Was wondering when your nickname will change from 'the whore' to 'disappointment.'"

Before my sister gets the chance to let out the rage that's burning in her eyes, my mother is escorting her away from me. Hopefully right back down the functioning stairs. A set of stairs I did not tell Aaron about.

"I didn't think your hatred went this… deep," he says as soon as our eyes meet again. "I suppose I should have guessed it would."

I lean down, my forehead pressing against his shoulder as I let out a quiet laughter. My body shakes, chest rumbles with a chuckle so soft, I never knew was possible. "Wait until you witness my father and I interact," I mumble, mostly to myself.

"What do you mean?"

I sit up straight, sighing. "I made sure he had a couple of difficulties with me ever since we moved here."

"Why?"

"Because I was mad. I didn't want to move here when I was seven. I didn't want to leave New City. Being the age I was, I didn't exactly understand why we had to move, and it made me furious that I had to leave everything and everyone behind just because my father had been given a better job in Munich." And *the* incident, but there's no need to tell Aaron about it.

He nods slowly as he processes what I'm saying. "So you turned rebellious?"

"Yeah, toward him. I only ever gave him short answers, if any. Or yelled at him. He had no control over me whatsoever. And by the time I understood why his job here was so important and far better for our family, I had no idea how to fix my relationship with him. So this time around, we're just co-existing." Though I know my father loves me in some ways, and I hope he knows that I love him. It's just difficult for both of us to approach one another without drawing out some rage from the other person.

All of a sudden, Aaron reaches a hand up to my face, his thumb stroking firmly along the skin right underneath my bottom lip.

I watch his face as his eyes linger on my lips. His features are soft, a glimpse of a smile tugging on the corner of his lips. His eyes full of admiration, and perhaps a hint of hope. Hope for what? I do not know, and I'm not sure I want to find out either.

"Red is not your color," I tell him, taking in the bits of red lipstick smeared not only on, but also around his lips. "Did you try purple? It's the complementary color of your eyes, so it should make them pop."

"That's what I have you for, Icicle," he answers. "You're all sorts of purple at all times."

I hate, hate, *hate* that he is right. I do wear a lot of purple every single day.

Aaron shifts underneath me, pulling out a tissue from his pocket. He unfolds it and starts removing the bits of lipstick on his lips without seeing where to wipe. Putting him out of his misery, I take the tissue from him and help him out.

Shortly after that, I have to deal with Aaron almost falling down the ladder while complaining about how insecure said ladder is, and that it should be put out of order, to which I remind him that this ladder is a simple ladder, not some fancy electric one that could malfunction.

CHAPTER 31

***"'cause in a sky full of stars / I think I saw you"—A Sky
Full of Stars by Coldplay***

Sofia

"I HEARD THEY'VE BEEN FRIENDS from a young age. That's probably the only reason someone like him would ever date someone like Sofia."

I roll my eyes at the voice of one of the gossip girls in the village. Lena has always been a diva. She thinks she's oh-so-amazing, has an opinion on *everything*, and is convinced she knows best. Always. She also never liked me, so I'm not surprised to hear her gossip about me.

But, hey, at least she's speaking in a language Aaron does not understand. I'm sure if he heard her say this, he would open his mouth and say some words *I* would end up regretting for him.

"Icicle."

I turn my head away from Lena and her *assistant*, to look at Aaron. You genuinely can't call Emilie her best friend, at least not when she does everything for Lena. Like, homework, *chores*, and more.

"Nix."

"Your father has been calling your name like five times by now."

I think he wants to talk to you."

My father? Wanting to talk to *me?* Yeah, I don't think so.

I look around the barn, searching for my father. To my surprise, when my eyes land on him, he is already staring at me, a hint of a smile on his lips.

Has he really been wanting to talk to me?

The smile on his lips disappears as quick as it came, a stern look covering his face. He motions for me to go outside, and when my eyebrows dip in confusion, he makes some sort of gesture that looks either like a lantern flying away, or he wants me to serve people? I'm just going to assume he means the former as this entire get-together is about lanterns.

It's something a couple of the villagers came up with after one of our neighbor's daughters has gone missing. They found the remains of her body three months later, or they assume these were hers. The body had skin missing, which—so I would assume—is to be expected when your lifeless body has been thrown into a lake filled with fish and other animals living in water.

Exactly nine years ago today, she went missing. She had just turned twelve that day. Nika and her friends wanted to stay out for a little while longer… but they never returned. Her friends came back two days later, disturbed out of their minds. Neither of them remembered what happened, but they could all say that something really bad did go down.

If it weren't for my father insisting I came home because we were to catch a flight early the next morning, I would have been a part of this group. I don't think I've ever been more grateful for my father's stubbornness, as bad as this may sound.

The year after, Nika's best friend's family suggested still throwing a little party for Nika, a lantern festival because Nika loved lanterns. It's now an annual thing. All her friends and family show up here, writing messages to her, or wishes we have, on lanterns before we send them up to the sky. It makes her parents and sisters feel a little better about their loss.

As my father makes his way over to Aaron and me, I grab my

fake boyfriend's hand and drag him out of the barn. He was smart to keep his jacket on, I, unfortunately, took mine off the second we entered the barn, which means I am now slowly freezing to death as it's approximately twenty-six degrees outside.

"You're shivering," Aaron says as he lays his hand on the small of my back, guiding me over to all the other people. They're spread all around the little field behind the barn, preparing their lanterns for take-off. Some are lit already, held on to so they won't fly up already.

"It's a bit cold." *No shit, captain obvious*.

Aaron chuckles, his hand retrieving from my body. "Should've put on a jacket." Just as we come to a hold and I'm handed a lantern and a sharpie, I can feel someone—most definitely Aaron—laying some fabric over my shoulders. He walks around me until we're face to face where he takes the lantern from me. "Put your arms in the sleeves."

I feel horrible because I do so without hesitation. It's my fault I forgot to put on a jacket before sprinting outside when I knew it was more than cold outside. I was well aware that it's snowing, and that the snow on the ground goes up to my calves. There is no excuse as to why I didn't put on a jacket. And now Aaron would rather freeze to give me his jacket than shrug off my stupidity.

"Thank you, but—"

"You're welcome." Aaron beams a smile at me. His smile is always so warm, genuine. It's inviting, truly. Just looking at Aaron challenges my mouth to keep quiet, fighting the urge to say the words I wanted to send him when I found his Facebook account a couple of years ago on accident.

And then he smiles… Oh boy, his smile.

It makes my heart squeeze in strange ways. In ways, it's never squeezed before. There's always a pinch of pain when I remember he's never going to be mine the way I want him to be. The way he *promised* he would be. But then again, he promised that when we were eight. Okay, *he* was eight, I was seven still. For two months, at least. Doesn't make it any better.

"So, what do we do with this?" he asks, holding the lantern in his hands up to bring it into my vision.

I sigh deeply. We have a little under two weeks to go, and I'm already spacing out, thinking, *dreaming* about Aaron when he is right in front of me.

"We send a message up to Nika," I tell him as I pull the cap off the Sharpie. Aaron looks a little confused but doesn't ask.

Right, he doesn't know what happened.

So I spend the next minute telling him about the horror night, what followed, and how it got to this annual lantern "festival". He doesn't get a broad story, just a tiny summary to know enough.

"Some send up wishes," I add at the end. "I always did." But I don't tell him that my wishes were only ever about him.

Yes, yes, I admit, that might be a little too over the top, but can you blame me? What good friend doesn't want their friends to succeed in life? What kind of friend wouldn't wish for the other to live happily ever after, make all their dreams come true, or be healthy? I never wished for Aaron to come find me or end up with him. All I ever wanted was for Aaron to be *happy*. So that's what I wished for. Every single year.

Aaron nods once, kind of like he's telling me he understood, but still has no idea what he's supposed to do now. He also doesn't ask *what* kind of wishes I sent up, and I genuinely appreciate that.

I wouldn't know what to tell him, and it sure as hell wouldn't be the truth. Plus, I'm a strong believer in that one sentence my father used to say a lot when I was younger. *"If you say it out loud, it's never going to happen."*

Now, I do think it's sort of the opposite of the truth since the law of attraction seems pretty legit. But I don't think he ever meant to say to *never speak* of your dreams. Only progress that's done to reach your goal as people are rude. They're cruel and a lot of people around you aren't always as they appear. Sure, they seem nice, but do they truly want you to succeed in life? Do better than them?

Of how many people in your life can you, with one hundred percent certainty, say that if you ever came out big, made it in the world, and made a *name* for yourself, they wouldn't get jealous? How many of those people in your life do you trust to not try and fuck it up? Throw dirt your way? How many of those in your life do you know genuinely *want* you to achieve your dreams, even if they seem silly and unreachable?

Not many.

So as long as you keep your dreams to yourself, work behind closed doors, and not have a single person know your plans, there is no one to try and get in your way.

It's why we don't kiss and tell on our birthday, right? Blow out a candle while wishing for something, you don't turn around and tell everyone your wish. It's for *you* to know. For *you* to hold on to. For *you* to achieve.

"Okay, so what are we going to wish for?" he asks, making it obvious that we have to share a lantern. It's what all the couples do to reduce waste and make it less harmful to the environment. I mean, we probably shouldn't be lighting even just *one* lantern, but reducing the amount is better than having double of it. And this tradition does happen to be very important to all of us…

I shrug because I have no idea. "You write something down on one side, and I'll do the same on the other side," I suggest. "But no peeking, alright?"

Aaron smirks, then presses his lips into a rather thin line. "No peeking."

He goes first, taking a whole two minutes to write on his side of the unlit lantern before handing it over to me.

I stare at the blank side, not knowing what to wish for. I mean, I *know* what to wish for, I'm just unsure of actually writing it down. If I write down yet another wish for Aaron, and he sees it, things between us could get awkward. So I have to make it less obvious… write way smaller than usual and put as many words as possible to reduce the risk of Aaron reading this.

Hi there, universe, me again. I'm not quite sure what's standing on the other side of this lantern, but whatever it is, I need you to make it come true. This is the first and last time the guy who's written on there will be here. He only gets one shot at this, wishing for things on a lantern in Germany, I mean. Or maybe not. Who even knows? But he won't be here with me next year to make another wish. And, you see, he's one of the most important people in my life, despite me knowing he won't be there forever. I've wished a lot of good things for him the past couple of years, so now I'm asking you to please *make his wish come true.*

Should be good enough, right? Or is it too obvious?

Honestly, I'm not even sure why I care so much about Aaron potentially reading this. So then he finds out I want what's best for him. Big deal. It doesn't automatically mean that I want to be in a committed relationship with him. Though I *do* want to be in a relationship with him, but he doesn't know that. And from a simple "I hope he does well", I highly doubt he would ever be able to tell.

"That's a very long wish," Aaron teases after a while. "You've been writing for like an eternity."

"I haven't." *Two minutes, max.*

As soon as our wishes are written down, my father suddenly approaches us. He's looking all kinds of loving toward my fake boyfriend, but completely ignores my existence. As he would most of the time so we wouldn't start yelling at one another.

He hands *my* jacket to Aaron like he truly doesn't see me around. I'm not going to lie, it kind of stings. Yes, I barely ever talk to my own father, only if necessary… but he doesn't have to act like I don't exist, does he?

"Don't catch a cold, son," he says, nodding at Aaron. Finally, my father looks at me, but the tension between us as our eyes lock seems to thicken with every second he stands there. The corner of his mouth twitches like he's wanting to speak but simply doesn't know what to say to me.

Until he does seem to find a couple of words. "Don't get too drunk tonight, Sofia."

"And what if I do?" Because I tend to get drunk every single year on this day. It's easier than to deal with an internal war.

I could have been one of those girls. Fuck, I could have been in Nika's place. The other girls were injured and disturbed, and yet they have absolutely no recollection of their memories from the days they've been gone. I'd rather not think about what could have happened to me if I stayed with them, and I can't help but feel guilty for getting out of it all unharmed.

It was one tiny decision I've made. Listening to what my father said, despite being majorly pissed at him for not letting me stay out with my friends. If I had disobeyed…

"Do you *always* have to do the exact opposite of what I say?"

"I do," I answer. "Do you *always* have to try and tell me what to do?"

He shakes his head disbelievingly, letting out a soft, pain-filled sigh. "I really tried with you, Sofia. I'm sorry I messed up with you so badly."

And just as fast as my father has made his way over to Aaron and me, he leaves again.

I want to scream. An anger-filled scream. Something loud and powerful enough to erase all the madness from my heart.

Why can't I be nice to my own father? Just for once.

"You need help?" Aaron asks as he hands me my jacket. To be honest, I expected him to ask about the way I spoke to my father, but he doesn't. The Aaron I knew would have jumped at the next best opportunity to find out, but this one simply ignores it. *For now*.

"Please." If it weren't for the huge lantern in my hands, I could take off Aaron's jacket and slip mine on all by myself. Well, I suppose I could also just hand the lantern to Aaron for a minute, but where would be the fun in that?

Slowly, Aaron removes one sleeve after the other. The freezing air hits me instantly, making goosebumps appear on my skin. I don't dislike the cold, which should be quite obvious given that I normally spend six days of the week in an ice rink, skating, and I happen to think I have quite the tolerance for what I find is cold and what isn't. Although I get the chills whenever I enter the rink, I still don't like the feeling of it. Don't think I ever will.

Once the jacket's off, I'm quick to slip into my own—of course, with Aaron's help. And just when he successfully put his own jacket back on, we're being told to light the lanterns and prep them for takeoff.

God, this sounds like we're about to catch a ride on a plane... or launch a rocket or something. We're merely sending lanterns up into the sky.

Letting them go is one of the most beautiful and magical sights anyone will ever see. So as soon as the first lanterns float up, my eyes are solely focused on the sky.

I love watching them fly away. I love the brightness of them, and how they get smaller with every meter they leave behind. The way they look like very bright, yellow shining stars when they're so far away, that they don't even look like lanterns anymore.

And the atmosphere... oh, boy. It's so cozy, even with the freezing temperature.

There must be at least half a hundred lanterns in the night sky right now, and it honestly makes me as happy as Rapunzel looked in Tangled when she first saw them from her window.

I wish I could watch them all night long. Watching lanterns brings some strange peace to me, and I honestly can't even tell you why. Maybe it's the fact that mine has a wish written on it—or more like two wishes—or maybe it's because they're simply magical. But they make me happy.

Watching these lanterns become the night sky's accessories for a short while teleports me into a whole other dimension. I feel like I'm part of the books I love to read and write. Like I'm at that very point in the book where everything's good again. The point in a book when the main characters find themselves together and get their happily ever after.

Or I'm in a movie. Just before the end credits roll, where the hero and heroine just got their long-awaited happy ending. They're sitting on the grass, cuddled up together while they're just enjoying each other's company. That's what watching those lanterns feels like. Happiness. A happily ever after.

Well, but once the people around me come back into the picture, I feel like this is just the beginning of a never-ending story.

"Let's go back inside," Aaron whispers into my ear right before he presses his lips to my cheek. And suddenly, another wave of happiness overcomes me. This time not from firey floating lanterns, but from the guy I have always had a crush on.

Damn him for making my head spin, and my heart crave him.

Oh, why did he have to promise me things we both knew he couldn't keep?

"Yeah," I agree. "I want to get wasted."

CHAPTER 32

"real sweet but I wish you were sober"—Wish You Were
Sober *by Conan Gray*

"SOFIA, MY LOVE, LET'S GET YOU—" Aaaand she falls onto her bed. Great.

When she said she wanted to get wasted, I wasn't expecting her to get *wasted*. I thought, maybe she would get a drink or two, not drown herself in liquor to the point where she can no longer walk in a straight line. Or any line, really.

She's still wearing all her clothes, accessories, *and* makeup. I can remove her earrings and hairclips, stuff like that. I'd even remove her makeup because I know how much she'll hate herself in the morning if she doesn't take that off before going to sleep. But I refuse to change her clothes. It's a privacy invalidation I am not going to mess with. Not in the condition she's in right now.

I'd gladly take her clothes off, but not when she's not stone-cold sober.

"Sofia," I say over and over again while I remove accessory after accessory. She just doesn't wake up. Every now and then I earn myself a grumpy groan, and a half-attempted slap… so at least I know she's *alive*.

Once I'm sure she won't poke herself with some bobby pins, or earrings, I look around her room and try to figure out where she keeps makeup wipes. That's what girls use to remove makeup, right? I'm not sure, but I swear Ana used to use those all the time, and they sound like they remove makeup, so why not?

I search through every drawer attached to Sofia's makeup vanity, and of course, I find an almost empty package of makeup wipes in the very last. At least I hope they're makeup wipes because I can't understand a single word on these labels. Luckily, the back of the package has an English translation, so now I'm relieved to know I won't accidentally burn Sofia's face off when I use them on her skin.

As I kneel down in front of Sofia, I take a deep breath before pulling one of the wipes out of the package and begin to remove her eye makeup. Is there a specific order in which makeup should be removed? If so, I most definitely am not sticking to it.

By the time I have most of her eye makeup removed, about five wipes have been thrown onto her nightstand because they're no longer usable. And when I add the sixth, Sofia suddenly opens her eyes and stares at me a little disorientated.

"Hi," she says a little slowly, sleepy.

Suppressing a chuckle, I continue to wipe off her makeup. "Hi."

She breathes heavily and rolls over on her side, slowly shaking her head at me when I get up and lean over her to remove the last bits of makeup. "I want to sleep."

"You think you can get changed first?" I doubt it but asking won't hurt.

Sofia sits up or tries to, so I pull her up instead. As soon as she sits, she reaches for the hem of her dress to pull it up, and she's quick to get frustrated when she's too weak to pull the fabric from underneath her ass. You know, the one she's currently sitting on.

I let her struggle for a little while longer, just so I can throw away the used makeup wipes and find something Sofia could wear to sleep.

Once I decide on a shirt of mine she can wear, and turn back around, Sofia is lying on her back again, having given up on getting undressed.

"I fell," she whines, struggling to sit back up. So I go to help her up... again. Sitting up straight once more, she tries her very best to pull up her dress but fails miserably. "Help me, Nix."

I decide to get it over with so she can go to sleep. Pulling Sofia off the bed, I set her down on the floor. She keeps her hands on my shoulders for balance while I pull her dress over her hips. With my eyes set on hers, I'm quick to lift it over her head and let the dress fall to the floor. All of a sudden, Sofia starts to laugh but doesn't keep me from pulling my shirt over her head and body to cover her back up.

"This smells like you," she says and grins widely.

"Yeah?"

Sofia excessively nods her head, and I can't help the smile that appears on my face. My smile doesn't stay unnoticed and seems to distract Sofia for a moment.

Her hands reach up to my face, her thumbs pushing the corners of my mouth higher up to which her laughter turns into a soft smile. "Did you know you have a lopsided smile?"

"Do I?" Of course I know that.

"Yes!" She sighs lightly. "I like it. It's cute. You're cute."

"You think I'm cute?" I pick Sofia up and lay her down on the bed again. As soon as she lies on her back, I pull down her tights but she's helping me—sort of—by kicking them off in the end.

Once that is done, I leave her to herself for a second, just so I can find some sweatpants to wear for bed.

"Very cute. I have tons of pictures of you," she admits. For her own sake, I will pretend like she never even said that. I've blurted out a couple of things when drunk, and I've got to say, admitting to certain ones of those still gives me the ick when I think about it. Some things are just meant to stay unsaid, and for some ears, these are meant to stay unheard.

After changing into some sweatpants and getting rid of my shirt, I sneak myself into the bed. Sneaking because as it seems, Sofia has fallen asleep.

She hasn't. Because the second I lie beside her, she turns on her side, facing me. One of her hands finds my face, her palm resting right on my cheek as she stares at me in the dark. And then she sighs, deeply, heavily.

"What's wrong, Icicle?" I ask, worried that she might have to puke or something like that.

"I held on to it," she says, scooching a little closer to me. So close, she now leans forward and rests her forehead against mine. "The promise you made."

"Which one?" Having made enough to last me a lifetime, I only roughly have an idea which one she's talking about.

"All of them." Her hot breath rolls over my skin as she exhales. "That you will come find me, and we'll get married."

I think my heart just stopped beating for a short moment. Being aware that this is mostly the alcohol talking, I tell myself to not get my hopes up. I, too, have been holding on to these promises. Truthfully, I wasn't expecting to ever see Sofia again, because trying to find her in a country without knowing in which area she stayed, I didn't even bother looking for her once I turned eighteen. And yet I never managed to move on from her.

Sofia has been who kept me from being with Winter, even though she hasn't been in the picture at that time. Being with Winter just felt wrong. My heart has always belonged to someone else, and it forever will. I know that now.

Liking Sofia and holding on to a couple of silly promises has never been just a mind thing. Sometimes souls connect way before they're meant to find together, but you just *know* you're connected to someone. Sofia and mine connected when we were little, otherwise the thought of her being with anyone but me wouldn't hurt as much as it does. And thinking of my future with anyone but Sofia by my side wouldn't disgust me as much if my soul didn't know I am supposed to be with her. Nobody on this planet could ever tell me that Sofia isn't meant for me.

But if we're going to have *this* conversation, I want Sofia to be sober and not say things because she couldn't keep her mouth shut.

"Go to sleep, my love."

She shakes her head. "I always had a wedding for us in mind. You probably won't like it, but it's my ultimate dream wedding. Want to hear it?"

I nod even before my common sense could kick in. If there are some things I should not be listening to when Sofia is drunk... it would be her professing her undying love for me, and *wedding* plans. Fuck, we're not even a couple and she has thought it all through.

Can't say I haven't, but still.

"I want it to be Tangled-themed," she says.

"Tangled? As in the movie?"

"Yes." She grins, I think. "Lanterns hung up above the tables like they're these floating ones. Purple everywhere, because, you know I love purple. I want to wear white while all my guests *have* to wear a light purple color, wisteria, how you'd put it. And you, Aaron, you, too, will have to wear white because that way we stick out from the purple crowd. My hair should be up in braids with flowers in them like Rapunzel had it when they got to the festival. I want white arches with lilacs throughout the aisle, but of course with some distance between them. A white cake with purple flowers, too. I want it to be out in the open, preferably in the dark so you can see the fairy lights better, but they'll be visible for the afterparty anyway, so that's not too much of a concern. I just want it to be *magical*."

"Go to sleep, Sofia." I certainly won't be able to anymore. Why did she have to tell me this? It only makes me want to make her dream come true so badly.

Sofia snuggles herself closer to me, and because I feel like torturing myself a little more, I close my arms around her.

She's been quiet for a while now, the only sounds coming from her are the usual breathing sounds. At least until I'm actually seconds away from falling asleep, even though I have had my bets set on not being able to.

I am tired, truly. It's been a long day and I haven't gotten much sleep the day prior. But when she speaks up again and completely messes with my head, I know I won't close an eye tonight.

"Promise me you will do everything in your power to make that dream come true, Aaron."

I promise, I say in my head but don't voice it.

Chapter 33

"soon you will be mine"—Fallingforyou by The 1975

I GUESS I DID END UP FALLING asleep because the last thing I remember is holding Sofia a little closer to me in case that would be the first and last time I got to do it. And now, she's standing in the middle of her room, currently stripping off my shirt.

She has already put on some leggings and must have brushed her hair because it doesn't look tangled *at all*. Her back is turned to me, so she doesn't know that I'm awake, and I do not plan on letting her know I am for a little while longer.

I try my best not to look at her when she throws my shirt in her hamper to get it washed, her back completely exposed to me. And I totally don't imagine walking up behind her, brushing her hair out of the way so I can kiss down her neck.

Nope, totally not doing that.

My dick jumps at the thought, and never in my life have I hated a boner more than at this moment.

Luckily, I don't have much time to admire her silky skin and make myself feel like a creep because her room door swings open without a warning.

Unfortunately, the person opening the door is none other than Leon, though, his appearance sure does help with my boner as that one's now no longer standing strong.

A nasty smirk tugs on his lips as his eyes linger on Sofia's chest a little too long before she covers herself up with her arms.

"Leave," she says… or so I would assume by the sound of her voice. Demanding, mad. I'm not even going to pretend I understood, but I love making up my own meanings.

"Fuck, you're hot, Sofia," he says and salivates. Okay, I'm kidding, that's my head speaking.

"Leon, LEAVE!"

He shakes his head, grinning so proudly, I would love to throw a fist just to fuck him up. That fucker doesn't even speak at first, he just stands there, staring. But when he does find his voice, he says all the wrong things. "Why are you covering yourself, Sofia? It's not like I haven't seen you naked before."

Now, you probably already guessed what happens next; I get up from the bed and walk up behind Sofia.

"Is there a reason you're staring at *my* girlfriend like you're starving, dude?" I ask, and because I am a petty and fucked-up man, I have the audacity to bring one of my arms around Sofia and lay it right over her boobs, to cover her up even more. As soon as my palm brushes her skin, I regret doing so immediately.

My dick hardens again, torturing me with a boner that most likely won't go away unless being taken care of. Just great. When I thought I hated the one before, it's nothing compared to this one.

"Why, got a problem with that?"

"I do, actually." I bring my other arm up to Sofia's chest, now covering her up with both of my arms while also pressing her closer to me. At this point, she might very well be able to feel my dick poking her, but I'm too focused on gatekeeping what's mine to care. "Your girlfriend not giving you enough to look at?"

He dodges my question. "I need to talk to Sofia."

"Hm, come back in an hour," I say unapologetically. "Or better yet, leave and never come back. Whatever you need to say to her, I just bet it's something stupid. So, spare yourself the embarrassment and leave."

Leon tries to find his brain in the back of his head and huffs in annoyance. Then he looks at Sofia, ignoring my presence. Not for long though, I'll make sure of it. "Sofia, I want you back."

She snorts, as so do I. "I decline, disrespectfully."

"But I love you!"

And I hate him. I did from the second Sofia told me about him, and my hatred only just got multiplied by seeing his face so early in the morning.

"You're a pathetic little shit, anyone ever tell you that?" I ask him because it's true. For all he knows, Sofia is in a committed relationship. Randomly showing up, barging into her room to confess his love in front of her boyfriend is… pathetic, and sad. Very, very sad.

"How can you even date him?" Leon points at me, yet his eyes stay on Sofia. "He's a dick. I'm so much better than him!"

"Better than me?" I laugh because this guy cannot be fucking serious, can he? But then I see his face, the expression of truly believing he's a million percent certain that there is no one better than him on this planet. "Ah, shit, you really believe that."

"Leon, just leave," Sofia sighs. "I really can't stand you. You're disrespectful. You're a *cheater*. God, seeing your *face* makes me want to puke."

"Do me a favor and take a step back," I say to Leon, and as stupid as he is, he does without thinking twice. Turning Sofia and me a little more sideways, I reach one arm out and push the door shut. Once shut, she moves out of my arms and speeds up to throw on a shirt while I make sure the door stays closed.

"I thought you were asleep." I watch as Sofia walks over to her makeup vanity, probably to remove the remains of the makeup I didn't get off. Or maybe not. The fuck do I know? I'm not even sure if I used the right makeup-removing stuff.

"Clearly I wasn't anymore." Bringing both of my hands up to my face, I *gently* slap away the feeling of Sofia's boobs in my hands. Unless I can genuinely enjoy the feeling, I don't want to have it imprinted in my memories, it would be nothing but torture.

Nonetheless, I allow myself a little joke to lighten up the tension. "You know, if you wanted my hands on your boobs that badly, you could just ask."

Sofia rolls her eyes at me, but I can see the little smile on her lips. She takes a seat by her makeup vanity and pulls out a bottle that looks like water with some oil swimming on top of it. Sofia then reaches into another drawer and takes out some cotton pads. "I'll remember that for next time."

Next. Time. Oh, fuck me. "They make a great bra, just saying."

She smirks but doesn't allow herself to laugh or even chuckle. I think someone may have forgotten that I can see her reflection in the mirror.

"Yeah? Says who?"

"Science has proven it," I answer immediately. No hesitation whatsoever. I walk over to her bed and take a seat, still making sure I see her through the mirror though. "I held yours for approximately a minute in total. You instantly felt better, didn't you?"

This time, Sofia allows the chuckle to come out. "If that keeps your ego unharmed, sure." Did anyone hear what she said before the word "Sure", because I certainly did not.

"You know what? I really appreciate that," I say. "Bruising a jock's ego can lead to fatal consequences." Consequences like... needing some extra cuddle time with the woman you wish to be with because jocks are the biggest babies to ever exist. Or I've just gone soft because of Sofia and only *I* have this strange desire to cuddle up to her for a whole day and do absolutely nothing else.

"Thanks for at least trying to remove my makeup last night, by the way." And she's not even asking about the consequences... what a shame. It would have been a great way to ease into a conversation we both know has to happen, but don't dare to start with.

"I did that bad of a job, huh?"

She shakes her head with a hint of a chuckle. "No, but you did use makeup wipes and not micellar water."

Yeah, I don't know the difference. And why the fuck would some water remove makeup better than something that's made to remove it? I will never understand it.

As I watch Sofia in silence, I start to think about what our lives would be like if we were to have a future together. Would I always watch her when she gets ready before we go somewhere together, or would I go do something else? Would I come home from a game and be greeted with a big teddy bear hug and thousands of kisses? Would she come home from work and tell me all about it?

I wonder if she would rather live somewhere on the countryside, or in a bigger city. Surely, I don't have many choices when I do end up playing for the NYR. I'd have to stay somewhere close to New York and the rink, ideally. Truthfully, for Sofia, I might even consider not playing for the NYR if she wanted to live elsewhere.

Would we have kids? It would be her decision because I'm good with either.

Would we argue a lot? I do think we wouldn't. And when we do, I hope they're easily fixable because I can't imagine staying mad at her for longer than an hour.

Would we go out a lot or would we be a rather indoorsy couple?

I don't want to ruin the vibe we have going, but… I think it's time we have *that* conversation. So, after taking a couple of encouraging breaths, I blurt out some words that I hope are, "Sofia, I hate to be that person, but we need to talk."

Chapter 34

"but when you told me the whole story, I felt like throwing up"—Daddy Issues (Remix) by The Neighbourhood, Syd

Sofia

THIS IS IT. THE PART in which Aaron will tell me I fucked up last night and he will fly home because he cannot deal with all of this.

And I *did* go a little bit too much into detail last night. *Screw you very much for that, drunk Sofia.*

I honestly wish I couldn't remember what happened after midnight, but I do remember... all too well.

I remember every single time I tried to kiss Aaron back in the barn, and the tons of times he kissed my cheek or forehead instead, then told me—loud enough—that he doesn't want people around us to feel uncomfortable if we kept on kissing all the time. But I didn't care, not then anyway. I just wanted to kiss him because these were my only chances I got.

He was the one to say if I wanted to kiss him I shall do so.

When he brought me home, helped me get changed, and removed my goddamn makeup for me because drunk Sofia was a tad too drunk, my heart melted. And thanks to my heart now taking over my entire body in its liquified state, of course, I would spill out some information that were never meant for his ears.

For instance, I imagined what our *wedding* would be like. Our. Goddamn. *Wedding*.

"What's keeping us from being together?" he asks, his eyes on me when I turn around to look at him because it would be rude not to. "You cannot tell me it's because you don't want to be with me."

Didn't think I could. I mean, you just have to look around my room and it becomes quite obvious. I suppose he made that connection the second he walked in here. And perhaps the fact that I literally admitted to having held on to his promises.

But that's not my problem. I *can* admit to wanting to be with Aaron. Because I do. I want to be with him so badly, I'd give up figure skating if that meant we could be together.

Unfortunately, my only reason not to be with him isn't as simple as that.

It's the fact that I can't be in New City or New York, and his entire life is there. His family, his friends, even his career is in New York. And I cannot ask him to give that up, nor would I ever. He's worked too hard to get to where he's now, and I wouldn't allow him to give that up for me.

I'm sure the NYR already have a spot reserved for him, and to turn down getting drafted by them would be insanely stupid. Especially when I know the New York Rangers have been Aaron's favorite hockey team since the beginning of time.

And I can't tell him why I will never be able to live in New York ever again. Going to St. Trewery was a risk, and I'm not going to lie, I was hoping to see Lily and Aaron one last time before we'd never meet again. But I now realize that I've only caused more damage than good.

"I'm only in America until the end of February, Aaron," I let him know. I leave early because I've been studying in Germany this entire time, and I will graduate from my university, not St. Trewery.

"But you can come back here." He sits up straight, eyebrows drawing together like he doesn't understand what I mean. And maybe he doesn't at first, but then his eyes widen when he connects the dots. "You don't plan on moving back, is that it?"

It's been my plan. I always wanted to come back to him. I always planned on spending my life with Aaron, but then the incident happened and now I cannot enter the New York state without thinking about *him*. Without feeling like I…

"You never planned to come back," he mumbles to himself, his eyes no longer on me but on the space of mattress in front of him.

I get up from my chair and walk over to my bed, kneel, and take Aaron's hands in mine. Hurting him is the last thing I want. I shake my head, feeling the tears build up in my eyes when I say, "We came back."

He looks up, confusion written all over his face.

"We came back when I was twelve years old." No matter how much this is going to hurt me, it's better to tell Aaron the truth so he understands that I never planned to leave him. I need him to understand that if I could, I would jump at the opportunity to be with him, to live the life with him he's promised me. He needs to know that I would do anything in my power to be with him if it weren't for that one obstacle that's like the gates of Hell to me.

And so, with taking one more deep breath, I tell him, despite having promised myself to never open up about it.

"We were visiting my grandparents the day we came back," I start, having his full attention. "I was so excited to see you and Lily again, that all day long, I was begging my parents to leave. We would spend the night in New York at my grandparents' house, then leave to see you and Lily in the morning."

His hand tightens around mine, giving it an encouraging squeeze. Aaron lifts my face to his, then motions for me to take a seat next to him, but I can't. Not before I have told him the entire story.

After this, he might never even want to speak to me ever again.

"I couldn't sleep all night long, and eventually I got thirsty, so I went downstairs to grab a glass of water. The lights were turned off because I didn't want to risk waking anyone up, which meant I was sneaking around, but that wasn't the problem." I feel like I cannot breathe, but I have to power through. I owe him that much. "At some point, I started to hear noises, like footsteps, and I knew they weren't mine. It freaked me out, so I started to run upstairs… until I felt someone's hand grab onto the back of my shirt. I started to scream, to cry, but I wasn't aware that it would only get worse."

Even though it's taking me an eternity to even find words, Aaron doesn't interrupt me. He sits there and listens patiently.

"I remember kicking around myself, and eventually that hand let go of me. But then I heard a loud noise. It sounded like someone fell down the stairs. My parents woke up from my screams and they came rushing to me. The lights turned on and when I looked down to see who was trying to attack me, I barely had a vision sharp enough to confirm what I saw." I break out into heavy sobs. "There was blood, Aaron. I have—" I hiccup "—I have never seen so much blood in my entire life. You'd think ten gallons doesn't sound too much, but it really is. And I didn't even see the whole ten gallons, obviously, and still, it was so goddamn much."

"I remember my father yelling at me, telling me that I'm out of my mind and that I'd spooked myself by watching too many of those criminal TV shows. And that—" I gasp for some air. I can feel my heart breaking, again. This was hands down, the worst night of my life. "He said that I killed my grandpa because I just refused to listen to him."

My father has told me over and over and over again to not watch these TV shows because I was too young and would be too spooked by them. He was right, of course. But did I listen? No. And why didn't I? Because I was holding a grudge for tearing me away from Aaron and Lily.

So, what did I get out of not listening? I killed my own grandfather.

It was an accident, so much I can see by now. I was scared, and I never meant to murder my grandpa, and yet I can't bear to be near that place.

In what must be less than a heartbeat, Aaron pulled me off the floor and sits me right in his lap. His hands come up to my face, his thumbs stroking underneath my eyes to remove some of my tears.

"That wasn't your fault, Sofia," he speaks quietly, softly. "Accidents happen. All the time."

"But I killed him." My arms sneak around his torso, my head pushing past his hands until my forehead rests against his shoulder. "I killed him, Aaron."

"Did you mean to do it?"

I shake my head instantly, praying that he can feel it as a head-shake and not a nod. Even if I ever had the desire to murder some-one, I'd be too chickenshit to go through with it. Not only would I rather stay out of prison and live in freedom, but it's also just not worth it to murder someone.

"You were twelve, Sofia. I highly doubt you even thought about someone being able to die right in that moment."

"My father hates me for it," I sob. Admittedly, I haven't made it easy for my father, as we have established before. But ever since that day… God, the look in his eyes, the anger, his *words*; I'll never be able to forget either of them.

"I think your father is smart enough to know you never meant to cause any harm, my love. It was a shock for him as well. People tend to say awful things when in shock," Aaron says. Why, oh why does he have to try to make me feel better about all of this. I thought he would hate me after this. Perhaps even see me as a cruel, vicious murderer that wasn't charged because my family told the police my grandpa tripped and never mentioned my name in connection with his death.

But my name *is* connected to his death. If it weren't for me, he'd still be alive.

"Have you talked to your grandma since then?" His arms close around my body, holding me just that tiny bit tighter.

"No," I answer. "I couldn't. In my mind, she doesn't want to see me, which I can understand. I visited my grandpa's grave a couple of weeks ago. I hoped that maybe I could get some closure, but I didn't."

Not sure how someone's supposed to get closure from visiting a grave and apologizing over and over again to a dead person, but I figured it was a try worth it.

"I couldn't stick around, Aaron. If I had stayed around New York, it would have killed me. Guilt would have gotten to me and I… I don't think I would have made it out alive." Staying around New York would *still* kill me. The incident still haunts me in my sleep, even my daytime. It's almost a miracle when I get a week without thinking about it.

A week when I'm *not* in New York. Ever since I'm back there, it's been haunting me daily. And I'm not sure I am strong enough to stick around without making everyone else around me miserable.

"Your parents permanently moved to Germany for you then?" I nod because they did. They didn't suggest leaving America for good, I did. I begged my parents to leave because sticking around wasn't an option for me. "If your father hates you as much as you think he does, I doubt he would have moved to the other side of the globe for you."

I keep quiet for a moment, trying to let Aaron's words sink in.

He might have a point there. If I hated someone, I wouldn't move far away from home for them. And he does pay for my current stay in America. He wanted to have me home for the holidays. If he hated me that much, wouldn't he want me to stay as far away from *him* as humanly possible?

Just yesterday he brought out my jacket because he saw I forgot it in the barn. If he hated me, he wouldn't do that. If he hated me, he wouldn't give a shit about me, but he *does*. He cares about me more than I ever allowed myself to see.

I need to apologize. To him. To my grandma. To everyone. I've been so caught up with making myself believe that everyone hates me for killing my grandpa, that I never even considered them seeing it as what Aaron has just pointed out, an *accident*. Surely, they know I never intended to murder someone. Not even my *sister* is that cruel and holds it against me, and I think we have already established that she just can't stand me. So if not even Julia mentions it with every—in her eyes—mistake I make, or to get me to do stuff for her… they cannot see me as a murderer, could they?

Pulling away from the hug, I quickly wipe away some tears before allowing myself to meet Aaron's eyes. And when they meet, I almost wish they didn't.

The look in his eyes is something I never expected to see again. Admiration. He wholeheartedly believes that I am a good person. Aaron doesn't see me as anyone below him even after my admission.

My heart skips a beat, butterflies in my stomach go wild and I can't help but pray I will sort this shit out because being with Aaron has been my dream for far too long to give it up now. Now that I *could* have it. He's within reach, holding his hand out for me to take, offering a relationship my younger self would kill me for declining. But all of this only *if* I manage to get past my trauma, grow as a person, and be able to give Aaron the love he deserves.

It's not fair to him otherwise.

Unless I can promise Aaron a future without him having to make a crazy and stupid sacrifice, I can't promise him forever. I can't have him get his hopes up only for me to end up running away.

And I believe it's important that I'm being honest with him.

"I can't promise you to stick around, Aaron. Being in New City, so close to Manhattan, where *this* happened… it shakes me up. Every single day I spend over there, I feel like the walls are caving in on me. I need to sort this out beforehand, otherwise, this would never be fair to you."

"We'll figure this out together, Icicle." He cups my face with his hands, forcing our eyes to stay locked. "I promised to marry you, and I am going to renew my promise now."

My eyes widen drastically, it feels like if they open just a millimeter more, they'll fall right out of my head. He's not—He can't possibly mean that.

"Sofia Michelle Carlsen, I promise you; you and I will get

married one day. I don't care how long it will take us to get there. I don't care what it will take us to get there, we *will* get married because no one in this entire universe could *ever* convince me of you not being meant for me," he says, being deadly serious.

This time, there is no goodbye after the promise. Neither of us has to leave and go catch a flight to another country. He hasn't just said those words because he is afraid to never see me again, he *means* it.

His lips connect with mine like he's sealing a deal. And with this kiss, he promises yet another thing. It's a promise of realness. He promises me years with him, a *lifetime*. In his kiss is the promise of a future, the sweetness of waiting for, and having found real *love*.

This isn't some movie or book-worthy kiss. It's far more than that. It's a step forward, a step into a passion that could easily catch on fire if handled wrongly. And yet, in his kiss I find home.

"And let's be honest here, no one but I would ever put up with a tangled-themed wedding," he adds as soon as we pull apart from the kiss.

I could swear my cheeks are redder than the wine I drank last night, but I also don't really care right at this moment. They only manage to deepen in color even more when I hesitate to ask, "Does that mean I'm your girlfriend now?"

Aaron suddenly reaches a hand out for my neck, tugging on my necklace that he did not take off before putting me to sleep. "We're way past the girlfriend and boyfriend status, my love. You've been my fiancée ever since I gave you this necklace." He blinks slowly, inhaling deeply like he can't believe he just said that. "We don't have to put a label on anything, but you sure as hell aren't just *anyone* to me."

CHAPTER 35

"everything that kills me makes me feel alive"—**Counting Stars by OneRepublic**

Aaron

IF I HAVE LEARNED ONE THING while being here in Germany… anything I thought I knew, everything I've thought of being amazing in America, Germany does it better.

Like the Christmas markets!

It looks so magical; I feel like I'm in one of the most popular Hollywood Christmas movies. Germans may not decorate their houses as crazy as we do in America, but holy fuck, their Christmas markets are everything.

There is not one stand that isn't decorated. Not one inch of this place that doesn't light up in Christmas lights, not even the outdoor ice rink is blank. Yes, you heard me right, an ice rink. I think you pay five euros to skate for an hour, but I haven't seen one Christmas market in the U.S. have an ice rink present.

Sure, we have some around a couple of cities during the wintertime, yet nothing quite like this.

But there is also one thing I don't understand about being here. Why are there so many *teenagers* sitting or standing by booths, drinking what Sofia has told me is called *Glühwein*—about the same as mulled wine? It's still strange to me that they can buy certain alcohol at the age of sixteen here, and that it isn't illegal to drink outside.

Seriously, they could walk around with any alcoholic drink in their hands, and they wouldn't face consequences here.

However, there is one huge downside. I do not understand a single word these people utter.

Sofia is currently looking at some glittery decorations, leaving me standing all by myself, and this man is trying to—so I would assume—sell me some weekend in Hawaii.

Maybe not that, but he sure is trying to sell me something.

Well, or he is offering me his daughter's hand. Either way, all I do is nod politely and smile at the man, praying I am not selling my soul to the devil right now.

"Aaron," I hear Sofia say despite being zoned out. "My friends and I are going to skate for a while. I figured you might want to join us?"

"Fuck, yes." I was praying she'd suggest that ever since I found out about the ice rink. If there is one thing I will never get enough of, it would be skating. I could spend a whole week on the ice and not get bored. A little freezing maybe, and catch myself a cold, but I'd find things to occupy myself with.

Okay, a week is exaggerated, but you get the point.

"Are they figure skaters?" I find myself asking as she pulls me away from the guy that now wears a huge question mark over his head. *Yes, dude, I was just as confused when you started talking to me.*

"No, but I suppose they know how to skate."

"I'm not teaching anyone." Except for Sofia, but she knows how to skate already.

What a bummer. Imagine the fun we could have on the ice.

Sofia constantly falling but getting excited when she made it a couple of inches without. Me holding her close to me as I guide her. Holding hands while skating, or her clinging on to my arm.

But her knowing how to skate also brings advantages... like, *races.* Yes. Who's faster on the ice? *Me.* Who's more comfortable on skates? *Me.* Who's better at ice hockey? *Me, obviously.*

Also, women that know how to skate, in my eyes, are a million times more attractive.

Sofia laughs and leans her head against my shoulder at the same time as her arms wrap around mine to hold on to me. "You'd be the worst teacher to ever exist."

I gasp for air, my heart feeling awfully betrayed by my girl-friend. Yes, *girlfriend.* Can you believe this? Because I certainly can't.

Okay, okay, I did say we won't put a label on our relationship until she feels comfortable enough with it, but that doesn't mean I can't still refer to her as my girlfriend. She *is* mine after all.

"I'll have you know, I am a *great* teacher, thank you very much."

"In your dreams, perhaps." Her head turns as she looks up at me, smiling like the little devil she is. Then her expression softens, her bottom lip sticking out as she pouts at me. "Did that hurt your feelings?"

I nod. It hasn't but she doesn't need to know that. "There's only one thing that could make the pain in my heart go away now." Sofia raises her eyebrows. I look away from her, up to the dark sky as I sigh heavily, a little dramatically. "You will have to kiss me."

She snorts a laugh. "What are you, twelve?" Again, I nod be-cause, no, but yes. "You'll get a kiss when you earned it."

How goddamn rude. I look back down at her, only to find her staring ahead to make sure we're not bumping into some strangers. I would do that too, but I'm kind of busy admiring Sofia. At least now I'm no longer a creep when I stare at her, and I also don't have to hide it anymore.

"My presence in your life earns me the right to get as many kisses as I want." She doesn't react, because Sofia knows as well as I do that we haven't shared one single kiss since we're in some kind of situationship slash actual relationship. To be fair, it hasn't even been a whole day yet, but according to the guy I've been before Sofia was back in my life, it wouldn't have taken me even one second to decide on a kiss. I wouldn't have hesitated, nor would I have been afraid to mess anything up.

Eventually, Sofia lets go of my arm, bringing an instant feeling of loss to my soul. Only then do I look around myself and find us standing in line for the ice rink, or more like getting some skates. Sofia's friends have already paid for our ice time.

"Why didn't you tell me they had an ice rink here?" I ask as we're about two people away from getting our skates. "I would have brought my own skates." You know, the expensive, blazer-sharp ones. The *good* ones.

"Yeah? Because flying back to New City to get your skates and coming back here to *skate* would have been worth it."

I shake my head. "They're in my suitcase. You think I'd go *anywhere* without my precious skates?" Sofia is obsessed with the color wisteria. She wouldn't go anywhere without having at least one thing on her in that color. I have skating as my obsession, and my skates that follow me wherever I go. "No, now I have to cheat on my babies."

"You'll live," she laughs, then starts speaking to the ice rink employee. After a short while, Sofia turns to look at me. "What's your size in skates," she asks.

"Like a 9." Honestly, it always depends on the brand. The ones I have are a 9, but they're from CCM. My former skates were an 8.5 from Bauer.

"Black or white ones?"

"Either way. They're skates." Ones I only "own" for approximately an hour. It's not like I'm up for a win against the *Sun Devils* or the *Falcons* and the game is televised. Fuck, even then they'd just be skates. As long as they're not bright pink or blue, or any crazy color, I'm good with it.

Sofia nods, then tells the guy my size. He asks something in return, to which Sofia answers with, "*Die in Hell*." I almost gasp in shock. Why the fuck would she just tell a random stranger to die in hell? What did that poor guy do to deserve this?

He disappears for a second, probably to get the skates.

"What the fuck, Sofia?" She looks at me, her eyebrows drawn together in confusion. "Why would you tell him to die in hell?"

It takes her a second to realize, but when my words finally settle in, she… laughs. A full-on, every-single-head-around-us-turns-to-look-who's-being-so-noisy kind of laughter.

I don't get it. What's so funny about me asking… "You didn't tell him to die in hell, did you?"

She shakes her head, thinning her lips to stop herself from laughing. "I told him we wanted the brighter ones."

"So, hell means bright?" Sofia nods. "Well… I guess hell *is* bright? With all the fire and… the fire only. Other than that, I'd say it's pretty dark down there."

"And I thought people who major in architecture are smart. Guess I was wrong."

I bring a hand up to her face, tipping her head up with my index finger, being seconds away from kissing that attitude out of her when the register guy comes back. With that guy back and him handing our skates over to Sofia, I let out an internal groan of frustration.

I don't think I've ever wanted to kiss someone as badly as I want to kiss my *girlfriend.*

"*Danke*," Sofia says and gives the register guy a warm smile. I'm just going to assume she thanked him. Honestly, ninety-nine-point-nine percent of the time when I hear someone speak in German, I am just making up my own stories. Every now and then I understand a word or two, but I certainly can't be sure they mean the same thing as they do in English.

Great example, me two minutes prior.

Sofia hands me my skates, then takes my hand in hers to pull me toward the benches. "Come on, my friends are waiting."

CHAPTER 36

***"have I known you twenty seconds or twenty years?"—
Lover (Remix) [feat. Shawn Mendes] by Taylor Swift,
Shawn Mendes***

"YOU'RE STARING AT HER AGAIN," Jane says with a chuckle. She leans against the railing of the ice rink, like I am previously doing to, apparently, stare at my girlfriend. "It's adorable."

"No guy *ever* wants to be called 'adorable.'"

She shrugs, I think. I'm not really looking at her, but from the movements I could see beside me, I'd say she did shrug. "I suppose not. But it *is* adorable. I haven't seen Sofia smile as much as she does recently, and I'm just happy to see her blossoming again, you know? She's been holding back on her happiness for a while now."

"Really?" I pull my eyes away from Sofia, averting them to Jane.

"Yes. And besides, I'm glad to know there are guys out there that are decent. Leon never looked at Sofia the way you do. He always gave me this strange vibe, and I told her, but Sofia wouldn't listen. Well, I guess you know how the story with him turned out. I'm not sure why, but you don't seem to be the guy to cheat."

Cheat? Hell nah. "I don't see the point in it," I admit, "Why stay in a relationship if you're lusting for someone else? Just end it and you're free to do whomever you want, *without* any stress, unnecessary tears, and a cheater title."

The second these words leave my mouth, someone skates into me from behind, arms come up around my torso. If I didn't know there's only one person that'd wear wisteria-colored gloves with a hint of glitter, I'd have been out of this hug way before it even happened.

Sofia comes up beside me. I lay one arm around her, pulling her close to me to keep her in my space. She looks up at me, smiling. "There are some guys over there, currently trying to remember your name, Sir Superstar."

My eyebrows dip. "Remember my name?"

"Yes. I'm assuming they've been keeping up with the U.S. college hockey. Probably livestreamed the games or watched them online somewhere. But they mentioned Colin's name, thought that'd be you. One of the guys said Colin's brunette, so this can't be you and now they're trying to figure out what your name is."

Now, I knew our games are televised, but I didn't think people outside of the U.S. really care about NCAA hockey.

"You probably shouldn't have worn this." Sofia reaches a hand up to the logo on my jacket. It's the St. Trewery hockey team logo, even bigger at the back of my jacket.

"Probably not." My hand slides down to her hip, tugging her just that *tiny* bit closer to me. "I didn't think people here watched our games."

Sofia grins, scrunching up her nose just a little. "Too bad they don't rent out pucks and sticks. You could have challenged them to a shootout. Being their age, you know they would have jumped at the opportunity."

"Wouldn't have been fair," I say.

"You know it's not a 4 vs. 1, right? It would have been fair."

I cock my head to the side, lifting my eyebrows. "Love, it wouldn't have been fair because I'm far better than all of them combined."

"Did you ever think about donating some of your cockiness? You have too much of it whereas others have none."

"What did you say about my cock? I know I've got a great one, but why should I give some of it to others?"

She sighs, dropping her head against my body. "Anyone ever tell you that you're impossible?"

I think for a second, looking up into the dark sky as I do. "You just did. But that's alright, I'll fuck the attitude right out of you sometime soon."

Her head snaps up, eyes wide and filled with a mixture of shock and confusion as they meet mine. God, she's so fucking adorable, it's giving me cute-aggressions.

Jane is laughing but stops when I give her a questioning, yet stern look. As quickly as she started to laugh, she's skating away to find her other friends.

"Come on." Sofia skates right out of my arms, interlocking our fingers to make me follow her. *I'd follow her anywhere.*

"Where are we going?"

Her sweet giggles sound through my body like it's fuel for me. Everything she does or says seems like a double shot of expresso with a little too much caffeine, giving me more energy than needed. "I bet I can skate faster than you."

She can't.

My little Icicle might be good with stunts and all, but faster? I highly doubt it. She never was.

I was right. She's not faster than me on the ice… and as it seems, a pretty sore loser. She's scowling, her arms crossed over her chest to show her madness. And yet, I can't help but find it cute.

Now I remember why I used to let her win all the time when we were younger, despite being a sore loser myself. Alright, and because of that stupid smile that sends electric shocks through my body whenever I see it.

We left the ice five minutes ago, and she's still grumpy, grunting answers if she even does, rolling her eyes, and sighing all the time. Either she's the worst loser alive, or my Icicle is a little hungry.

When we were younger, Sofia used to get *really* moody whenever she was hungry. She would act like a total asshole, snap at people, and give the shortest answers known to humankind. Until she finally got food, and just like that, her mood was turned around again.

"How about we go drink some *Glühwein*, sit inside, and just spend some time catching up? Kind of like letting a get-together sound itself out before we all head home?" Emma suggests. The other girls agree almost instantly.

Is this what they do here? Go out and then let the evening "sound itself out"? If so, it doesn't make sense. Just leave whenever you want to, honestly.

Either way, I still hate wine, and as far as I'm concerned, *Glühwein* is wine, heated and with spices and stuff. But wine.

Anyway, Sofia agrees with Emma, and I couldn't possibly speak against it now, could I? I'm already outnumbered, being the only man with four women. So what I do instead only makes sense to me. "Sure, but can I borrow Sofia for just a minute? I need her to be my translator for something."

The girls laugh, all except Sofia, of course. My little Icicle still hasn't defrosted.

"Sure, you go do your thing." Pia waves us off. "We'll order for you then, okay? Don't be too long!"

As we part ways with Sofia's friends, I bring my hand to the small of Sofia's back, guiding her toward wherever we will find food. It shouldn't be too difficult as this entire goddamn Christmas market is made of food stalls, Christmas lights, a good amount of gaming stalls, carousels, and decorations.

I told myself I'd buy Sofia whatever she wanted to eat, but she's a little stubborn, so when I ask her what she wanted, she responds with, "I'm not hungry."

"Yes, you are, Icicle."

She rolls her eyes, letting out a disagreeing gruff. "Am not."

"Okay." We stop in front of a food stall that seems to be only selling chocolate-covered fruits. It's not exactly what I had in mind, but it'll do for now. I turn to Sofia with a smile. "Could you order *me* something then? I still don't speak German."

Earning myself yet another eye-roll, she obliges. "What do you want?"

"Anything you like." Mainly because I'm certain that I won't get a single bite from that thing. The second it's bought, she'll look at me with those puppy dog eyes, asking for just a small taste to check if it's good, and before I know, she'll have it eaten up.

But that's okay, I'm not that much of a fan of chocolate-covered fruits anyway.

Sofia orders a chocolate-covered banana, and it's suddenly even *better* that I won't have to eat it because bananas are nothing but disgusting. They have a way too dominant taste. Put it in a smoothie, just the tiniest piece of it, and you now have a banana smoothie, despite the million other fruits you threw in there.

I hand her my wallet at the same time as she hands me the banana on a stick. She pays for it, then walks somewhere next to the stall with me.

The second we stand, I hold the banana to Sofia's mouth, waiting until she takes a bite. And she does, without questioning me. Perhaps she didn't think about it twice, but I'm sure she knows what I'm up to.

If there is one person in this world that *always* knew what I thought, and why I did certain things, it is Sofia. Even now I'm sure she had her assumptions the second I said she shall choose whatever *she* wanted.

"You're mean, you know?" she says right after she swallows, yet she takes another bite.

"Just taking care of you, my Icicle."

Sofia smiles softly, even more so when I bring my free hand underneath the banana to stop the chocolate from crumbling all over the floor.

"You didn't have to do that, you know?"

I shake my head. "I know, but you get all grumpy when you're hungry."

It takes her a little while to eat that nasty thing, but I'd rather spend ten minutes watching Sofia eat a banana than sit in some booth and have to smell this heated wine for an hour.

When I get back from throwing the wooden stick away, I notice Sofia shivering slightly. I mean, I get it. She might be wearing a winter jacket, but perhaps putting on a goddamn skirt wasn't her smartest decision. And I highly doubt these wisteria-colored stockings that only go to her mid-thighs do anything to warm her legs.

She looks sexy as hell, but I've been wondering when she'd start shivering.

Before I get to ask Sofia if she's cold, which she would answer with yes, she's already bringing her hands to my face, carefully pulling my head down until our lips meet.

She's kissing me.

Sofia is *kissing* me.

Not for the first time, mind you, but it's still... wow.

No, that's false, it *is* the first time *she* is kissing *me* without me daring her to.

I'm not surprised that it feels right, a little too right, maybe. But then again, I'm convinced that Sofia and I were meant to be together from the second we met, so maybe "too right" isn't a thing.

Now, I'm not some believer in everything supernatural, or people being destined for one another. For the longest time in my life, I didn't even think soul mates were a thing. But Sofia proves me wrong.

She *is* my soul mate, and I will never believe anything else.

The way her tongue sweeps over my bottom lip startles me for a second, but fuck, I want her to do it again.

The banana taste is still there, but I don't give a fuck. If I had to, I'd eat tons of bananas for her. I'd eat one or ten a day if she asked me to. Perhaps I'm a banana-lover after all.

Her mouth brushes mine, over and over again, and when I try to pull away from her to take a quick breath, Sofia finds it much better to slide her tongue into my mouth.

I'm not going to complain. So then I will die of oxygen deprivation. At least I died a happy death, having kissed my childhood crush, my now girlfriend, for the last thing I did with my life.

As her hands slide down my neck, gripping my jacket tightly into her fists, an all too familiar desire surges through me and rushes right down to my balls.

I promised myself to not move too fast with her. We might have rushed into our relationship, but we also had to go a whole thirteen years without any sort of contact. Nonetheless, I want to go at her pace, do only what Sofia is comfortable with… and yet when her tongue touches mine, and she lets out the softest of moan right into my mouth, I'm so close to tipping over, losing the ground beneath me, that I barely realize what I do next.

Taking Sofia's hands from my body, I interlock one with mine and make her follow me behind the rowed-up food stalls.

Nobody is back here, nobody and nothing except for a couple of extra trashcans from the stalls. Not sure if anyone is ever going back here either, or if they do, they'll hopefully leave as quickly as they came.

CHAPTER 37

"And you keep on falling, baby, figure it out"—Falling by Chase Atlantic

MY BACK HITS THE WALL OF one of these food stalls, but I don't care because the second it does, Aaron's lips are back on mine.

I meant to kiss him all day long, was waiting for him to kiss me… but it never happened. Admittedly, I didn't want to weird out my friends by kissing Aaron randomly in front of them, and I assume he thought the same.

But now we are kissing, and fuck, I do not want to stop. Ever.

I'm not sure if it's a lack of oxygen in my brain that makes me think making out in public isn't inappropriate, but right at this moment, I don't give any fucks. Besides, nobody's here, now, is there?

"I lied," I admit once Aaron gives us a second to draw in ragged breaths.

"I know."

"About the kiss not meaning anything, I mean." His lips press to mine again, quickly, shortly. Not nearly long enough to put out the fire it was lighting up.

"I know, love."

Leaning my head against the wooden wall, I draw my eyebrows

together, bringing a hand up to his face to keep his mouth parted from mine. "You knew?"

He nods with a smirk. "You're an awful liar, Icicle." Aaron lays the palm of his hand right over my heart, his eyes holding mine. "Your heart's always betraying you. It beats faster when you lie, and you get these guilt-filled eyes. One side of your lip twitches for a short second, and oftentimes, you close your eyes to take a deep breath before lying."

"I hate you."

His mouth crashes down to mine, bringing back unwanted butterflies. "Liar," he whispers.

"I didn't lie." *I did.*

"Mhm." His hands travel down my body, stopping by my hips. "So, if I snuck my hand underneath your skirt, I wouldn't find you wet at all?"

I shake my head. "No." His eyes dare me to challenge him, waiting for my consent to touch me. Suddenly I remember one text Aaron received a couple of days ago, a perfect way to challenge him. "You wouldn't even dare to touch me if I begged you."

He winks, then in the blink of an eye, he turns me around. My palms press against the wood as he pushes my legs a little further apart, enough to sneak a hand underneath my skirt.

The tips of his fingers gaze my panties, a soft shiver running through my body. I can hear his heavy breathing, hot air blowing on my neck. He wastes no time to gently push my panties aside, sliding his fingers through my slick folds.

I can hear a low groan coming from him, his head dipping down until his mouth is close to my ear. "You're a little liar, Icicle." His voice is raspy, whispery, I could die hearing his voice.

A moan escapes me as one finger sinks inside me, and it takes all my willpower not to hit my head against the wood in front of me.

His erection presses against my lower back, an instant wave of lust washing over me at the feeling. Truthfully, I've never been one to find the feeling of a dick hot, but everything seems to be different with Aaron.

"Can you feel what you do to me?" he asks, pressing his hips a bit harder against my body.

A satisfied grunt leaves him when I nod in response.

As Aaron pushes yet another finger inside me, I lean my head against the wooden wall, not caring whether this might get me a splinter or not. All I truly care about is the ever-growing desire to come and the sudden heat that my body is met with.

"Tell me how badly you want to come," he says in a low tone, planting a kiss behind my ear.

I don't answer, but instead, I moan a little breathlessly.

"You need to answer me, love."

If only words were still present in my head. "*Please*," I manage to spit out, desperate.

Hearing a soft, breathy chuckle coming from Aaron is almost as hot as his raspy morning voice. And believe me, I've been trying my very best not to cry in desperation every single morning since we've come here. Now, I no longer have to pretend that either of those doesn't turn me on. Because they fucking do.

It isn't until I hear a woman's laughter that I'm reminded of Aaron and my surroundings.

"Aaron," I force out, "we're in public."

"So?"

"Anyone could see us."

His fingers pull out of me, the loss being awfully disappointing. Why do we have to be outside, surrounded by hundreds of people? We could have had something really good—

Aaron turns me back around, pressing my back into the wall. His mouth comes down to mine, yet our lips don't meet. "What? You're scared of getting caught?"

"Kind of." Am I though? What's supposed to happen?

Someone will see us, big deal. Like they've never opened Google to watch some porn. Now, they'd see it in person. Lucky them.

Aaron is about to take a step back, clearly validating my

decision. And, fuck, does it feel great knowing he respects my choices, unlike a certain ex-boyfriend.

"Actually, no. I'm not scared of getting caught."

He halts, looking into my eyes. The light shining on us from the lamppost that's good thirty-two feet away illuminates his face, highlighting all the right curves and making him look five times as handsome as he is. "You sure?"

I kiss the corner of his mouth. "I'm sure."

As our lips lock and my hands find into his hair, Aaron undoes his pants, pushing them down enough to free his erection. I want to reach down, stroke him, but I keep myself from doing it. With my friends waiting, and the possibility of someone finding us, we're on some kind of time limit after all.

So I just wait. Wait until he has pulled out his wallet, taken out a condom, then let the wallet fall to the floor like he has no care in the world.

After that, he tears open the foil, takes out the condom, and quickly rolls it onto his dick.

But then I have to wait another moment because Aaron just keeps looking into my eyes as though he can't believe we're doing this. Neither can I.

"Aaron," I say under my breath, just to make sure he's still present.

"Did you know you're really fucking beautiful?" He lifts me off the ground, my legs wrapping around his hips at the same time as my arms find their way around his neck.

"Figured." My breath hitches when Aaron slides the tip of his dick through my folds, then slowly guides his tip inside of me.

"How so?" He sinks in a little deeper, so slow, I will quite literally explode with exasperation if he goes any slower.

"You keep staring at me like I'm the most beautiful thing you've ever seen."

I thought he was at least halfway inside of me by now, but I'm being proven wrong when Aaron suddenly pulls me down onto his cock. I suck in a breath, feeling unusually full.

One after the other, Aaron brings one arm underneath my legs so it's easier for him to hold me up, only that the change of arm placement pushes him a little deeper inside me, eliciting sharp gasps from me.

"You're not an object, Sofia," he whispers into my ear, then leaves a kiss right behind it. "But yes, you're the most beautiful person I have ever laid eyes on."

He kisses my lips, down my jawline, the parts of skin on my neck he can reach. And when I part my lips to suck in some air, Aaron takes full advantage, bringing his mouth back to mine and sliding his tongue in.

My heart almost combusts at the contact. He tastes like himself, something masculine and a little mix of my lipstick.

Aaron thrusts deeper inside me, letting out a raspy groan, his fingertips pressing into my skin where he holds me up. I moan in response.

My eyes roll back in my head, seeing stars for a second there. And holy fuck, I don't think I've ever felt my orgasm build as fast as it does right now. But quite frankly, I don't really care either.

I clench around Aaron's dick, and when a hoarse grunt leaves him, I know he can feel it.

"Fuck, Sofia," Aaron rasps as he thrusts faster inside me, leaving kisses along my jawline. "I want you to come on my cock, love." Like I'm not literally seconds away from doing just that.

It's approximately thirty-seven point four degrees outside, and yet my skin feels like it's on fire. There's nothing I'd rather do right now than strip down and cool off, but since we're in public, that wouldn't be my best decision.

Aaron captures my lips with his and pushes his tongue into my mouth as my breathing grows more and more irregular, gasping and panting for air. I moan, feeling my body shake as I squeeze his cock and explode around him.

My eyes squeeze shut, my head falling against the wood behind me and my hands close into fists around his jacket as I let the power of my orgasm consume me.

He doesn't stop moving. Aaron just keeps pushing inside of me, his pace gaining some speed. He's kissing me hard, even though I barely manage to kiss him back.

My wet folds make it easy for him to thrust in and out of me with a ferocious velocity.

I tighten my arms a little around his neck, then lean into him. Moans spill out of me without a second thought, at least not until I hear yet another laughter that didn't come from either Aaron or me. That's when I bite my bottom lip to keep myself quiet.

"I want to hear the noises you make, Sofia," Aaron groans, forcing himself even deeper inside of me like he's trying to explore every inch of me. My eyes shut tightly, my mouth falls open, a cry leaves me.

"Aaron." I chant his name, at the same time as I felt another knot in my stomach grow, ready to let go and feel like falling and diving into a pool of ecstasy.

When I let the sweet relief consume me, allow tingles to run over the surface of my skin and my eyes roll back; legs shaking, my vagina clenches around Aaron's cock.

"Fuck," he grits out, the tips of his fingers pressing right into my skin as he squeezes my ass.

Seconds pass until Aaron eventually stops pumping into me and his body tenses as his orgasm hits him. Aaron leans his forehead against mine, panting, letting out gasps and a couple of curse words.

I'm officially ruined. Like, I knew my heart would always belong to Aaron, no matter how hard I'd have tried to replace him with another guy, but now I know for sure that it's never going to be possible.

There's a fine line between a casual hookup with a stranger and a hookup with the guy you've had feelings for since the moment you've laid eyes on him. I'm not even anywhere near the line, I'm entirely on the Aaron-fucking-Marsh-can-own-my-soul side.

With one last kiss Aaron peppers on my lips, he pulls out of me and sets me down on the floor. He still holds me up a little, making sure I don't tip over, which I'm thankful for because honestly? I would have.

"That was more than 'head in and done'," I chuckle, to which Aaron just casually winks like it's nothing.

"Was it?" His lips press to my cheek. "Shit. I hope it was still okay."

"Meh. I was expecting a quick fuck."

"Next time," he promises with a smile. "We should go to Vegas and get married."

I shake my head, bursting out into laughter. But the worst part, I almost agree, wouldn't that idea be totally crazy. We're only twenty-one. Well, he is. I won't be for another two days. And besides, he doesn't even mean it. It's the post-orgasm talking. "I'll take that as a compliment, you know."

He snorts. "What for? I did all the work."

"Excuse you? You got to hold me in your arms and look at me. That's pretty tiring, you know? Plus, my pussy isn't accessible for every guy I tumble across, so technically, I did more work than you."

Aaron removes the condom from him, knotting it, zips up his pants. He picks up his wallet from the floor, then starts looking around us. When he spots a trashcan that must be owned by one of the food stalls, he turns back to look at me. "To no one but me."

My eyebrows lower. "What?"

"Your pussy is not accessible for anyone but me, Sofia." He reaches underneath my skirt, pulling on my panties to let them snap back into place.

"Aaron…"

"I mean it," he says and walks toward the trashcan to throw the used condom away. It's a miracle they even keep some back here. "I just fucked my childhood crush. The one I promised to marry in the future. There is no fucking way I will ever allow any other man but me to touch you, Sofia. Not *one*."

CHAPTER 38

"you're not ready to feel what I feel"—I Am Falling in Love by Isak Danielson

Aaron

"ARE YOU COMING WITH US TO the cinema?" Sofia asks, currently putting her hair up into a bun. She spent the last thirty minutes doing her makeup without saying so much as a word to me, so excuse me when I flinch when she suddenly starts to speak out of the blue.

I shake my head, though she probably can't see it. "Nah. I wouldn't understand a single word anyway, that would be a waste of money for me. You have fun though."

She turns around on her chair, pouting at me. I almost cave at the expression, simply because she looks so goddamn adorable that I feel bad for saying no. But I have things to do, things to organize for tomorrow.

"So, uh, I was wondering," I start, "what if Colin and Lily came here for New Year's? Colin said they were looking to go somewhere else for New Year's because Italy is getting boring, or so he believes. I doubt Lily feels that way."

Sofia shrugs. "Sounds good. I always wondered what spending New Year's with you and Lily would be like, so, please, invite them."

"Thought about me a lot, huh?" I smirk at her sheepishly, earning myself an annoyed eye-roll which only makes me chuckle.

"They could stay here. I bet my parents don't mind them staying in our guest room for a day or two."

"Alright. I'll ask them then." I mean, ask her parents because, well, it will be a little longer than just New Year's and the day after, but Sofia doesn't know that yet.

She gets up from her seat, walking across the room to get dressed. I'd love to just sit here and watch, but that feels a little too creepy, so instead I take my phone to send Colin a text.

Aaron: How about you guys come to Germany for tomorrow?

Colin: Why, getting bored of spending time with Sofia one on one?

Aaron: It's her birthday tomorrow, moron. I thought it'd be cool if she could spend the day with Lily as that was off the charts for years.

Colin: Leaving during the night to be there tomorrow morning! Grey and Miles coming too?

Aaron: Doubt they'd make it. And as far as I know, Miles is off to California with Brooke, is he not? Think they wanted to go to Disneyland.

Colin: Right. Grey's probably going with them then. Too bad. But Lilybug and I will be there, promise!

And that's only one part of the surprise for Sofia. God, she's going to either hate me for all I've planned or fall in love with me. I hope for the latter, but I doubt it. It's just a silly birthday present.

"I won't be back for a couple of hours," Sofia says, grabbing a jacket from her closet. "What are your plans for the while being?"

"Watch some tapes." I hold up my phone, though I don't plan on watching tapes. "We have a game the first Friday after the break so I might as well study my opponents' move in advance."

Sofia nods slowly. "Boring."

"It's better than spending money on a ticket for the movies only to end up not understanding a word." Though, I would go with her if it weren't for her birthday tomorrow and the millions of calls I have to make still. Hopefully with the help of Sofia's parents because I sure need someone to translate.

"True." After putting on her wisteria-colored jacket, she grabs a white purse to fill with stuff like lip gloss, tissues, and, obviously, some extra money. Her phone chimes and she immediately checks who texted, only to look up at me again. "Emma's here to pick me up."

As my little Sofia is about to open her bedroom door to leave, I hold her back. "You forgot something." She turns around, looking at me with a mixture of confusion and anticipation. "As your boyfriend, I deserve a goodbye kiss whenever you're leaving me."

Just like that, she hurries over to me. She stands between my legs and leans down to press a kiss to my lips. "You're a whiny little baby, you know that?"

I nod and wrap my arms around her lower back to keep her close to me. "For that comment, I demand a second kiss or else I won't let you leave."

Sofia giggles softly, running a hand through my hair. "And for this demand, I should get a free pass."

I gasp in shock. "How dare you say that?" Looking up at Sofia, I pout at her, pretending to be butt-hurt. "As your boyfriend, I get to demand as many kisses as I'd like."

"As your girlfriend, I get to decline as many kisses as I'd like."

"As your boyfriend—"

Sofia leans into me, her lips brushing against mine, interrupting me mid-sentence.

"You're really lucky, you know that?" Peter says just as he hangs up the phone call with the flower shop. "They're not open tomorrow, but they said they could squeeze your order in to be delivered in a couple of hours. But that will cost you a hundred euros extra. We could pay that for you if that's out of your budget."

"Nah all good. I have a pretty decent trust fund to steal money from." I'm already grateful that Sofia's parents even agreed to help me out today. Peter took the day off work only to help me out, that's how last-minute all this is. "Plus, Sofia's my girlfriend, isn't she? Might as well go all out for her birthday."

"Are you sure it's not a little too much?" Karin asks, crossing off yet another item from the list. "That must be thousands you'll be paying, Aaron."

"That's fine, really. At least I don't have to rent a location last minute as well." Because I can use their barn, which is fortunate for all the decorations. "Colin and Lily will be here tomorrow by five in the morning to help me do some more touch-ups."

This could be a *really* stupid thing I am doing. Sofia wasn't talking about her birthday at all in that sense, and here I am making it possible anyway.

Karin smiles softly, laying a hand on my shoulder. "Sofia knows they're coming?"

"No, it's kind of a surprise. She only knows they'll be here for New Year's." And quite frankly, I think Karin is more excited to see Lily again than Sofia is. But I can't blame her, I was pretty excited to see Sofia's parents again, and by the looks of their faces when they saw me, they were almost as shocked and happy to see me.

We spend the next three hours organizing a couple more things until everything on that list I have written is crossed off. Now… it's only a matter of time and skill to make tomorrow as special for Sofia as humanly possible. There's one thing I know for sure, though, Leon will not be able to top my surprise for Sofia and make her birthday be forgotten.

Chapter 39

"sit tight like bookends / pages between us / written with no end"—**Strong by One Direction**

Aaron

SOFIA IS STILL FAST ASLEEP BY the time Peter and I get to the airport to pick up Colin and Lily. Or so Karin told me in the texts she's sent me. I mean, someone kind of had to stay back and keep Sofia busy in case she wakes up, right?

I doubt it, but what if Sofia were to question where I am at, this early in the morning? It's easier to say I'm out with her father to catch a couple last-minute Christmas presents instead of somehow having to explain why all three of us were gone.

Though, maybe Sofia wouldn't believe the Christmas present excuse because as far as I've been told, stores aren't open on holidays, and Christmas Eve here is like their Christmas day? It's confusing, really. At least for me.

It's so much more logical to wake up on Christmas morning and open presents than hand them out on Christmas Eve after dinner or something like that.

"Are the stores open today?" I ask Peter as we wait. I'm not asking because I need one more present to buy, but because I'm genuinely interested in finding out. Germany's business hours are confusing as hell.

Peter nods. "Until two p.m., as far as I know. You need anything?"

"No, I've got all my presents. I was just wondering." Yes, I even have a present for Colin and Lily, believe it or not. I've had that idea of inviting Lily and Colin for Sofia's birthday ever since I knew I'd be here for it, so I bought a couple of just-in-case presents.

Then, finally, Lily and Colin come walking toward us. Having to keep myself from snorting out loud when I find their hands interlocked, I manage to not gag and appear happy to see them both. I am happy to see them, I just don't like seeing them being so… in love. It's kind of strange, especially when my best friend has his tongue stuck down my sister's throat.

I'm happy for them, truly. I couldn't imagine anyone better for my sister, and I know Colin makes her really happy. Perhaps I'm still a little weirded out by what I had to witness on my birthday.

"Please cover up your face, my eyes cannot take this ugliness," Colin says instead of a heart-warming greeting. But that's him, I guess. I'd be worried if he were to shake my hand as hello or give me one of his all too loved bro-hugs *only*. I get those when he's drunk all the time, or when he has something up his sleeves. "Man, my eyes were just recovering from the last time I saw you, and now all the progress is down the drain."

Instead of a hug or anything alike, Colin is holding his fist out to me, naturally, I give in to the fist bump because you never ignore one. Ignoring fist bumps or high-fives? Super uncool.

Then I move over to my sister, pulling her in for a brotherly hug. She chuckles, but eventually closes her arms around my torso to reciprocate the hug. "Didn't get enough affection the last few days?"

"I did, but I figured a hug won't hurt because you guys have a lot of work to do. So see this as my form of payment to you."

We pull away from the hug, and I grin at the stunned face she makes. At least until Lily turns away to greet Peter.

Shortly after a couple of "How was your flight" and other small-talk attempts, we're finally on our way back to the Carlsen's house, or more like their barn. We haven't quite managed to finish decorating everything before Sofia came back home yesterday, and as I didn't want her suspecting anything, we all had to be back at the house to seem as unsuspicious as ever.

But now we only have a couple more hours to finish, tops.

It's around six-thirty in the morning when we get back to the house and storm into the barn. Peter is kind enough to take Colin and Lily's luggage into the house for them, that way there is less of a chance for Sofia to spot them in advance.

"Oh, there are clothes for each of you in your room. I'd like to ask you to wear them, even if it's not your color," I tell them both, not bothering to explain any further.

"You really did mean *big* plans," Colin says, looking around the mostly finished decorated barn. "Looks good."

Lily does the same, just looking around with a rather impressed expression. "I start to understand why the party starts as soon as the sun sets."

Makes sense once you see this. The number of goddamn lights everywhere… they'll only look good in the dark. With sunlight shining through the two windows, it just looks weird.

"Yeah. But we still need to take care of all the flowers. They delivered them last night. Karin only had enough time to put them all in some water, so we have to put them in different vases now and, you know, make them look pretty all around here." That's going to be more work than I imagine, won't it?

Of course, it will be. It's always more work than people imagine.

"I do wonder, though…" Colin turns to look at me, slightly narrowing his eyes. "It's just Sofia's birthday, right? Why go so over the top for it?"

"Because her stupid ex-boyfriend is planning to propose to Julia."

Lily gasps, bringing both of her hands to her mouth. "No way."

"Yes way. Can you believe that guy *cheated* on Sofia? Like, who the fuck would do that?" My blood still starts to boil whenever I think about that. Sometimes I wish Sofia hadn't told me, because every single time I see Leon's face, I want to do nothing more but make him taste my fists and give him a free nose job.

Colin walks over to where the flowers are separated into five huge buckets. "Sounds like you're really mad about it, babe." He takes one bouquet out, looking at it like he's questioning every single decision he's made in his life.

"I am."

He grins, though turns to not let me see he is. Too bad, I've already seen it.

"You know, for someone that claims not to have feelings for her, you get quite upset with shit that isn't your fault and involves her." Colin walks over to the table in the middle of the barn, putting the flowers in a vase. "The last and *only* time I got that upset about anything that wasn't in my hands, it was connected to Lily, and we all know how that turned out." He smiles at my sister, then winks when he finds her smiling back at him. "Okay, and maybe the shit Maeve is pulling with Miles. But that's still a different kind of madness."

Sighing, I start to do the same Colin does. Take a bouquet of flowers and put them in any of the empty vases. "I'm not like in love with Sofia. I just don't like her getting fucked with."

"Because you'd rather *you* fuck her," Lily says, brushing off some hay from the chairs.

I groan. "Don't say that." Seriously, she's my sister. If Colin said that, it wouldn't bug me nearly as much as when Lily does it.

"It's the truth though. You could barely keep your pants on with Winter around. I can only imagine how awful this must be for you when Sofia is around," Colin adds for my sister. "Ever thought about just telling her how you feel?"

"I did." They both look at me with raised eyebrows. "Kind of." Sitting down on one of the chairs, I kick some hay in front of me away, tapping my foot on the wood. "We're dating, you know. Like, genuinely. She's my girlfriend now. But it's… complicated."

"Really?" Lily comes running over to me, kneeling while keeping her hands on my knees to keep herself steady. "You didn't mention *that*."

"It's not that big a deal." It is though, to me. I've been holding on to a promise for years, not knowing whether we'd ever get there or not. And now Sofia and I *are* dating, still, there's a huge possibility that it's all for nothing. "She just might not ever come back to America after she's graduated."

"What?" Colin drops the bouquet in his hands in the vase, his head instantly snapping over to me. "Why the hell not?"

"For reasons I cannot say. But it's huge and I'd totally get if she didn't come back, you know. It's just…"

"You'd be separated from an ocean again with almost to no way of seeing the other regularly," Lily fills in for me when I just trail off. I only manage to nod. "You could move to Germany, though, right? I mean, you'd have to learn a whole new language because I doubt you could live here for the rest of your life depending on Sofia to translate."

"I can't." Moving to a whole other country, that's difficult as fuck. Getting a temporary work visa, or one for traveling is much easier than *moving* to the country you're visiting.

"Yeah, he can't," Colin says. "He'll be drafted to go pro, and that sure as fuck won't be in Germany."

"I'd drop hockey for her, but I doubt I'd be happy so far away from everyone."

"And you say you're not in love." My sister rolls her eyes, plopping down to sit in front of me now. "Ever thought about that maybe Sofia wouldn't be all too happy being away from her family either?"

I've thought about that just around a million times for two days.

"Besides, Ron, if you don't think your relationship is going anywhere, why bother being in one in the first place?" Lily asks.

"Because I'd rather have limited time with Sofia than none at all."

"Holy shit," Colin says, followed by a long groan. "You were right."

Right about what? I didn't say anything.

Lily laughs, and for once it doesn't bug me as much when she laughs without me knowing why. I used to hate it because I always thought she was laughing about me. But recently, even if she were laughing about me, it's better than to never hear her laugh ever again. "Told you, Aaron *is* the dating type."

All right. Yeah, that's definitely laughing about Colin for, apparently, thinking I wasn't interested in dating.

I am not. Not unless it's Sofia I am dating.

Colin pulls out his wallet from his pocket, opens it, sighs, and closes it again. He then looks up at Lily. "I don't have money on me. But the second we're back home, I'll give you your fifty bucks."

My eyes almost pop right out of my head. "You were *betting* about me ever dating someone?"

Colin shakes his head. "Nah, we were betting about you dating Sofia. I said no way, you're too much of a pussy for that. Lily said you'd totally go for it the second you get the chance to."

"I hate you guys so much."

The audacity of them. I am having a real crisis here, and they're making bets about me and Sofia dating. *Unbe-fucking-lievable.*

"Ah, shut it. You've done the same with Miles and Grey about Colin and me," Lily says, waving me off.

"I did not." I made bets with the entire *team*. I won.

"Oh, you so did. Miles told me about it."

"When the hell did you speak to Miles?" Colin asks, now more concerned than he is whenever we're about to lose a game.

Lily shrugs. "I don't know. That one time on campus. He said Sofia and I wouldn't have to watch Brooke during practice because Emory would have her."

"And you proceeded to talk beyond that? *Mi sol*, he's ready to jump your bones."

"He is not," Lily and I say in unison. Miles wouldn't ever go for a dude's girlfriend. Especially not his best friend's girlfriend.

240

"Besides, I am pretty sure he has a crush on Emory."

I slide a hand down my face, muffling a laugh whereas Colin lets his slip out like it's nothing.

"Lils, Miles *loathes* Emory."

Lily's nose wrinkles. "Then how come she's always around. Well, not always, but I see them together a lot. And she does get mentioned a hell of a lot of times."

"Emory is Brooke's aunt. Millie's sister."

"*Twin* sister," Colin corrects. "And they dated once before him and Millie did, so she's also his ex-girlfriend."

And here I thought my love life was complicated and pitiful.

Chapter 40

*"I can be temptation / You can be my sin"—Come My
Way by PLVTINUM*

Aaron

"Leon has been walking around with that smug smile all fucking morning. It's like he knows I know he's planning on ruining
my birthday all over again," Sofia says, plopping back down onto
the bed right after her shower.

Colin and Lily both have been ordered to stay in the guest room
until either Sofia's parents or I come to get them. Until then,
they're supposed to stay quieter than a mouse. Since we finished
decorating before Sofia woke up, I managed to sneak back into bed
to make it look like I'd been there all this time.

I must have fallen asleep though, because when I woke up
again, Sofia was gone, and I could hear the shower across from her
room running.

Well, and now she's back here… in just a towel, lying down on
her bed right next to me.

My cock is almost jumping out of my pants seeing her half naked and *knowing* it'd only take one slip-up and she would be lying
here in all her naked glory.

Rolling over onto my side, I just look at Sofia for a whole

minute, admiring her beautiful side profile before I find words to say. "He won't succeed though."

"How would you know? My parents didn't even say happy birthday to me when I passed them in the kitchen."

I need to press my lips together to refrain from smiling. Obviously, I know why they haven't. No, I promise you, this is not some kind of "We'll pretend to forget it's her birthday" kind of bullshit. Maybe some form of it.

"Well, miss birthday girl…" Once again, I roll over, but this time to be on top of her, holding myself up with my arms. She shrieks a little, followed by laughter when I kiss up her cleavage, over her neck until my lips attack hers like I was deprived of her mouth. *I sure was.*

"Happy Birthday," I whisper in between kisses, over and over again. At least five times, I swear, but only because I can't bring myself to stop kissing her. Slowly, I kiss my way down again, before I suddenly get up, turn her around slightly and pull her to the edge of the bed.

Kneeling in front of her, I nudge her legs apart and reach my hands up to her towel. I keep my eyes on hers as Sofia props up on her arms, looking down at me with a lust-filled gaze. "Want my present for you now or later?" I ask, smirking.

"Now *and* later?"

My heart does a little backflip, threatening to jump out of my chest. "Let's see what we can arrange."

I pull on one side of the towel, unwrapping Sofia like she's *my* present. And thinking about it, she really is.

My breath goes lost in my lungs when one half of her body is revealed to me, and it stops when I lift the other side as well, exposing her faintly flushed skin to me entirely. My God, she really is the most beautiful person I have ever seen.

Our eyes meet, a thought passing between us that seems impossibly intimate, yet not intimate enough to make it something too deep. For a moment, I just stare into her eyes, feeling but not acknowledging the corner of my lips tugging upwards into a soft smile.

It isn't until Sofia smiles back and therefore crushes my entire world in a matter of seconds that I remember I was about to eat her pussy. I certainly wouldn't want to disappoint my Sofia, so I lean down and drop a couple of kisses on her silky-smooth skin, kissing my way up her thigh and aiming for her pussy.

With every new kiss I lay on her inner thigh, Sofia grows more restless, moving her hips and reaching one hand down into my hair. "Aaron," she says, sounding a little strained, "Please, touch me."

So, I do. I trace the tips of my fingers up her sides, letting goose-bumps appear on my girlfriend's body.

For as long as I can remember, I could only ever imagine what it would be like if I had my head between Sofia's thighs, what she would taste like, what kind of sounds she would make, and now I am happy to report, every single aspect about sex with Sofia is the absolute best.

Her pussy is bare and glistening, making me salivate and wanting her more than ever.

The further I slide my hands up, the closer my lips get to her pussy, and the second my hands cup her breasts, I plant a kiss to it before flattening my tongue and going in for one long stroke, licking from her entrance up to her clit.

What we had yesterday at the Christmas market, it's nothing compared to my tongue on her, getting a whole new taste of the woman that has stolen my heart years ago.

Stroking my thumbs over her hard nipples, and sucking her clit into my mouth, Sofia arches her back, her head leaning into her neck as a moan slips past her beautiful lips. The sound of it travels through my body, right into my balls.

As much as I'd love to hear them in their full power, I'd rather not have the whole house hear her. "You've got to keep quiet, love."

Sofia shakes her head, moaning a little louder when I push my tongue inside her and lick back up to her clit only to close my lips around it and suck, again. "Let them hear. I don't care."

"You have absolutely no idea what you do to me, do you, Sofia?" Not letting her answer, I push two of my fingers inside her wet pussy. Her hips buck against me, pushing herself a little closer to me and I just can't help but chuckle to myself.

I suck on her clit, curling my fingers up inside her only to hear her whimpers and moans. When her strength leaves her and she lies in front of me, no longer propping herself up, her pussy clenching around my fingers, I know she's close.

"Aaron!" she cries out, her muscles clamping tightly around my fingers as I keep on pumping them inside her. Her other hand finds into my hair, tugging on it. "Fuck."

Sofia's back arches off the bed, so naturally, I squeeze her boob while pushing her back down. "Come for me, love." My cock is throbbing, begging to get inside her. But not right now. First, I want to eat her for as long as possible. Unfortunately, she will no longer last for that long, I can feel it.

She gasps for air, panting heavily. "I… yes."

Her nails dig into my scalp, her moans growing louder every time my tongue sweeps over her clit and my fingers push inside her. Until eventually, she lets go.

CHAPTER 41

"you're buried in the pillow, yeah you're so loud"—Slow Down by Chase Atlantic

AARON CRAWLS UP MY BODY the second after he has put on the condom. He kisses every inch of me, making me feel incredibly wanted.

It's something I never thought was possible to feel. *Wanted.* He wants me, right now. Sure, it is sex, and he wants me for my body for the moment, but that doesn't change the little hint of something deeper, something *more* in his kisses, his words.

My lips part when I feel his cock against my pussy, and Aaron uses that moment to slide his tongue inside my mouth. Every single time he kisses me, it gets more and more intoxicating. Adrenaline rushes through me, igniting every imaginable cell in my body.

"Aaron," I say a little breathless. "What do I do to you?" The question has been running through my mind since he asked me if I had any clue what I did to him. But he was quick to shut me up and forget about it. Until now.

His eyes are a little hazy when he looks at me, dazed and filled with lust. "What you do to me?" he repeats back to me, reaching a hand down between our bodies only to slide the tip of his cock through my folds. "You're driving me insane."

He pushes inside of me all at once, making me gasp for air.

"You invade my mind all day, every day." He pulls out and thrusts back inside, this time a little slower than before. "You keep me up at night because I'd much rather think about you than sleep." Aaron kisses me, pumping his hips in a sweet, yet slow rhythm. "But when I do sleep, you're in every single dream of mine."

I moan into his mouth, wrapping my arms around his neck to pull him down.

"You're the first thought sneaking into my head when I wake up." He pushes into me. "You're the last thought in my head when I lie in bed and fall asleep."

His cock fills me up, and I love every second of him inside me. The feeling of Aaron, on me, around me, inside of me… it's everything I have ever wanted.

"You're in everything I see, in every single thing I do."

A tear rolls down my face, not from sadness, but just emotions.

He kisses my tear away, then presses his lips back to mine. "Oh, Sofia…"

"Aaron."

When his head comes down, resting next to mine as he thrusts just that tiny bit deeper into me, and I find my hands stroking down his back, I finally realize that ever leaving him again will be the worst thing to ever happen in my entire life.

I can hear his pants, his small groans, and huffs, and they're one of the most erotic sounds I have ever heard. Aaron isn't my first time, but I sure wish he was.

Aaron is sweet with me, listens to what I want, and makes me feel good. He cares about me, *my* pleasure, not just his own.

"Fuck," he rasps just as my hands grip his biceps, my fingers dipping into his skin. "You were made for me, Sofia."

No, you were made for me, Aaron.

He brings a hand down to where we're joined, pressing his fingers to my clit, rubbing me. "I need you to come for me, love."

My eyes roll back in my head, my chest pressing against his as my back arches away from the mattress. I know he can feel me clench around his cock because he groans into my ear, his voice low and hoarse.

"Come with me, love."

I let go at the same time as he does, crying out in pleasure and not caring a single bit about my family being in the house. All my mind is focusing on is the sweet, sweet relief and the orgasm rushing through my veins, tensing up my body and going boneless a moment later.

Aaron collapses on top of me, heavily breathing and panting.

Why has nobody ever warned me about getting intimate with the guy you have an awful amount of feelings for? No, it's great, really. I love every second Aaron and I spend together being intimate, vulnerable to each other. I just don't like feeling the emotions, the negative ones. The ones that have me fear losing him again because I still haven't worked through my trauma.

I told Aaron I wouldn't know if I could ever live in New City again, or the state of New York. He knows, and yet I feel bad for not having the guts to face my fears.

This man here followed me to Germany to get back at my ex-boyfriend, yet I'm here questioning if it's even going to be worth his time.

I should suck it up and face my grandmother, leave the trauma behind, and start living the life I *want*. With Aaron by my side. Every step I take.

CHAPTER 42

"there's a future in my life I can't foresee"—Ready to Run by One Direction

Sofia

AARON TOLD ME TO DRESS NICE because he is taking me out. Unsure of where he will take me, especially on Christmas Eve with only churches being open and, if you're lucky, a way too fancy restaurant way outside of my little village here, I decide to go a little classier than I usually would.

Instead of a black dress with my purple bow, Aaron made me go with all white. A cute short dress, showing some cleavage. It's tight and has a little cut-out triangle going from right underneath the middle of my breasts. Perhaps I should have chosen to wear sneakers as it's still snowing outside, but they wouldn't have fit the outfit, so I will have to suffer.

And, of course, my favorite piece of jewelry. *The* necklace. The Lego necklace. At least there is one thing in purple on me today.

As I finish the last touch-ups on my face, Aaron comes walking into my bedroom. He stops in his tracks when his eyes find me, scanning my body from head to toe. "That's what you're wearing?"

I nod. "Got a problem with that?"

Aaron steps closer, closing the door behind him. "I do,

actually." He walks up behind me, turning my head to face the mirror together with him. One hand of his strokes up my hips before they settle to hold me by my waist. "You're too stunning. I might get a stroke looking at you."

He leans down, placing a kiss to my shoulder. Tilting my head to grant him a little more access to my neck, I suck in a breath when he actually leaves kisses there.

"Aaron…" If he continues to kiss me like that, this will end with us on my bed again, and as far as I know, we don't have enough time for that.

"Just…" He turns me around, lifting my face to his. "One." The space between our lips disappears, and before I know, Aaron has his pressed to mine. My heartbeat quickens, even more so when Aaron pulls my hips closer to his own body.

Never in my life have I thought I would ever stand here, kissing the guy of my dreams. I never want him to stop doing that, ever. I never want to stop feeling his hands on my body. I never want to stop feeling like he's part of the oxygen I am breathing.

When we pull away from our kiss, Aaron hands me a piece of folded paper. I honestly expect him to just hand me an empty paper or read words my mind will wish I have never read. God knows what his mouth says when he's in a certain mood.

Before I even get to read what it says, I have one more question I need answered. "Do you think this dress is too revealing?"

I'm not sure what he has planned for tonight, but I'd rather not enter anywhere fancy with tons of old mediocre white men staring at my boobs the entire time. Or get off on the slit that goes up my leg. Who even knows what these people consider as getting-off material?

"Who cares?" He reaches a hand up to my face, tugging a strand of my hair behind my ear. "I'm tall and know how to fight. Someone looks at you a little too long, I intimidate them. Someone touches you, I punch them."

Aaron's hot breath rolls over my skin, tickling with electricity on the surface.

"Wear whatever you want, Icicle. I'll look out for you." No doubt he would.

Finally, I look down at the paper in my hands, and what I read instead of the nasty nothings I had in mind, only makes me want to cry happy tears.

"You're the most beautiful, most incredible, and most annoying girl in the whole world."

"Most annoying?" I look up at him, raising my eyebrows.

Aaron shrugs a little unbothered, though he keeps a smile on his face. "Yeah, you're a restless sleeper, you know? You tend to kick me during the night."

Now, he may suffer the consequences of his words by feeling my hands slap against his chest repetitively.

It doesn't last very long because Aaron's quick to stop me, pressing both my hands against his chest rather than have me slap him. My palms rest right over his heart, feeling it beat a little faster than what's normal.

He hasn't been running around, that much I know for sure. "Nervous?"

"No, but you're looking at me and that seems to be enough to make my heart want to leave my body."

Mine, too, Aaron. Mine, too.

"Now, come on, let's go before they're making up stories as to why we're late." He grabs my hand in his, pulling me after him as we leave my room. "Might get cold for the time we're walking over there."

"Where?"

"The barn, Icicle. It's Christmas Eve. You think I found somewhere fancy to go for us?"

"Honestly? Yes." No, really. For some reason, I figured if someone were to make the impossible possible, it would be him. "You made me overdress, didn't you?"

Aaron chuckles like it's a yes, but he shakes his head. "Well, it's your birthday and you're supposed to stand out love."

I hate him. No, really, I do.

At least he was decent enough to wear a suit, a white one, mind you, and not let me suffer all by myself.

By the time we reach the barn, I actually do feel like an icicle for once. My legs are as cold as one, so are my arms despite me having put on a thin jacket. And don't even get me started on my feet. Walking in a meter-high snow in heels? The worst possible decision I have ever made.

Fortunately for me, Aaron carried me after about two steps I took because he feared my toes falling off if he let me walk. I'm sure they would have.

Our barn isn't in our backyard but probably a good five-minute walk away from the house. So, yes, I might have gotten to it with blue toes. At least the inside of the barn is heated.

As he lets me down, Aaron quickly pulls on the back of my dress, covering up my ass again as my dress must've ridden up when he put me down. "Scared someone might see my ass?"

He slaps a hand to my ass, making me yelp. "Not scared, but I'd rather only me see it. Plus, your ex-boyfriend is in there and I have to hold myself back from punching him plenty as it is. Couldn't promise not to freak out when he stares at your ass as well."

Why does Leon have to be here? Like, I know he's Julia's boyfriend and he's been here last year as well, but it's annoying nonetheless. It's *my* birthday, and I believe I should be the one to decide whether I want my ex at my party or not.

The answer to that would be that I do *not* want him here. At least Aaron is with me this year, so even if everyone forgets it's still my birthday and not my sister-received-a-great-present day, there will be at least one person that wouldn't forget about me.

Aaron intertwines our hands, then looks at me one more time before he opens the door to the barn and walks us inside.

My eyes almost fall out of my head when I look at the hung-up fairy lights. Not just *any* fairy lights… they're floating lantern fairy lights, hanging all around the barn and especially over the huge table in the middle of it.

The next thing I take in are the flowers. So fucking many of them, it's impossible to count them. And like I'm not already close to bawling my eyes out, the bouquets are a mix of light purple lilacs, purple hydrangeas, and wisterias. A few are lined up on the floor to make up an aisle to walk toward the table, an aisle like you'd get on your wedding day, only this one seems a little less professionally placed. But I am in love with the look of it anyway.

And then I spot my birthday cake in the middle of the table, gasping when it's a white two-tier cake with purple flowers all over the cake.

"Aaron," I manage to force out, my voice strained from the force of tears I try to suppress.

"I couldn't give you a wedding yet, but I could make your birthday almost as magical."

This is crazy. *He* is crazy.

It gets even crazier though. Aaron managed to make every single person in this room wear light purple clothes. Even my goddamn sister and ex-boyfriend. And to make it *even* crazier… Lily and Colin are here.

How the fuck did he do all this? How did Aaron manage to pull all of this off without me noticing? He never left my side, he had absolutely no time to plan any of this… except for yesterday. But surely all this isn't a one-day kind of work.

"You made my wedding dreams come true." I hiccup lightly as I can feel a tear roll down my cheek. "For my *birthday*." Still can't believe it. All this seems a little… surreal. With every second that passes, I wonder when I will open my eyes and wake up from my dream because there is no way this is real.

"You like it?" He turns me around to look at him, bringing his index finger underneath my chin to lift my face.

I shake my head. "I love it, thank you." Bringing both of my hands to his jawline, I pull Aaron down to me, pressing my lips to his without caring about my family and friends… and Leon watching us.

Aaron lays his hands on my waist, pulling me into his body like he does every single time when we kiss. I never thought getting pulled into someone's body was going to make my head spin, but it sure as hell does with him.

"Sofia!" a little boy yells from the enormous table, followed by a giggle.

I pull away from Aaron, looking at Nick with a huge smile. Nick is the son of one of our neighbors, five years old, and always up to spend his time here in the barn. He also happens to be Jane's younger brother, so naturally, he uses every chance he gets to come here.

"Mommy said Santa won't come until you open your birthday presents," he says, running toward me. Once he reaches Aaron and me, Nick holds onto my hand, trying his best to pull me after him. "Please can you open your birthday presents so Santa can come?"

Aaron looks at me a little confused, and only then do I remember that he didn't understand a single word of what Nick has said. It doesn't matter anyway, wasn't his conversation.

So I kneel to Nick, still holding his hand. "Did you get me a present for my birthday?" He nods proudly. "Can I open it first?"

"*JA!*" He jumps up and down excitedly, making me chuckle. And just like that, he runs off towards the table filled with surprisingly a hell lot of presents.

I get back up but instead of looking at Aaron, what I've wanted to do, my eyes find Julia's. She looks mad, as though she's moments away from bursting into flames because today isn't about her. And when Leon whispers something into her ear, her frown only deepens.

That's new.

Leon gets up from his chair, asking for everyone's attention. That fucker. He's really going to propose to Julia on my birthday, isn't he?

Nope, he isn't. Because the next thing I know, Aaron reaches for my hand, intertwines them once more, and leads me down the flower aisle to get to the table. "Thank you all for sacrificing your Christmas Eve to be here tonight."

I look at Lily, finding her forcing a serious expression. Colin has an arm swung around her shoulders, doing the exact same face as her. Something's up. I'm not quite sure yet what it is, but I suppose I will find out sooner or later. I just hope Aaron hasn't lost his mind completely and planned to top Leon's proposal by pulling one himself.

Attempting to ease my anxiety about it, I just have to ask. "You do not plan on proposing to me, are you?" It's quiet enough for only Aaron to hear.

He laughs. "Not tonight, Icicle. That's my plan for New Year's Eve."

Again, Leon tries to get everyone's attention. He starts to speak about having some kind of big thing planned but then he gets interrupted again. This time by Colin, not Aaron.

"So, how's this whole thing work here? I've never celebrated a birthday on Christmas Eve."

Leon rolls his eyes.

My mother basically gives Colin a rundown of a traditional German Christmas Eve, only that we're not going to church tonight and instead of just eating dinner, we'll have a birthday party as well. All while Aaron leads me over to our seats. I sit down, he doesn't.

Nick comes back from the present table, standing next to me as he hands me his present. I take it, only for him to quickly run back to his seat, watching me open it.

I open it, being more-or-less surprised when the paper-thin present contains a drawn paper. I thank Nick wholeheartedly, though I have no idea what I'm supposed to do with the drawing. But it's the thought that counts, right?

For the next fifteen minutes, Aaron hands me present after present. They're all beautifully wrapped, with only a few exceptions. I've gotten quite a variety of products, some more useful, some less so. Everything's within the range of drawings to clothes and jewelry, facemasks and bath bombs, there is everything. And yes, even books.

But now that there is only one present left and Aaron is smirking at me, I'm honestly a little scared to open it. When he hands it to me, I thank him.

"From me," he says as if I hadn't figured that one out already.

"Nix, I bet you already paid for all of this, and even if you didn't, making this"—I gesture around the barn—"possible is the best gift I've ever gotten."

"Shut up and open your present, Icicle."

And so I do. Slowly, because there might very well be a very flat-pressed spider inside of this present. A little too hard for it, but it's possible, alright?

However, as soon as the present is opened, my jaw drops when I find a CD in there, with Aaron's handwriting on it.

I look up at him, still shocked by the words I've just read, yet also intrigued to find out what songs he thought of putting on this CD.

"What's so shocking?" Julia asks, being a nosy nelly as always.

Aaron leans down, his mouth close to my ear when he whispers, "Read it out loud."

I shake my head instantly. "There's a five-year-old at the table."

But of course that isn't an obstacle for him. He asks Jane to cover her brother's ears, so I could read it out loud.

Now that I no longer have an excuse apart from my parents literally being two meters away from me, three at most, I take a deep breath, telling myself that I got this.

"Icicle, read it out loud."

"I hate you," I grit out, mentally having murdered him at least five times by now.

"You say that now, but we both know that's not true."

It is right now.

You got this, Sofia. They're just five silly words.

"Songs I—" I make one huge mistake, looking at my father. He closes his eyes, already knowing what this says. But his annoyance only gives me more courage. "Songs I'll fuck you to."

"YES! WHORING!" My brother yells, making everyone laugh

after the shock of their life. Well, Lily and Colin were already about to burst out into laughter, so now they can finally let it out. "I LOVE THAT GUY!"

Aaron leans my head back in my neck, bringing his face over mine. Saying, "It's a promise, love", before bringing his lips down to mine to seal his promise with a kiss.

CHAPTER 43

"you're the only one that my heart keeps coming back to"—Always Been You by Shawn Mendes

Sofia

AFTER WE ATE DINNER AND opened Christmas presents—*yay, more presents*—my guests start singing *Happy Birthday* to me right before I'm supposed to blow out the candles on my cake and cut it.

It's awkward. Really damn awkward. Like, what am I even supposed to do while they're singing? Just stand here and look embarrassed, apparently.

As soon as they finish singing, I suck in some air, ready to blow out the candles on my cake when Leon makes yet another attempt to ruin my birthday.

"Before Sofia blows out the candles," he says in German, getting up from his seat again. Only this time, he kneels in front of Julia immediately instead of holding a whole ass speech beforehand. Julia brings her hands to her mouth, gasping.

I'm about to scream and freak out on them both when Aaron takes my hand, kisses the back of it, and tells me to just watch. Squeezing his hand in either anger or an attempt to calm down, I do as he says… watch.

Everyone watches them, actually. Listening to the god-awful cheesy words Leon has to say.

And then he takes out the ring box, opens it, and continues to say cheesy words until my ears fall off. Looking around, I first see how everyone else isn't exactly fazed by Leon's proposal. In fact, they look quite annoyed, kind of like they already knew—

"You told them," I accuse a little shocked. Aaron nods. "Why?"

"Because it's disrespectful. They all agreed. Besides, nobody should be proposed to on the holidays, how unoriginal." I want to believe him, I do believe him, but there's still this tiny grin on his face that tells me there is something else to come. And honestly, I am not sure if that should scare me.

When my sister says yes to the proposal, everyone is quiet, still just watching. Except for my parents, they're both kind of looking happy for my sister, although still a little too pissed to be one hundred percent happy about that. Then, Leon takes the ring out of the box, ready to put it on Julia's finger, only he doesn't get that far.

The second he takes the ring out, the part that held it up jumps out of the box, followed by what seems to be blue ink, exploding and dripping not only over his hands, but also hitting his and my sister's, chin, and their clothes.

As far as I can tell, every single person present gasps out loud, except for four. Aaron, Colin, Lily, and Lukas. All four of them start to laugh like little kids that just pulled off the best April fool's prank of their lives. Only that it's not April fools and they just ruined Leon's proposal to Julia.

It's hilarious, so much I can admit. Mean, but hilarious. They deserve it though.

So finally, I join my laughing friends and brother. I lean my head against Aaron's shoulder as I laugh to the point of my stomach hurting, but it's the best laugh I've had in a very long time, so I don't care much about it.

"Why did you do this?" I ask Aaron, whispering so nobody else would hear. Though, it wouldn't matter because everyone most definitely knows this is his doing.

"Figured having people remember your birthday as the day when a proposal got ruined would be better than having them remember it as your sister's something-good," Aaron says, sneaking one arm around my shoulders. "Besides, this was Colin's idea and his execution. I don't know how the chemistry and physics behind all this works."

"I hate you."

Just as the words leave my mouth, I can feel Aaron gently press his lips to the top of my head, whispering, "I hate you, too."

Chapter 44

"but even superwoman / sometimes needed superman's soul"—Helium by Sia

SOFIA CUTS INTO THE CAKE, swatting my hands away when I'm ready to serve it for her.

"Aaron, this is Germany," she says like it's an explanation to me. "Here, the guests are just that, *guests*. They don't serve or help, that's all on the hosts or rather the person whose birthday it is."

"That's stupid. It's your birthday, you should be served."

Still, instead of letting me help her, Sofia insists on doing the work all by herself, she won't even let me give her a helping hand.

"You already planned all this, Nix. You've helped enough." She gives me a gentle smile, trying to push me away.

Only that I won't let her get rid of me that easily, so instead, I lay my hands on her waist, pull her close to me, give her the tiniest and quickest kiss in my entire life, and swing her over my shoulder.

"Aaron!" she shrieks at the same time as her hands slap against my lower back.

I pull on the end of her dress, keeping the fabric in my hand to cover up her ass, at least until I have her carried over to her seat and put her down to sit. "Let me do it," I say, quiet enough for only her to hear. She sighs a little defeated but isn't arguing back, that's a win on my part.

So I spend the next ten minutes cutting more cake and handing it over to every single person—even Leon, though I don't think he's much of a person—in this barn.

After the ruined proposal, I figured Julia and Leon would leave and not return, but they didn't, much to my dismay. I still don't understand how an older sister can be this cruel, wanting to see their younger sibling suffer and get embarrassed.

I admit, ruining a proposal is a shitty move, but it was about time someone showed them what embarrassment felt like because, clearly, they haven't experienced it nearly enough. It's obvious they're a little embarrassed by what happened, the ashamed looks and the lack of the sounds of their voices making it very obvious. But I just can't feel bad for them.

Good thing tonight is about Sofia and not them.

As my eyes fall beneath the table for a split second, I notice Sofia's leg shaking. I look at her shaking leg suspiciously, my hand then instantly finding her thigh.

Ever since I've known her, Sofia would fidget with her fingers, bracelets, necklaces, even her hair if she couldn't find anything else when she was nervous. Whenever we sat somewhere on the benches in the arena, I would notice her legs shake to the point that it would annoy me. Back then I thought it was because of the cold, but nowadays I know it isn't.

Her head snaps toward me the second my hand finds her thigh, but she doesn't ask questions. And so I do instead. "Are you okay?"

Sofia nods quickly, now bringing her hand over mine, clutching it tightly. "My grandma tried calling me. She tries every year but I... never pick up." Her voice gets quieter with every word that leaves her mouth.

I lean into her, resting my head against hers when I say, "Maybe you should."

"I don't even know what to say."

Getting up from the uncomfortable chair, I pull Sofia up on her

266

feet as well. At first, she looks at me with a little questioning look, but then tells her guests we'll be right back. I wouldn't have done it, so at least she did. I mean, it's nobody's business anyway.

Leading Sofia over to the stairwell—the one I only found thanks to having decorated this entire barn, otherwise she wouldn't get me up here ever again—that leads upstairs to her favorite spot, she seems to calm down a little each step we take.

As we reach the hay bales we sat on last time, Sofia falls down on them and suddenly starts to cry. Her shoulders shake, gasping for air rather than taking normal breaths. It pains me to see her like this, and yet the only thing I do is sit beside her and close my arms around her body.

I don't even dare to speak, just letting her cry it out and calm down. Everyone's allowed to break, right? People are supposed to *feel* their emotions, and if I tried to calm her, I fear it'd only make it seem like I don't want her to feel them. I mean, sure, I do not want to see Sofia cry, but if that's what it takes for her to allow herself to feel, then I am okay with it.

"Why does she keep calling?" she cries, pressing her face into the front of my shoulder. "I don't get it, Aaron. She just…" She hiccups, her hands closing tighter around my shirt. "She tries every year to reach me, and I don't understand why. I *killed* her *husband*."

"You did not kill your own grandpa, Sofia."

"But I did. I scared him and he fell and—"

"Sofia," I interrupt, "You did *not* kill your grandpa."

"Then why does it feel like I did?" If only I knew… "Can you call her back? Tell her to not call me again?"

"Sure. If that's what you want."

Sofia hands me her phone, and so I immediately go to call her grandmother back. It takes her a short while to answer, but she gets there in the end. "Sofia?" she says, sounding more excited than Sofia may ever believe.

"Mrs. Carlsen? This is Aaron, Sofia's boyfriend." I'm not sure if she remembers me, but that's not important anyway.

"Aaron?" she repeats back to me. "Where is my granddaughter, Sofia?"

I reach for Sofia's hand, holding it in mine because from what I could tell, Sofia is about to run for an exit. "She's next to me. Unfortunately, she does not feel up to speaking with you just yet, but maybe I can forward a message?"

"Oh," Mrs. Carlsen sighs deeply, almost painfully. "I call every year, but she never picks up. I thought, maybe she has a different number but that couldn't be because her father gave me this one. So, I keep calling in hopes that one day she might answer me."

Why did I say I'd call her? This is tougher than I thought it would be. Especially when Sofia's grandmother sounds like she is fighting her tears. "I understand, but like I said, Sofia doesn't feel comfortable talking to you yet."

"But why? Is she still upset with me because I didn't bake cookies when they visited last?"

This might be a little bit of a reach, but is it possible that Mrs. Carlsen has absolutely no idea why Sofia has never reached out to her after her grandfather's passing?

"Uh, no, I don't think she's upset because of cookies. I will ask her, though. Alright?"

"You do that, Aaron." Another heavy sigh comes through the phone, as though she wants to say something else but doesn't quite know how to phrase it yet. Eventually, she finds her words though. "Can you wish her a happy birthday for me?"

"I will." I look at Sofia just in time to catch her wiping away a tear. Not hanging up the phone, I say, "Your grandma says happy birthday."

Sofia's eyes close as she takes a deep breath. A hint of a smile tugs on her lips, but she doesn't quite let it show. "Tell her I said thank you."

I don't have to, because Grandma Carlsen heaves a sigh, followed by what must be a hiccup from a silent crier. "Oh, was that her? She sounds so lovely, so grown up. Tell her to come see me sometime, will you, Aaron? Please ask her to come visit me, she's my little Sofia. I don't understand why she won't see me anymore or talk to me. I really miss her; can you tell her that?"

I'm sorry, Sofia. "Maybe you tell her yourself, okay?" Instead of waiting for an answer, or letting Sofia react in any other way than her widened eyes, I hold the phone up to her ear.

Sofia's hand immediately covers mine, tightening her grip as her grandmother must be speaking to her. Sofia doesn't answer, but she listens, and the only way for me to tell she is listening is from the way her hands loosen around mine and her expression lightening.

The heavy weight she's been carrying from ignoring her grandmother's calls for years, missing someone whom she'd thought of hating her just lifting off at the sound of her voice.

A minute passes until Sofia finally speaks. "I… miss you, too."

Chapter 45

"slide across the floor, I'm forever yours"—dancing in the kitchen by LANY

Aaron

COLIN AND LILY HAVE BEEN staying here all week long, taking busses and trains to see the country or rather Bavaria. Well, at least they're out of my hair, right? Because I fully planned on spending as much time with Sofia as humanly possible. *Only* Sofia.

Having Colin and my sister around once or twice isn't bothering me but imagine if I had to deal with them every single day until New Year's when I could use that time more wisely. I mean, fucking my girlfriend or going on little dates sounds much more intriguing when it's just the both of us.

Anyway, we've spent all day with them today, so when they finally decided to go to sleep, I was a little relieved to have some alone time with Sofia… only that she went to bed as well. So, now it's two in the morning and I am here, standing in the kitchen and drinking a glass of warm milk with honey to *hopefully* get sleepy as well.

Five minutes must have passed since I've been standing here, and yet I feel nothing. Nothing except for that aching erection in my pants. I'm not even horny or anything, it's just… Sofia has changed in front of me, and I caught a glimpse of her perfect boobs. Ever since then, my dick's been a slight problem.

"Can't sleep?" a sweet voice comes from behind the open refrigerator door, followed by a little giggle that travels right through my body.

"Not really," I answer Sofia, setting the mug in my hands down just before she stands in front of me. She lays her hands on my naked torso, lightly tracing her fingers over the ripples of my abs. "I thought you fell asleep?"

Sofia shakes her head. "I tried, but my brain just won't shut up."

"What's your brain complaining about?" I take her into my embrace, soothingly stroking a hand up and down her back while leaning my chin on top of her head.

"Too much," she admits, nuzzling her head right into my body as her arms close tighter around me. "I can't stop thinking about what I will say to my grandma when I go to see her."

So she did decide to try and sort her problems out. That's a start, no? A good one.

I can't help but smile a little at the thought of Sofia *wanting* us to work out. If she didn't, she wouldn't want to try and face her fears, right?

Ah, well, she should find closure even if it wasn't for the chance of an *us*. And being with me isn't nearly as important as her health.

"I'm not sure if it's smarter to see her the second we're back in the U.S., or when I have to leave again."

Leave again… I don't want her to leave, ever.

My body tenses, something in my chest starts to hurt just thinking about having to say goodbye to the love of my life.

No. *No*. Not love of my life. Not yet. She… She can't be, right? That's impossible. We've only just met again. We've only recently started dating. I can't think of her as the love of my life, that would be insane.

I knew she was my soul mate, came to terms with that ages ago. But love of my life? No. Not yet. *Please*. For my own sanity, I cannot consider her to be just that when it's not one hundred percent guaranteed she'll also stay in my life for the rest of it. To let me love her for the rest of it and beyond.

"I think it's time I give us both the chance to figure some things out. Get closure, maybe? I don't know, but I want to see her. I want to *speak* to her."

"Sounds like you've made your mind up about it?" Which I do hope she did. Not for the sake of Sofia and me finding a way to make my promise come true, but for her own good. Sofia *needs* closure, with me still in her life or not.

"I have."

Pushing Sofia away just enough to take her hands in mine, I twirl her around. "Dance with me, Icicle."

"Now?" I nod. "Without music?" Another nod. "In the middle of this kitchen, with no light except the one from the refrigerator?" And one more time, I nod.

"It's either that or a quick fuck in the shower."

"Can I get both?"

"You can get anything you want from me, Sofia." I keep one of her hands in mine as my other lays on her hip. "Just say the word and it's yours."

I can barely make out her expression, but the faintest blue light ever highlights the smile on her lips, the same chubby cheeks I love seeing more than anything being highlighted like whoever's out there to make miracles happen *wanted* me to see it again, knowing it was my favorite sight.

Well, seeing Sofia is my favorite sight, but that smile… it's getting damn close to my favorite.

We move to no sound other than our breathing and the sound of bare feet on kitchen tiles. The only other sound is the beating of my heart, beating in a rhythm that I am praying is the same as Sofia's. She can't hear my heart beating, and neither can I, but I can feel it.

Never have I hoped for someone's heart to beat at the same pace as mine, wanting the same as me, yet here I am, silently begging the universe to never take my Sofia away from me ever again.

I'm not sure when I started to need her in my life, but I finally realize that I do. I need her to breathe, to feel happy and complete.

Both our eyes fall to my wrist as I hold her. I'm still wearing her wisteria-colored ribbon around it every single day, and I do not plan on ever taking it off. Ever since I took it from her, I've been wearing it without having had it off, with only a few exceptions. I do not wear it for hockey, for multiple reasons. For one, and probably the most important one, I am not even *allowed* to wear any kind of bracelets, rings, or necklaces during practice or games. Other than that, I only take it off to work out as I don't want it to get all sweaty and disgusting.

"Aaron?" she says quietly, looking up at me through her lashes. Her voice is the most beautiful one I have ever heard, and hearing her say my name never fails to make my heart skip a beat or two.

"Sofia?" I push a strand of hair that fell into her face back behind her ear.

"Can you promise me something?"

"Unless you want me to leave you and move on, yes." I doubt I could, even if I tried to. Leaving her and moving on? No, it's impossible.

"If we do somehow manage to make your promise become reality, promise me not to say, 'I love you' for the first time on my birthday."

We stop moving, but despite the little anxiety and shock in my bones, I still reach my hands up to her face, cupping it. "Why not?"

"Because I would never be able to celebrate one happy birthday again if we broke up. It would be ruined for all of eternity, haunting me. It would remind me that there was a time when you loved me, and we were together. You would have made a special day in my life more special and then taken the magic away without leaving crumbs."

I kiss her, gently, deeply, like this is the last time I'd ever get to kiss her. As we part, the words, "I promise" leave me in a whisper. With the kiss that follows, I also promise her not to say these words for the first time on *any* day that is supposed to be special to her.

Like Easter, Christmas, or any other holiday that exists. Though, it wouldn't make a difference because when I say those words, they'll be forever, and there will never be a way back from them.

Chapter 46

"hold your hair in deep devotion"—I Wanna Be Yours by Arctic Monkey

"Close your eyes, love," Aaron says, as he washes off his hands from my shampoo, then takes the showerhead in his hand. "I don't want you to get shampoo into your eyes."

I close my eyes but am kind enough to let him know they're closed. Even if we decided to turn on the ceiling light and not just the ones around the mirror, he wouldn't see my eyes as my back is facing him.

He brings the showerhead to my hair, having turned the water a little hotter as he knows I prefer it that way.

The second we stepped in here and I had turned the water to "boiling-hot", so Aaron insists it was, he had me turn it colder. At least now that he is washing my hair, or rather rinsing out the shampoo he so gently massaged into it, he has turned up the temperature again.

Once my hair is washed, we'll be good to go back into bed and catch some sleep, but I'm still kind of hoping for the shower sex I was promised. To be fair, I did kind of ruin the whole mood by making him promise me not to say "I love you" on my birthday, which would be a year from now as my birthday was only a week ago.

Buuut, the boner he is sporting still lets me hope, okay? Sue me.

And not to forget, Aaron has put on the playlist he created for whenever we have sex just before we stepped into the shower. He didn't use the CD he gifted me, but as far as I can tell, he has the same playlist on his phone.

"Stop moving so much," he grunts, pressing a hand to the top of my head to keep it in place. "You're the worst possible shower-buddy I have ever had."

"Who else was there?"

"My rubber duckies and the shower gel slash shampoo bottles lined up in my shower. And yes, they're a better audience than you are."

"No other woman?" *Why, Sofia? WHY?*

He snorts. "Nah. I am not giving free shows of my dick to any-one."

"Yet here you are giving me a free show."

Aaron turns me around, holding the showerhead right into my face. I almost choke on the water but am lucky enough not to actu-ally inhale it.

"Oh, sorry, did that hit your face?"

He moves his hand away from my face, putting the showerhead back in its place and switching on the big ceiling rain shower in-stead. All the while he's being attacked by my hands that keep slap-ping him for his rudeness.

When my hand finds his ass—logical consequence from him not reacting to any of my other beating attempts—he faces me. His eyebrows are currently visiting Jupiter, that's how high he's raised them. Aaron's jaw is slightly clenched as he keeps himself from either laughing or spitting out some words that no holy person would ever appreciate hearing, and without throwing at least three liters of holy water at them. Might as well drown him in it at this point.

"Did you just *slap* my ass?"

278

I shrug. "I don't know. Did you feel *my* hand on your ass or someone else's?"

"Having a smart mouth now, huh?" He comes a little closer, I take a step back. "How smart is that mouth of yours going to be when I push you up against this glass?"

He's speaking of the only barrier that's separating the bathroom from the enormous walk-in shower my parents thought of being practical to get. I never understood why we'd need a huge shower here, but for once I'm quite grateful we have it.

In a heartbeat, Aaron turns me back around, presses my body into the glass as he stands behind me. The cold of the glass makes me gasp, but not nearly as much as Aaron does when he nudges my legs apart and reaches his hand down to cup my pussy.

"How smart is that mouth going to be when I do this…" Two fingers slide through my folds until the tips of them dare to sink inside me. "Or this." They push inside me, and I would love to say the water kind of makes it a little more difficult, but it doesn't. I'm as wet as I have been the last couple of times Aaron and I had sex, which seems a little embarrassing if I'm being honest. Not enough to mortify me though.

"Always so ready for me," he rasps, leaving kissing down my neck. "Do you want me to stop?"

"I will murder you if you do." I shouldn't have said that, because it only makes Aaron pull his fingers out of me and chuckle. "Aaron Phoenix Mar—"

My voice gets lost when he spins me around and lifts me up. A soft huff leaves me, which he is quick to swallow because his lips are on mine so hungrily, it almost appears as though he hates it when he can't muffle me with his own mouth.

"You better keep quiet this time, Icicle," he warns, then brings his mouth to my breasts, capturing one of my nipples between his teeth, licking it then sucking it right into his mouth.

I whimper, then groan in frustration when he releases my nipple with a slight pop.

"I mean it, Sofia." His fingertips on my ass dig deeper into my skin as he squeezes it. "Make a sound and I'll stop."

"Why?"

"Because the entire house is asleep, and I refuse to let my soon-to-be in-laws get woken up by me fucking their daughter."

My heart makes a jump. Or two. Or twenty. *Soon-to-be in-laws.* I like the sound of it… maybe a little too much.

We. Are. Not. Anywhere. Near. Engaged. So suck it up, Sofia.

"You guys keep condoms in the bathroom?" Oh. Right.

I shake my head. "Not that I know of it."

"Dare to go bare or should I run over to your room and get one?"

He already knows I'm on the pill, or at least I think he does. Aaron has witnessed me taking them, and I doubt he's too clueless to know what kind of pills I've been taking at the very same time, daily. "Are there any STDs you have I should know of?"

"Funny." He laughs sarcastically, setting me down on the floor. "Got tested the week before we got here."

"Me, too."

"Good." Aaron lifts one of my legs, hooking his arm underneath my knee. With his free hand, he grasps his dick, gives himself one long stroke then slides the head of his cock through my lips.

My mouth opens, a whimper about to leave me when Aaron's mouth comes slamming to mine instead.

He pushes inside me, his hand moves to my waist, just holding me close and steady. Though, I wish I could say the same for my breathing because that one sure as hell is far from steady.

My arms come up around his neck, hands finding into his wet hair.

The hot water raining down on us does nothing for the heat increase my body is met with every time Aaron slides out of me to push back inside.

He kisses my lips, my jaw, down my neck, and wherever he can reach. I moan, leaning my head back against the glass only to realize my mistake. I have made a sound.

Aaron pulls out of me, punishing me. "Aaron," I groan, angry at the loss and deprived of an orgasm I could feel building up already.

"I warned you."

"It's a natural reaction," I argue. Like, come on. He cannot seriously punish me for being vocal. After all, it is Aaron fucking me, making me feel good. He should be *proud*. "Please."

He turns me around, my hands flat on the glass. I can feel Aaron wrap my wet hair around his fist before his other hand settles on my hips and he slams into me again. This time, Aaron doesn't punish me for moaning out loud, and thank God he doesn't.

I'm far too sensitive to his touch to control what comes out of my mouth right now.

My moans grow louder with every thrust. Another gasp for air follows when Aaron covers one of my hands with his and my eyes find the light purple ribbon around it. I'm not sure why this turns me on even more, but it does.

He pulls on my hair, my head tilting back until our eyes meet. My mouth stands open, my eyes half-lidded as my legs start to feel weaker.

"You like this?" He thrusts into me a little harder, letting go of my hair only to bring his arm around my body to hold me close to him.

"Yes," I gasp, meeting his thrusts.

"WOULD YOU QUIET DOWN!" a deep voice with a heavy German accent screams, banging against the bathroom door.

I would be terrified if I didn't know this was Leon. Aaron seems to know as well, or he simply doesn't care who's on the other side of the door.

"Jealous you couldn't get her to be this loud?" He slams into me a little harder, eliciting a moan from my throat that's almost loud enough to wake the dead.

"Are you seriously carrying on? Who the fuck does that?" God, Leon is getting on my nerves. We've established this before, but right at this moment, I wish I had a knife with me to stab him with.

"Sure. Want to come in and watch?" The door is locked, Aaron knows that.

"I'd rather die."

"Then why are you still standing there talking to me?"

Judging by the lack of comeback, either Leon has now left, or he is being a weirdo and pretends to have gone back to my sister's room. Either way, I couldn't care any less.

I clench around Aaron's dick, tingles running down my spine. "I'm going to come," I cry out.

"Fuck yeah, you are."

He chases my orgasm with possession like he knows he owns me even if I would never tell him because I'm still my own person.

My brain shuts off, vision going dark as my eyes roll back and I cry out in pleasure. The rush of my orgasm sweeping through my body.

Aaron comes inside of me, panting just as heavily as I am.

For a short while, we just stand there with Aaron still buried deep inside of me. Our breaths trying to calm down but not seeming to do so any time soon.

By the time we exit the bathroom and are back in my room, I am officially exhausted enough to fall asleep within the second my head hits the pillow.

We both fall down on the bed, not caring that neither of us wears any proper clothing. Aaron only threw on some boxer briefs while I allowed myself to steal one of his sweatshirts. I don't even wear anything underneath, but it's not like Aaron hasn't seen me naked, so who cares?

As we lie and my eyes close, Aaron rolls over, right on top of me, resting his head right on my boobs. It's a little difficult to breathe, but not enough for me to push him off.

"Good night, my love," he mumbles, my heart melting at his sleepy voice.

"Just like that?" He nods very slowly. "On top of me?"

"Yup."

I bring my arms around his body, gently tracing my nails over his back for some backrubs. "Okay," I whisper, "Good night."

"Good night."

He already said that, but I'm too tired to tell him.

Just like that, I drift off to sleep with my favorite person right on top of me.

Chapter 47

"when we were younger / we wore our hearts right on our sleeves"—Little League by Conan Gray

SOMEONE KNOCKS ON MY DOOR just a second after waking up.

For the first knock, I am sure it was just in my dream, but then that certain someone knocks again, making this pretty realistic.

"Who's there?" I call out, not bothering to even get out of bed yet.

It's not Aaron, that much I know for sure. He would be barging in here, possibly even throwing himself on top of me only so I would get up or give him some cuddles.

Who would have thought Aaron Marsh would love cuddles? Not me.

And besides, Aaron has left to help my parents with grocery shopping. Or I just dreamed that when he woke me up and told me. Either way, I don't really care.

"Uh, Lily. Can I come in or is this a bad time?"

Lily? Oh. Lily.

She's been staying here for a week. I cannot believe I haven't *once* asked her to see my room. Is that what people do? Show their friends their rooms?

No? Alright.

Anyway.

"No, yes. Come in." I sit up, running my hands down my face to… what? Make myself appear less asleep? Rub the sleep off my face?

The door opens and she comes walking inside, stopping half-way through the door. "Oh, wow. This is… purple."

She looks around my room until they eventually settle on the frog on my bed. She comes walking in all the way, closing the door. In what must be a heartbeat, she's over by my bed, taking the frog in her hands.

"So you guys really did switch them, huh? I thought Aaron made that up so I would be… I don't know, less suspicious about your relationship when I used to hate it," she says.

"Wait, *switched* them? Aaron gave me his because I lost mine." I don't remember anything about *switching* my stuffed frog with his.

Lily chuckles, putting the frog back down on my bed. "Yeah, he told me you stopped by before you left for Germany so you could switch the frogs. Apparently, you liked his better and he didn't want to be mean and say no when he didn't know when he would see you again."

"I… I never asked for his. I stopped by to say goodbye and then I told him I lost mine. He just gave me his."

Shrugging, Lily walks over to my dresser, looking at the pictures standing on it as well as the ones on my wall. "I suppose he just wanted to keep something of yours, so he stole it and gave you his as a replacement."

"He had the necklace."

Lily doesn't even look at me when she waves me off, not agreeing with my words. "Yeah, but the necklace didn't *smell* like you."

"We were eight, Lily." I get off the bed, walking over to her. Well, to my dresser because I should really get dressed sometime soonish.

"Mhm, and I was blind as fuck, clearly." She points at one of the pictures on my wall. It's a picture of Aaron, Lily, and me.

The picture was taken on one of Lily and my competitions. We just received our medals for second place as Aaron had run across the ice to get to us.

The camera captured the moment when Aaron ran into my arms instead of his sister's to congratulate us on our win. You can't exactly see my face, but I know I was smiling widely, even more so when Aaron was hugging me.

And Lily? She's looking at the camera, holding up her medal like a proud mother.

I remember when Lily turned around and had just forced herself into the hug because she thought it was a group hug rather than Aaron being proud of me.

But then again, we were like six years old, it's a little less deep considering our age.

"You weren't blind, you were a child," I kindly let her know while quickly putting on some underwear from my dresser as I am still in Aaron's shirt *only*.

"Ah, well, I should have known," she says, turning around to look at me. Her eyes follow me as I walk over to my closet and take out a pair of black leggings. "I did kind of plan a wedding for you guys though."

I laugh. "That one time we were playing house does not count."

"You guys made me be your *dog*, what the hell else was I supposed to do?"

"I don't know, Lily, what do dogs do?" I put on my leggings, then go and find myself some socks because it's getting quite cold. "Bark and, I don't know, pee, I guess? But they definitely do not plan weddings."

She holds up her hands like I was holding her at gunpoint. "I was a very talented dog. Even to the point where I could hold the entire ceremony."

Being a child really is magical. You find joy in everything, and your imagination doesn't hold back. See a stick? No, it's now a wand. See a leaf and have sand? No, it's now a weirdly shaped, self-built cup with tea.

I take a seat on my bed again, taking a deep breath before letting out a question that's been on my mind since she got here for my birthday. "You're not mad at me for being with your brother, are you?"

Lily frowns at me like she's seconds away from bursting out laughing. She shakes her head, making her way over to me only to take a seat next to me. "I am sorry for you. I always thought you were smarter than dating someone like Aaron."

"What's that supposed to mean?"

"Ah, you know. Only that he is the worst human imaginable?" She leans her head on my shoulder. "Like, did you hear him talk? He's worse than Colin, ego-wise, I mean. Aaron truly believes he's the best of the best."

Yeah, okay. I can't argue that. But Aaron does happen to be pretty good at hockey, so I can't blame him for being proud of himself for it.

"No, seriously, Sofia, I am happy for you. I told you, I don't care, it's your life. Besides, I always wanted to hold a great wedding speech and not have to lie about liking my brother's spouse. I can include how you guys excluded me when we were younger and only did the exact opposite of what I wanted. So, it's convenient."

"I thought your last one was great. With all the *woofs* and growls."

I don't remember exactly what Lily had said back then, but not a lot. She was supposed to be a dog after all.

"Well, if you would have had a child instead of a dog, maybe you would have gotten some words, too."

I truly wish Lily and I could have gone to school together, grow up together. Imagine all the stories we would be able to tell, all the things we would have experienced together. Though, unfortunately, life doesn't always give you want you want.

"Oh, uh, what I actually came here for," Lily says, sitting up straight again, "Colin wants to go to a bar for New Year's, and he was wondering if you would come with us. We'll even make an exception for Aaron."

"How gracious of you."

Chapter 48

"I swear that I'll be yours forever, till forever falls apart"—*Till Forever Falls Apart by Ashe, FINNEAS*

Aaron

"ANOTHER ROUND OF SHOTS?" Colin asks, though he has already ordered four new ones and is currently setting down all four of the shots on the table.

"Tequila shots?" Lily asks, though before receiving an answer, she has put some salt on the back of her hand, licked it up and downed the shot, then shoves a slice of lime into her mouth.

Colin kisses the side of her head before downing his own shot.

Sofia looks at me, the same mischievous spark in her eyes as the first time we took shots together. She has a better tolerance for alcohol than me, which I blame on Germany, to be honest. But, fuck, is it hot when she's near sober from four shots and whatever drink she had, whereas I am barely keeping up with my beer and two shots.

She leans into me, her mouth to my ear when she says, "I bet you won't drink yours."

If she thought, I'd ever back out of a challenge... I might have to show her why I wouldn't. Like, come on, if you don't want a guy participating, don't challenge him. He'll take on the challenge, even if there is a higher risk of him dying than surviving.

We both put some salt on the back of our hands, counting down from three. Only when we reach one, Sofia doesn't lick the salt on her hand, she leans over to me, her tongue gliding over my neck before she downs her shot.

My jaw drops, as so does the shot glass in my hand, spilling its entire contents on the table. *Luckily,* it's the table and not my pants.

As my head shoots toward my girlfriend, I find her laughing uncontrollably. She falls back into the booth, smoothly sliding over until her thigh presses against mine. "I won," she spits out through laughter.

She has the most infectious laughter I have ever heard; so genuine, loud, and joyous. It is almost a shame that not every single living being will experience her laughter.

Hearing that laughter confuses something inside me though. I never know if I want to laugh with her, kiss her breath away, or fuck her nine ways to Sunday. Maybe all of the above, but even then, in which order?

"You cheated." Turning slightly in my seat, I lift her head from my shoulder then hold it in my hands, looking at her. My heart beats faster in my chest, and it's driving me insane. Why does it keep doing that? "Licking me wasn't part of the deal."

She grins. "I never stated any rules."

"You and your smart mouth."

Our faces are so close together, I can feel her hot breath roll over my skin. Soft lips only millimeters away, so kissable, and sweet. Her eyes are shining even through the dark light of this bar, building a passage right into my soul when she looks at me. But that's alright. Eyes this beautiful are bound to find a way to someone's heart, even if you weren't aware of falling for them.

"Oh, my God. They just opened the stage for karaoke!" Lily pulls on my girlfriend's arm, forcing her away from me. "We *have* to sing a song together!"

"I'm the worst singer to ever exist," Sofia replies, yet following Lily to the stage. Whatever Lily says next, I cannot hear but I know better than anyone that my sister can't sing to save her life. So this is going to be fun.

Not so much for everyone's ears, but fun, nonetheless.

"Let's do a Spanish song!" Lily speaks, forgetting that the microphone is already picking up their voices. But the look on Colin's face is totally worth it. My sister knows a total of zero Spanish words, maybe the basics like *hola* or *sí*. You know, the words everyone knows, basically.

Now, you may wonder why my sister attempting a Spanish song would be as shocking and horrifying to Colin as it is. Easy, his mother is from Spain, and therefore I would say he knows his fair share of Spanish.

This night keeps getting more and more hilarious.

And when Sofia and Lily start singing, standing on that stage arm in arm, barely hitting any tones, nor saying *any* of the words right, I can no longer keep my laughter in. It just spills out of me without me having a say in it.

But they're both laughing at themselves, making everyone inside this bar join in, even the bartenders. When I look at the security guard by the entrance, I even find him smiling the faintest smile possible.

So then neither of them has a great voice, and neither of them knows the words, but they're a great spirit.

My eyes are now focused on Sofia, and without noticing, I no longer laugh but instead smile at her and enjoy the view. She's so effortlessly beautiful, it kills me every time I look at her.

There is one more thing about this whole awful karaoke performance that leaves me love it despite the great spirit. Seeing my sister happy.

I can't remember the last time I've seen her this free, this light. So if it takes a karaoke night for her to be happy, I'd drag her to a karaoke bar every weekend if I have to.

"Have you ever seen my sister this happy?" I ask Colin, noticing how his eyes are only on her. Perhaps I do not need to drag my sister anywhere after all. My best friend seems to be doing the job just fine, keeping Lily happy, I mean.

"I have," he says as a matter of fact, "In my bed with me buried deep inside her."

Unfortunately, I no longer have a drink I could throw at him, so gagging will have to do. "Gross."

He grins cockily, then winks at me like he wants me to beat his ass. "Wish that was you, huh?"

"Definitely." I gag yet again, memories of that one night we spent together making its way through to me. "Did you ever regret it?"

Colin laughs. "Being with your sister? Nah, dude. She's my everything."

I throw a tissue at him, the one I used to clean off the tequila from the table. "Sucking me off, I mean." We never spoke about that night ever again. It happened, and although Colin and I both seemingly went to tell Grey about it, which ended up with Grey laughing for a good thirty hours straight, *we* never really talked about it.

Not sure what there was to talk about. I don't talk about the sex I had with whoever I fucked either. I always just leave and that's it. But still, I had always wondered if he regretted it.

"I regret having told Grey," he says, "but only because of his comments and the laughter. And perhaps because he told Miles so he wouldn't be the only one laughing."

He didn't mean any harm, we both know that. And he wasn't making fun of us, he was just a little surprised. Plus, we were like nineteen or something. Guys that age make fun about almost everything, teasing each other. We still do, even two years later.

"So other than that, no regrets?" Colin shakes his head with a slight shrug. "Did you tell Lily?"

"I have. I wanted her to know before one of our friends lets it slip out on accident and she'd think I cheated on her or something. She took it well. Though, she was a little grossed out because I was talking about *you* and me, not some other guy. But other than that, I don't think she's mad at you."

"Why would she be mad at me?"

He winks. "You know, because I had my mouth on your before I had it on her."

"Gross, dude."

By the time the song ends, some people are screaming for Lily and Sofia to sing another one. I do not understand why, because my ears need a break, but sure, why not?

And of course they give their fans what they want and start yet another Spanish song. This time, however, Colin isn't having it. "I cannot let them continue to ruin Spanish songs like that," he mumbles and walks up to the stage.

Lily welcomes him with open arms, holding her microphone out for him or at least enough for them to share it because, God forbid my sister disappoints her millions of fans.

Sofia's laughter fills the room, before she jumps off stage to dance instead of making up new words to a song that's named after her. Well, probably not after *her* but I'm pretty sure the song is called "Sofia".

Some guy then approaches Sofia, but at least he isn't invading her space too much, I guess. I would love to get up and tell him to fuck off, but then Sofia turns around, pointing at me. She waves, and I wave back.

The guy nods his head at me, so I do the same as some form of acknowledgement. He then says something to my girlfriend before making his way back to wherever he came from. Only then do I notice how tense I was. Subconsciously, I have clenched my hands into fists, ready to use them in case that guy were to touch what's mine.

Sofia comes running over to me, panting like she's been dancing for hours. "How'd you like my performance?" she asks, plopping down beside me.

She leans against me, putting her legs up on the seating space.

"Loved the parts when you didn't know the words or didn't hit any tones. They were my absolute favorites."

"Mine too!" She then turns her phone on the table to face her, tapping on the screen for it to light up. "It's almost midnight."

"Five more minutes."

"That's going to be my first ever New Year's kiss," she admits, taking my hand in hers to look at my wrist. She twists the ribbon, looking at it from every possible angle.

"Who says I'll be kissing you?"

Sofia lets go off my hand, letting it fall right down to her body. "Who says I will be kissing *you*?"

Nope. That's it.

The hand she had just held in hers is now pulling on her hair so that her head leans into her neck, forcing Sofia to look up at me. I may be upside down to her, but the possessive, claiming kiss I lay on her lips still gets the message across.

She is *mine*. And mine alone.

My tongue finds into her mouth, brushing hers.

Only when she smiles into the kiss do I eventually let her go again. "Don't say shit like this, Icicle. You'll regret it."

"I will if that means you'll kiss me like this more often."

"Aaron, Sofia!" Lily shrieks. "Let's go outside to watch the fireworks."

I thought we'd just be inside the bar, counting down from ten then scream *Happy New Year* and go back home ten minutes later… apparently, I was wrong.

So now we're standing outside, me keeping Sofia in my arms because this woman forgot her jacket inside and is freezing her goddamn skin off. And she keeps wondering why I nicknamed her icicle. She literally *is* one.

Eventually we can hear the people inside the bar start to count down from ten, I hope. Somehow, I keep forgetting they speak a whole other language here.

Anyway, Colin and I join in starting at eight because we were confused at first. Lily and Sofia follow suit.

Fireworks keep going off although we have five seconds left, but there are always some stupid people wherever you are in the world.

"Three!" we yell.

"Two!"

"One!"

While Colin and Lily yell out "Happy New Year", I already have my lips attached to Sofia's.

The night sky gets swamped with firework after firework, and the entire street is suddenly filled with people that just came out of their houses to light up even more fireworks on the street, small ones, bigger ones, every possible firework imaginable.

"Happy New Year, my love," I whisper into Sofia's ear, waiting until she has said it back before my lips are back on hers for another New Year's kiss, because, why the hell not?

CHAPTER 49

"*'cause without you, babe, I lose my way*"—*Falling Like The Stars* by James Arthur

Sofia

"CAN YOU NOT LEAVE YOUR CLOTHES all over the living room?" Winter says as she barges into my bedroom, throwing my jacket at me.

We've been back in New City for a week now, and with every passing day, this woman gets more annoying.

Being back here also means that I no longer see Aaron every day, but he texts me… hourly. Well, I do see him daily, either because we eat lunch together or at hockey practice when Lily and I watch Brooklyn for Miles. But we no longer sleep in one bed together. At least not unless he spends the night here or I spend the night at his house, which hasn't happened yet.

I get it, though. I wouldn't want to spend a day in this dorm room either, if I had any other choice. Winter is a pain in my goddamn ass, worse than my pedophilic uncle. Yes, I said it. She is worse than *him*.

"You always leave your stuff *everywhere*. Are you a hoarder or something?"

She irritates me, a lot. I always thought I was good at finding

words to say or know what someone is about to say but with her…
I just don't ever know.

"You do know that a hoarder isn't the right term, right?" Plus,
I left my jacket hanging by the coatrack, not anywhere else around
the living space, so what the hell is she on about?

"Doesn't matter. You are annoying me with your dirtiness."

"My… What?"

"So now you don't even understand English. Just great." Winter
inhales deeply, then repeats what she had said *very* slowly.

"I did understand what you said, Winter. I *am* from New City.
I was *born* here. I speak English fluently. You just don't make
fucking *sense*." God, please, let me go back in time. Preferably to
the beginning of whenever Aaron and I became just that; an *us*, we.

"You are a horrible person," she mutters under her breath, then
has the audacity to look around my room like she hasn't been
snooping around while I was gone for a little over two weeks. "You
got a lot of pictures of Aaron. You've got a crush on my boyfriend?"

I almost laugh right into her face at that. "*Your* boyfriend?"

"Yes."

"You are delusional, Winter Varley." And I absolutely stand by
that. How in the world has Lily managed to share a space with this
woman since freshman year? I barely made it a full month in total,
and I would rather sleep on the streets than spend another day in
her presence.

"What? You think you're his girlfriend?" She laughs, once.
"Honey, you do know Aaron only hangs around you because of a
bet, right?"

"Once you're done talking bullshit, close the door when you
leave."

She takes a step deeper into my room. "You don't believe me?"

"I don't ever believe a word you say." Can she just let me get
back to my assignment? Doesn't she have her own schoolwork to
do anyway?

My phone chimes, and while Winter keeps babbling about that

stupid bet she just made up, I check my messages.

Aaron: I can't sleep, my brain won't stop thinking about you.

I smile to myself, quickly shaking that smile off my face because what the actual fuck? I do *not* smile at messages from anyone. Ever.

Sofia: Aw, miss me?

Aaron: Nah. But your cute butt rubbing against me when I try to fall asleep, that I do miss.

Aaron: Also, I was thinking about something else…

Sofia: Oh, no. Nothing good ever comes from that one.

Aaron: Listen here my little ketchup packet. I will literally come over right now to shove a pillow into your face if you say that shit ever again.

Sofia: Little ketchup packet? What?

Aaron: Yup. That's your new nickname now for whenever you're on your devils week. You better learn to love it.

It's a genuine sport trying to understand how his mind works. His new nickname for me sits a little heavy in my heart, but I suppose I can get used to it.

At least it's only a once-a-month kind of thing.

Sofia: Hold on. Winter is talking to me.

"Can you just leave, my God. Do you need me to spell it out for you or something?" I snap when she sits down beside me and tries to look at my screen.

What is her damn problem with me? I don't walk around here marching into her room to speak to her either, so why the fuck would she do that to me? Come to think Winter doesn't just hate me, she envies me for some unknown reasons.

Alright, maybe not all too unknown, but like, just give it up already. By now, she should have gotten the hint that Aaron and her will *never* happen.

"Have you listened to anything I just said?"

"I have not." Nor will I ever listen to what she says.

Seriously, the entire building could be on fire, and I would not believe a thing that came out of her mouth, let alone even *hear* it. She's tuned out, constantly.

"You're digging your own grave with this one, Sophie. I am telling you." She gets up from my bed, walking toward the door.

Jokes on her, I already have my grave dug.

As soon as the door closes behind her, my eyes are back on the screen.

Aaron: I told Lily it would be a bad idea letting you stay with Winter.

Aaron: She's jealous I have a way better and deeper relationship with you than I ever had with her.

Sofia: Already figured that one out two seconds after I moved in.

I wish I was lying, but I'm not.

From the second I stepped foot in this dorm room with Aaron by my side, she has hated me. The disgusted looks I've had to put up with was only a small indicator.

Sofia: Anyway, what were you thinking about?

Aaron: Never mind. Already figured it out.

Chapter 50

"no one ever makes me feel like you do when you smile"—
Nobody Compares by One Direction

Aaron

I DIDN'T THINK I'D BE BACK AT the dorms any time soon. At least not by the time I helped Sofia move in here. Now, I cannot deny I would be back here all day every day if that meant I could see my girlfriend.

Unfortunately, Winter is also here, and I just bet everyone in the building can hear because this woman is screaming so loudly, I can hear it the second I exit my car.

This is bad. Really bad.

Storming inside the building, I almost reach their room in no time. Must be my new record, for sure.

I bang on the door, waiting for someone to open it. I'm more or less surprised when Winter opens the door instead of Sofia, but I couldn't care less anyway. Someone opened the door, that's all I needed to get inside.

"What the hell are you screaming for?" I ask Winter, walking inside the room without asking for permission. I have my girl-friend's, that's enough.

"Well, if you didn't bring your new fuck buddy into the same room as me, maybe I wouldn't be yelling," Winter answers, crossing her arms over her chest.

I sigh, pinching the bridge of my nose. "She's not my fuck buddy."

"Well, have you told her that? Because she insists you are together which would be totally absurd."

Seriously, how could I ever think Winter was a good fill-in for the void in my heart? She isn't. Yeah, sex with her was great, but the couple of months we've been in a relationship...? How did I survive those?

"You're not dating her, are you, Aaron?" Winter's hands are now on her hips, her chest pushed out like she's trying to stand her ground, being the dominant person.

"I am."

"What the *fuck*, Aaron!" I can hear a door open, which must be Sofia's then, clearly having heard Winter talking to me. "You told me you weren't going to start anything."

"I never said that." Maybe in her dreams, but I know for sure those words would have never left my mouth, ever.

Winter could have promised me a million dollars and I still would have stood with my hopes; if there is a chance for me to be with Sofia, I will jump on it.

"Sure you did. Remember the bet we made? When I said you wouldn't be able to hook up with Sofia without catching feelings." Her eyebrows rise as the smuggest smile known to humanity appears on her lips. "When she moved in here, remember that? We talked in my room, and we started this bet."

I exhale deeply, bringing both of my hands to either side of my head, rubbing my temples. I spot Sofia standing in the door to the living room, leaning against the frame. Her eyes are on me, and for once I have no idea what she is thinking.

Does she believe Winter? I sure hope she doesn't because none of the shit she is saying is remotely true.

"You *threw* your stuff at me, Winter." I swear to everything holy, if Winter is going to be the reason Sofia and I will break up, she can go find herself a cozy coffin to spend all of eternity in. "Don't make up a ridiculous lie because you don't like seeing me with someone that isn't you."

"I am not lying!"

"Fuck this, Winter." I storm past her, grasping my girlfriend's hand in mine and pulling her back into her own bedroom.

Sofia closes the door as I let go of her hand and make my way over to her bed, needing to take a seat and just breathe for a second.

This is why I don't do girlfriends or fuck buddies. Hookups, sure, it's one time and forgotten, but everything that goes beyond that… I should have never even entertained Winter's ridiculous friends with benefits proposal years ago. Worst decision I have ever made in my entire life.

"Sofia, I swear to you, I have *never* made any bets with Winter," I finally say when she walks over to me, her arms finding around my neck when she takes a seat on my lap instead of the bed space next to me.

She lifts my face to hers, smiling. "I am not going to discuss this with you, Aaron."

"But—"

Sofia shakes her head, covering my mouth with her hand. "I do not believe a word she says. And I'd be surprised if you had a bet with her going about not catching feelings for me, because you lost that one at the age of eight."

My arms sneak around her waist, pulling her so close to me, I fear I might squeeze her to death, but she isn't complaining, so I don't bother losing my grip.

In a moment like this, I do wonder how I have gone through life without her by my side. We've always had a connection, that much I am sure about. I just never understood how deep this connection could go, until I'm in her arms, relieved that she doesn't believe whatever my crazy ex-girlfriend had to say.

If I had lost Sofia because of a lie… I wouldn't know how to ever recover from that.

Having lost her once broke me. Losing her again will destroy me.

"By any chance, did you happen to bring some chocolate?"

Sighing deeply in faked defeat, I reach one hand into the pocket of my jacket, pulling out the same kind of chocolate bar she had wanted to buy when she first got to New City in October. "You already know I did, my little ketchup packet."

After handing it to her, I reach into my pocket one more time, pulling out a pack of tampons. "I figured it wouldn't hurt getting these too."

Sofia is quick to turn one of her hands into finger guns, holding them up to my temple. "Any last words before I murder you?"

My jaw drops a little. "Here I thought I was being a great boyfriend and you want to kill me?" Girlfriends these days… can never make them happy. "I do have some last words."

"Yeah? Better spit them out fast."

"I lo—" She hits the imaginary trigger.

Alright, I'll play.

I fall back on her bed, pulling her down with me. The package in my hand falls down to the floor, making for a super dramatic death.

My eyes close and I hold my breath for a whole five seconds before I rip open my eyes again, drawing in a deep breath like I was swimming up after being two whole minutes underwater.

"Kidding, didn't hit me," I say, clamming my arms around Sofia's body like some clamshell, not planning on ever letting her go again. "I have a bulletproof brain. It bounced right off."

She laughs, once again to the point where these cute chubby cheeks start to show.

God, please let this be the last thing I see before I die.

CHAPTER 51

"I always thought I would sink, so I never swam"—Malibu by Miley Cyrus

MY HANDS ARE SHAKING as I stand in front of the house. The same one I ran away from years ago.

I promised myself I would face it. My fears. My past.

I want the future I've been promised. I want to grow old with Aaron, marry him in a couple of years and start a family. I want all this, but I know I will never have it if I cannot face what I ran away from first.

It's easy staying in a city that seems to only have your walls cave in, at least when there is one thing that keeps you there. But I don't want to be a burden to Aaron in the future.

For now, it's fine. I can breathe without feeling like I am choking on air. But what will happen in ten years? What will happen in a few years, when I find out the only grandmother I have left has passed away?

Once she is dead, I will never find closure. I will never get answers to questions I'm not sure I have. Maybe one, but even just one question can change a person's whole view on the world.

I refuse to promise Aaron forever when I cannot even promise

177t

myself not to run away when going gets tough.

Taking a deep breath, I lift my fist to knock but somehow my stupid knuckles just won't touch the wood to make a sound. And when I try to ring the doorbell, my finger refuses to hit the button.

I am supposed to be at my boyfriend's hockey game in two hours. If I keep standing here not doing anything, I won't be anywhere near his game in time.

Suck it up, Sofia.

"Easier said than done." Great, and now I am talking to myself.

Not having knocked yet, my breath gets lost in my lungs when the front door suddenly opens and an elderly woman with grey hair looks up at me.

She looks a little lost, her eyes moving from left to right, up and down trying to place me anywhere.

"Sofia…" My grandma brings a shaking hand to her mouth, covering it. "Oh, dear."

Her eyes begin to water, an unknown pain stabbing me right in the heart at the sight.

"Come in, dearest, please." She steps aside, a little wobbly on her feet but she has always been ever since I can remember.

I shake my head a little too automatically. Standing outside of the house it all happened is one thing but entering is a whole other topic.

"I'd rather not." Does that seem mean? I hope not. My grandmother must understand that standing here is probably the hardest thing I have done in almost a decade. Apart from, you know, killing my grandfather. Though, maybe that was less difficult as I didn't intent to murder him.

"You came all this way, Sofia." More or less a long one considering that I am currently a student at St. Trewery University, but she doesn't know that. "Please, do come inside. I won't bite you, dear."

I mean, there is still a chance that she hates me and only wants me to come inside to poison me and watch me die, but sure.

She wouldn't do that, right? She is my grandma still, even after what I have done.

"Alright."

One tiny step at a time, I walk into the house, breathing in the familiar scent of home and love I was met with whenever we came to visit when I was younger.

The house hasn't changed much. The half cupboard in the corridor still has the same dent it always had. Not always, but from whenever I was six years old, and my brother and I decided to play hide and seek in the dark. I ended up walking into the coatrack, which then fell and put a dent into the wood of the half cupboard.

I wasn't in trouble for it, despite thinking I'd get the beating of my life.

The walls are covered with pictures of my siblings and I, my cousins and aunt and uncles, even pictures of my father when he was younger, or my parents' wedding day.

And then there are a few family photos with my grandpa. As much as I want to look at them, I can't bring myself to do it, so I walk past them a little quicker.

I follow my grandma into the living room, closing my eyes as I have to walk past the stairs. She must have noticed because when my eyes open again, she smiles at me a little, but at least she doesn't comment on it.

When she sits, my grandma gestures for me to do the same. For once I do without hesitating. Being turned away from the stairs will at least give me some peace. Not a lot, but a little, maybe? It will keep me from bursting into tears any second.

Or maybe not, we'll see.

"Can I get you a glass of water, Sofia, dearest?" I shake my head, doubting I could down *anything* right now. "Alright. So tell me, how have you been? You haven't come to visit much in the last couple of years, I was wondering when I'd see you again."

Come to visit? I didn't even speak to her in years all because I felt too guilty to do so.

Even now I am not sure if I should tell my grandmother all about me when I came here for closure. Or at least trying to understand why my family hasn't abandoned me yet.

So, instead of answering the question I've been asked, I say, "Are you not in the slightest mad at me?"

Chapter 52

"don't tell me that it's over, the book of you and I"—The Book of You & I by Alec Benjamin

Aaron

THE GAME'S GOING RELATIVELY SMOOTH.

Parker, our goalie, hasn't let a lot of pucks in, if any. The opponent's goalie, however, he seems to be having a bad day.

Nate isn't a bad goalie. I know because I've spent hours watching tapes and analyzing the *Red Hut's* moves. He has skills, so what the hell happened?

Every other puck my team shoots goes in the net. It should make me happy that we're winning, but at what costs? Winning because the opponents have a shitty day and gave up just isn't the same.

By the time the third period starts, my team is in the lead by 16-2. Honestly, we could just end the game right fucking now, it's not like they're going to catch up with us.

I was excited to be back in the game, but if I had known this game would be like playing against toddlers, I would have pretended to be sick or something.

Since I am forced to be on the ice for the last five minutes, I decide to skate in circles. Yes, that's how boring this godawful game is.

Passing opponents with a sympatric smile and nodding at them like we're here for a coffee date. They know they suck today, everyone knows, so there is no use to deny it. At least they take their loss with pride. I mean, it's quite the achievement, right?

For the last two minutes, I decide to just look for Sofia in the audience, not even caring when the puck zooms past me. At this point it's just getting kicked around to pass the time, so why bother?

It takes me a whole twenty seconds until I find Lily… by herself. Sofia was supposed to be with her, watch Brooke like they do for every game. She couldn't have known Miles wasn't going to show up today and that's why she didn't come, so where the hell is my girlfriend at?

I pound against the tempered glass, trying to catch my sister's attention. She's busy scrolling through her phone.

It takes me a whole three hits until she eventually looks up. I nod toward the free seat next to her, she shrugs, knowing exactly what I am asking.

Alright, so Lily hasn't heard from Sofia? That is totally not a reason to freak out. Maybe she fell asleep. Let's not overreact here.

As the timer runs out and the sound of sirens going off shrills through the arena, it's to nobody's surprise when St. Trewery won. In record time, everyone leaves the ice, just wanting to get back home because this was a waste of time here tonight.

Walking into the locker room, I sprint toward my locker, open my bag, and take out my phone to check if maybe Sofia has texted me with an excuse as to why she couldn't come. But there is nothing.

I send her text after text, but none of them even say delivered, they're all pending. And when I call, I get send straight to voicemail.

"Grey!" I yell out the second he steps inside the room, stopping in his tracks with a shocked face. "You heard anything from Sofia?"

He always knows everything, so there is a chance. "No?" Grey comes walking toward me, sitting down by his locker across from mine. "Isn't she with your sister?"

I shake my head, fighting the urge to throw my phone against the nearest wall.

Now, I know I may be overreacting despite saying I shouldn't, but something just feels off.

I can't describe the feeling, but it's like I know there is something wrong. Sofia doesn't just *not* show up when she said she would. She would have called me or send a text, and if not me, she would have told Lily. If neither Lily knows where Sofia's at, nor I do, then this isn't normal.

Today of all days I have decided to not take my car here and caught a ride with Grey, so I can't even storm off and get to her dorm to see if she's there.

"What the fuck was that?" Kaiden asks just the second he enters the locker room together with Zac and Colin.

"I almost fell asleep on the ice," Colin adds, laughing. "I'll try to find out what happened and let you assholes know." He stops by his locker, immediately stripping off his clothes to go take a shower. Only that the second his eyes land on my face, he halts mid taking off his shirt. "You good?"

"Sofia is missing," Grey says for me when I don't speak and only stare at my best friend. He then pats a hand on my shoulder. "Or so he believes."

She *is* missing. What else would she be? Certainly not have been abducted by aliens.

"Missing?" Colin makes sure he heard that right. "Like she got kidnapped or something?"

"No, dickhead. She isn't responding to any of my texts or calls. Not even Lily knows where the hell she's at!"

Colin lets his shirt fall again, sighing. "So you think she ran off, just like that?"

Do I? It wouldn't be the first time that Sofia disappeared out of my life without giving me a heads-up first. Sure, I knew she was leaving for four years... but even after those four years, she never showed up, never even let me know she wouldn't come back. So is it that wrong of me to think she might have left without saying a word?

"I doubt it," Kaiden says, like he has any clue what has been happening in my life over the break. Maybe he does. Everyone has been sending pictures of their holidays and such in our team group chat. Plus, we always have the other's location and know of everyone's plans. "Everyone knows you guys are like crazy in love."

"Even the blindest, most dense person can see that," Zac adds.

I wave at them dismissively. This isn't about me being in love with Sofia, it's about me not knowing what is going on and her just being... gone. Unreachable.

Okay, and maybe it's a little about my fear of her leaving me again as well.

"Can I take a shower before you make me speed us back home?" Grey asks, already having a towel thrown over his shoulder.

This is ridiculous.

Sofia is an adult, surely, she wouldn't just run away again, she's better than that. Maybe her phone just ran out and she's stuck in traffic. You know, with the car that she does not have.

Why does my heart feel so heavy? I don't understand. I know I have been in love with Sofia for a whole while, but why does this feel like an end?

CHAPTER 53

"and I lost you and I lost my mind"—Turn Back Time by Daniel Schulz

Sofia

"AND YOU HAVE BEEN STAYING with Nicole and that…"

I nod, chuckling softly. "Her pedophilic boyfriend? Yeah, unfortunately."

"I cannot believe she is still seeing him," my grandmother says, letting out a long sigh while picking up her teacup.

My Grandma and I have been talking for a while now, I'm not sure how long exactly, but enough for me to get more and more comfortable with the second. She's asked me so many questions about what I've been up to, what it's like for me living in Germany, whether it was difficult to learn German or not.

She's also told me all about her elderly neighbor that keeps stopping by every morning to bring her some fresh milk because she once told him she preferred the fresh one over these packaged milk containers. I thought it's cute, in some ways.

We still haven't gotten to why I suddenly showed up here, but I'm not exactly upset about it either. Just having a short while with my grandma, talking to her like nothing ever happened is something I might never get ever again, so I will take every moment I can.

Oh, she has also told me about how Keith, the elderly neighbor, has fixed the fence in the front yard for my grandma. Apparently, my grandfather wanted to do that but, well, he never got to do it.

I thought this might be a great chance to ask her why she's not mad at me for pushing her husband down the stairs, but then she changed the topic and talked about her newest addition to her flowerbed. She has started growing lilacs because they reminded her of me, and since she never got to hear from me ever, it was all she had left of me. After telling me this, she even asked if I still liked them or if she has to find another flower to keep alive.

My heart was doing all sorts of things when she said this. Mostly hurt.

The tears in my eyes are threatening to swell over with every new topic she starts to talk about, especially the ones that remind her of me and how I used to always come around the house to help her bake cookies on Saturdays.

Between you and me, I only ever wanted to bake cookies because I knew I'd see Aaron the next day, and I tried to impress him with my baking skills. It didn't work, but still, I tried every week again.

"Your boyfriend," my grandma starts, a small smile tugging on her lips as she speaks, "is he the little boy you always liked when you were younger?"

"He is," I confirm. It's kind of weird how life turns out. Sometimes one door closes and another opens. Other times one door closes, and ten doors open, making you choose. Then you choose the wrong one, and for a while your life seems great, but it turns into one big mess because that door wasn't for you. So now you somehow have to find back through the chaos to the door that was supposed to be yours.

I think Aaron and my relationship was part of that whole choosing-the-wrong-door escapade. But, hey, years later and I finally found the right one.

"So, is he finally taller than you are?"

I chuckle, nodding.

For a short time, Aaron was shorter than me, and I always made fun of him for that. Even Lily used to be taller than him, but he still always insisted he was the tallest. He was the whiniest little boy known to human history, that's what he was.

Anyway, no more beating around the bush.

Inhaling deeply, I finally rush out a couple of words that could lead to a very bad ending to all of this. "Listen, Grams…" My lips tremble when I speak, but I push through. "I actually came here to speak with you about something else."

She nods like she knows. "Figured," she says with a smile. "You brought flowers to your grandfathers grave."

Okay, how?

There could have been at least a million different other things I wanted to say, how would she know it is my grandfather I want to discuss?

"I… Yes. But I wasn't going to say that." Here goes absolutely nothing, nor will here go anything if I keep rambling and not saying what I have to say.

"I know, Sofia." She leans forward, reaching a hand over the small coffee table to grasp mine. "You're not as secretive with your motives as you think you are."

"What?"

"Dear, I've always known when you were upset. And I admit, for a while when you were ignoring me, I thought it was because you were upset with *me*, when I should have known you were upset with *yourself* all along."

Upset with myself? That's quite an understatement. I *loathe* myself for what I have done to my family, to her, to my very own grandfather.

How could she say I am *upset* when I had wished to exchange my place with my grandfather's since the day he has passed?

I am not suicidal, but if there would have been a chance, I could've brought him back to life in exchange for my own, I would have taken it rather than live with the guilt of having killed him by accident.

The tears in my eyes become too much and swell over, one after the other running down my cheeks faster than I thought they would. Even when I wipe them away, they keep on coming.

"Oh, Sofia," my grandmother sighs with sympathy, carefully forcing herself to get up from her seat. She walks over to me, sitting down beside me. "There is no need for you to cry."

I shouldn't do this, and yet I wrap my arms around her. My shoulders shake as I sob, tears falling onto her shirt, but she doesn't tell me to move, instead, her arms come around my body, holding me.

"How are you so…" I gasp for air, my breath shaking. "How are you still willing to speak to me?"

Her hand strokes through the length of my hair before eventually feeling up the bow on the back of my head. "Why wouldn't I, Sofia?"

"Because I killed your *husband*?" I break away from the hug, scooting a little over on the couch to bring some space between us.

I barely have enough courage to look my grandma in her eyes, but I do so anyway. Facing my trauma means *facing* it. I don't start shit and then back out; I pull through with it.

When our eyes meet, she looks horrified. It's like she has no idea what I am talking about. But she should, she was there. I mean, alright, she didn't *see* me push my grandpa down the stairs but I'm sure my father has told her.

"Your grandpa died because of a heart failure, Sofia. What are you talking about?"

A heart failure? No. No, that can't be. I specifically remember him grabbing on to my shoulder, holding on to me when I wanted to run upstairs. I kicked around myself and could only listen to the painfilled groans before he let go of my shirt and fell.

There is no way I made that up.

"He fell. There was blood everywhere. I kicked him and he fell."

"He fell because he had a heart attack. The autopsy confirmed it. Your grandpa was sick, had a weak heart. We didn't know how long it would take until he could finally rest, but we were all aware of it happening sometime soonish," she says, laying a hand on my leg. "You were twelve, honey, even if you had kicked him down the stairs, it would have been an accident. You are not a bad person, sweetie. Especially not a murderer."

So… she's telling me I ran away from my home, my friends and family for nothing? I felt guilty for something that has never been my fault in the first place?

Either she's lying to make me feel better, or my parents have done a shitshow of a job to console me.

CHAPTER 54

***"it's like a knife that cuts right through my soul"—Only
Love Can Hurt Like This – Slowed Down Version by
Paloma Faith***

Aaron

IT'S TWO HOURS LATER when I finally get home.

Sofia still hasn't reached out. Grey has brought me to the dorms first to check if she might be asleep, but she wasn't there. Neither were her belongings.

Winter told me Sofia moved out and back to wherever she came from, which could only mean her aunt, but when I got there and asked Nicole if Sofia was there, I've been told she hasn't seen Sofia ever since she moved to the dorms.

I must have sent her millions of texts, none of which went through to her. If I haven't already been freaking out, I sure as hell would be now.

Though, when Grey parks the car in front of my house—he usually does and walks over to his house through the backyard we share—and I get out, I almost choke on my breath when I find Sofia sitting on the steps to the house. She's got her suitcases next to her, looking almost identical to when I first saw her in the grocery store the day she arrived.

"What the fuck, Sofia!" I shouldn't yell, but it just comes right out of me anyway. "Do you know what kind of fucking heart attack you gave m—" My words die out when I notice she's crying.

In less than a heartbeat, I drop my bag and I'm kneeled in front of her, holding her face in my hands as I wipe away the tears. The thought of her having gone missing for hours disappearing like it was never there.

"What happened?"

Grey walks past us, not saying a word but even if he did, I'm not sure I would have paid any attention to it. What's important is finding out why my girlfriend is sitting on the steps to my house with her suitcases, crying.

The front door closes after Grey walks into the house, giving us some privacy.

"I went to see my grandma," she says, her voice almost a whisper.

I guess that would be a step forward… if it weren't for Sofia's suitcases. Yes, I admit, these stupid silver suitcases give me major anxiety.

"Okay?"

Her breath comes out weakly as she exhales. "I have to talk to my dad, Aaron."

"In person?"

She nods, breaking out in sobs. I fall to my knees, not caring whether the stone would rip my pants or not when I pull Sofia in for a tight hug.

This is goodbye, isn't it? She's here to tell me she has to leave, and she won't return.

"Listen…" She tries to break apart from the hug, but I'm not letting her. If this is the last time, I'll ever get to hold her, then I won't let her go before it is truly necessary. "Aaron, I love you."

My arms tighten at her words, my heart aching regardless of me having thought it would be overfilled with joy when I got to hear her say them for the first time.

Remember when Sofia asked me not to say it to her for the first time on her birthday because it would ruin the day for her after we break up? I now realize, it doesn't matter what day they're said on. Hearing her say this is the best and worst moment in my life, and the day has nothing to do with it.

I will always remember this day as the one she loved me enough to admit to it, and I loved her back, yet it still wasn't enough to keep her.

"I promised you I would try, and this is me trying. I went to see my grandma, talked to her, fought for us," she says. "There are a few other things I have to sort out before I can give myself to you. I think there might have been a huge misunderstanding between me and my father, and I couldn't live with myself if I didn't fix this before it's too late to do so."

I let her go, sit down on the concrete, and just look at her through the dark as hot tears roll down my cheeks. It takes a lot for me to cry, apparently saying goodbye to Sofia is one of the rare things that get the better of me.

She gets up just as a car stops behind me. Sofia grabs her suitcases, making her way past me. Only that she doesn't get very far because I grasp her wrist in my hand, holding her back.

Her eyes are red from crying, and I hate the sight more than losing a game.

"I need you to promise me something, Sofia." Usually I am the one to make promises, but this time I really do need her to give me her word. "I need you to promise me that you won't move on."

She looks away from me, avoiding my eyes but her hand stays in mine. Maybe she doesn't notice it, but I sure do when Sofia interlocks our fingers and squeezes my hand.

"Promise me you won't try to forget me and try to find someone else to fill in my space." If she means what she said, that she loves me, this shouldn't be that big of a deal, right?

"Aaron…" When she looks at me again, it's almost like looking at a whole different Sofia. This one is sad and broken, unlike the one I know. Or maybe this is the real her, the one that has been fighting demons for too long and is finally starting to breathe fresh air again.

Either way, I don't need Sofia to be fixed, I don't need her healed and unbroken. I only want *her*. With the broken parts and everything.

I get up from the floor, still holding her hand in mine. My eyes find to her hand, my thumb stroking over her cold knuckles.

"Please," I beg, looking up to meet her gaze, "I wouldn't be able to take it. When I come look for you in eight weeks and find out you're in a relationship with someone that isn't me, I don't think my heart could survive that. It will crush me, Sofia. Because in my story, you were never meant to be with anyone but me. I cannot allow some fucked up plot twist and even more misery to happen to us. We both need a happy ending, and we deserve it. So please, I am begging you, don't rewrite what we have with someone else."

Sofia takes a step closer to me, bringing her other hand to my face as she gets up on her tiptoes to plant the softest of kiss right to the corner of my mouth. "I never said this was a goodbye, Aaron. But now, I will be expecting you to come find me and give me all the reasons why I should move back here for you."

Chapter 55

"I'm so sick and tired / of feeling sick and tired"—I THINK I'M LOST AGAIN by Chase Atlantic

Aaron

"SUCK IT UP, DUDE," Miles says as he seats himself beside me. "She said it wasn't a goodbye."

It's been a week since Sofia left, and all I did was sulk and drink myself to oblivion.

I never said this was a goodbye, then why does it feel like one?

She doesn't even respond to my texts. I mean, she reads them but apparently responding takes up too much of her time.

"Have you ever been in love?" I lean my head against Miles's shoulder, and maybe if I weren't as drunk as I am, I would have been smarter than to ask *him* this.

He brings an arm around me, patting me on my shoulder. "You do know I have a daughter, right?"

"Mhm. But Brooke wasn't planned, so that doesn't guarantee you were in love with Millie. And you're not in love with your wife either."

"Alright." I hear Colin chuckle just before he's in my face and takes my beer away from me. "Think you've had enough."

"Nah," I say, "I think I could use another beer." Or another five.

I don't even like beer, tastes like piss. Colin walks away with my beer in his hands, ignoring me wanting another one. Fuck him, nobody needs Colin anyway.

That's not true, love that man. But fuck him anyway.

"So, Miles, how'd you get over Millie?" I look at him with half-opened eyes, barely even seeing him though. He's all blurry and I'm not exactly sure why.

"Ah, well, you know, she died." He snaps his fingers against my forehead, and I fall back on the couch like an old sack of potatoes. "Took some time to adjust."

"Then you fucked her twin sister," I comment, then immediately slap a hand to my face. Not because I regret saying it though. "Miles-y has a type."

"I dated Em even before I was with Millie, Aaron."

"Like I said, you've got a type. Blondes with green eyes." I gape at him at the realization. "Do you have a thing for my sister?" If he does, I'm sure Colin won't like hearing about it.

Miles sighs deeply, shaking his head.

"For me then?"

"I don't like dicks."

"Good, because I really don't like you that way man. Like, I love you, but I definitely love Sofia way more. And I—"

"Shut up, Aaron." Grey laughs, laying his hand on my shoulder as he stands in front of me. "You'll regret all the shit you're saying right now."

Probably, yet I ignore him anyway and turn back to look at Miles. "Do you miss Millie? Because I feel like I will never not miss Sofia. And she is alive." *Just shut up, Aaron. You're not helping anything.*

He hesitates to answer, his head slightly tilting. Miles doesn't talk about Millie much. To be fair, neither of us knows her personally, only from what he did tell us about her.

Alright, *I* know Millie, because my sister used to be friends with her but other than that, not a clue who she was as a person.

"Aaron, stop bothering Miles. He's got enough shit going."

Grey pulls me off the couch, hooking an arm around me to lead me away from my fellow blond friend.

"But he hasn't answered me yet."

"She is *dead*. Of course he misses her." He leads me around the couches, making the room spin like a merry go round.

Can he stop making the room spin? It really makes me want to puke.

Then, out of nowhere, my head snaps back around to look at Miles. "Where is Brooke anyway?" Maybe I'm blind, but I don't see her around, nor do I *hear* her being here. She's always giggling or making some noises to make her presence known.

I love her little giggles, they're so pure and pain-free.

Why do humans grow up and their laughter's automatically no longer honest? Why do we have to suffer when nobody even asked us to be on earth anyway?

And why the hell am I becoming a philosopher?

"She's with Emory so I can be here and help our friends take care of your drunk ass," Miles answers.

Hm. Checks out.

"Do you miss Izan?" I slurp on my words, feeling my head pounding a little.

Grey shakes his head at me, I think? Could be the room spinning, too.

"I'll take it from here," my sister says, coming up behind me as Grey and I reach the stairs.

"You sure? He'll be a pain in the ass to get upstairs."

"Why am I going upstairs?" I ask, almost falling into my sister's arms.

"Because it's late and you should go to sleep," Grey tells me. But he is lying because it is still light outside. Not daylight-light but enough to see the streets still, and the trees and sky and everything.

Whatever, right? Maybe catching some sleep will do me good. Though, probably not because the second I close my eyes, all I see is Sofia. She is everywhere, haunting me.

Lily leads me into my bedroom, right over to my bed so I can fall down on it with a huff.

So now I lie here, my legs dangling down the side of my bed while I stare at my blurry ceiling with stupid salty tears just casually leaving my eyes like I gave it permission to do so.

The mattress slightly dips next to me as Lily takes a seat. "It's only seven more weeks until graduation," she says, taking my hand in hers.

"Seven too many."

What does it change if I fly to Germany and get my Sofia back now or in eight weeks? Alright, seven, now that one has passed already. What does Sofia need eight weeks for? Talking to her father shouldn't take this long.

Right—she didn't even give me a specific time period in which she'd be back, or I could come visit her. I made that time up because when she said she'd leave, in my head, I knew I'd be coming for her the second I'm free to leave the U.S., no longer bound to school.

"You're whinier than I was when I wanted to kill myself."

I laugh, once. One little "Ha", like what she said was the unfunniest of funniest things I have ever heard. And maybe it is. She may joke about her depression, but to anyone that loves her, it's more like a mini heart attack every single time she jokes about it.

"Because you have room to talk," I mutter under my breath. "Your boyfriend didn't run away from you."

"Sofia didn't run away from you either, Ron. She is trying to fix her life and become someone you can love without her making it unnecessarily difficult."

"But I already love her," I groan. "I love her, Lily." I sit up a little too fast, my head spinning like crazy, but I don't care enough to lie back down. I look at Lily, my lungs fighting for air when all I take are shallow breaths. My voice small and quiet when I repeat, "I love her…"

"I know you do." She rests our hands on her lap, her eyes staying on the ribbon around my wrist. "That Sofia's?"

I look down, blinking a couple of times to make my eyes focus on the wisteria fabric. "She loves this stupid ribbon." I groan in pain. Not physical pain, the shit that's invading my heart. "Why do I feel like this, Lils?"

"Because you drank a little too much and your girlfriend is kind of an ocean away."

Like I didn't know that. Can't she just gaslight me into believing I'm alright? "Thanks for making all this more depressing."

"Aaron, you will be all right. You'll stay sad for a while but it's going to be forgotten the moment you see her again."

"I'd rather be angry." Anger seems less painful. I could be mad that Sofia just left me, and I have no idea if she's ever coming back. Sure, she said it wasn't a goodbye, but that still doesn't guarantee me she will be back *here*.

In addition, she could at least answer my goddamn texts. Perhaps that would be enough to stop me from crying like a baby.

"You don't. Anger is basically sadness in fight-mode."

"You seemed to prefer anger to sadness." I raise my eyebrows at her, or one. Maybe I don't even raise one. I'm not sure how much control of my own facial features I have at this point.

"Yeah, because I was suicidal and needed my feelings to stop in order to keep myself alive. It was exhausting to be angry at everyone and everything." She gets up from my bed, letting go of my hand as well. "Sadness is a bitch that pulls you under water, expecting you to be able to breathe. Anger just likes to hurt everyone around and yourself. Anger makes you forget whereas sadness lets you feel. I'd rather be sad than feel nothing at all, and so should you."

Lily makes her way to my door, ready to leave. Only as she reaches the door do her words finally settle in.

Perhaps she's right.

"Lils?" I call out louder than expected. Her hand halts on the doorknob. She turns around, waiting. "Did you talk to her?"

She nods. "Yesterday."

"Is she okay?"

"As okay as it gets. She misses you, Aaron. It's not easy for her either, but I bet you know as much as I do that Sofia *needs* to figure out her situation before there could ever be a chance for you two getting a happily ever after." Lily smiles at me warmly, maybe sympatric even. "You've gone thirteen years without talking to Sofia, I think you will survive eight more weeks."

"Seven."

"Seven then."

Chapter 56

"all that time just thrown away"—love, death and distrac- tion by EDEN

"SOFIA!"

I can't help but roll my eyes at her voice. I truly believe my sister has the most annoying voice in the entire universe.

"Did you take your last exam yet?"

"Just this morning." Not that she cares. Julia is counting down the days until I graduate so I can move out. Though, she is twenty-eight years old, still living at home and wanting to get rid of me? If she's so sick of me, how about *she* moves out?

"So, when will you know if you passed?" She leans against my doorframe, crossing her arms over her chest.

"I don't know, Julia. In a few days? Weeks?" I was supposed to leave the U.S. by the end of February, well, I left early. I only needed six weeks in an English-speaking country anyway, so it wasn't that big of a problem.

Anyway, me leaving early lead to me also taking my final exam earlier than planned. Again, it doesn't really matter. Germany doesn't have much of a graduation party. Once you passed, you passed. That's it. No party, no fancy ceremony.

So I could have waited another month or two to take my exam, but why should I? I was ready to take it, plus I wanted to clear my head a little.

For the past four weeks, I've been distracting myself with studying and now that I no longer have something to distract myself with, I think I'm ready to face my father.

I wanted to do so the second I was back here, but I needed a break. Finding out I was hating on myself for murdering my grandpa when it was never my fault in the first place was more than a big pill to swallow. It's why I needed to leave Aaron for a while as well.

I knew if I stayed for the month still, I would have been nothing but a burden as my emotions were all over the place. I simply couldn't do that to him, especially not with scouts still coming to his hockey games and him having to study for his finals etcetera. He needed as much of a break from me as I did from him for the time being.

It broke my heart having to leave him, and I admit, I did spend the first week back here in my bedroom, crying my entire heart and soul out, but like I told him, this wasn't a goodbye.

But now that I am done with figuring out what to say to my father and being done with university, it's about time I get this shit over with.

"Mom said you're thinking about moving into the city. Is the tiny village *you* chose not enough for you anymore?" Julia asks, pouting at me mockingly.

"What the hell is your problem, Julia?" I don't remember one day of her ever having been nice to me. Not *one*.

"You are my problem," she says, laughing ironically. "Ever since you were born it's always about *you*. You didn't want to be back in the U.S., so we moved here for you. Did you ever consider that maybe Lukas and I wanted to be with our family and friends, and yet when you said the word, our parents jumped and did. And you don't even appreciate the sacrifices we made for you."

"You've hated me long before that."

"I never hated you. Not until you turned out to be... this." She gestures toward me. "You've had the best life imaginable, one neither Lukas nor I got. You got to have hobbies from the mere age of two, an expensive one as well. When I was six and wanted to have a stupid ice cream, I've been told we don't have the money for it. Now, imagine my surprise when two years later, you were born and another two later you got to take skating lessons."

How is this my fault though? I didn't know my parents were struggling with money before I was born.

"Don't get me wrong, Sofia, I'm glad you didn't have to grow up being told no to things you wanted because we had no money. The older I got, the more I understood why I've been told no, and you weren't. Though, at ten years old, I sure as hell didn't understand a thing about it. Then we moved for only a couple of years, and even here it was always about you. What we could do to make *you* feel better because you did nothing but cry over Lily and Aaron. Even when *you* ended up wanting to move here for good, you still cried about them when you knew damn well you could have reached out to them."

I couldn't reach out to them because I had no idea if I would ever see them again. Getting in touch with them only to potentially having to say goodbye one more time wasn't worth it. Especially not the pain.

"And then you went and fucked my boyfriend? What was that for? Revenge for being stupid and wanting to stay in Germany?" The words just so happen to spurt out of me without my brain ever consenting to it.

Julia shakes her head. "He was *cheating* on you, Sofia. You really think I would have been stupid enough to fuck your boyfriend and get caught doing it? I *wanted* you to see it, because if I had told you I saw Leon with some other girl you wouldn't have believed me, am I right?"

She's got me there. I really wouldn't have. "Then why are you still with him?"

"To keep him away from you. You would have been naïve

enough to take him back if that little love for me in your heart wasn't holding you back," she says. "I knew if you kept on thinking I loved him you wouldn't get back with him even if he begged for your forgiveness. You may be a little stupid at times, but you would never intentionally hurt someone, no matter how much hatred you might have for them."

Her arms fall to her sides as she sighs. "God, do you know how often I yelled at him for treating you the way he did? The proposal on your birthday? I was *glad* Aaron and his friend ruined it. I was just waiting to break up with Leon, but I couldn't do that before I knew you wouldn't take him back because you would empathize with his lying ass."

"Do you mean that?" I get up from my bed. She nods.

"Sofia, I hated the thought of hurting you. You're my sister, I was just trying to protect you."

I walk over to her, the tears in my eyes no longer only threatening to swell over, but actually doing so. For the first time ever, I wrap my arms around her body for a hug. She closes me in, holding me tight.

Feeling Julia press a kiss to my head is strange, but for once, I don't exactly hate it. To be fair, she's never done it before either, but still.

"I didn't get to say this before, but Sofia, I'm happy for you," she says quietly. "Even when you were younger, everyone knew you'd eventually be with Aaron. You guys were disgustingly close, and as it seems, you still are."

My hands clench around the material of her shirt as she mentions his name. It still hurts to think about him, though I know we're not broken up. I hope he knows that, too.

"You should text him back though. He retrieved to sending *me* messages and asking how you are. And I think we both know he doesn't like me very much," she adds, making me laugh through tears.

We pull apart and I wipe my nose with the back of my sweatshirt, needing that stupid drop of tears to be gone. "I owe you an apology…"

Julia shakes her head with a smile. "Nah, I kind of fucked your boyfriend. We're good." We both laugh. Never in my life have I thought I'd be *laughing* at something my sister has said, yet here I am. "Speaking of him, I have someone to break up with. Finally."

Chapter 57

"I know that you're the feeling I'm missing"—If I Can't Have You by Shawn Mendes

Sofia

MY DAD SHOULD BE BACK HOME from work in thirty minutes.

I've been sitting in the living room, waiting for him ever since my talk with Julia.

It's still crazy to think that we might actually get along. Though, for how long? I don't have much time left before I potentially move out and I doubt I'll see much of her after that.

Anyway, Julia is not the problem, nor has she ever been, really. I need to sort shit out with my dad, not her.

While waiting, my phone keeps chiming, but I don't dare looking at my screen. There's a high chance it's Aaron again, but I'm not sure how long I can keep going with ignoring his messages.

The question is, *why* am I even ignoring his messages in the first place? Fear, perhaps? But what am I afraid of?

I know I said I want him to focus on his studies and hockey, and I needed to focus on my school and my issues… but now that I no longer have either of those—except for the long talk I'm about to have with my father—what is holding me back from sending him just one silly message?

The least I can do is see what he might want, right?

And so, I take my phone from the coffee table and check.

Aaron: Kinda really miss your biiboes.

Aaron: Bppburs.

Aaron: Boobies. Got it.

It should be a little too early for him to be drunk enough to mess up words like that. If I'm not mistaken, it's only five p.m. for him.

Please tell me I have not caused him more problems with leaving…

Lily said he was heartbroken when I left, but that was to be expected. Now it's four weeks later and he can't possibly still be that down because of my absence, can he?

Looking around myself, I try to see if someone is anywhere nearby. But who should be? Julia went out with some friends; my mother is at some neighbor's house and my brother has long been moved out. So it's only me at home. For now.

And my dad won't be home for another twenty-something minutes.

Which means…

I take off my shirt, followed by my bra. God, I've never sent nudes to anyone, let alone taken some but I suppose there's a first time for everything. Lying down, I open the camera and bring my phone up high enough to capture me from my waist up.

Yes, yes, it's smarter to take a picture without your face in it in case they get leaked, blah blah. Aaron wouldn't leak them, he's a bit too possessive of me to do so.

After taking at least fifty pictures, I quickly put my clothes back on before spending some time deciding which one's the best. And once I found it, I select it and send it before I could overthink this.

From the moment I send the picture, it doesn't take long until my phone starts ringing in my hands. Despite the little kick of anxiety in my stomach begging me not to pick up, I do.

"Sofia?" Aaron's voice comes through the phone. He sounds a little breathless, but not drunk at all. "Did someone hack your phone?"

I laugh, only to stop when I hear Aaron gasp.

"You sent me a picture of your boobs, Sofia. And trust me, I know they're yours because yours are basically burned into my memory."

He wanted it, did he not? "You indirectly asked for it."

"Yes, but… Damn." He clears his throat. "Alright, uh, if I had— wow. If I had known it'd only take me asking for nudes for you to respond, I would have asked four weeks ago."

I wouldn't have sent it then, but I'm not saying that out loud. Instead I say, "Should've tried."

"Fuck," he cusses, and I just bet he's got his eyes closed. "Sofia? I just want to let you know you killed me with that picture."

I get up from the couch, pacing up and down the living room. "Where are you?" I ask, hearing some muffled chatter and music in the background.

"Brites with the boys," he answers, his voice choked like he is holding back tears. "Jesus, I'm so fucked. I'm sorry."

"Figured. Took you three whole tries to spell boobies," I chuckle.

He groans. "Don't say boobies, Icicle."

"Why not?"

"Because I will have to sit down in Colin's car and whack one off if you do."

I'm about to respond, tease him a little more when I hear the front door open. My father is home early, and that I did not count with. "Listen, my dad just got home…"

"Uh-huh." He breathes heavily into the phone. "Can I call you later?" He sounds a little scared, reluctant. Like he fears that the second we hang up, he'd never get to speak to me again. But he will.

I smile, knowing he can't see that. "I'll call you back when I talked to my dad, alright? I still haven't gotten to do that, but I think it's about time."

"Okay."

"Aaron?" He hums, letting me know he is still listening. "Don't drink too much, alright?"

"I promise."

"I love you." It's no surprise to anyone how easily those words roll off my tongue when said to him. I think deep down I have always known it was either going to be Aaron I fall in love with, or nobody. "Don't say it back."

"Okay."

We say goodbye, and I hang up because he wouldn't if I didn't. To my utter surprise, I feel lighter now that I have talked to Aaron, even if it lasted a whole two minutes only.

Hearing his voice never fails to ease my nerves so much more than I think possible. Every time I believe it won't work, it surprises me when the sound of his voice alone makes my heart beat faster with love for him, and my anxiety vanish into thin air.

"Dad!" I call out, knowing the first room he's about to enter is the kitchen to get himself an after-work-snack before mum cooks for dinner.

I can watch him stop in his tracks by the door to the living room, a little shocked to hear me call for him. I would be too if I were him.

"Yes?" He drops his bag by the door, walking into the room.

"Can we talk?"

My father nods carefully, slowly coming closer. "You're not like pregnant or anything, are you? Because if so, you should ask your mother for advice, not me."

Bemused I shake my head. "No, I am not pregnant, dad."

He blows out some air, being visibly relieved. My dad takes a seat on the armchair next to the sofa, looking at me without saying a word.

Just spit it out right? Get it over with.

"Do you believe I pushed my grandpa down the stairs and killed him?" *Maybe a little too straight-forward?*

To not drag this out too much, here's a little summary of how our talk turns out.

My father ends up saying he never thought I murdered my grandpa, what turned out to be true as it wasn't my fault. Someone seriously should have told me this years ago, would have prevented a lot of sleepless nights and trauma for me.

The reasons my father and I haven't been getting along all these years is apparently because I just shut him out, which I did. I did because I thought he blamed me for the death of his father-in-law. And, well, I love holding grudges, apparently. I'm still a little mad he made us move in the first place, but I suppose it's time I finally let go off of it.

Moving to Germany has been hell for me at first, but my life here turned out to be great anyway. Apart from the cheating boy-friend, the father I didn't exchange a word with, and the sister I thought hates me.

And maybe the schools. They're shit too.

But aside from that, my life here was great, so there is no need to keep on holding a grudge for something that did turn out to be okay.

Besides, I am dating Aaron now, aren't I? So my dreams did end up coming true even if I was an ocean apart from him for thirteen years.

"So, uh, dad. We might have to talk about me moving…"

Chapter 58

"but I know now I found the one I love"—I GUESS I AM
IN LOVE by Clinton Kane

Aaron

WHO WOULD HAVE THOUGHT trying to get to a stupidly small village by public transport would be an Olympic sport? Not me, that is for sure.

But now that I have been in Germany for six hours, currently still waiting for my stupid bus to take me to Sofia's village, I am starting to believe I should have rented a car. Though, apparently, I am not allowed to drive here because I don't have an international driver's license.

I've read somewhere that I can still drive a car up to six months of being here, only then would I need a German driver's license, but I'd rather not end up in jail for getting my facts wrong.

Could I go to jail for driving a car with a license that is not accepted here? What if I just said I didn't know? Because I didn't until Sofia told me that one time, and nobody could ever proof I did know.

Anyway, I am currently missing my graduation party for this. Yup, as it seems, I'd rather spend one fourth of a day waiting on busses and trains and tractors to get me to Sofia instead of partying and celebrating finishing college.

Oh, yes, tractors. I came across one of Sofia's neighbors and they took me to the next bus stop because I was too stupid to find it. He said he would take me to her house, but I refused. I didn't want to be a burden or make his life difficult.

Sofia doesn't know I'm coming today, she thinks I'll arrive tomorrow morning, but I just couldn't wait another day. These past eight weeks have been torture without her. The first half more than the last.

While waiting, I decide to send Sofia another of those texts I've sent her a month ago, only to make her believe I'm wasted and will definitely not show up in hopefully an hour or two at most.

Aaron: I want to fuck you so bad right now.

It's not even a lie. My dick is aching to get back inside her, fucking my hand for a month straight really isn't doing it. One month only because the one before was filled with pain and the worst hangovers I've ever had.

Worst bit, even though I get to hold Sofia in my arms again starting today, I still won't get to fuck her though.

Sofia: I had a great day, thanks for asking, Sir always-so-romantic.

Aaron: Sorry. Let me try again:

Aaron: I have the strong desire to roughly insert my dick inside of you. I might even light up a candle, my little ketchup packet.

Sofia: Are you on drugs?

Rude.

Am I on drugs? If being in love counts as one, then yes,

unfortunately.

I never wanted to fall in love, so what the fuck happened? Sofia, I suppose. Glad it's her, I don't think I would have much love inside of me for anyone but her anyway, but seriously, come on. I am pussywhipped, and I cannot, for the life of me, understand why it had to be the one woman who lives on a whole other continent than me.

An hour later, I finally made it. Only that nobody is at home.

I rang the doorbell like six times, but the door stays closed. Just great.

After spending hours on an airplane and at least seven hours on the road to get here, I am exhausted. Now imagine my annoyance having to find out that nobody is at home.

Just when I drop down by the front door, ready to wait for the rest of the day until someone comes home, the front door of the house across from the Carlsen's opens, and Jane appears.

She smiles at me even before jogging over to me. "Didn't think I'd see you again," she says, laughing a little.

"Why not?" I'll be here whenever I'm off from hockey, so much I can promise everyone. The second I have a couple of days to spare, I'll be on the next flight to see Sofia. A long-distance relationship isn't ideal, but it hasn't killed anyone yet, right?

Right????

"I don't know, I figured Sofia would move in with you, now that she's done with Uni, and I believe so are you?" Jane takes a seat on the concrete across from me, crossing her legs. "I watched the Carlsen's put moving boxes into their car all morning. Haven't gotten to ask Sofia about them yet, but it looked awfully a lot like she's moving. From what I could tell, every box had her name on it, nobody else's."

Please let this be a joke. I cannot take another couple of hours driving all through Germany to find her.

"She hasn't said anything." I think I would know if Sofia planned to move in with me, right? It wouldn't be a problem, in fact, I would prefer this over long-distance shit, but I will not persuade her into moving to the U.S., and I know she doesn't want me giving up hockey for her, so going long-distance is all we have.

"As far as I know, Sofia went to the barn. Or at least that's what it looked like, so maybe try finding her there."

Sighing heavily, I get up even though my bones are begging me not to.

I swear, traveling for a whole day is worse than hockey practice.

Chapter 59

"when the world don't feel like home / I'm a place to call your own"—ROOM FOR 2 by Benson Boone

Sofia

I THINK I GOT IT NOW. The first few ideas for the book I want to start writing. At least I got the right guy to be inspired by for the love interest.

So, I set my pen down, falling back on the hay bales like I always do when live overwhelms me a little.

Only eighteen more hours, and then finally, I get to hold Aaron in my arms again. I should have been there for his graduation, watch him walk up and down the stage and celebrate with him. But it was impossible, unfortunately.

But I mean, at least we get to spend all day tomorrow celebrating. Hopefully more than just both of us finishing university.

I close my eyes, fantasizing about how tomorrow will go down. Hopefully he will agree with what I am about to drop on him tomorrow.

But that's not important right now.

Ever since Aaron has sent me this stupid message, I can't stop thinking about it either. It's been months since Aaron and I had sex, and it's killing me. I mean, I've been celibate before him for a year, but ever since Aaron is in my life, I think the maximum we went without sex would be four days, and that only because I was on my period.

Truthfully, I wouldn't be opposed to try it during my time of the month, but Aaron kind of has this thing that he gets lightheaded whenever he sees blood, so that might not be a great idea.

The entire barn is quiet as I am the only one in here, or so I thought until I hear one of the wooden stairs creaking. That's the thing with old structures, everything makes sounds.

But the only people coming in here would be my parents or Jane, so I'm not worried.

Just, when I open my eyes and catch a masculine figure holding a bouquet of flowers, I no longer lie on the hay bales, I am sat up in what must be less than a blink of an eye.

My jaw drops when I find Aaron smiling at me, his head slightly tilted, his eyebrows raised like he knows exactly what kind of naughty thoughts went through my head.

Once off the bales, I run over to him, jumping into his arms. I don't even question what he's doing here, nor how he found me, it's the least important thing right now. He is *here*, holding me, filling my nostrils with his scent again.

Did you know you could miss someone's perfume? Because I just realized I missed his. The smell of rich, yet musky perfume mixed with fresh laundry and a hint of cinnamon.

When I look up at him, barely a second passes before my hands are on his jawline while his free one holds me by my waist and our lips connect. An instant tremor runs through my body, my nerves shaking with the love that I feel for him.

A part of my heart melts when he pulls my hips into his body, his tongue pushing into my mouth to brush mine.

Kissing Aaron is the best feeling in the world, and I do believe a kiss of his could fix everything from this day forth.

The other half of my heart melts the second we break apart and he grins at me with this dimple-inducing smile before he says, "I love you, Sofia."

My eyes water with joy and I gasp for air, though I already knew he did. Aaron didn't have to use words for me to know he loves me, and yet finally hearing him say it brings more malfunctions to my body than any factory could ever claim to have.

Slowly, I feel my lips pull into a huge smile, so huge, I can even feel my cheeks getting chubby again. I hate when this happens, but as soon as Aaron pokes one of my cheeks with his fingers and looks at me like these stupid chubby cheeks are the cutest thing he's ever seen, I simply can no longer hate them.

"I love you, Aaron."

Aaron licks his lips, closing his eyes for a moment as if to find a place to store my words in. But then he shakes his head. "No, you don't understand, my little ketchup packet. I love you. I have always loved you. And I will love you until I take my very last breath, even beyond that. I swear to you, the spirit realm better be real because I will not accept *not* haunting earth together with you after our death."

"You mean, you will haunt earth and I will have to clean up after you?"

"Yeah, that." He grabs my hand in his, giving it a squeeze. "You think ghost sex is a thing? If not, we'll make it one."

"Aaron!" I slap my palm to his chest, laughing.

"Sorry, I'm horny *and* exhausted, it's the worst combination *ever*."

My eyes then snap to the lilacs in his hand, internally cussing him out for spending yet another fortune on flowers for me. "Are those for me?"

"Nah. Bought them for myself, figured I earned them."

"You don't even like purple."

His shoulders lift into a shrug. "It's my favorite color, didn't you know? My girlfriend is so obsessed with everything wisteria, I sort of had to learn to love it."

"It's still light purple," I correct.

"Icicle, it will forever be wisteria." Eventually, he does hand the lilacs over to me, quickly pressing his lips to mine one more time before he walks us both over to the hay bales to sit. Come to realize, he does look a little exhausted. How long has he been on the road for to reach *this* level of exhaustion?

I lay the lilacs down on the floor, leaning into Aaron's body as his arm loops around me to pull me close.

"Jane told me you're moving?"

Oh. Alright, makes it a little easier on me to start this topic off. "Yeah, uh, I might move to NYC."

"You are?" His eyes widen drastically, a lot of emotions crossing his face when he realizes what I just said. "Wait, New York City. Like where I will be?"

"Yeah, I just need to find the courage to ask my boyfriend if he would like to move there together."

He looks at me with a serious expression now. A mix of confusion and concern hiding in his features. "Together-together?"

I nod, fearing his answer. Even if he says no, it wouldn't be the end of the world, right?

Slowly, and I mean *very* slowly, one side of his mouth tips up into a lopsided smile. "You sure you thought that through? Because I heard living with a pro hockey player can get *really* tiring. Especially when they come home late at night from a game and just throw their bag anywhere and fall right into bed."

My jaw drops. "You got drafted?!"

"Don't be so surprised."

A joy-filled shriek leaves me before I fall all over him, pushing his back into the hay and swinging a leg over his body to sit right on top of him. My hands rest on his chest, feeling his heart beating under my palm. "I always wanted to date a pro hockey player."

Aaron holds me by my hips, making sure I do not fall off him, or simply because he wants his hands on my body. Either way, I am not complaining.

"I've got good news for you then. You'll be marrying a pro hockey player in a few years."

Now that, that I can live with. Under one condition. "That guy better be you or else I don't want it. You just told me hockey players can be tiring, and I won't put myself through that exhaustion for anyone but you."

"Oh, shit. I kind of promised you to Miles but let me just cancel everything then."

And so I suppose, after thirteen years apart, I will finally get my happily ever after with the guy I couldn't get out of my head since the beginning of my time.

EPILOGUE

"I like shiny things, but I'd marry you with paper rings"—
paper rings by Taylor Swift

Sofia

Three Years Later

"YOU CANNOT SAY A WORD to Lily before I found a way to tell my friends without hurting their feelings," Aaron says just as we enter our apartment.

It's a super fancy apartment complex with a lot, and more importantly, huge rooms. The apartment is way too big for Aaron and me, but since we might never move out, it could make for a great space to raise kids together. Not yet, but sometime in the future.

With two extra bedrooms apart from ours, of course, a total of four bathrooms, an enormous living and dining space plus kitchen and balcony, I'd say we don't even have to buy a house. Unless, of course, Aaron still wants to design a house for us to live in. I'd be okay with that, too. But a bonus for the apartment complex is, the other guys live here too.

Not in our apartment, obviously, but we're neighbors.

No, seriously, Colin and Lily live right across from us. It takes us a good three steps until we can reach the other's apartment door.

Grey and Miles aren't on our floor as it's only two apartments on each, but they're in the building as well. As so are some other of the NYR players. Yup, we moved right into an apartment complex that's basically owned by jocks because it's the most fancy *and* closest building to the arena.

I don't mind it though. It sure as hell gets annoying when one comes knocking on the door—or just barges in because all three of my husband's friends have a spare key—while Aaron and I are busy doing other things, but it's manageable.

Oh, yes. You heard me right. *Husband.*

Aaron and I just kind of eloped. Without telling a single soul. Not even my parents know.

It started off as a joke, a simple: "You know, I think we should elope", when Aaron came home from early practice. Little did I know an hour later I'd find myself signing a marriage certificate. Some part of me wishes I would've gotten my big wedding venue plans with him, but then again, I did when I turned twenty-one.

"You think they'll cry?" What I found out in three years of living with a jock and constantly having other's around me, they're dramatic as fuck.

Aaron snorts a laugh. "Probably."

He holds his hand out for me and I take it only to be pulled right into his embrace. My favorite place on earth; his arms.

When it finally draws on me that Aaron and I *really* got married. Like, this is *real*. Not us stupidly talking about it and making up unrealistic plans for our wedding, a shiver runs down my spine. A shiver that's so much more than *just* a shiver. It's excitement. Happiness. Accomplishing a long-anticipated dream. Maybe a little anxiety for the future, too.

"You don't think this was a little too early?" The words leave my mouth before I could stop myself, my fingers playing with themselves, picking on the skin around my nails as I wait for a response.

Aaron must have noticed because in seconds he has laid his hand over mine, interlocking our fingers. "Love, we've been together for three years and *exactly* two months," he says like it explains everything. He chuckles at my lack of reaction. "I wanted to drag you down that aisle when we were eight, Sofia."

"Yes, but that's… you know. It's not valid because we were children and that was just plain stupid."

I can feel him shake his head. "Alright, let me say it in clearer words then; I do *not* think we got married too early."

My head bobs up and down, taking in his words. God, it was a stupid question to begin with, I now realize. He was the one to suggest it, of course, he doesn't think it was too early.

"Does your manager know you got married?" He should know, right? Because I'm pretty sure once the media finds out, there will be a wave of interview requests coming in for Aaron.

To be honest, I still don't understand why some people care so much about someone else's private life, but sure, why not, I guess? I don't mind the media. It only bothers me when I can't even walk down the streets with Aaron without having our photo taken every step we take. But I suppose that comes with his job.

It's been three years since Aaron started playing for the pros, and to this day, people coming up to us and asking for his autograph or a picture with him still seems odd. I'm okay with it, obviously, it's just strange anyway.

Knowing strangers all over the world have pictures of my husband on their phones, doesn't sit right with me, but I am adjusting and learning to live with it. It just takes me a little while.

People know he's in a relationship. Though it doesn't stop a good number of women from flirting with him or sliding into his DMs with nudes, Aaron ignores all of them.

There have been tons of interviews online in which he talks about how we met and stuff like that. It's weird having almost my entire life with him out in the open world, but Aaron never told anything I wasn't okay with people knowing. He always makes sure he gets my permission to share first.

"Not yet. I should probably give him a heads-up though, huh?" Aaron picks me up, my legs wrapping around his hips before he walks us right into the open kitchen and sits me down on the kitchen island, standing between my legs. "But I think for now, I'll just keep you as my wife in private and not tell anyone."

His lips press against my neck, leaving soft kisses on my skin, my head leans back immediately.

"We'll go on a private honeymoon, masking it as a normal vacation, once the season ends in a few weeks," he says, then begins to kiss down my neck at the same time as his hands sneak underneath my shirt. "We'll go wherever you want for a whole month. Just you and me."

"Aaron…" I moan, sliding my hands down his back. Bringing them around to sneak underneath his shirt and catching a feeling of the muscles he's always trying to hide.

"How does that sound, Mrs. Marsh?" His lips find mine, the tips of his finger tracing along my bra to find the back.

Mrs. Marsh. God, I could get used to that. Not could, *have* to. I did just marry the guy I loved from the second our eyes met.

I don't have to answer Aaron, he knows I love his idea. A month just with him? None of his friends walking in on us? Yes. Sounds like heaven.

As soon as he hooks his fingers into my bra to unclasp it, a groan leaves me because I can hear the sound of a key jiggling in our lock. Aaron must hear it too because he removes his hands from my body, plants an apologetic kiss on my lips, and stares at the door to see which one of his friends decided to interrupt us this time.

Only that it isn't his friends and rather the daughter of one of them.

"Uncle Ron?" Brooke yells out as soon as the door is opened, as usual forgetting to close it behind her when she steps inside.

"What can I help you with?" Aaron asks, making his way over to her.

I go to close the door, only barely resisting the urge to bang my head against it while doing so.

She giggles when he picks her up and throws her over his

shoulder before carrying her into the living room. He throws her on the couch, and she starts to laugh harder than before. Brooklyn then crawls into his lap when Aaron sits down beside her.

His hands instantly go around her body, holding her steady to keep her from falling.

He then turns around, his eyes finding mine. "Come here, love."

"Yes, Sofia. Come here."

And so I do, walk over to Aaron and Brooke, and take a seat on the couch with them.

Once I'm seated, Aaron repeats his question from earlier. "Tell me, little princess, what can I do for you?"

"You know how it's my birthday this year?" Brooklyn starts, her eyes shining brighter than the sun as she looks at Aaron.

"No, no. Your birthday was last year, I'm pretty sure."

Brooke giggles, scrunching up her nose. "But Uncle Ron, I turn eight this year. Last year I turned seven." Mind you, her birthday is in September and it's currently March.

"Yeah, no. I'm sure your birthday isn't until next year. You keep growing up and we cannot let this happen."

Watching Aaron interact with Brooke has always made me question what he would be like with his own children. He's the best uncle, though I might be a little biased, and imagining what he would be like as a father sure brings dangerous thoughts to my head.

I do not want children yet. It's a little too early for my liking, but a woman can dream, right? Besides, I have my books for that part. Anything I want and cannot have, I'm sure there is a book for it somewhere out there that I can read. And if there isn't, I'll just write it myself.

That's not entirely true. I do think I might be a little too young to have a child, but Aaron and I had this talk a couple of months ago and we decided that if it happens, it happens. Meaning, we won't excessively try to get me pregnant, but we're not *not* trying either.

Whatever Brooklyn has said about her birthday next; I didn't hear because I was too in my head with picturing Aaron as a father. But I do hear her say, "Did you know Emory looks exactly like my mom?"

"Did she tell you that?" Aaron asks in return.

Brooke shakes her head. "Daddy did. We talked." She sighs *very* heavily, leaning back in my husband's arms like she's trying to show him how boring the conversation was.

Someone knocks at the door, but before I get the chance to get up and open it, Brooke has jumped off Aaron's lap and storms toward it. "It's my dad. I have to leave now for my dance class. But I'll come visit again!" And out the door she is, this time closing it behind her. Or maybe Miles did it for her.

I lay down, my head resting on Aaron's thighs. "You think someone is going to come march in if we tried again?"

Aaron looks down at me, bringing a hand to my head, lifting it enough to quickly remove the bow from the back of it only to allow me to lie back down.

"Probably. Colin saw us coming back home, so there's a high chance he's running some errands and then shows up here to watch whatever stupid game is on TV." He runs a hand right through my hair, then gently starts giving my scalp a rub that's almost as good as having sex, while the other finds a cozy spot on one of my boobs.

Such a boobs guy.

"I vote for exchanging the locks and—"

Aaron covers my mouth with his hand or rather my face. "Shut up and get naked, wife. I'll hang up a 'do not disturb' sign if I have to. We have a whole ass playlist to fuck through." He pushes me off his legs and the couch, slapping his hand to my ass once I stand.

"And they say romance is dead."

Holding eye contact, I reach my arms underneath my shirt, unclasping my bra. Then, as Aaron would say it, I use my magical-woman powers to take it off in seconds from right underneath my top, pulling the bra out from under my shirt and tossing it on top of my husband's head.

He pulls it off and gets up. The bra then falls to the floor as he lets go of it, only to lift me up instead and throw me right over his shoulder. Aaron slaps his hand to my ass, again, chuckling when I gasp instead of yelp.

It doesn't take him long until he has me in our bedroom, standing in front of our bed with his hands all over me.

"I love you," he whispers after kissing behind my ear, moving down my neck.

Over the last three years, Aaron has said these three words at least once a day, if he felt extra romantic, a couple more times, and still, they never fail to make me weak in the knees.

"You only say that so you can get in my pants."

"Obviously." He pushes my top up, lifting it over my head before throwing it somewhere across the room. "But I'd get there without the perks of being in love with my wife."

If someone had told me five years ago that Aaron Marsh has kept his promise, fell in love with me, and we ended up getting married, I would have laughed right into that person's face.

But as it turns out, miracles can happen if you hold on to the thought for a little while longer. Even when it gets ridiculous.

THE END

Extended Epilogue

"darling I want all the strings attached"—Strings by Shawn Mendes

Aaron

Four Years Later

WE LOST. WE FUCKING lost the entire damn season. I could smell the win and then… I couldn't anymore. All because of that one stupid mistake.

I swear to you, it only needs a second to ruin an entire game. And it's the worst feeling ever.

At least now I get to go home and get babied by my wife. Sounds annoying, but it's the best feeling in the world. She'll cuddle up to me all day long and get madder than the entire team is, and Sofia doesn't even give one shit about hockey.

It's cute.

When I get home that evening, exhausted from all the traveling, I'm glad to find my wife on the couch, cuddled up in a blanket while watching some kids' movie.

"Daddy!" Jamie jumps up on the floor as soon as I'm through the door, running toward me.

Sofia doesn't react though, so I'm assuming she fell asleep

while rewatching that movie for the sixth time this week.

I hold my arms open for my son, kneeling so it's easier for him to actually end up in my embrace. And once he's close enough, I close my arms around him "Did you make your mommy fall asleep again?"

Jamie shakes his head against my chest, giggling. He then turns in my arms, pointing toward the blanket on the floor. "Kieran, too."

"I see."

Jamie and Kieran are both three years old and the most exhausting duo you'll ever come across. It doesn't help that Kieran is being raised by Colin, the man whose middle name is "crazy". For whatever black-magical reasons Sofia and Lily get pregnant at the same time. It was the first time, but it seems not the last. They're both pregnant *again*, but this time like four weeks apart.

When the TV automatically turns off, I'm suddenly reminded of the time. It must be after ten p.m., which means Jamie should have been asleep hours ago. I let him go, giving him a mini push so he'd walk when I say, "Come on, let's get you to bed, okay?"

Jamie yawns, rubbing his eyes, then runs off toward his bedroom. He's already in his pajamas, so I'm guessing Sofia got them both ready for bed already. Or just Jamie? I'm not sure. Surely Lily would have picked up Kieran by now if he isn't supposed to spend the night, right?

Placing the flowers in my hand on the kitchen island, I walk around the couch and pick up Kieran from the floor, careful not to wake him up because it's a pain to get him to sleep, unlike Jamie.

Just as I make my way to my son's bedroom, the door to Sofia and my apartment opens and Colin comes marching inside. "Have you—Oh. There he is."

"Yeah, where else would Kieran be?" They don't exactly spend much time with Grey, apart from the daily visits. And Brooke is a little annoyed by them, so sending them to Miles isn't going to happen.

"I don't know, Lily is asleep so I couldn't ask."

Making my way over to my best friend, I hand his son over to him, only to watch him roll his eyes when he sees the tiny frogs all over Kieran's pajama. "Someday I will lose my mind. She keeps buying frog-printed clothes for him."

Suppressing a smile, I look at Colin's shirt. "Not only for him."

He looks down at himself, then back up with closed eyes. "Excuse me while I go murder your sister."

"DADDY I IS WAITING!"

"You have fun doing that. Let me know how it went." Because even if he tried to kill her, Lily would turn the tables around and end up killing him instead. "Close the door when you leave."

Twenty minutes later, Jamie is all tucked in and sleeping. Now it's only a matter of skills to get Sofia into bed without waking her.

Unless that is no longer necessary because when I enter the living room, my wife sits on the couch, slurping on a glass of juice.

"How was your signing?" I ask, remembering the one she had this afternoon. Unfortunately, I couldn't be there this time, make Sofia sign yet another set of her porn books for me, because I was outside of New York.

She shrugs. "Fun. Though, the same people that always show up to my signings here seemed to miss you interrupting every twenty seconds."

I never interrupt. Only… every time I feel like I need my wife's attention, which, okay, might be a lot of times.

"How was your game?" Sofia reminds me that I even had one.

"We lost."

Sofia's sleepy smile falls, her arms immediately open for me. Like I'd say no to a hug.

Walking over to my wife, I instantly take a seat next to her and welcome her hug. Sometimes I need her hugs more than my next breath, today isn't one of those anymore, but I still take them whenever I get them.

I pull Sofia into my lap, her perfume filling my chest with a familiar warmth. Apparently, I don't even need Sofia's hugs to feel better, just knowing she's around makes life seem less cruel.

As she sits on my legs, her head resting against my body and I look around myself, I finally realize what I should have four years ago. "We did it, love."

Sofia breaks away from the hug, one hand reaching for the necklace around my neck, the other for her own. She brings both parts of the stupid Lego heart together, clipping them to the other with the words, "We did, huh?"

I'm still wearing Sofia's wisteria-colored ribbon around my wrist, though it no longer looks as fresh as it did seven years ago. That means I might have to steal another one, Sofia certainly has enough of them. She keeps telling me I should use a new one, but something about the original ribbon seems too valuable to just get rid of it, exchange it.

"Did you get the flowers?" Sofia asks, excited to see them.

Every time I'm gone because of a game, I come back home with a bouquet of lilacs to make being gone for days up to Sofia. Though, to be fair, I get her some flowers every Monday anyway, exchanging the old ones for new ones, you know? They're usually less expensive, like roses or sunflowers or whatever I find pretty that week, even though I have the money to afford weekly lilacs.

"Sorry, it was late, and the flower shop was closed," I say with a betraying grin. She already knows I brought them. I always get them, even if I have to board the plane with lilacs in my hands.

"You are such a liar!" She slaps a hand to my chest, so logically I cover hers with mine and keep it right on my body.

"Colin came to pick up Kieran, by the way. Why was he here?" Jamie and Kieran have sleepovers all the time, but with both my sister and Sofia pregnant, dumping an extra toddler on one mother only should be illegal.

"Came to steal milk because Lily wanted to bake but he never left again."

"And she didn't come looking for him?" I just know Sofia would have checked what's taking so long at least thirty seconds after Jamie was gone. And mind you, Sofia would've walked him to the door, watched as he entered, then wait for him to come back, all right by our apartment door.

"She called. Then told me to keep him because she'd have big plans."

"Well, Lily fell asleep." I laugh and Sofia joins in.

"So was I, but not anymore…" Her hand slides down my chest, her lips pulling into a faint smirk.

"Hm, I see." I lift Sofia up with me, kissing her lips deeply because a greeting kiss is long overdue, then carry her right into our bedroom.

No, no, don't think too nasty thoughts, we're solely lying in bed all cuddled up while finally managing to continue watching that show Sofia is so obsessed with. Not sure what it's called, or what it is about, really, I spend most of the time watching this show with Sofia, looking at her and thinking about other stuff I could do to her.

Like all the ways I could fuck her.

Come on, we all know I was going to go there.

Even now, while she's watching her show, I can't help but look at her, smile at every smile that comes on her face, or get mad when that stupid show makes her cry. Oh, and I do think about fucking her, obviously.

Sofia is the best that's ever happened to me.

Being forced to spend thirteen years apart might have been the worst that happened to us. It robbed us of growing up and getting through all our firsts together but looking forward, there are way more years to come for us than the silly thirteen years we spent apart.

And although for a long time in my life, I wished for her to be all my firsts, and I would have been hers, I eventually came to realize that it doesn't matter who came first because what's more important is that I was her last first and will forever be, like it is the other way round.

If I had the chance to change our past into us experiencing life together right from the start, I wouldn't do it. I wouldn't because I like the way *we* turned out now, and I wouldn't ever dare change that for anything.

Aaron's Playlist

I wanna be yours – Arctic Monkeys
The Take – Tory Lanez (feat. Chris Brown)
Sex Sounds – Lil Tjay
Often – The Weeknd
Sex, Drugs, Etc. – Beach Weather
Earned It – The Weeknd
Mount Everest – Labrinth
Love Is a Bitch – Two Feet
The Hills – The Weeknd
I Feel Like I'm Drowning – Two Feet
Naked – Jason Derulo
Swim – Chase Atlantic
Streets – Doja Cat
So High – Doja Cat
Go Fuck Yourself – Two Feet

Acknowledgments

This is just a quick thanks to my friend Jane. Thanks for having been excited for me to finish this book. Without your anticipation to read Aaron and Sofia's story, I don't think I would've ended up finishing the first draft as fast as I did.

Also, thanks for beta reading, again, your few mid-reading updates were hilarious, and I enjoyed them more than you could imagine.

And to my mother, for being supportive and telling me that I do not have to be embarrassed about reading certain scenes out loud to you. It will never, *ever* happen, but thank you for trying to make it less awkward!

Made in United States
Orlando, FL
15 June 2023

34172055R00224